I0831808

united states

a novel

Printed in the United States of America.

FIRST EDITION, Silver Horse Press, 3834 Mt. Philo Road, Charlotte, VT 05445

Cover illustration by Irina Solatges/Shutterstock.com
Cover design and interior by Custom-book-tique.com
Silver Horse Press logo by Danielle Monsarrat

Library of Congress Control Number: 2014911173

ISBN: 978-0-9960176-1-9

united states

a novel

NICK MONSARRAT

Silver Horse Press

For Barbara Ann Curcio

Chapter One

New York City, May, 2038

Quayle heard the horsemen of the Brigades before he saw them, the iron shoes of their mounts clattering behind him as the riders slowed to cross the cobblestones of the same Central Park bridge he had just traversed. The lead horseman launched his mount into a gallop off the bridge, and Quayle leapt aside to allow the squad of a half-dozen uniformed men to gallop past. The riders' apparent quarry, a balding middle-aged man in a running suit, forged on with arms pumping, headed toward the safety of the traffic of the West Side. The lead horseman overtook him and, wheeling his horse into the man's path, shouted a command across the grassy plain that separated him from the runner: "Stay where you are, Kidman! We've got you now!"

The man swerved down a steep embankment, then reappeared on the far slope of the next grassy rise. Scrambling up to its crest, he let out a groan. He had blundered into the center of a second tightening noose of riders. He was surrounded.

Quayle moved ahead, then stepped under the cover of a towering oak's low branches.

It was always dangerous to be conspicuous at interventions, the security cameras everywhere. Even innocent observers were vulnerable to roundup, their own backgrounds subject to checks, their faces broadcast if the Brigades found their behavior even slightly suspicious. As chief publicist for the Enterprise, one of the most powerful corporations in the world, Quayle could ill afford negative notoriety.

Along nearby walkways, strollers slunk off. A foreign-looking woman in flowing black skirts and a white caftan suddenly passed him. She halted, took in the scene, and drifted back beside him, glancing at Quayle, her face uncovered for a moment.

"That poor fool," she whispered under her breath. She tightened her scarf below her eyes. "He's actually thinking of standing up to them."

"He'll be lost if he does," Quayle said. "They'll make quick work of him."

"You are police?" Her dark eyes fixed on him.

Quayle shook his head.

The woman's face was smooth, cheekbones angular, sharply defined. She appeared Arab, her accent possibly French, her age around thirty-five, although appearance-enhancers now made anyone's true age hard to gauge. She seemed an unlikely ally of the police, although ever since passage of the Emergency Decrees, foreign-looking strangers could not be ruled out as preying on their own kind; there was money to be made in such complicity.

"News reports this morning called him some sort of dangerous agitator," Quayle said.

"Sometimes the harmless-looking ones turn out to be most difficult," she said.

"So it is you who are with the police then?"

She smiled --- ironically, he guessed --- such tests of allegiances common in this climate of suspicion. " I have nothing to do with them. I offer healing services to people who are in distress---deep meditation and massage, holistic medicines, natural lotions." She nodded. "Perhaps a prosperous-looking man such as yourself would require such services? You seem familiar to me. I have seen you someplace before?"

Before he could respond, the lead horseman, a helmeted, fair-skinned youth with wire-rimmed spectacles, smiled an unnatural smile and spurred his roan forward. Jaw thrust out, he leaned forward. "Speak up, Kidman. Save yourself! You know it's useless to resist."

The fugitive's lips quivered. He shook his head. "I demand to know the charge."

Onlookers ahead and behind surged forward, bypassing the ravine and moving to the grassy plain where the circle of horsemen now stood; Quayle and the woman felt themselves drawn forward with the crowd.

The commander of the brigade pulled a folded sheet of yellow paper from his uniform and declared in an officious tone: "You know the charge. It's been announced. It concerns the playwright John Dalton Bright."

The fugitive's eyes widened. "You dare confront me with him? His play was an attack on all immigrants, vilifying all who seek refuge here, simply for the crime of breathing. I merely gave it a truthful review."

"You misunderstand. It has become a criminal matter."

Kidman's mouth fell open. "Is it now a crime to criticize a poisonous play? I tell you, as I informed my readers, the play was a crime against truth, not to mention an affront to the audience's kidneys. At four hours and five acts, the idea that this man might sit in judgment of what is admirable in our nation and what is not is insane."

The horseman rose in his saddle, held up the damning document and calmly spoke so all could hear: "Do you deny, citizen Kidman, these are your words: 'Mr. Bright's play, *A Season of Peace*, is the spring season's most shining example of shallowness, its subject matter grotesquely sentimental, its premise childish---pure rubbish---the very length of the work a deplorable, unendurable insult.'" The Brigadesman lifted his eyes from the document. "Are these not your exact words?"

"If you read the full review, you'll see I also made several positive points. I wrote that the special effects were imaginative and that the view of the stage was adequate even from the cheap seats."

"You dare mock me?" the Brigadesman snapped. "Do you not know the truth?"

"What more is there to know?"

"Citizen Bright has killed himself; his suicide note has blamed you."

Kidman stared, his gaze slowly assessing the ragged perimeter of the encirclement; all avenues of retreat were gone.

The fugitive finally answered: "I am aware only that last night the rest of the media called the show a triumph---hardly a surprise, given the fact this dismal work was financed by those who so profusely praise him. Why would it matter so much to him what one negative review said unless he knew I wrote the truth?"

The Brigadesman brandished his yellow sheet. "You are not appreciating the severity of this."

Kidman shook his head. "What can one say about such an absurd response to a mere theater review. You have trumped all this up for some reason I do not understand."

"This is no trivial matter," the Brigadesman repeated. "Your sympathies for enclave appeasers and certain indigent factions opposed to the Emergency Decrees are well known. The evidence is clear; the polls have been taken. Unless you can convince us there are mitigating circumstances, we will have no choice but to pronounce you guilty of provocative acts leading to the death of an innocent man. That is your crime, sir."

Kidman trembled, his face an angry crimson. "Provocation? Is it now unlawful for a theater critic to condemn the fascist propaganda of a half-witted playwright? Are you saying the decrees should extend to criticism of art? Or perhaps it is all thin cover for ridding yourselves of a Jew who has taken up the rights of immigrants and other indigent people inside the enclaves, including Islamists, for whom you and your Directorate appear to have disgraceful, racist contempt."

The Brigadesman wheeled his mount. Quayle grabbed the woman by one arm and forced her back, sparing her from being trampled.

The Brigadesman shook his head. Facing the crowd, he began to shout his response to this verbal attack: "You see this man's deception? He turns this into a political matter, when his own reckless acts are solely to blame. In the Directorate we care nothing about politics. Public safety---the public order---that is our charge. Homicide is a crime---a crime against order." He dropped his eyes back to the yellow sheet, then slowly raised them again; the lenses of his glasses flashing in the sunlight. "The Emergency Decrees declare that the use of incendiary words is the same as detonated bombs. Citizen Kidman cannot deny that his words have led to the death of an innocent man; no reasonable citizen could. You, the public, agrees, as the morning polls confirm; this man has committed a crime and must confess to it or automatically pay the extreme penalty. So the decrees have proscribed."

"I will not confess," the fugitive repeated. "I have committed no crime."

Quayle and the woman exchanged glances. Since the Christmas bombings, the Directorate and its Brigades, the security arm of the city's largest corporations, had received extraordinary new powers. The same thought seemed to pass between Quayle and the woman: the fugitive was defying the Directorate; he appeared to be inviting his own death.

The Brigades commander reined in his mount. Rocking back, he again spoke directly to the crowd:

"As always, we are prepared to consider mitigating circumstances. A temporary insanity. An impairment of judgment. Divorce, alcoholism, illness, some similarly serious mitigating circumstance to explain the commission of a grievous libel against an innocent man." He looked down at Kidman as if addressing a child. "Do you understand?"

"I make no such claim," Kidman retorted. "The thought is absurd. I merely wrote what I thought about a bad play, nothing more. A bad writer who saw the world through a twisted lens has chosen to kill himself---- an act proving the depths of his self-delusion. I do not consider his death my responsibility. It would make more sense for you to condemn him as his own killer."

"You would mock me?" cried the horseman, pointing a finger at Kidman. "With freedom comes responsibility; that is the point, and you know it. You have killed a worthy citizen as surely as if you had held the gun to his head. Incendiary words or incendiary bombs, it makes no difference, you have committed murder."

"I repeat: I emphatically deny it."

"A pity," the horseman said, with a look as cold as Quayle had ever seen in any corporate boardroom.

Word of the fugitive's predicament was traveling fast, people converging from all corners of the park.

"There being no statement from the accused," the Brigadesman interjected, returning to his officious manner, "it is our conclusion, and the conclusion of public opinion, that you, Israel Kidman, must be held accountable for the untimely death of the aforementioned John Dalton Bright." He motioned a cameraman closer. "As required by law, I hereby notify you that we will now document everything, cognizant of the fact that we are publicly accountable for all charges filed and all sentences meted out. Israel Aaron Kidman, I ask you again: Do you have anything to say in your own defense before final judgment is passed?"

The accused raised his head: "I will not be an accomplice to injustice; I will not participate in my own condemnation. You wish me to confess to a crime I have not committed, and to absolve yourselves of a crime you yourselves are about to commit. So let the record show I refuse...." He pointed a finger at the film crew drawing up to the encirclement and spoke directly into the camera's red eye. "Citizens, this man's words are a sham, only spoken for public effect. You must not believe any of this. These are all lies."

"This defense you choose to offer is no defense," the horseman answered back. "The decrees declare this unlawful, the equivalent of an admission of guilt. Do you not know this?"

"I insist on an authentic defense, not a charade." Kidman shouted, then lowered his head. The rush of midday traffic on the West Side could be heard, the occasional laughter of children in the distance. Slowly, he lifted his eyes. "I have nothing more to say."

The head horseman began reading from the scripted charge. "You have the right to appeal for clemency. You have the right to cite mitigating circumstances. You have the right to express remorse."

Quayle knew how the body would be disposed of; the newly-enacted Emergency Decrees had proscribed this well, evoking pity in him for this stranger. The corpse would be dumped in a potter's field in an unmarked grave, his survivors denied his pension. On every television channel nightly-news loops would play, then replay, selected segments of the Kidman intervention, until his face and carefully edited responses were imprinted on millions of minds, fair warning to all why the emergency decrees' recent curbs on dissent must be obeyed. How much less extreme for Kidman to confess publicly to his breach of decorum, then accept whatever lesser penalty the Brigades' tribunal might impose, fair warning enough in its own right.

From the yellow sheet, the Brigadesman read the final interlocutory:

"Are you Israel Aaron Kidman, of 2019 Avenue of the Americas, City of New York, Borough of Manhattan, son of Spellman and Constantine Kidman, both deceased?" The horseman paused. "Let the record note the accused has failed or refused to answer. "Do you admit to having authored the damaging article, appearing on page 13 of the 'Theater-in-New York' section of *The New York Spectator*, dated May 6, 2038, which has been found to have led to the untimely death of one playwright, John Dalton Bright, of 42 Spring Street, Soho, New York, N.Y., found deceased of a self-inflicted gunshot wound to the head on the 14th of May in this year of 2038?"

Kidman again refused to respond.

"There being a note discovered in the deceased's own hand blaming the accused, Israel Aaron Kidman, whose long-standing malicious contempt for the deceased has been confirmed by the wife of the aforementioned Kidman....flash polls also having identified these inflammatory words as crimes against the public order... and there being no statement of mitigating circumstances on the part of the accused, despite repeated efforts to afford him that right, it is my duty to exercise the completion of the warrant as proscribed by paragraph 3, subparagraph (b) of the Emergency Decrees of December last, in the year 2037, by administering the proscribed sentence."

He raised his pistol. The fugitive raised his head. For an instant their eyes met, the fugitive's still wide in apparent disbelief that this could happen, Then the shot cut Kidman's skull in two. His body tumbled to the grass, blood pooling around his splintered head on the bright green grass.

Beside him, Quayle noticed the woman in the caftan. She was

writing something in a small black notebook.

Two riders dismounted and lifted Kidman's remains into a zippered rubber bag. Closing it, they lifted the corpse over the first Brigadesman's horse, remounted their own, and trotted swiftly away. The intervention had taken less than thirty minutes.

Quayle attempted to move back to the path, but the woman stopped him, staring directly into his face. "I know you," she exclaimed.

Quayle, still stunned by the circumstances of the intervention, stared back blankly.

"You are Benjamin Quayle of the Enterprise," she insisted. "I have seen you on television as a corporate spokesman. You are an important man. Please take this." She pressed a business card into his hand. "I wish to be of service to you."

Quayle looked at the card without expression: "De-Stress, Inc.," it read. "Raisa Amin, Doctor of Meditation." Below the elaborate gold script were a Park Avenue address and a communicator number.

He tried to hand the card back.

"You do not understand," she insisted again. "I must speak with you in private. It's very urgent."

Before he could refuse a second time, she turned away. Swiftly, she walked up the path, away from the departing Brigadesmen, her long skirts billowing. In seconds, she was gone.

Chapter Two

Smoke rose from the morning cook fires of the sprawling tent city that had sprung up overnight along the East River embankments of the Bronx, Queens, and Brooklyn enclaves. Quayle watched from the rooftop squash courts of the Roosevelt Island Racquet Club as hundreds of plumes spindled high above the river, then drifted eastward into a blood-red sunrise. The sliver of urban island where Quayle stood marked the invisible line between Manhattan and the immigrant high-rises erected inside the most destitute sections of the three easternmost boroughs. The granite towers, a dozen in all, were now bursting at the seams with new arrivals.

The security crackdowns had assured the relentless overcrowding. Since enactment of the Emergency Decrees, Directorate spies were everywhere, watchful for signs of anyone in the enclaves planning to export more violence into Manhattan. On the list: anyone associating with banned groups; any artist or writer expressing public sympathy for such groups; anyone suspected of fomenting violence inside the enclaves themselves; anyone, foreign or native-born, regardless of locale, known to be harboring or assisting agitators.

Longtime residents of the three boroughs had bitterly protested the enclave designation, taking to the streets to shake their fists at the Directorate's armed trucks invading their neighborhoods, the waves of suspects being trucked in to the overcrowded towers---Middle Easterners at first, soon all colors and nationalities, plucked from every corner of the city for the slightest infractions---suspects whose cases could be sealed unless grounds were found for the Directorate's main tribunal to order a public trial. These borough protests had no more swayed the wider public opinion than they had in 2020, when the first enclave designations had been announced and the Patriot Acts reenacted.

Now, Quayle watched the squalor of tent cities emerge before his eyes and knew just what a power shift had been unleashed in yet another cyclical swing of the pendulum from the renewal of hope under Obama to the rebirth of suspicion and fear.

Jack Flyte, president, founder, and chief executive officer of the Enterprise, stepped to his side. The two were opposites, Jack impeccable in his squash-playing whites, tall and lean and darkly somber in his demeanor, Quayle fair-skinned and sandy-haired, even-tempered and politic to Jack's unpolitical impulsiveness. Both took in the scene with an identical intensity.

Bulldozers were starting to clear the last of the Queens waterfront. As they watched, a phalanx of earth movers burst through the remaining warehouses, sending clouds of dust billowing up over what remained of the once-reclaimed commercial river front.

Flyte shook his head. "This wasn't what we bargained for," he said, and slipped his racquet from his shoulder. Removing the cover, he cast a wary eye back at the embankments.

"We should have refused to get involved from the start. It was wrong to let that damn chief of security talk us into it. I've decided it's time to tell the board to reconsider. I don't care what

Thompson says about our vulnerability."

Quayle nodded in agreement. Flyte had just returned from Hong Kong; Quayle had not had time to describe the intervention he'd seen the day before, or the woman who had asked to speak to him. He felt sure it would confirm Jack's own growing concerns about having been so quick to buy into the Directorate's consortium. They moved into the more predictable arena of the squash court. Jack closed the door, shutting out the outside noise. Quayle palmed the hard rubber ball, pausing before taking his drop "I witnessed an intervention yesterday. I was there."

Flyte nodded. "I saw the news reports on the plane back. I thought I caught a glimpse of you in the crowd. The usual lies and distortions, I expect?"

"The accounts were mostly accurate, actually. I monitored them all. They kept most of it in the broadcasts, including Kidman's final defiance. Fair warning, I suppose. Convenient of Kidman to give them the pretext."

"I knew that man. Israel Kidman. A thorny one, all right, always spouting about some cause. I'm not surprised he incited them. But he was a harmless type. What they did was a disgrace. We should wash our hands of the whole apparatus."

The ball rocketed off Quayle's racquet and Flyte stepped back, preparing to launch a return. At that instant, the back door to the court swung open. Two uniformed men faced them. The taller, with red sideburns trimmed down to his jaw line, demanded, "Is one of you Jack Flyte of the Enterprise?"

"I am Jack Flyte."

"This entire building must be evacuated, Mr. Flyte. We've had a report of a bomb. Both of you must come with us."

Quayle stepped forward to retrieve the ball.

"At once, sir!" the officer exclaimed.

Quayle nodded and turned quickly to accompany Jack to the exit.

Outside, the rooftops of the sprawling Racquet Club stood bathed in yellow haze. Across the river, the growl of earth-movers continued, the din even louder than before.

The Brigadesmen escorted them to the rooftop elevators. At the basement level, they brought them through a corridor into the racquet Club's brightly-lit men's locker room. There, a tiny, olive-skinned woman, long strands of colored beads clicking in her tangle of coal-black hair, sat on a bench; both hands lay clasped uneasily in her lap. Standing over her was a heavyset, balding man in a rumpled suit. One fleshy hand held a notebook, the other a pen. He snapped the pen open and shut noisily as he spoke. "I will learn your name soon enough," he said. "You might as well tell us what it is now."

The young woman kept her eyes down. Her skin was weathered, but Quayle guessed she was not more than twenty years old. When she raised her dark eyes, they shone with a strange black luminescence.

"How long have you been employed by this club?" the inquisitor demanded.

She shook her head.

"You know exactly what I am saying; don't pretend you don't." Bending low, he peered into her eyes. "Listen to me. You are lying. I know you spoke with the watchman before. I want you to tell us what you know."

"She has no papers," the shorter Brigadesman said. Leaning close to her blank face, he said, "If you do not answer this officer, you will be deported. Do you understand?"

Quayle stood motionless just inside the doorway. Jack's locker door stood wide open, a small black airline bag imprinted with *Air Algérie* inside. Jack was staring at it, too.

"Is this your property, sir?" the plainclothesman asked and pointed to the bag.

"I have never seen it before," Jack said.

"This gypsy told the night watchman the door to your locker was closed when she started cleaning this section earlier this morning. She said she had nothing to do with this. Yet, not ten minutes ago, the watchman says he saw her return. He said she used a key to unlock the door and place the bag inside. " He turned back to the woman. "When he demanded to know what she was doing, she ran. She was caught at the elevators attempting to escape. The Directorate's bomb disposal team has disarmed the device and is now examining it." The interrogator narrowed his eyes at her. "What was in the bag, gypsy? Who instructed you to place it in this particular locker? You will have to confess eventually. If you do not, this will go badly for you."

The woman did not speak. Quayle could see her trembling. Her green dress and matching apron were standard fare for the club's janitorial staff. Her cleaning materials stood in one corner in a plastic bucket, along with a half empty jug of pink solvent beside it. Her small hands twisted and turned in her lap. Quayle could not remember if he had seen her before; he and Jack had been coming here for a year for their daily morning exercise.

Jack took a step toward her and spoke to her firmly. "You must tell them what they want to know. Do you understand? If you do this, I will see to it you are released. I am a powerful man. Without the support of my company, these men are powerless. They do not want you, only the people who have paid you. If you help them, I promise you will not be harmed."

The gypsy sat motionless on the bench, silent.

"I am not like these people you fear," Jack pressed. "My word is good. One word from me and I promise you they will have to free you."

"That's not exactly the case, Mr. Flyte," the interrogator interrupted. "As you well know, we are authorized to act independently of the consortium. Our mission is security, nothing can supersede that. We shall see what this gypsy has been up to. There will be no talk of bargains just yet."

Flyte looked at the gypsy. "You've frightened her again."

"I knew *gadji* word no good," the young woman spat, meeting the interrogator's angry glare with defiance.

At that moment, the door to the room flew open. One of the club's watchman strode in, his uniform distinct. "They've disarmed the device. As we thought, it's a communicator-triggered bomb, identical to the architecture of the Christmas bombs on the Flatbush, Asbury Park, and Fulton Street trains."

"Is this the woman you saw place that bag in the locker, officer?" the interrogator demanded.

The watchman nodded.

"What do you have to say for yourself now, gypsy?" the interrogator demanded.

The gypsy looked up, trembling again. "He know I catch him stealing stuff. He just want me fired so I not tell. He the one telling lies so I don't tell."

"That will be all, officer," the interrogator said. He turned to Flyte. "You see what we have here? These types have their people everywhere. If this bomb had gone off, you and your colleague would most certainly have died; it was lucky we found you during our evacuation; we almost didn't come to the roof." His eyes narrowed. "I have heard it said within the Directorate, Mr. Flyte, you do not fully support the Emergency Decrees. Now, sir, here is an example of why we must have them. Violence must be contained. You and the city and your corporate community have declared it. We have been authorized to do what is necessary to keep the city secure. As you can see, we are only doing our duty."

"Where will this young woman be brought?" Flyte demanded.

The interrogator shrugged. "That is up to the Directorate's special tribunal. If she does not tell us who has paid her, and she turns out to be an illegal, of course it will then become a simple matter of deportation." The interrogator addressed Quayle. "I understand you are the publicist for the Enterprise. You must understand, sir, the media aren't to be informed of this incident, unless and until we find that the case warrants advancement to the courts. We can't have groundless alarms sounded about supposed holes in security before we have fully investigated. I will be filing a confidential report about the tribunal's recommendation soon enough. Perhaps, you and Mr. Flyte will be so good as to inform them yourselves how efficiently you have seen us work. Perhaps you will even say how you owe your lives to the Directorate, and how very grateful you are."

"And if the tribunal does not turn this woman's case over to the courts?" Flyte asked, ignoring what the interrogator had just called for.

"As I said, I will file a confidential report detailing the tribunal's findings and recommendations in triplicate, one for the mayor's office, the second for your consortium---of which, if I am not mistaken, Mr. Flyte, you are an executive board member---and the third will go to the courts. If you will recall, this is the procedure that was decided by the mayor's office under the December decrees. I believe you signed on to it yourself as a member of the consortium."

"You needn't remind me, sir." He glared at the man. "I take it from your answer, then, anything the tribunal decides not to take to trial can be indefinitely sealed."

"That is correct."

Quayle saw the gypsy shift her position on the bench. One of the Brigadesman placed his big hands on her shoulders.

She shook her head violently, then suddenly leaped up, lunging toward the bucket of cleaning materials.

"A cagey bird," scoffed the Brigadesman meanly. "You think you can fly away?"

She dropped to her knees, brought her face close to the bucket. She appeared about to be sick.

"Watch out, you fools," snapped the interrogator, "she's up to something." Before any of them could act, she twisted off the cap of the cleaning fluid, put the jug to her lips, and drank.

The two Brigadesman tried to wrench the jug away, but she kept swallowing, then choking, before a Brigadesman's hand could knock the jug away. She fell back with a crash and erupted in a coughing fit against the lockers. Her eyes began rolling.

The interrogator grabbed her arm, rolled her onto her stomach, and pounded her back. "Damn it, I told you you should have tied her hands. Get an EMT in here! Fast!"

The young woman moaned, her small feet kicking. The Brigadesman turned her back over, slapped her cheek, then reached into her mouth and freed her tongue.

An EMT team arrived, one member kneeling over her, the other two holding her flat on the floor. A bilious stream of pink liquid gushed from her mouth. Her small body shook and twitched before she let out a wail and began violently vomiting.

"*Romani* trash," the interrogator said, and tossed a wash rag from the bucket to the EMT. "Even Arabs despise these damn gypsies. No loyalty to anyone but their own kind."

Flyte stared. Quayle knew that look. It came whenever Jack saw a line being crossed. "I plan to file a report about this," he said. "In my opinion, this entire matter has been mishandled from beginning to end."

"You may file any complaint you wish," the interrogator said calmly, "but I guarantee this is not the end. I have no time for you now. If there is a wider plot under way, we must discover it. Now, move away, sir, or I will have you arrested for impeding this investigation. I assure you, we have the full support of the city's most senior elected officials. Don't bother filing any complaints there."

"We'll see about that," Flyte said.

Quayle knew the interrogator spoke the truth; the city's corporate community had bought the mayor's people a long time ago. Still, there was something about the gypsy's story Quayle could tell Jack was inclined to believe.

Flyte motioned to Quayle to use his communicator to film the scene. Immediately, the interrogator seized it, removed the disk, and thrust the device back into Quayle's hands. "This is an official investigation. Filming is not permitted." He stepped back. "I will have my officers escort you and your associate to the funicular at once for your return to Manhattan. If you refuse, we will be obliged to use force."

"That won't be necessary," Flyte said calmly.

Preparing to leave, the EMTs lifted the gypsy, now motionless, onto a gurney. She opened her eyes and raised her head; with great effort she tried to speak to Jack in her strange language.

Jack leaned down and touched her hand. "Listen to me. You must reveal what you know; your life will depend on it. If you have done nothing wrong, the decrees say you must be freed. That remains the law no matter what this man says." He retrieved the rag from the EMT. Gently, he wiped disinfectant from her chin.

The interrogator opened the door to the hallway and ushered them both out behind the rolling gurney.

"They think us fools for our compassion, Mr. Flyte," the interrogator said. "It's mother's milk to them. If I were you, I would leave dangerous matters like this to us. I am sure you will see the truth of that good advice soon enough."

Chapter Three

At the corner of Fifth and East 65th, Jack told the driver to pull over. Seated beside Quayle in the expansive back seat of the limousine, both lanky legs stretched out before him, the Enterprise CEO carefully examined the card Quayle had just handed him. "What urgent business could this person have with us?"

"I thought you would know. She knew I was with the Enterprise; she said she'd seen me on television, probably at some press conference."

Jack examined the card. "Sounds like some sort of holistic healer---harmless enough; they've got them on almost every block now."

"But at that Park Avenue address?"

Jack removed his communicator from his briefcase. Tapping into the Web, he did a search for De-Stress, Inc. He read what he was finding and frowned. "Its main business seems to be imports---jades, silks, special perfumes, hard-to-find exotic merchandise, rare paintings--- branch offices in New York and London---headquarters in Algiers."

"*Air Algérie*," Quayle said.

"It could be a coincidence, I suppose. Most likely she wants help with some trade problem; she probably knows we have influence with congressional committees."

Quayle frowned. "I had the idea she wanted to talk about a

service she had to offer us, not the other way around; it sounded urgent."

The light was turning green, the way back onto Fifth clearing. Jack remained silent as he stared blankly at the business card. "I think you'd better get out," he said suddenly.

Quayle looked at him.

Jack nodded emphatically. "The restaurant's just across the park. You can walk it easily. I need to get back uptown. Tell Cecil I'm sorry to miss her. Tell her we'll have to make it another time."

Quayle shook his head. "She's been begging me to have you to lunch for weeks. She has an idea involving Governor Wainwright. She needs to know if you think she's getting ready to run."

Jack leaned over and opened the door for him. "You can tell her my sources have told me Genesee's definitely planning to run. Also, tell Cecil I'll call her in the morning; she can explain her idea to me then. I promise to do whatever I can, but right now, I need to check out this woman. I've just remembered something."

Quayle stared at Jack. This nugget about Genesee was real news. The governor remained one of his wife's closest college friends. The other two---Olivia Gardner Steele, the new director of the Fifth Avenue Gallery, and Sabrena Tah, publisher of *In*, the city's most prestigious celebrity, fashion, and political Web-a-zine ---had proved far less reliable. While those past friendships had recently given way to rivalries, Genesee Wainwright still never failed to return Cecil's messages and calls.

"She'll appreciate that news very much," Quayle said, and stepped from the plush carpet of the car into the street. He waved as the driver pulled from the curb and continued south down Fifth.

Navigating the pedestrian crush, Quayle turned into the park, striding past the intervention site and swiftly on through the park to the West Side, the memory of the encounter he'd witnessed two days before firmly in his mind.

* * *

Cecil hurried into the restaurant of the Empire Hotel ten minutes late and sat down beside him at the long walnut bar in a puff of Chanel No. 5. Attracting stares, she was dressed in a red tailored blazer and navy-blue skirt, her auburn hair bobbed just above her ears, Clara Bow-style,. Her sharp blue eyes and finely defined cheekbones startled him each time he saw her, or passed newsstands where her face appeared some magazine cover, usually accompanied by a saccharin cover story about her supposedly glamorous portrait-artist lifestyle. In truth, neither of them went out much anymore, and when they did, it was more out of necessity than enthusiasm.

"I'm sorry I'm late," she said. "Some guy's out front selling tickets to the Eugene O'Neill revival *The Times* has been raving about it. The guy was unbelievably persistent."

Quayle stared at the tickets in her hand: "Long Day's Journey into Night."

"A fabulous play, of course, and the man selling the tickets obviously needs the money. He's one of the teachers they fired last month for requiring his students to study the play. You remember: the school board called it depressing and morally depraved."

"Yes, and brutally truthful," Quayle said. "Still, why taunt the authorities when you know it will have such dire consequences? That's all I'm saying. Life is too short."

"Of course you don't mean that, Ben." She looked at him askance, then scanned all the empty bar stools, finally frowning. "You did remember to ask Jack to meet us here?"

"He promised to call you tomorrow morning. He said to tell you Genesee's going to announce an exploratory committee in the fall."

"Just as I suspected. Good for Jack for confiding it; if anybody knows the inside scoop, I'm sure he does." She stared into her martini pensively. "Olivia won't dare be so dismissive if I can persuade Genesee to pose for me; this could be just the nudge she needs. I don't know why she's been so opposed to an official portrait."

"Quintessential Genesee," Quayle said. "The less she markets herself like a typical politician, the more her celebrity stature grows. Smart PR, that's all."

Cecil nodded. "Speaking of which, I finally got to see Olivia this morning about the spring showing. She kept me waiting an hour. For God's sake, how many years have we been friends? More than either of us cares to admit. Still, I couldn't get her to promise anything except that she hopes it can be my work can be included in the spring show at the Fifth Avenue Gallery sometime in August---in August, when absolutely no breathing human being is in town. Then she had the gall to say she's decided to hang all my portraits in the dreary lower gallery and my best political mural upstairs in the back gallery. The back gallery! Honestly, you'd think I was nobody. You won't believe what she said then about the portraits z when I complained." She stared fiercely into her nearly empty glass before draining it, then motioned to the bartender for another.

"What did she say?"

"'You're not abstract enough,' she said. 'Too Sargent, dear. Abstract is all the rage again now.' To my face, in front of my five most important uptown clients she decides to say this!" Cecil's jaw quivered. "You ask me why I spend my spare time doing guerrilla art?" She raised her martini and quickly drained it. "Sometimes I think I'd rather be like that wild man Banksy was, or fucking Zorro." She slashed a Z in the air with a forefinger. "Viva la truth, damn it!"

"Well, you were very smart to get the show contracted before Olivia landed the gallery directorship. Once she got what she wanted, she could have cut you out of the space altogether. Try to be patient; she'll come around. First, though, I don't think you should risk doing any more of those provocative political murals. It's too dangerous for you and the career."

Cecil shot him a sour frown.

"I'm serious, C. It's not just the Kidman intervention. This morning there was a bomb threat at the racquet Club. Jack and I were detained for an hour while the Brigades questioned some poor cleaning woman, a gypsy from the enclaves. I don't think the woman knew a damn thing about it, but they scared the hell out of her with their interrogation. She panicked and tried to poison herself. Jack suspects the Brigades may have staged the whole thing, probably to convince Jack and me to keep the Enterprise supporting the decrees. Before the scare, we saw the Directorate building encampments in the enclaves---tent cities with barbed wire, for God's sake, probably to hold a new wave of suspected illegals. The encampments are going up along the entire river. We saw it!"

Cecil shook her head. "We can't just pretend it's not happening." She paused, staring into her empty glass. "Last night, I had to watch Olivia fawn over that dreadful Tommy Sung's new-wave debut---scrawls not fit for a bathroom wall, and there everyone was, goo-gooing over him; it was too fucking humiliating. Somebody's got to start standing up to this sort of fakery. Nobody dares tell the truth about anything anymore. What's it going to take to drive people to the barricades?"

"A lot more than Israel Kidman, I'm afraid. No one's going to mourn that sort of unpleasant fellow. If he had admitted to something--- anything--- they would have gone easy on him. All they really wanted was a confession; they would have broadcast it on the evening news as a public warning about so-called inappropriate speech and hooliganism been done with it. He might have been given sixty days, all but a week suspended. I really think he thought he could bluff them out of it. Instead that bloody kid, that Brigadesman, shot him where he stood."

"Taunting an obviously unstable man, I think it's outrageous," Cecil said, "You know damn well they knew what they were doing. As you say, I think they need some blood now."

Quayle shrugged. "Still, when you come down to it, there's nothing we can do about it. And I'd keep my voice down, if I were you."

They moved to a window table and ordered. Quayle looked out across Columbus Circle to the Plaza where the horse-drawn carriages were rolling out, the memory of the foreign woman in the park returning to his mind. Strange how she kept materializing like that.

Quayle looked at Cecil and said: "Jack told me something else this morning. He's just found out Israel Kidman was Nonnie Schoenfeld's brother-in-law."

Cecil stared at him. "You can't be serious. That's absolutely horrid. She's organizing the party for Jack's fortieth birthday Saturday evening. That's tomorrow, Ben; everybody in the world will be there. How can she explain this?"

"Again, it's just the point I've been trying to make. Nobody can afford to be under suspicion, even by association."

Their food arrived.

Cecil picked up a fork, then set it down. "All the more reason for us to encourage Genesee to run. This repressive return to all that post-911 fear-mongering has been an absolute disaster."

"I agree, of course."

"As for Olivia," she interrupted, "frankly, I'm very tempted to invoke my release option right now and take my whole spring show over to the Orion on Madison just to spite her."

Quayle shook his head. "Listen to me. Put Olivia aside for just one moment. I have an idea about this business about Genesee.

This is a delicate matter, and it needs to be handled delicately. That is, if you'd like to hear my idea."

"Of course. I'm all ears."

Cecil and Ben's relationship had begun much this way, Jack ordering a mural for the sprawling lobby of the Enterprise's new headquarters building, Cecil, the elusive Soho portrait artist and muralist, resisting Quayle's initial overtures. Her dramatic, decorative tableaus had been appearing all over the city on exterior and interior walls of the city's most prestigious public spaces, but this was too purely commercial, she'd protested; "bank-vault art," she'd called it. Quayle had persisted, reminding her that powerful corporate figures would be streaming through the soaring Enterprise lobby each day, the exposure to her work bound to expand her list of corporate portrait clients exponentially. She would be foolish not to accept the work. "You'll have a week to show Jack something original," he'd advised her. "He's a big believer in spontaneity. He'll like what he sees or he won't. Just give him something surprising that he won't be able to forget."

Persuaded, she'd played to Jack's sense of the heroic, proposing a tableau of vast splashes of color---yellows, oranges, reds, shocking pink---a soaring, dramatic backdrop for a flotilla of Enterprise tankers, container transports, and its signature casino ship, the Starfire, all of them steaming out of New York Harbor in single file, lights blazing, the conglomerate's myriad of cargoes aboard---the entire scene framed from marble floor to vaulted ceiling of the lobby by a dramatic, futuristic silhouette of the Manhattan skyline.

The preliminary sketches had disarmed Jack. "Beauty, brains, and talent," he'd exclaimed to Quayle. "Hire this woman; marry her if you can!"

Quayle had willingly, eagerly, complied on both counts.

Quayle went on: "You need to be politic and a little mysterious about this. Tell Olivia someone powerful and influential has agreed to sit exclusively for you---a big commission---someone soon to become an even bigger celebrity. Tell her if she can't do better than this for your spring show, you'll take your new client elsewhere in the Fall. Let her wonder for a week or two about who you've landed." Quayle paused, watching the idea sink in. "In the meantime, ask your friend Sabrena at *In* if she's interested in you doing a formal portrait of the governor for the November cover, sweetened with your promise to persuade Genesee to sit for an exclusive interview. If she buys it, approach Genesee with the proposal. How can she refuse? A Cecil Collander portrait of her on the cover of *In*, the city's most influential magazine, the same week the original portrait itself is unveiled in the front window of the Fifth Avenue Gallery, the very same day she is announcing her exploratory committee for president of the United States?"

Cecil flicked the olive into her mouth. "This is a very, very naughty idea."

"I was thinking the Upper West Side Orphanage might be a good venue for the interview, a perfect tie-in for Genesee's Hunger and Immigrant Relief Initiative."

"And not coincidentally," Cecil added, "the neighborhood of choice for countless political donors and wealthy civic-minded activists."

Just then her communicator vibrated on the table. She picked it up. "Nonnie, yes, yes, I just heard the news myself from Ben. Don't worry. Are you all right? No, of course I don't. But Ben is with me now. Why don't you ask him? What could you possibly have known about any of this?"

Quayle took the communicator, Nonnie was already talking. "I know, I know," he said, "it must be very distressing for you. "First, tell me how you found out."

As he heard her answer---a business reporter had called---he knew this might be more complicated than just her worry about what Jack might think. Schuyler Schoenfeld was Nonnie's husband, a powerful Washington lobbyist; also a private fund-raiser for many of

Jack's interests. If any even remotely negative connection were made publicly between the Kidman intervention and Schoenfeld, Keller & Sharp, it would not go well for the continuance of that long-term relationship.

Quayle interrupted. "Nonnie, listen to me. Jack knows all about this; he knows you and your cousin's husband were never close. You don't need to worry about what he thinks; he'll back you up. If other media call, just tell them what you just told me: you were related to Israel Kidman only by your cousin's marriage to him; you knew nothing about his actions; you were as surprised as anyone about what happened with the Brigades. If they ask what you think of his review, you say it was disgraceful and unforgivable and the suicide of Dalton Bright was absolutely tragic. Believe me, Kidman could have saved himself; I was there, I saw the whole thing. If the man had only confessed to acting recklessly---simply let them make an example of him---I am certain they would have spared him. Did you say Schuyler already knows? All right, good. I want you to keep planning for Jack's party. There's absolutely no reason not to." Quayle paused, his eyes drawn to Cecil. She was nodding approvingly.

They both had always appreciated Nonnie despite her exhausting neurotic tendencies; she helped people with her many philanthropies, and she had a genuinely good heart.

"Nonnie," he said. "You can trust Jack to be with you on this. And, of course, Cecil and I both are, too. Don't worry about this. In a day or two, not a soul will remember it; the gossip mongers will be onto something else, I guarantee it."

Quayle handed the communicator back to Cecil, returning to his lunch as Cecil gave Nonnie her own reassurances. When she broke off, he looked at her. "I mean it, C. If you're thinking about tweaking the Brigades over any of this---sending that crazy guerrilla crew of yours out to slap up one of your clever pieces of street art in the dead of night, don't. They could be seen or traced back to you. It's too dangerous now for pranks, even clever ones."

He saw he no longer had her attention, her eyes widening. She was gazing out the window. He followed her gaze. At the curb, the hotel doorman was waving the fired teacher away from the entrance to the restaurant. Cecil got to her feet, picked up her purse, and started toward the door.

"Where are you going?" Quayle asked anxiously.

"Outside," she said, not looking back.

Reaching the street, she stepped off the curb and grabbed the doorman's arm. Removing cash from her wallet, she handed it to the startled teacher, who looked at it, then traded it for the entire batch of unsold tickets. Cecil stuffed the tickets into her purse and stormed back to their table.

Quayle smiled as she sat back down. 'Feel better?"

"Don't be condescending, darling; that wasn't the point. Now, what were you just saying?"

"I was saying that after ten years of marriage, you'd think I would learn not to give you advice I know you will completely ignore."

She shook her head. "Not this time, Ben. I heard you."

Chapter Four

After lunch, Cecil returned to the Fifth Avenue Gallery. Olivia stood in the front display space, her braided wheat-colored hair coiled atop her head like a python. Statuesque and immaculate in a cream-colored pantsuit, she was issuing commands into the receiver of a wall phone. Silently, she mouthed to Cecil, "I'll only be a minute."

To one side, nearly covering the gallery's largest display area, was another Tommy Sung, a canvas Cecil had not yet seen, an undulating trail of raised white acrylic, slathered liberally over vivid shades of pinks. by Olivia's precious protégé. The collective mass formed an abstract rendering of a spectacular orchid in full bloom. "Orgasm," the title read.

No kidding, Cecil thought.

As Olivia hung up, she turned to Cecil and appraised her coldly.

"Hello, Livvy," Cecil said with an equal measure of frostiness, "we need to talk."

Olivia frowned unpleasantly. "Again with the time and display issues, C? I thought we settled all that. I'm awfully busy right now. I told you before, we'll come back to you in August when the tourists are in town. They never tire of portraits and urbanscapes."

"If I'd known you were going for laughs," Cecil shot back, "I would have painted one of my own orgasms."

"Don't be vulgar, darling. We'd barely gone online yesterday with this before we were taking thousands of orders for silk-screen prints and greeting cards. A lot of people are depending on me to show a profit in the first quarter. It's not just about your art. It's about my career, too. I'm just trying to be honest with you."

Cecil's face turned livid. "Olivia, what the hell's the matter with you? This is me."

Olivia shook her head. "You used to be such fun, C. Now you're so damn serious. Tommy's experimentation is thrilling; he evokes such naughty and amazing reactions from people. He gets people's minds off these events like this horrid intervention in Central Park you were going on about at the debut last night. I mean, what can be done about that?"

"Well, there are people dying and suffering, and not just in the enclaves. Absolutely no one is paying attention to any of this. Where in God's name did you find this Tommy Sung character? Nobody's even heard of him."

"He's Ambassador Chu's son. You remember, we met them both at the benefit for Genesee's Hunger Initiative in the Hamptons last fall."

"Ben and I left early, I don't even recall them. I detest Hamptons people."

"Tommy had only just arrived in America. He showed me some of his work and I offered to show him around. He'd been in the country just three months, but his father was pressuring him to sell something. I assured him Tommy had talent, and that I would look after him personally. Of course, he hadn't the slightest idea what Tommy was painting. My decision has had nothing to do with my not loving your work---I want yours to be shown in the proper time and space, that's all---*Feng Shui*, darling." Her pencil-thin brows arched. "Don't be that way now, damn it. I know how seriously you take the political realm, but let's keep this in perspective. Politics isn't commerce, darling, and abstracts are the rage now. *The Times* plans to mention Tommy's debut last night in Sunday's Arts section. That's big news, and you know damn well it is. Also, Ambassador Chu can be a very powerful entree to Chinese collectors in the highest places. Supposedly, Tommy's been associating with some very unsavory people, and his father's not happy about it. He's going to need my support."

"So it's about politics after all.

"I suppose a little. It can't hurt."

"If it's damaging your judgment and my career, you're damn right it hurts. I'm negotiating a very important commission now---a major celebrity who's about to become even bigger---bigger than you can imagine. If you really want me to work with you, I want my new work to have the display it deserves, and I want prime time---top billing in November. Otherwise, I will not renew our contract. I will take everything to Dorian Day-Allen at the Orion, and I will make a stink about it. *Feng shui*, darling!"

"You don't mean that."

"Absolutely, I do."

Cecil examined Olivia's surprise. She had sensed friction from the moment Olivia had won the directorship. Olivia had always envied Cecil's greater talent;. Increasingly, this felt like payback.

"Let me remind you, Livvy," Cecil went on, "there are people who still believe in doing something to benefit mankind. I remember when you believed that, too. Now you tell me I must compete with an exploding vagina? I won't do it!"

Olivia's nostrils quivered. "What sort of commission, dear? Who?"

"I can't say right now, but it will cause a much bigger stir than this, though, I can promise you."

"Don't make me do all this schedule juggling without a damn good reason, Cecil. I mean it."

Olivia started to continue but abruptly stopped when Tommy

Sung, a blue silk jacket draped over one shoulder, stepped through the front door and scanned the apparently empty space nervously. He was almost six feet tall, slender, too dark-skinned to be pure Asian, more Indian, except for two black, almond-shaped eyes Cecil remembered from the debut; they had both seemed to be drilling straight through her. She wondered if he had overheard any of their conversation.

"Tommy, you remember Cecilia from last night?"

Tommy Sung nodded half-heartedly, his attention on everything but Cecil or Olivia. Glancing furtively at the door to the street, he seemed to be expecting someone.

"She was just saying how much she admired your work."

Tommy shrugged and finally looked at her. "You anybody important? I forget."

"She's a well-known portrait artist and muralist," Cecil said earnestly. "I'm glad you've come. I have something to tell you about the fall show we were discussing last night."

Tommy Sung once again was not paying attention. Outside the main display window, two bearded, shabbily-dressed men seemed to be waiting, languidly smoking cigarettes.

Olivia touched Tommy's arm. "What's the matter? Why are you here?"

He swung around and faced her. "I speak to you in private, all right?"

"You can speak freely. She's a friend."

"I need the money we talked about last night."

"I told you. I have to discuss it with my board. You're right. This is not the time or place to discuss this...."

"I need it now," he demanded, his voice rising. Cecil saw the artist's fingertips grip one of Olivia's wrists. They looked like talons. He spun her around toward the window. "You see those guys? They will kill me if I don't come out of here with the money. You understand? You said you would advance it to me. That's the word? Advance, no? Like a loan? You make a call for me. You call this board of yours now."

"Tommy, no. You're hurting me. " She pulled away, the spoiled way she often did with men. "I told you last night I can't do this quickly. We won't meet until next week; several members are out of the country." She glared at him. "You are asking for a lot of money. This is your first American show. The board will want assurances you will maintain your marketability. I told you I would speak to them. Now I want you to go. If your father knew you were here making a scene, he would not like it."

The artist scowled. "He is not my father now."

"What are you talking about?"

"This morning he informs me I am no longer his son. He calls me depraved, my art decadent. He had one of his men spy on my show last night. He said he will have me deported if I do not pull this art off your walls right now. He says I bring our family shame. I need the money to pay those men to make sure he cannot have me deported."

Olivia paled. "All right, calm down. I am sure he can't do that. There are laws that must be followed. This is not China. I will phone you as soon as I have the authorization to give you the advance. I am sure it can be worked out. However, I warn you I will not be bullied into doing what's not in the gallery's best interests. Do you understand?"

"Ok, ok.. But you tell them, they not give me the money, I take back my work. You tell them that."

"You can't do that, we have a signed contract, you must be patient. I believe in your work. I have told you that many times. If I have to, I will speak to your father. Perhaps he simply does not understand your work."

The artist glanced again at the street. The two men were still there, pacing and smoking.

"Why don't you leave by the back?" Olivia asked.

Tommy shook his head. Slowly, he walked back to the front door. Outside, the two men confronted him. But he pushed by them rapidly, hurrying to cross the busy street. The two men dropped their cigarettes and darted into traffic in pursuit.

"What have you gotten yourself into, Olivia?"

Olivia's face was ashen.

Chapter Five

Quayle stood on the lower terrace of Jack's East Side penthouse suite and observed the crowd assembling for the Enterprise chief's fortieth birthday. On this balmy May evening, an eclectic mix of about fifty of the city's most powerful leaders---politicians, financiers, corporate executives, publicists, people whose assets and liabilities Quayle kept catalogued in his head for the greater good of the Enterprise. Far below the terrace --- one of two that projected into New York's air space from the top-most floors like double bowsprits of a schooner---the East River ran fast and wide.

Nonnie Schoenfeld, flushed and agitated, walked toward him through the crowd. She steered him off the terrace and into the front room and adjoining library. Closing the door, she said: "I haven't heard from Jack. Have you?"

Quayle turned off the television set. The news channels were still obsessively replaying the intervention footage, his own face popping up over and over. Quayle looked at Nonnie and shook his head without concern, although thirty-five minutes into the party, Jack had yet to appear. "He's most likely upstairs in his office planning next week's agenda," he said calmly. "He never likes to be interrupted at this time of day. I'm sure he'll be down soon."

"Why did this happen?" Nonnie demanded. She stared dumbly at the blackened screen. "I've hardly slept since it happened; I couldn't believe it when that reporter called to say it was Israel

Kidman. Why on earth would anyone bother with him?"

Quayle nodded sympathetically. "I know. It shocked me to have to witness it."

"Why did they do it? It was so extreme."

"I'm afraid they may have had their reasons. Jack and I had our own encounter with the Brigades just yesterday morning---a bomb scare at the Racquet Club--- a device a gypsy appeared to have put in Jack's locker. It was probably some sort of reaction to the Brigades' erecting the new immigrant encampments. That's ironic, because Jack was one of the only members of the Brigades' advisory consortium to speak against them; he predicted it would make matters worse. Of course, none of them listened."

Nonnie frowned unpleasantly. "I hope they don't question me, I couldn't bear it. And Schuyler---he will be very upset to have his name even remotely associated with such a sordid matter. You don't think they will interrogate me, do you?"

"As I told you on the phone, just tell them you had nothing personally to do with Kidman. You'd never have known him at all if he hadn't been married to your cousin."

Nonnie nodded but bit down on her lower lip, unconsoled. "I'm sure they will interview Ruth, though. I have no idea why she stayed with him; she was always trying to please him. The conversations we had over lunch over the years were always about how difficult he made her life when he was so critical of the authorities. He was always being rounded up and questioned by them. I felt so sorry for her. I will give you her address. Can you make sure she doesn't mention me when they question her?"

"She will probably have no reason to, but you never know. I will do whatever I can. You know how much we depend on you and Schuyler."

She removed a pen and paper from her purse and wrote down the address. "I can't thank you enough, Ben. This is so unnerving."

* * *

The front room was growing crowded with new arrivals. Quayle greeted the always-prickly Mayor Francis Shrum and his wife as politely as he could manage and steered them and their aides toward the terrace and the open bar. Across the terrace, he could see Cecil and Robert Thompson abruptly parting company, the Enterprise's chief of security striding away. Cecil waved at Quayle and headed toward him.

Behind her, he could see the horizon turning pink. Lights started to wink on all over the city, except for the enclaves where the eight o'clock curfews would soon take effect; all but essential lights were prohibited after that hour.

"What was that about with Thompson?" he asked Cecil once she had threaded her way through the crowd. "He looked quite annoyed with you."

"Just the usual---Mr. Officious being officious. I asked him where Jack was, and he walked off. I think he needed to make a call." She leaned closer. "Where is Jack? Nonnie looked worried with you just now. He's not going to miss his own party, is he?"

"He's probably still upstairs making some deal, as always."

"Why don't you have a drink? You look like you could use one."

"No drinks for me. It's early." He walked her to the foyer and the elevator. He looked at her worriedly now. "I do think I'll go up and have a look."

He punched the "up" button as she trained her eyes on him. "I'm glad you look a little jealous whenever I mention Thompson. When I see how some of these women look at you, I want to do something drastic myself."

The elevator doors opened. He stepped inside and turned back to her. "Believe me, when it comes to our chief of security, jealousy's the least of my gripes with him."

As Quayle ascended, his wife's encounter with Thompson was quickly replaced by his recollection of Nonnie Schoenfeld's abject fear. It seemed just what the Brigades had intended when they had executed Kidman.

One flight up, he stepped from the elevator. In the front alcove, Jack Flyte's uniformed guard, Henry Kemp, sat slumped fast asleep in a chair. Quayle shook the man by the shoulders, and as the guard sprang to his feet blurting apologies, entered the expansive conference room with its panoramic view of the East River and eastern boroughs. Tucked into one wall to the right was a small side kitchen stocked with spring water, Cuban cigars, every imaginable cheese, wine and brandies, vintage champagne; to the left was Jack's private office and bedroom. Photographs of the Enterprise's fleet of super ships had been hung alongside old pictures of the vintage container ships of Jack's father's era, all that remained of the senior Flyte's union-organizing days, Jack's memory of his unwitting role in his father's untimely death was still far too painful to memorialize beyond these impersonal photographs. Through an expanse of sliding doors, Quayle and Kemp scanned the empty terrace, scoured all the rooms of the penthouse, and returned to the conference room.

"Well, Kemp, where the hell is he? Did he tell you he was going out?"

The guard anxiously glanced at his watch. "He said he was going to be working in his office for the rest of the afternoon."

Jack's red telephone's warning light began to blink. Quayle lifted the receiver. On the other end a man's voice spoke softly through a crackle of static: "Play 7 on the red."

"Who is this?" Quayle demanded.

No response, then the line went dead. Frowning, he cradled the receiver, staring hard at the bodyguard. "Mr. Flyte could easily have left without your knowing. When I came in you were asleep."

"No, sir. It would be impossible for him to pass me without using this." He groped in

his breast pocket and withdrew a color-coded elevator key card.

Quayle said: "He could have slipped that from your pocket while you slept, used it to activate the elevator, then put it back in your pocket. Call security. Get them on this, now!"

Sweating, the guard activated his communicator. "We have a 10:65 for Prime Time. Can you check?" He listened for a few moments, then muttered to Quayle: "They haven't heard from him. He's not reported a change of location, and he's not answering his communicator or the emergency number. They're checking the building's security cameras."

Quayle glanced at the logs himself: Housekeeping had brought up the lunch tray with two meals at noon, while Thompson had arrived at 12:25 and left at 1:46. Housekeeping had picked up the tray at 2:00. Between then and now, a span of nearly five hours, the log provided no clue about Jack's whereabouts. Meanwhile, the security cameras, he knew, fell notoriously short when it came to providing full coverage of this old building.

"When did you last speak to Mr. Flyte," he demanded finally.

"Right after Mr. Thompson left. That's when he told me he would be working here the rest of the afternoon. I'm sure of that."

Quayle said sharply: "Call security back. Tell them they'll need to start checking the usual places he meets people outside his offices. He's probably turned off his communicator if he's gone to this much trouble to slip out. And make sure this stays in-house."

Quayle walked back out to the upper terrace, the party clearly audible below. He stood at the rail overlooking the river. In the deep channel of the Hell Gate Narrows, currents were whipping up whitecaps, luminous under the last rays of sun.

He returned to the conference room as Kemp returned, his expression even more sheepish than before. "Still no sign of him, sir. Not at the Enterprise offices, either." The bodyguard winced as he explained the next piece of news: "His car is gone from the garage; the security cameras picked up his driver taking it out without a passenger."

"All right. He's probably been called away on some sort of business. He managed to evade the security cameras himself and had the driver pick him up outside. You know how elusive he can be when he puts his mind to it. Let me know at once when he's heard from."

"Yes, sir. Sorry about this, sir.

Quayle took the elevator back down to the lower penthouse. As he told Cecil the news, her eyes grew wide. "For God's sake, can't you call him on his communicator?"

"He's not answering. Something's come up. You know how impulsive he is---it's always the deal first."

"I'm worried."

Quayle leaned closer: "Pretend you're not." Then he stepped to the buffet table and tapped a glass. "Welcome, friends. My apologies to everybody. It seems Jack's been delayed. He should be here momentarily. In the meantime, I'm sure he would want you to continue enjoying the evening."

Amidst the disappointed murmurs, he moved back to the bar.

"What's going on?" Nonnie said softly behind him. "Is he coming or not?"

"I don't know. It appears his driver's taken his car out of the garage."

"Well, where would he have gone? All these people, Ben."

"Security's checking. It's probably easily explained. It usually is with Jack."

Cecil stepped closer. "Robert took a call on the terrace while we were talking. He left when I came over to see you. I don't see him anywhere."

Quayle's communicator sounded; Kemp again: "You'd better come back up. Something here you need to see."

Quayle looked at Cecil without expression. "They want me upstairs again. Just hold the fort for me down here."

"Ben, what is it?"

He frowned. "I don't know."

On the elevator, Quayle's mind sifted through the events of the last two weeks for clues as to what might be happening. There had been several briefings Quayle had attended on potential problems that might rise to a level of public interest, one in particular involving a major acquisition that had been on the table for the past week involving the Hong Kong casino operation. Also, some discrepancies Chief Auditor Julius Rabinsky had detected in some staff expense vouchers. Jack had told him to investigate and report back. Neither incident had seemed particularly urgent.

Back in the foyer of the top suite, Quayle found the hallway filled with uniformed Enterprise security officers. On the balcony outside, Kemp looked even more unnerved. Three security agents were examining a short length of rail dislodged from its corner supporting post and projecting outward into air space. Beyond it over the river, three jetcopters of the Metro Police hovered, their searchlights trained down on the whitecaps of the Narrows.A short distance away, a Coast Guard cutter was moving up river, its own searchlights sweeping the river.

"The tide will be turning soon," Kemp said. "If anybody's out there, they'll be taken down the moment they hit the riptides."

"Who called Metro Police?" Quayle demanded.

"Bob Thompson. He felt it would be wise to launch a search at once."

"I should have been told before he authorized this," Quayle said, punching a number into his communicator. He got Thompson's voice mail. "Bob. Where the hell are you? I'm in Jack's upper suite. I need to prepare a media statement. You and I need to get on the same page here."

Quayle snapped the communicator shut. He turned back to the foyer. The elevator doors were opening. He was still half-expecting Jack to materialize, but two Metro Police officers strode into the penthouse instead.

Quayle stepped forward and blocked the way. "We're conducting our own investigation here, officers. Would you mind not interfering?"

"I am Detective Navarro, Metro Police." He showed his shield. "Your chief of security has asked us to investigate a possible missing person. Who are you, sir?"

"Benjamin Quayle, Jack Flyte's chief publicist."

The detective nodded. 'If you'll step away, we're going to need to have a look."

Quayle stood his ground. "There are fifty guests of Mr. Flyte's below us who will be very alarmed if I don't have a plausible explanation to give them about what's going on here, to say nothing of the media who aren't likely to miss this incident report on their police scanners. I should tell you, it's not unusual for Mr. Flyte to go missing of his own accord, always for legitimate business reasons. Also, his personal car is not in the garage. He simply appears to have gone out."

Navarro nodded, looking unconvinced. "We are aware of that. But we have been told there is the possibility of an accident --- a faulty deck railing on this floor." The detective's gaze met Quayle's. "I assure you, we have no intention of making this public. If the media ask about the activity on the river, we'll say our aircraft are searching for a Rikers Island escapee reported missing several hours ago."

At that instant, one of the jetcopters swept a searchlight across the building's upper facades, then banked away toward the Hell Gate Narrows further up river, its engines shrieking.

"Your people are making this difficult, detective."

"Maybe you'd prefer the Brigades handled this?"

Quayle shook his head. "That won't be necessary."

Chapter Six

Robert Thompson shouldered his way through the foyer of the crowded upper penthouse. At six feet, three inches tall, with a closely shaved pate and oversized jaw, he was an imposing figure. Barely acknowledging Quayle, he approached two uniformed policemen standing watch over the terrace's broken guardrail.

He shook hands with Detective Navarro and provided an update on his security team's findings so far: no signs of Jack in the building, his town car observed by security camera exiting the lower garage without a passenger and no response as yet from his driver; no sightings at airports, helicopter services, cab companies, bus stations, train stations, hospitals, or morgues. No incoming or outgoing calls from his communicator or land lines from 2 p.m. on; all his outside dealmaking haunts still in the process of being checked.

"When was the last time a safety check was done here?" Navarro suddenly asked, his gaze on the broken rail.

A security man stepped forward. "We inspect monthly because of the winds. A week ago, the rails were sound on all terraces."

Thompson's communicator buzzed. He answered, listened, and pocketed it. "Jack's bodyguard has just reviewed camera tapes, all the ones between 2 p.m. and the last hour. Jack's driver just reported in. He was only going out to gas up for what he'd been told by Jack's secretary would be a run out to the Hamptons. Jack had that on his schedule, a lunch with Schuyler Schoenfeld, the financier and lobbyist. His wife is here tonight; she confirms they were planning to meet for a luncheon in a day or two."

Quayle checked his communicator and nodded. "That's right. It's penciled in on his schedule."

Navarro nodded. "So we're down to two possibilities: He used his private elevator to leave the building through his private entrance, which isn't covered by cameras, or..." He pointed to the damaged railing, "... he went through the railing and is in the river."

The group stared where the detective's eyes were riveted, the river far below a black mass illuminated randomly by a jetcopter's searchlights.

Quayle turned back to Navarro. "What are you telling the media about the reason for all this commotion?"

"That we're searching for a prisoner who escaped from Rikers. We've been looking for this guy since this morning. There's no reason for us to mention any of this." The detective paused. "There have been executive kidnappings abroad, as we all know; we can't rule that out. Also, any unusual event involving any employees, any insider who might have reason to want the company or Mr. Flyte harmed? Anything of that nature?"

Thompson did not answer at once. Quayle sensed something in the silence.

"There has just been an incident with our chief auditor," Thompson said finally. The officer made a note. Quayle stared at Thompson.

"I had to fire the man."

"Go on," Navarro said.

"The matter is still under investigation. I prefer not to go into it right now."

"I see," Navarro said, making a note. "The man's name?"

"Julius Rabinsky. That's all I can tell you right now. It's an internal security matter."

Quayle was about to interrupt when Navarro raised his hand. "Was there anything in your last discussion with Mr. Flyte earlier today that might have had a bearing on his decision to leave the building instead of attending his own party? Something involving this matter with the auditor?"

Thompson glanced at Quayle. "We discussed the audit problem briefly. It seemed worth bringing up to him --- a computer glitch concerning some casino receipts reported by the Hong Kong office. He told me to do what I thought the situation required. He seemed very distracted; he'd been discussing some commodities transaction. I wasn't aware of the seriousness of the computer problem until my security people discovered Rabinsky clearing out his office. When my people attempted to question him, he managed to slip out of the building with files."

The officer made a note. "He quit on the spot, did he?"

"He refused to explain what he was doing. My people were about to interrogate him when he suddenly left the building. We had no idea about his intentions. It wasn't until we went into his encoded computer files we noticed some expense account records were missing. At that point, I asked the Directorate to have the Brigades detain him so we could question him." His eyes narrowed. "It's important, detective, this remain an internal matter until we get to the bottom of it. This could easily rile markets."

Navarro nodded, turning his attention back to the broken railing. "Our lab boys are going to need to do some forensics here. I'll also want to interview Mr. Flyte's bodyguard when he gets back."

"Anything you need, officer," Thompson said. "We want to cooperate in any way we can."

Quayle waited for the detective to rejoin his men on the balcony, then motioned for Thompson to join him. The security chief followed him into Jack's penthouse office and Quayle closed the door.

"Why wasn't I informed? You called in Metro without consulting me. What if the media had asked me? I would have looked like a fool."

Thompson's lips tightened. He stood a full head taller than Quayle, his broad shoulders squared as if confronting a subordinate. "I did inform you about the Rabinsky problem."

"What are you talking about?

"I left you a voice message early this morning. I said Rabinksy had quit out of the blue and that we'd found discrepancies in his computer files. As for consulting you about calling in Metro, there wasn't time. If Jack's body's in the river now, the tides will take it into Hell Gate Narrows damn soon. He might never be found. Still, Metro's got the best search-and-rescue operation in the city."

Quayle was about to protest again, then stopped. He remembered now. A garbled message had appeared on his communicator before he'd come to the office; it must have been about this.

"All right, calling in Metro's your decision, I agree," he said finally. "Let's start this discussion again. All public statements are my decision, after consultation with you, just as Jack has called for in his absence. No deviations from that policy, and no comments to the media until I say so. The reporters are used to dealing with me, they trust me; I should handle all inquiries."

Thompson shrugged. "Agreed."

"I will tell them if they ask that Jack has already left for the International Monetary Fund meeting in Dubrovnik. That's four days from now. But it wouldn't be unusual for him to make other unannounced deal-making stops beforehand and not bother to tell us. There's no reason he should be missed until then. Now, I want to know the details of the Rabinsky matter. What reason did Rabinsky give for quitting?"

Thompson shook his head. "He refused to say. He said he

would be sending Jack his formal resignation. We think he was worried we'd caught him manipulating the Hong Kong casino accounts, which we found later to be a mess, and then he panicked. We're still trying to figure out exactly what he was doing and how many documents he actually got away with."

Quayle stared at Thompson. "You're telling me Rabinsky was stealing? Our Rabinsky?"

Thompson nodded.

"Not possible!"

"Maybe unlikely, but impossible? In my world, nothing's impossible. In fact, my people intercepted an encrypted message sent from Rabinsky to one of the low-level auditors in Hong Kong three days ago. He'd been demanding an accounting of all our Orient Casino's cash-flow for the past two years." Thompson paused, his eyes narrowing, revealing a mounting impatience at all these questions. "By the time I was told, he was already out the damn door. Some of the expense-account records are also missing from his electronic data base---purged just before he cleared out. Our forensics people are going through all the data bases now for discrepancies."

Quayle paused, trying to make sense of this. This could be about one of Rabinsky's spot audits. "Maybe he had suspicions of his own about those accounts," he suggested. "Maybe that was the reason for the Hong Kong inquiry. Maybe it was you jumping to conclusions here."

"If he had nothing to hide," Thompson said, "why did he run? Why didn't he just tell me what was going on? I would have helped him investigate the damn problem myself."

Quayle shook his head. Nothing about this was making sense now.

Chapter Seven

Quayle pressed the buzzer beside the wall scanner and waited for the occupant of Apartment 22B to acknowledge him.

"My name is Benjamin Quayle," he said in response to a woman's husky voice. "I am from the Enterprise. I need to speak with Mrs. Kidman."

"Please go away," the voice rasped. "I've already told the authorities all I know."

"I'm not with the authorities, Mrs. Kidman. Your cousin, Mrs. Schoenfeld, asked me to bring you her condolences. I know it's very late, but I must speak with you. She will be very upset if she knows you have refused to see me."

There was silence. The door locks finally buzzed, and he stepped inside the small vestibule; one flight up he found the apartment. Through a crack in the door, a silver-haired woman in a housecoat and slippers examined him suspiciously, then slowly unlatched the chain.

The apartment he entered was modest in size, dominated by a combined living area and library bounded floor to ceiling by books---the space where the city's most influential theater critic must have passed much of his time. Mrs. Kidman, obviously just awakened, pinned a stray lock of hair back over one ear and sat down at the dining room table. There, a sympathy card lay conspicuously against a vase of freshly cut flowers.

Quayle removed Nonnie's note from his jacket pocket and

handed it to her. "Your cousin wanted you to have this."

Her eyes fell to the envelope. "What is it?"

"Her condolences, Mrs. Kidman, and, I believe, some financial assistance."

She opened the envelope. A check dropped out, and she stared at it as if it might be dangerous. As she read on, however, tears welled up in her eyes, and her hands began to tremble.

"She wanted to do something to help you," Quayle said. "It's been all over the news that you could be denied your husband's pension because of this."

She shook her head slowly. "She's been foolish to do this. Tell her if they find out it could cause her a lot of trouble. Also, I may never be able to repay her. Please, Mr. Quayle, I can't accept this."

"I'm sure she doesn't expect you to repay it, and no one will ever know."

"You don't understand. I am sure I am being watched. If they ask you why you have come here, what will you say?"

"I am not afraid of them."

She held his eyes for a moment; his resolve seemed to reassure her. "Our lunches together were always so enjoyable. She didn't care much for my husband; she knew the strain Israel was under, having to answer to my friends for his notoriety, but I always defended him. We didn't dare go out sometimes after one of his reviews, but Nonnie was always sympathetic and understanding. I have always had my antiques store, so I have had my own life, too; she was very interested in that and brought me her friends to consign wonderful things." She shook her head sadly. "In some ways he enjoyed being a pariah, never so glad as when he made important people angry. It always got him the attention he craved. My husband was not an easy man---without a heart, people said--- but he measured all his work by the amount of truth he told in his reviews, how much hypocrisy he could expose on any given day without bringing down the Valkyries, as he called them; he was well-respected in some quarters for always challenging the censors, even within *The Times*. I suppose that's really why they had to kill him--- he was too clever for them. They needed to send a warning to those who read and admired him not to challenge the status quo in the same way. The Brigades asked me so many questions about friends they claimed he had ---people I knew nothing about...."

"What sort of people?"

"They asked if he had met with foreigners. I told them foreigners were often directors and playwrights for the stage. They said he had been observed making contact with known agitators in the enclaves. Did I know anything about this? I said I did not. I don't think they believed me. They ordered me to report anyone who contacted me." She compressed her thin lips; her eyes shone fiercely. "Then they took away all his papers, his two computers and other communicators, files and writings, notes, everything that mattered to him. If I did not cooperate, they said they would make certain I did not receive any of his pension. After they left, I heard the downstairs buzzer again. I thought they had returned to arrest me. Instead, there were flowers with this card left for me."

"That card looks familiar. May I see it?"

Quayle saw the familiar embossed letters of gold---Raisa Amin's name and number and the services her firm offered: "De-Stress, Inc."

She looked at him. "Is this a trick? If I respond to this, will they have me arrested?"

For a moment Quayle did not answer. "You must tell me, Mrs. Kidman. Did your husband ever speak openly against the Brigades?"

"You can't expect me to answer that. How do I know I can trust you, Mr. Quayle? Just because you say you come from my cousin? Why should I tell you what I would not tell them when they asked that same question? Even my own friends will not answer my calls now; my cousin is the only one to offer any sympathy at all, besides this woman I do not even know; I've had vicious messages on my machine ever since the intervention appeared all over television. What if they have seen you come here?"

"I will tell them I was simply bringing condolences from your cousin; a natural thing for a relative to do. However, I must be honest with you. I am also in a difficult position here. The Enterprise is one of the companies that pays the Directorate for its external security; however, we are now considering discontinuing this security relationship. Please, you must not repeat what I have just said, or that I have suggested you seek this woman's help. Consider my confiding this as a down payment on your trust. Call Mrs. Schoenfeld yourself right now, if you doubt me. She will be happy to tell you who I am."

"That won't be necessary, Mr. Quayle. Please sit down and forgive my rudeness. I must tell someone or I will burst; yes, I am sure Israel would want me to. Please believe me when I say he never discussed politics in my presence. However, I know he had friends who were very political---artists, writers, composers, actors--- the sorts of people who had chosen in recent years to settle in the boroughs to escape interference from the censors. Sometimes they came here, and I heard some of their discussions. They were often very heated. Many had chosen to stay in the enclaves in spite of the new conditions created by the Emergency Decrees.

The men from the Directorate who came to question me seemed to know all about these people, but I confirmed nothing. I know they were trying to implicate me in whatever suspicions they had, but I told them that Israel and I led mostly separate lives. I have always put my antiques business first, and Israel always supported me in that. I told these men I had nothing to do with politics, which was the truth. Of course, I had my opinions, and Israel was not wrong about his distaste for those who would tell him what he could or could not say in print."

"And this playwright Berger. Did your husband ever mention him?"

"The night he'd come back from seeing his play, Israel closed himself off in his study; I assumed he was writing his review. I sensed he was very angry, but I did not ask why. The next day I read his report in the newspaper, and I knew why he was so angry. He felt the play was thinly disguised propaganda in support of the ethnic-cleansing program---Berger, a Jew, one of us, was obviously advocating through his characters a general displacement of all new immigrants to these new encampments in the enclaves. It was an abomination to my husband that such a play would be performed and be so well received---as it was to me. My grandparents were also Jews. They suffered their own difficult times. They say they are fencing off the encampments with barbed wire to make them prisons. Is this true?"

Quayle turned away, then back to her. "Your husband's execution is a warning to these dissidents, I am convinced of it. They have executed him to send a message, no doubt to your husband's friends, but also to others. We also have only the Brigades' word that Berger's death was a suicide. I doubt that as well."

"Then they are the criminals."

"Yes, but you must not repeat this allegation to anyone. It will be dangerous for you." He pressed Raisa Amin's card back into her hand. "Instead, speak with this woman. I think she is prepared to assist in discreet ways. Unrest in the enclaves cannot be allowed to become a pretext for the Brigades' injustice, but I am certain it cannot be fought in any conventional way."

Mrs. Kidman looked at him. "Thank you for your kindness, Mr. Quayle, thank you." Clutching the card, she dropped her face into her hands and quietly wept.

***

As Quayle's cab neared the townhouse, he motioned for the driver to stop. Punching a number into his communicator, he waited for his messages. He listened, made a note, and rang off. Paying his fare, he stepped from the cab and looked up. It was now nearly eleven o'clock; he had stopped at two of Jack's lesser-known haunts on the way back from Mrs. Kidman's, but no one had seen him. He looked up and saw the sitting-room lights still on.

Cecil looked up from the couch when he came in and frowned. "You're late."

"I'm sorry, I went to see Nonnie's cousin, then out to check some places for Jack. I lost track of the time. Anyone call?"

"No. I'm worried now."

"It's not the same as before with his vanishing acts. This has a different feel to it."

"You had a visitor an hour ago---a courier from the Enterprise. He delivered this."

Quayle took the pouch she handed him and stripped it open. Inside was a brown envelope addressed to him, sealed with the official double-eagle stamp of the Enterprise. He began to read the contents.

Outside, it had begun to rain---a downpour. Drops the size of nickels beat against the windows.

"Well, what is it?" Cecil asked.

"The board has called an emergency meeting in two days. They want to discuss a succession plan. These are all the legal documents involved."

"Now, I'm scared," Cecil said.

Quayle stared silently into the downpour. Across the wet street stood the walled compounds of the Croninshields, Dustins, and

Carmodies---three of the city's 100 most influential and powerful families, two born to the city's most important corporate board rooms, one---Michael Carmody---a pretender to that capitalist elite, a union-boss turned corporate tyrant. The names of all 100, including Carmody's, could be found in "M," the exclusive, unofficial social registry of the city, most of them descendants of families who had held sway in the city's earliest days. Each year, without public fanfare or official announcement, a few new names were chosen by living members to replace those who had died. Two weeks before, Jack Flyte's name had appeared, his photograph, biography, and contact information included for the first time within the silver boards of M's elaborately bound Book of Names. Behind this, Jack had sensed once again the clever hand of Carmody.

Tossing the book into the trash, he had said to Quayle: "What do you suppose the son of a bitch wants from me now?"

Chapter Eight

Quayle stood dockside at Pier 17 near the Battery and waited for the launch to take him out to the Enterprise's Starfire Casino conspicuously anchored near mid-channel. Under the advancing sunrise, jet foils sent their rooster tails sky-high as the crafts crossed over to Manhattan from Staten Island and Brooklyn, loaded to the gunwales with early commuters on their way to Wall Street. There still had been no sign of Jack, and Quayle watched the East River waterfront come to life trying to put a damper on his growing dread.

Few signs remained of the old waterfront of a century ago. The smoky taverns, perfumed brothels, and flea-bag hotels of that era had been yielding for years to the glittering South Street tourist attractions and an ever-expanding forest of financial towers that now dominated the neighborhood. The long, grim piers where fast packets had once unloaded and the knives of drunken sailors had flashed were now chic boutiques, restaurants, and outdoor cafes. What remained of the old East Side docks, where Jack's father had once loaded and unloaded trucks for Michael Carmody's trucking empire, now bristled with the masts and tangled rigging of restored eighteenth-century ships, while along the western side of the Battery, jutting into the Hudson like half a dozen long thumbs, stood the shiny tubular warehouses of the Immigrant Selection Center--- the new Ellis Island---a warren of interview cubicles, offices, cavernous dining rooms, and temporary housing quarters, the fenced compound divided into two separate but similar parts: one for men, the other for women. Those fortunate enough to have proper papers and sponsors processed out quickly upon their arrival; however, the remaining legions of undocumented immigrants could expect to experience interminable waiting, their only diversion an idealized version of America's past projected night and day in black-and-white film footage on a wall screen at the rear of each bunkhouse, buoyed only by whatever hope had brought them. Their best chance to avoid deportation was to be moved from here to the enclaves, where there would be more interminable waiting, screening, questioning, but at least still a chance of finding a proper sponsor, placement in a job, and their ultimate release into the public domain. For the rest, deportation was almost inevitable, the solemn, imperfect solution to the immigrant problem spawned by years of trouble. Indeed, to Quayle, it was a marvel that so many still wanted to endure these hardships. Governments wherever these ports of entry existed had long since washed their hands of the matter, handing over security aspects to privatized, specially- appointed private security apparatus like the Directorate. Even now, as he watched from the dock, a van flying the black flag of the Brigades was moving out of the nearest compound trucking out another load of hapless immigrants, most likely headed for the newly constructed compounds in the Bronx, Queens, or Brooklyn enclaves, each sorted according to regions of origin.

Quayle stepped into the launch amidst the crush of the Starfire's crew change. Stewards, croupiers, dealers, floor managers in their distinctive orange jackets clamored aboard. Beyond the pier, close to mid-channel, a half-mile south of the Brooklyn Bridge, the Starfire rocked at anchor. At 300 yards in length, 52 feet of beam, the ship was the largest gambling vessel of its kind, twice the size of Sun-Yung Resorts' casino ship out of Shanghai. At 5 p.m. sharp each day, with a blast of horns, the ship's nuclear engines fired up and sent the ship noiselessly and effortlessly toward the 3-mile limit. There, beyond the reach of laws save for its own, she stood at anchor until 1 a.m., its two casinos packed with players and hangers-on, then slowly returned with its decks awash with drunken revelry.

The Starfire's launch left the dock, and soon the ship's gangway was clattering down from above. Captain Treadway was peering over the rail of the bridge, spectacles propped precariously at the end of his nose, finally coming to rest on Quayle. When he was sure he'd caught Quayle's attention, he angrily jerked a thumb toward the ships starboard rail. Quayle looked. Two Coast Guard cutters, engines full ahead, were bearing down fast, on a course precariously close to the ship. As the passengers began to board the gangway, the ship rocked and shuddered in their heavy wakes, and a doubly exercised Treadway beckoned Quayle to come up to the bridge.

In the wheel house, Treadway glared at Quayle with displeasure: "They've been making wakes all morning, damn it. Navigation's been trying to find out what the hell it's about. So far they won't answer our signals. They tell us we're supposed to consult you about it. They've been at it ever since we back came in this morning. Isn't there something you can do about this? You're the PR man."

"I'm aware of what's happening," Quayle said. "Tell Navigation this may go on for a while--- a routine counter-terrorism exercise. The passengers will just have to put up with it until you weigh anchor again."

"Just following orders," Captain Treadway snapped. "Passengers first, you know--- as per Mr. Flyte's instructions. You happen to know where he's gotten to? My chief steward's been trying to raise him? He's gotten no response."

"On his way abroad; it's confidential for the moment. Anything you need in his absence, ask me. I'll call Metro police from his stateroom to make sure they give you a wider berth. Tell the steward I'm aboard in case somebody calls for me."

Treadway looked at him strangely. "Your security man Robert Thompson already called for you. He's after me to beef up ship's security. I told him I would need to check that out with Mr. Flyte first."

"It's all right. I'm sure Mr. Flyte would want us to cooperate. Metro Police is looking for a Rikers escapee." The captain had proved himself competent and totally loyal; however Quayle dared not provide him with more information than necessary. "Is that all Thompson said?"

"Aye, sir." Treadway raised the intercom to his lips and began barking orders. Quayle left the bridge and descended to second deck, walked into the main casino, passed through an army of cleaners and worked his way around the banks of slots, crap tables, and blackjack tables. At Jack's cabin, he stopped and unlocked the door. Closing it, he went directly to Jack's wall safe. He did not know what he might find---in the event of something urgent, there were supposed to be sealed instructions about how to launch the emergency plan. At a minimum, he hoped for a note, some clue to Jack's whereabouts. Quayle consulted the list of combinations on his half of the worldwide inventory of safes, matched the Starfire's with the half Thompson had grudgingly left him at their brief morning meeting, and punched in the completed code. He had found it curious in their brief conversation Thompson had not insisted he be present when he opened it---almost as if he had already guessed whatever he might find inside would be of no consequence. In fact, there was no sealed envelope and Quayle shook his head, disappointed. Had Jack decided not to leave emergency instructions after all?

Instead, he found the usual stack of recent corporate contracts, both recently completed and still pending; a thick sheaf of other correspondence bound in rubber bands, along with folders stacked alphabetically by country, each containing individual accounting ledgers. He took the material to the desk where Jack did much of his private paperwork and sat down to work through it. The stateroom began to rock. Two more cutters were passing at a high rate of speed, heading north. He punched up Metro Police on his communicator. The operations sergeant answered. After he identified himself, he was informed the number of search ships had been increased from two to four.

"Has there been some sort of sighting?"

"No, sir. Standard procedure when the 24-hour mark has been reached without a find."

"Very well. I'm aboard the Starfire. My captain is concerned the search ships are cutting too close to us. It's bound to disturb our passengers."

"I'll patch through and tell them to give you more leeway."

"Also, leave a message with the Detective Division for someone to call me. I should be aboard at least another hour. They have my number. I want an update."

Quayle returned to the clutter on the desk. Before him lay recent contracts between the Enterprise and a variety of entities, all projects familiar to Quayle. Among them were Pretoria Diamonds, S.A., Colorado Basalt, Inc., and Allison Tungsten. Each deal, he knew, had helped solidify the Enterprise's mineral holdings in the last year, the exact purpose of which was not immediately obvious to the sellers but always, in Jack's way of doing business, a means to larger ends---horizontal integration in business-speak---if you could control all pieces of a manufacturing process, you could corner large parts of the raw materials and gain the benefit of profits at each step of the process. In this particular instance: diamonds to make drill bits for new oil exploration near Murmansk, basalt and crushed stone for building roads into the new wells, tungsten carried in by Enterprise ships to harden the steel for building those new Murmansk refineries.

It was all perfectly legal in the deregulated global environment that no longer regarded monopoly as a crime. As in each field the Enterprise chose to dominate, it was usually only a matter of time before weaker, less integrated competition fell victim to higher costs---all but Sun-Yung Resorts, whose moves, motives, and methods were as secretive and shrewd as any of Jack's, thanks to the usual active help of the Chinese government.

Quayle continued to pour through the contents of the safe, but found no specific guidance, just contract after contract. He assumed all the other safes around the world, fifty in all, would hold their own separate records of similarly far-flung deals, useful to any succession team in the event of Jack's demise but impossible for any prying outsider to discover or exploit without all the codes.

He replaced the documents, then paused and withdrew from a rear shelf a dust-covered book, its jacket badly torn. The author's name seemed vaguely familiar but the title did not, Dietrich Bonhoeffer's *Letters & Papers From Prison.* The volume appeared to be a diary from World War II---one of Jack's passions lately. The shelves of his Enterprise office had been filling lately with such writings---- Churchill, Roosevelt, Lindbergh, Eisenhower; also, Shirer, Gerhardt Boldt, and Rainer Zitelman on fascism; even an early edition of "Mein Kampf" itself. His conversations had been sprinkled with references to these writings, along with musings about the mystery of how a race so intellectually advanced in so many ways could sink so easily into barbarism. Quayle thumbed through a synopsis stuck between the brittle, yellowed pages of the prologue. In the spring of 1945, just weeks before the Russian liberation of Berlin, the SS had hanged the imprisoned thirty-nine-year-old pastor and scholar, Bonhoeffer, having finally pieced together his shadowy association with the plot to kill Hitler. A deeply religious man, Bonhoeffer had been working to further an assassination. What had Jack found of such special interest?

Quayle paged through the frail pages, stopping to take note of Jack's underlinings, circlings, and notations:

"The great masquerade of evil has played havoc with all our ethical concepts. For evil to appear disguised as light, charity, historical necessity, or social justice is quite bewildering....

"...The fact could not be escaped that the German still lacked something fundamental: he could not see the need for free and responsible action...in its place there appeared on the one hand an irresponsible lack of scruple, and on the other a self-tormenting, punctiliousness that never led to action....

"Civil courage, in fact, can grow only out of the free responsibility of free men. Only now are the Germans beginning to discover the meaning of free responsibility...."

In the margin beside this last encircled sentence was a question, written in Jack's familiar hand: "Who now among us is such a man?" He looked at the margins of the next page: Again in Jack's hand were scrawled more familiar names---Merton, Rand, Friedman, Galbraith, Aquinas, Plato, Hegel, Kazantzakis, Lao Tsu, some of the thinkers and writers whose often contrary views of the world were essential to their surviving freshman philosophy at Yale. For a few months, Jack had expressed intense interest in these works, arguing for hours in his study group about the pros and cons of a contemplative life vs. one centered on money and power. He'd worn out Quayle's patience with probing questions about these and other similarly abstract of ideas, such as the precise point where the spiritual and temporal meet, the meaning of civil responsibility in the midst of a political crisis, and the ethics of employing violence to oppose evil. For months afterward, long after the course was over, he had kept the volumes in a cardboard box in the corner of their dorm room, continuing to devour them deep into many long winter New Haven nights. Then, one morning in the spring of their graduation year, Quayle noticed the books gone. "Sold," Jack had said when Quayle had asked. "What matters is opportunity, not philosophy. In all things, above all else one must be practical." Quayle had guessed this dramatic change of mind had had something to do with his father, who several days before had come unannounced to see him. Quayle had taken a ride with his father---in Michael Carmody's limousine, as he would learn---joining Carmody at his private club, the three of them discussing Jack's future. Afterwards, Quayle had seen the change in Jack's outlook. What had been an open, questioning mind had turned to a cold determination to exploit the opportunity with which he had just been presented: a loan from the Teamsters Pension Fund that had allowed Jack to buy and refit his first cargo ship, a loan for which his father had agreed to cosign and for which Carmody would later exact a steep price---a first claim for the Teamsters to all future Enterprise shipping contracts. It was then Jack had begun talking in earnest about forming the Enterprise, a plan Quayle had readily agreed to join. Now, however, Quayle wondered what had occurred to draw his friend's attention back to his original Platonic ideals, an even more abrupt sea change of mind that seemed to be related to the evidence in recent days of the Directorate's gathering, intrusive powers. There was no question these events had rattled Jack's reality, just as they were rattling his own: Kidman's execution, the arrest of the gypsy, the relentless expansion of the immigrant enclaves. And now Jack's unaccountable disappearance.

Where the hell was he?

He slipped the book back into the safe, locked the door, and went next to Jack's desk. But there was nothing to be found there, either, once again no written instructions as the emergency plan proscribed, no hints in correspondence of pending trouble, no sign that everything wasn't as it should be. Jack, from all appearances, had fully intended to follow through with his usual morning routine of on-board paperwork before the ship sailed. Jack might have broken through the railing, after all, plunging from the terrace into the river below, just as Thompson was intimating.

A knock on the door. The chief steward. He stood stiffly before Quayle in his pressed whites. "Sorry to bother you, sir. I just thought you should know. There's been talk. A rumor Mr. Flyte has been reported missing."

Quayle looked at the man. He knew him as extremely loyal, British-born and a stickler for detail. "I appreciate your reporting this to me, Shields. However, Mr. Flyte is en route to a very important business meeting abroad. He was supposed to appear at his birthday celebration last night but was called away beforehand. This may be where the rumor originated."

"Yes, sir. Very good, sir. I just thought I'd better reassure the crew. There's been quite a buzz going on about it this morning."

"Understood," Quayle said.

He watched the man leave. Normally, by now he would have heard something from Jack. Yet he'd been repeatedly trying his secure channel without response. It was clear from this encounter, he might have less time than he hoped before the rumors got out of control. Overhead, the whine of an arriving jetcopter could be heard. He went to the porthole and watched as Metro Police #5 set down on the starboard heliport. His communicator sounded almost immediately.

"Mr. Quayle? This is Detective Navarro of Metro Police First Squad. We've just come aboard. There's been a report of a body washed up. We need you to come with us at once."

Quayle's jaw hardened. "Is this a secure channel? I warned you people not to go public with this?"

"It's secure. There will be no leaks from my department, I assure you."

Aboard the aircraft, Quayle sat strapped in beside the detective, caught in the rush of air pouring through a wide open door as they lifted off. The aircraft banked and headed directly away from the Starfire, aiming toward the spider-web spans of the Brooklyn and Manhattan Bridges. Passing directly over them, they accelerated along mid-channel and began to head due north, the same path the Coast Guard cutter had taken earlier. He watched Manhattan's towers pass by, among them Jack's own penthouse, for a moment its distinctive double-decked terrace clearly visible, the distinctive white railing of the topmost terrace, its broken section boarded over now, looming precipitously over the river. As much as he wanted to rule it out, Thompson's assumption that Jack had fallen through that rail could not be easily dismissed.

From the cockpit radio, the voice of an air controller suddenly warned the pilot to shift east away from mid-channel. They slowed, rolled right and moved in closer to the Brooklyn side of the river before rising and leveling off, heading swiftly north again.

Through the open bay of the aircraft, the southern finger of Roosevelt Island appeared. At the northern tip, just before the Hell Gate convergence, the Landmark Light tower was visible. The stone tower seemed to be the scene of some commotion. The jetcopter rose. It banked sharply and began to slowly circle the scene. Below, Quayle could see the airspace starting to fill with news choppers, dipping and swooping like gulls over the lighthouse, call letters of their stations plainly visible on their sides as the pilots jockeyed, playing a dangerous game. Along the road leading from the Hospital for Indigents and foreigners, a single-file line of horsemen could now be seen, trotting north up the island river walk toward the light. Sunlight gleamed off the tops of their black lacquered helmets. Quayle could see the apparent focus of their attention: a lone man standing before the lighthouse facing them. Navarro urged the pilot to loop around again, both he and Quayle scanning the scene with electronic binoculars. The man below was plainly visible as the jetcopter swooped past, his frightened face springing into Quayle's lenses---the face of Julius Rabinsky.

The Enterprise's chief accountant stood motionless, looking agitated and very small.

Navarro ordered the pilot to hover. With a jolt, the stabilizer rockets ignited and halted them in midair, the craft held motionless by its stabilizing thrusters a hundred feet above the scene.

"You know him?" Navarro shouted at Quayle above the racquet.

"Yes, Julius Rabinsky. He's our chief accountant."

The detective opened his communicator and spoke into it. "Detective Navarro from Metro Police here. I need to question that man." A voice crackled back in a way Quayle could not clearly hear. "I see," Navarro said. "Then I want access to him at your earliest convenience."

Navarro closed his communicator and shook his head. "I'm sorry. It's outside my jurisdiction. What do you think this is about?"

Quayle looked again at Rabinsky through the powerful binoculars. The little man held a revolver in his right hand. He had it pointed straight down at the ground. Sunlight shone off his bald pate.

"My jurisdiction ends somewhere between this door and that point of land down there," the chief of detectives continued loudly. "As far as any questioning is concerned, we will have to wait our turn. This is Brigades business, it seems. "

"He has a gun," Quayle interrupted, lowering the binoculars and handing them to Navarro.

The detective snatched his communicator out of his pocket again. He shouted into it against the din of the jetcopter's engines: "This is Chief of Detectives Navarro from Metro again; that man is armed."

"We know that," a voice barked back. "Now, keep this fucking channel open or you will be reported as interfering with an arrest."

Navarro snapped his communicator shut. "These pricks," he growled. "They're running around invoking these Emergency Decrees every damn day now. The mayor's created a monster with these paramilitary units."

Quayle understood perfectly. This was supposed to be Metro Police's jurisdiction, and the Brigades had been allowed to impose their own order wherever they chose. They sounded rattled, too.

Backing up, Rabinsky had now reached the island's northernmost point. The seawall and the river were at his back. He stared at the phalanx of horsemen facing him, his escape blocked. A horseman spurred his mount forward and stopped just feet from the fugitive. Slowly, he raised his pistol. Rabinsky did not move. The rider motioned him forward.

A plume of smoke erupted from the muzzle of Rabinsky's gun. The shot blew a piece of his skull skyward as his short, frail frame hurtled backwards from the force of the shot. His body came to rest atop the seawall, his short legs folded under him. As the jetcopter hovered, Quayle could see two horsemen dismount, one with the now-familiar body bag slung over a shoulder.

The police jetcopter banked sharply away from the island to avoid a swiftly approaching news chopper, the intruder's television call letters practically filling the jetcopter's bubble-domed windshield as it shot skyward, then banked back toward the river. With a deafening roar, its whirling blades passed just feet away from the open doorway.

The police crew cursed as they passed.

"I will need to know everything you know about this man," Detective Navarro said as he ordered the pilot to resume the flight north. "If you think there is any connection between this and Mr. Flyte's disappearance, I need to know that, too."

Quayle nodded. "Of course."

The jetcopter dipped low over Hell Gate's whitecaps, heading eastward almost at wave top, slipping around Rikers Island and under the heavy LaGuardia air traffic. Across the mud flats of Flushing Bay, the machine accelerated for another quarter mile before setting down on a spit of land within view of the sprawling Rikers prison. A hundred yards further east, near the Whitestone Bridge, they could see the water's edge. It was low tide, and the mud flats stank of every imaginable smell. They got out and walked toward a cluster of uniformed police waiting beside a corpse encased in clear plastic.

Quayle watched as an officer draw back the sheet of plastic.

"Dead not more than twenty-four hours, I'd say," the officer said to Navarro. "No I.D. on him."

"Look carefully," Detective Navarro insisted.

Quayle was shaking his head. "This is not Jack Flyte. Nothing like him."

"Look again. You must be absolutely sure? The river can change a person's appearance very fast."

With a lump in his throat, Quayle studied the remains of the face, its bruised, torn, and swollen features still possible to faintly distinguish despite the beating it had taken in the narrows. The features and build were nothing like Jack's. He said in a voice breaking with relief: "The age appears right, that's about all."

"There's been substantial disfigurement from the body's passage through the river debris," Navarro insisted. "Please look again."

"No, I'm certain," Quayle repeated.

Navarro nodded. He drew Quayle aside as they moved back toward their transport. "When we make a positive identification of this man, I will make it clear he was the reason for our search. I now have five men on the investigation."

"Thank you, detective. I will get back to you about Rabinsky as soon as I can."

In minutes, the jetcopter was airborne again, Quayle aboard, headed for the Midtown Skyport where he would be dropped off before the body was unloaded at the Bellevue morgue. As they again crossed Roosevelt Island, Quayle could see half a dozen Metro Police cars escorting an ambulance from the scene as uniformed workers hosed down the site. On the path back from where the horsemen had closed in, two mothers pushed baby strollers back through the barricades and hurried toward the safety of the looming apartment complex from which they must have come. The media were long gone.

Chapter Nine

Cecil sat sketching in the front room of the townhouse, her taut, angular face bathed in warm midday sunlight pouring in from the street. Nearby, Quayle kept watch on the flickering wall screen for news of the Rabinksy intervention. It was just past noon, an hour since he'd left an encoded text message for Thompson about the Riker's body not being Jack. Still, he'd received no word back.

He heard the main international alarms in fragments: "Pentagon reports U.S. Navy ships entering Taiwan Strait...Washington warns Beijing of reprisals if U.S. relief efforts to Taiwan are blocked...President counsels calm..."

The media overload was unmanageable now. Even as a publicist, Quayle had grown adept at screening out false, manufactured media alerts, but these new Chinese tensions were real. The Enterprise's Shanghai casino business would be disrupted if new regional unrest broke out, as would the conglomerate's cruise-ship and oil-tanker traffic.

Suddenly, the wall screen filled with the Metro Report. He turned up the sound. Rabinsky's bespectacled, terrified face filled the wall. The newscaster shouted over the jetcopter's whine: "An attempted apprehension on Roosevelt Island today has come to a bloody end. A man authorities are identifying as a high-level employee of the international conglomerate the Enterprise has taken his own life." The camera overhead panned the scene, then flashed back to the face of the Brigades' quarry. "Julius Rabinksy, chief accountant of the company, was being sought for questioning in connection with an undisclosed matter. In dramatic WESN film footage some may find offensive, the fugitive can be seen refusing, then ending his own life with a single shot to the head. All efforts to revive him failed. A spokesman for the Directorate says an investigation is under way."

"My God," cried Cecil. "I saw Rabinsky at Jack's party."

Quayle looked up quickly. "You're certain of that?"

"Absolutely. I'd arrived early. He was standing at the elevator in Jack's lower suite when I got off. You hadn't arrived yet. One of the security men was preventing him from going up to Jack's penthouse suite on his private elevator. I remember it distinctly. He was being ordered back down in the public elevator. I thought there was something very odd about that."

"Do you remember what was being said?"

"Something about Rabinsky needing to speak with Jack about a business matter."

"Who was preventing him?"

Cecil thought for a moment. "I am sure it was one of Thompson's security men."

Quayle's lips tightened. He turned back to the wall screen. The reporter was shouting above the roar of the jetcopter's engines: "A spokesman for the Directorate has told WESN News that an urgent appeal to the public has been issued. Anyone with information about associates or friends of Julius Rabinsky of 145 West 122nd Street is being urged to contact the agency's Citizens Watch number at once. All calls will be handled with absolute confidentiality."

Already, Quayle knew, the Directorate's electronic kiosks positioned all over the city would be projecting the phone number for all to see.

Quayle opened his communicator and punched in Thompson's

secure number. This time

Thompson answered.

"Where the hell have you been," Quayle shouted angrily. "I've been trying to reach you all morning. Are you monitoring Channel 7?"

"Yes, of course."

"How the hell did this happen?"

"I only informed the Directorate to have the Brigades be on the lookout for Rabinsky. I told them I only wanted him detained, so we could question him. Rabinsky panicked."

"Damn it, Bob. Look at this mess! We've been through all this already. Jack's emergency instructions weren't in the safe when I looked. Where the hell are they?"

There was a pause, then finally Thompson answered: "The directors have rescinded them. This is an internal security matter now. I've had all the envelopes removed and couriered back to me. There's no telling how much Rabinsky has compromised security. There's more. The directors have called an emergency meeting of the executive board. The day and time are still to be decided. I sent you a memo by courier. Did you get it?"

"Yes."

"Also, Jack Blackwell just called from Legal. He wants you to put out a statement to all media that the Enterprise has had an ongoing investigation of Rabinsky for some time. We need to cover our asses on this."

"Cover your ass, you mean. Why am I hearing all this from you now? Why haven't you contacted me about this before?"

Thompson remained silent. Slowly, his ice-cold voice came back on the line. "Here's how it is, Ben. From now on, the board wants you to report directly to me. You'll hear all about it at the meeting. I was planning to give you a heads up when you got here. Nothing personal. This is my problem to handle now. It's to be strictly a security operation."

Quayle fought to control his anger. "I should warn you, Bob. I'm going to fight this. This is not what Jack intended. Telling the media about an internal investigation is like pouring gasoline on a fire."

"Ben, the directors will be expecting you to be a team player on this...for the good of the Enterprise"

"And I am telling you, damn it, this is about to become a PR disaster. You fired Rabinsky before we could evaluate exactly what he'd done. Then your people let him get out of the building before we could vet him. It could have been done far more discreetly. The Brigades are totally out of control now; Jack's been increasingly concerned about them. He would never have let you turn the Directorate and the Brigades loose on Rabinsky like that."

Thompson uttered a derisive grunt. "Rabinsky was bound to go to the media with some lie to cover his butt. Is that what you would have wanted---an even worse PR mess--- simply because you and I couldn't get our acts together? Face it. It was Rabinsky who overreacted. It wasn't the Directorate's or the Brigades' doing. We've got all of Rabinsky's codes and files now; we have what we need to prove what he's been up to. We don't even need him to complete the picture. I'd say the documents and his snuffing himself pretty well settle it."

"For the record, Bob, I would be very surprised if Rabinsky was skimming any casino accounts, much less cooking any books. Jack has trusted him implicitly and absolutely as long as he has been with us, and that's long before you got here. For your sake, I hope you do have the goods; the executive committee is not going to be pleased if you don't."

"Let me worry about that, Ben," Thompson snapped.

"As you damn well should," Quayle said sharply, and closed his communicator, ending the conversation.

Cecil stared. "What on earth is that man up to now?"

Quayle did not respond. His attention had been drawn back to the wall screen. Across it now streamed old file film of a Taiwanese destroyer firing rockets over the Taiwan Strait --- alarming file images from the first Chinese-Taiwanese conflict of twenty years before. The media were adding new propellant to the crisis; damage control would be needed here as well.

Turning back to her, Quayle said to Cecil: "I just remembered something one of Rabinsky's auditors tried to tell me a few weeks ago. It seemed trivial at the time, some expense account matter he'd been looking into. I put him off. Now I wonder if it might be significant after all."

Cecil was no longer listening, staring instead through the open curtains of the front window. "Ben," she said.

Quayle stood up and went to the window. Two men in well-tailored suits were crossing the busy street, approaching their stone stoop. Seconds later, their buzzer sounded.

Chapter Ten

The headquarters of the Directorate---overseer of the Horse Brigades---could have housed any manner of bureau, agency, or office. Its two nondescript granite towers rose ten stories from a blind alley off Foley Square, rows of bronze-burnished windows positioned to draw in outside light while concealing its true function. No sign stood outside, no numbered address appeared on any wall, no actual street address existed that Quayle had ever seen. All that distinguished this from all other buildings encamped around City Hall was its solitary entrance, imbedded several yards back inside the shadowy confines of a dark alleyway, where a small bronze sun stood at the center of a blast-proof door.

Inside, Quayle and his two escorts stopped at a security desk and waited as a uniformed guard scanned his magnetic ID, then directed them all up a long staircase. Second-floor-only access to elevators was the standard defense now against street-level explosions.

From Level 2 , they took an elevator to Level 10 and stepped into an empty, brightly-lit corridor. At the far end stood a glassed-in waiting room. Quayle entered with his handlers and sat waiting.

Suddenly, incongruously, a violin began to play --- Stravinsky, Quayle guessed. Save for the halting, occasionally off-key notes of the instrument, no sounds came from the rows of other cubicles lining the waiting room. Soon, the music ceased, and a rather curious gentleman popped his head from a rear cubicle and beckoned to him. He had a broad brow and a thick head of snow-white hair, matched in color and texture by thick, unkempt brows and framing intense, opaque eyes. His overall appearance was of an eagle examining a morsel of prey.

"Please, take a seat," the man said curtly, violin in hand. "I'll be with you in a moment."

Quayle guessed at the accent: upper-class British. It was not uncommon for the Directorate to draw on ex-MI5 talent for its investigative branches, shunning former CIA types as potentially too close to a U.S. security apparatus that lately had proven itself inept. Private security operations like the Directorate were now regularly soliciting and winning lucrative contracts from anxious corporations no longer trustful of government.

"You are Mr. Quayle?"

"Yes, sir, I am."

"I am Noel Gatwick, the Directorate's commissioner of inquiries. He raised the violin and plinked a string. "I seem to have mauled a note." He struck the bow lightly against the strings and produced a sweeter tone. "Ah," he said, "my crime against *Histoire du Soldat* is redeemed." Replacing the instrument in its case, he looked at Quayle more closely. "What sort of name would Quayle be--- Scottish then?"

"By origin. However, my grandparents were French-born; my parents American-born citizens after the Algerian War of '62."

"Yes, so it says in your file." Gatwick peered at him inquisitively. "Technically, though, I see it says here your grandmother was actually Arab? Is that correct?"

"Yes. Algerian French and Sunni Arab. She married my grandfather in Algiers when he was stationed in one of the French ministries during the violence."

"Yes, that *pieds-noirs* business," Gatwick said. "Very instructive for us when we attended the London Security Academy. De Gaulle caught flat-footed on that one, eh, ordering everybody back home after one too many FLN bombings? He didn't earn any thanks from the colonialists, did he, or from the home-fronters, either? Only the bloody Arab terror squads and their bombers got what they wanted. What did your grandparents make of all that?"

"They were civil servants, not political. To them, the *pieds-noirs* were innocents---farmers, patriots, settlers---not occupiers, not political at all. They thought de Gaulle sold them out, just as many of their Arab friends did once the violence started. They believed they were pawns in that struggle for independence."

"And your grandparents came to New York after the evacuations were ordered. Is that right?"

"Yes."

"Instead of returning to France as so many of the other ex-patriot *pieds-noirs* did, I see they came here with their son---your father."

"Yes."

"And your father became an important man, did he not? A skilled stock trader with one of the important brokerages?"

"Yes. Cantor Fitzgerald."

"And he met and married your mother, who was also of Algerian-Arab background?"

"Also Sunni Arab, yes, though she had also come to New York from Jeddah, with her own family. She was also very young then."

"And they met and married, then in 1998 you were born?"

"Yes. But you must know all of this from my file as well. I still don't understand why I am here."

"We will get to that. First, I always like to make certain our records are accurate. Go on, I find this very interesting. Describe in your own words what you came to learn about the events of September 11, 2001."

For Quayle, this was nothing new; he had explained it all so often in the year he'd spent in therapy at 16, it scarcely brought up any disturbing feelings anymore; it had become someone else's story. Still, within this coercive context and under Gatwick's intense gaze, he felt unnerved. He cleared his throat and said: "They were both working in Tower II when it fell. Neither made it out. I was only 3 years old when it happened. Eventually, I was sent by child services to live with my grandparents. They raised me."

"You were fortunate. Some children of victims had no one. What did your grandparents teach you about that terrible event?"

Quayle paused. Personally, he remembered nothing. However, the media coverage and constantly replayed images he saw later remained seared into his mind as if he had in fact witnessed it all---especially, he remembered, those images of people jumping; he had learned later his parents had been among them, sometimes seeing them appearing in his dreams, falling and falling, never landing.

"They told me I must keep the events in context, that these terrorists had been people on the margins, people with personal grievances, misunderstandings, and greed not unlike the hypocrisies of those demanding their rights and independence in the Algerian violence. I would find, my grandfather said, many past centuries littered with similar unfairnesses, all with one common thread: tribal grudges that always, without fail, spilled blood, yet produced no lasting solutions.

Quayle remembered this---the day they had tried to explain it to him---and he could sense what was now coming. Gatwick wanted to know whose side he was on. He wanted his unconditional support for the Directorate's Emergency Decrees.

Then, there it was: "With such a history," Gatwick began coldly, "you must resent people who would do such a thing. You understand what we are up against with the enclaves, do you not?"

Quayle sensed the trap. He must tread carefully. He averted his eyes, slowly shaking his head. "This happened to my parents a long time ago." He looked up then, and rather than appear evasive suddenly met Gatwick's intense gaze directly. "The grievances of those in the enclaves are happening today, right now; some may be justifiable, some may not be. I am in no real position to judge."

"No you are not. But you do understand why the public must respect the judgment of those who do know, and that it's most urgent we all remain unified against violence, whatever form it takes, This is also why the corporate consortium to which your company, the Enterprise, belongs must proceed with unwavering confidence that all the consortium's members are in full agreement that these decrees are right and necessary?"

"Yes, I do understand that."

Gatwick nodded, but went on as if Quayle's response had not yet struck him as emphatic enough. "Should the enemy detect the slightest weakness, they will take it as an opportunity to foment more violence. Indecision on any of our parts is not an option. The consortium has engaged us to ensure that companies like the Enterprise remain fully free to conduct their business in safety, despite these so-called enclave grievances. The Emergency Decrees are vital to future security."

"Why do you raise these questions with me? Of course I agree with all that. Why do you think I would not?"

Gatwick's gaze narrowed; his smile was no longer congenial. "There has been a report...." He turned back to his computer. "... a report that Mr. Flyte, your CEO and friend, has been expressing doubts about our methods. We understand that he has suggested it might be a wise step for the Enterprise to withdraw its support from the Directorate and leave the consortium. Perhaps, you would care to comment about those reports?"

Gatwick's frosted winged brows had risen, his eyes had become more piercing. "Let me be more precise, Mr. Quayle. I need your absolute assurance that these rumors are unfounded."

"I think that is a question better put to Mr. Flyte," Quayle answered quickly, trying to keep his voice from quavering.

"We haven't been able to reach him. Therefore, it would be very helpful if you would tell us if you have heard from him or where we might locate him. I will repeat this message to you as often as it may be required: You must cooperate fully with us, not only at this moment as we speak, but for as long as the Emergency Decrees may be in force. Is that understood?"

Quayle's expression remained impassive, but inside him was turmoil. He knew now: the squash court, the locker room, maybe other places, had been bugged. Gatwick knew what Jack had said; The Directorate's chief of inquiries had been a direct recipient of that information.

"I do recall a conversation about the new encampments," Quayle answered finally, "I don't believe, however, our discussion was particularly original; encampments with their barbed wire enclosures were a topic of conversation all over the city that day."

"Let me be more direct, Mr. Quayle. Did Mr. Flyte express to you his intention to recommend to the Enterprise board that it cease its association with the consortium and with the Directorate?"

"I would prefer that you ask him that. I insist on it, in fact."

"No. My question is being put to you. I insist you see the gravity of this situation. As you know, from your own experience at the racquet club and the unexploded bomb the Brigades found there, the hatred of certain enclave elements now threatens to spill into the greater metropolitan area. I'm sure neither you nor Mr. Flyte would wish to be responsible for encouraging that. Please understand, as reluctant as we have been to fortify security within the enclaves, it is a step that is both logical and necessary. I repeat: We must have your cooperation."

Quayle dropped his gaze, then looked up with his jaw set. "I am sure Mr. Flyte will explain his thinking when he feels he has reason to do so."

"Then you are telling me you personally will not cooperate?"

"Yes, I will cooperate to the best of my ability. However, it is not my place to characterize what the Enterprise as a company may or may not choose to do. Until I have spoken with my employer, that is all I can say about this."

Gatwick's enigmatic smile crept across his lips. "You have been a busy man over these past few days, haven't you, Mr. Quayle? Present at the Kidman intervention, then a witness along with Mr. Flyte to the Brigades arresting a suspect in an attempted bombing. Both of you could have been killed had it not been for the Brigades' alertness in stopping that attempt. And now..." his voice dropped pointedly, "...the Enterprise's chief accountant has taken his own life, rather than submit to questioning about a criminal matter that your own chief of security had brought to our attention and asked help with. Yet, you still seem less than enthusiastic about cooperating with us." He met Quayle's gaze directly. "Can you tell me why we should not hold you for further questioning?"

"I can assure you," Quayle snapped, "I have no special knowledge of any of those events you mention, or any others You will be wasting your time and mine to hold me, and I am sure Mr. Flyte would be exceedingly displeased."

"I wonder," Gatwick said with that smile.

"Look. When he returns, I will be happy to give him a report about our conversation and pass on to him your concern about his position on the decrees. As you must know from past media reports, unannounced absences are not uncommon for Mr. Flyte. I am sure I will be hearing from him before his upcoming meeting in Dubrovnik in three days."

"You should understand we are continuing our investigation of the Rabinksy matter and will need your further cooperation on that matter as we proceed."

"Again, I assure you that I am cooperating within the limits of my capacity as chief publicist of the Enterprise. I am sure you wouldn't want me to break a corporate confidence, an action I have no authority, by the way, to do."

Gatwick's eyes narrowed. "Indeed, if we had reason to believe this Rabinsky matter posed a danger to the general public safety, I can promise you we would insist upon it. Don't mistake me. While I admire loyalty and discretion, I must repeat: Whenever the security of the consortium is involved, loyalty must come second."

"I will pass that message on."

Gatwick held Quayle's gaze, slowly nodding. "Then I think we have had a satisfactory meeting, Mr. Quayle."

The commissioner of inquiries faced his computer screen, typed several lines, and printed out what he had written. "Your interview has been duly noted. Take this to the security men waiting for you at the elevators. You are free to go."

***

Outside, Quayle stood for a moment in front of the Directorate observing the food vendors serving the last of the lunchtime crowd. Heavy traffic was circling Foley Square, while overhead the whir of north-south trams could be heard, the bright red cars taking their passengers along the wires at a rapid speed. The time. according to the huge clock on City Hall tower, was now five minutes past 1.On the east side of the square, around one corner, a motorcade appeared. Quayle watched a stream of cars sweep past, police materializing out of nowhere to halt traffic to allow them to move swiftly through the main intersection, then swing around the far side of the park and down a broad apron of concrete into the depths of an underground garage. Quayle crossed the park and came to the entrance of the garage, walking slowly down the apron of concrete into the cavernous space. He entered just as the main barriers came plummeting down behind him. Some distance away, in the back reaches of the garage, he could hear car doors slamming, then the repetitive dings of arriving and departing elevators.

He could not be entirely certain this garage served only the Directorate towers. Its elevators might just as easily open onto the floors of City Hall, or any one of the handful of other adjacent buildings within the Foley Square government complex. The disembarking passengers might have been headed anywhere in the buildings above.

He walked several yards further into the garage where scores of passengers now stood waiting at a rear bank of elevators. From the last and longest limousine pulling up, a short, squat man emerged---the easily recognizable mayor of New York City, Francis Shrum---followed by a second---tall, square-jawed, and broad-shouldered, his pale countenance also recognizable to Quayle as he stepped out of the rear seat into the glare of the overhead lights of the garage---Thompson, the Enterprise's chief of security.

The two men stood conversing, then quickly stepped into the arriving elevator together. The mayor clapped Thompson on the back as they both vanished behind the closing doors.

Chapter Eleven

Cecil's taxi swerved onto 42nd Street in a downpour, the driver braking hard to avoid a young couple opening a red umbrella in the crosswalk, then turned into the curb at New Media Tower. Cecil paid her fare and raced under the canopy of the entrance. She was twenty minutes late, a sure way to tax Sabrena's short attention span.

Just below the rain clouds, a biplane banked low, then began a slow climb back skyward. It was clearly visible from where she stood, trailing a banner that read "Be alert! Report!" She took out a sketch pad and noted the toll-free number it included, fodder for the new public mural she was planning for a blank wall she'd spotted near the Whitney. Her purse slipped from her shoulder, and she stooped to retrieve it. From directly behind her came a loud pop, like a cap pistol going off. A beat more and a deafening explosion rocked the block. In the instant it took for the shock wave to strike her, she felt herself pitching face down onto the concrete apron of the entrance. Dazed, she opened her eyes. Untangling herself from her purse strap, she tried to look back from where the explosion had come. There, on the street, she could see a cab on its roof, wheels spinning. Shards of glass, steel and reinforced concrete were strewn everywhere. Traffic had come to a standstill. Geysers of steam hissed up from manholes, their covers strewn like poker chips across the block. Under one of these circular slabs of concrete, a young woman lay in a pool of her own blood, one motionless hand gripping a red umbrella. In the distance, sirens began to wail.

Cecil felt nausea rise and roll over her. She began fumbling for the contents of her purse--- lipsticks, compact, comb, brush, wallet, sketchpad, pencils, pens, packet of Kleenex, communicator---her mind focused on them, repulsed by the rest of the scene. Finally, she raised her eyes. A shard of steel stood buried at an angle in a pillar nearby. It had missed her head by mere inches. Outside, a chorus of sirens grew louder. She caught a glimpse of an ambulance, then another, and another.

She felt herself lifted to her feet and led slowly to the rear of the lobby. There, she sat down in the armchair. She said she was all right, thanked her helpers. She sat for a moment, catching her breath, then slowly punched Ben's number into her communicator. She got Voicemail. "It's me. You'd better turn on the news. There's been an explosion across from New Horizon Media, Sabrena's building in midtown. I'm all right. I'm going up to try to go up and see her now. I'll call you later."

In the ladies' room, she examined herself. Except for scraped elbows and knees, she seemed unscathed. She discarded her torn hose, washed blood off her knees and elbows, and redid her makeup. Back in the lobby, people were flooding out of the elevators, no one going up. She stepped into an empty car, speed-dialed Sabrena's number as the doors closed, and had to contend again with Voicemail. "It's Cecil. I hope you're still there. There's been a bombing. I'm all right, but I'm coming up."

Exiting at the forty-fifth floor, she pushed her way past a crowd waiting to enter her elevator and threaded her way past the double-glass doors into reception.

The plush waiting room stood empty, remains of elaborately framed screen shots of *In*'s Web-a-zine covers strewn across the floor in broken glass, their display cases blown from the walls.

Sabrena's door stood ajar. She called her name, and the door flew open. "Cecil, thank, God," Sabrena said, cradling a phone against her cheek and waving her to a chair. She spoke into the phone: "I don't care, I'm not evacuating. Tell security they'll have to come up here and haul me out themselves. No, I don't care what the mayor's orders are. I've got a magazine to close tonight; we're not about to walk away from what may be the year's biggest story."

Sabrena ended the call and punched in a new number. "Jimmy, tell everybody to their asses back up here. Round them all up even if you have to do it yourself. I want this story on the Web site in an hour, updates every fifteen minutes. And I want as many images, details, and eyewitness accounts in the print edition as we can get when we close tonight. Make sure you tell Freddie he's in charge of all coverage. Our security cameras probably caught the whole damn scene. We need to make copies before the police confiscate them as evidence. Well, find Freddie , damn it. Tell him to get back up here now!"

Cecil took a seat in one of the arm chairs lining the room, the space designed more for meetings than Sabrena's private office. The room was relentlessly white---walls, furniture, carpets, draperies accented in pastels, all of it complemented by an expansive scenic mural that took up three walls---a Cecil Collander original, also dominated by white. Six panels rose on each wall from floor to ceiling, the collective scene depicting a river of milk winding through an emerald green valley splashed from above by luminous rays of a tangerine sun. "Milk and Honey," Cecil had entitled the work, which had pleased Sabrena so enormously she had featured its unveiling in the Web-a-zine.

Sabrena paced behind her desk, still speaking rapidly into her communicator, then pausing as she pulled back the drapes and stared out the window. "Jesus Christ, can they make any more of a mess out there? Was anybody killed?" She combed her nails nervously through her wheat-colored mane as she waited for an answer. "God. Five so far? Are they still counting? Yes? Damn it. The mayor's people have continuously assured us this wouldn't happen to Manhattan. Now, here it is, on our own bloody doorstep."

She stopped pacing, cupped the phone, and looked at Cecil. "You're all right, aren't you? You weren't hurt?"

"Only some scrapes, my nerves are like a Mixmaster, but I'm fine."

"Thank God for that." She returned to her call. "Don't tell me to calm down. I'll get calm when I'm good and ready. For the last time, Jimmy, tell security we're not evacuating until we've got our work done up here." She ended the call and dropped into the chair behind her desk, letting out an exasperated sigh. "So the shit storm begins: more crap from our own security people about fortifying departments and entrances, more bullshit excuses from the mayor's office about clearing all stories with them, an economic bloody nose for the downtown boutiques and our ad stream and we can't get any fucking facts without mud-wrestling an army of the mayor's flaks. It's hard enough getting the Chanel people and the Versace mob to cooperate without a war between the crazy Achmeds and Mayor Shrum ruining business downtown. Tent cities, for God's sake! What did Shrum think was going to happen when he ordered those up. And with his non-negotiation malarky, the Imams have no reason at all to restrain their radicals over there. There won't be a moderate left for anybody to talk to if this keeps up--- on either side of the damn river. Now a bombing in Midtown? It's going to be a total fucking disaster."

"That's not all," Cecil said quickly. "Someone planted a bomb in Jack's locker at the Racquet Club yesterday. Fortunately, the Brigades found it somehow and disarmed it."

Sabrena shuddered. "For God's sake. Shrum's such a hopeless

specimen."

"I have an idea, ' Cecil said. "It's not exactly why I first asked to see you, but now that

I think of it, it's close enough." She drew a deep breath. She had Sabrena's full attention now, she could see that. A rare moment these days when she was so infernally busy with the magazine and all its ancillary media ventures. In school, whenever she needed advice, it was Sabrena she'd go to first. In this case, no one had a better bead on the cultural and political moshpit inside City Hall than Sabrena did, *In*'s army of reporters and bloggers notorious for finding dirt. The Web-a-zine and its various bloggers were also a must-read for the politically savvy, mixing inside celebrity gossip with in-depth political analysis; there was nobody more tuned to politics, local, state, and national, than *In*'s chief national reporter Julian Fabreeze.

"Ben has a source who is almost certain Genesee plans to announce for the presidency in the fall," Cecil said. "I know she's been denying it publicly, refusing interviews, but Ben's heard privately she's on the verge of naming an exploratory committee. He says she'll need two hundred million dollars just for next year's primaries. I was thinking if we could convince her to go on the record with us first---in an exclusive interview with *In* about this security problem in the city--- it might be a way into the bigger question of her presidential ambitions."

Sabrena blinked. "Two hundred million. That sounds plausible. And she'll need at least that much lead time to raise that much. Go on."

"This Midtown bombing may be just the pretext for her to announce a bold new initiative on managing this security problem. As you said, Shrum's consistently ruled out negotiations with anyone in the enclaves. Now this. He'll be sure to escalate the crackdown. This could be a perfect moment for Genesee to intervene."

"She's said so far she won't. She's keeping it Shrum's problem. So is the White House. I think they're all perfectly content to let Shrum experiment with the decrees and hand off the dirty work to the Brigades. I think they want to see if it works, so they can decide if it makes sense to replicate it elsewhere."

"Ben witnessed the Brigades' intervention the other day," Cecil broke in. "Kidman, that theater critic. They said he was having secret dealings with enclave radicals."

"I read all about it in the *Post.* No trial under the Emergency Decrees, either. People are starting to think that's just a more efficient way of doing things. I didn't see a single blogger, commentator or letter to the editor complaining about it. Not a fucking peep."

"Someone's got to persuade Genesee to stop this."

Sabrena nodded, her eyes brightening more. "Except, she won't answer my calls. She's still pissed off at me for not sending someone to Albany to cover her upstate antipoverty initiative. I told her our readers don't give a damn about what goes on up there; Albany might as well be a foreign country. Syracuse and Buffalo, for God's sake--- nobody sells newspapers, magazines, or air time talking about them. That's all Albany's problem."

"I want you to let me try to pitch an idea of mine to her. The whole country is going to be talking about this. There will be more calls for security crackdowns and all of that, just as you say. But what if Genesee were to decide to run against that tide?"

Sabrena bit her lip. "She really does need to stop being so damn cautious. I don't really understand why she's been so silent about all this. I've been wondering if Shrum's got her compromised in some way. It would be just like him. Tell me more."

Cecil leaned forward. "As we're saying, Shrum has refused to negotiate, like he wants this all to blow up in the city's face. Then and the City Council can find ways to make the Directorate even more powerful. But suppose Genesee went into the enclaves with her own people, bypassing Shrum and the city---an impromptu inspection of all the enclaves' encampments, escorted by a group of moderate Imams. Nobody really knows what's been going on in there since way before the Emergency Decrees were even ordered; in the past year the mainstream media haven't even tried; their coverage so far has been from the air. I tried to get into the Brooklyn enclave last month to do sketches for a mural I had planned, and they stopped me at the area they've now cordoned off with barbed wire. There were already bulldozers in there. They wouldn't let me pass, told me it wasn't safe."

"What's to keep Shrum and his people from telling her no, that it's within the city's jurisdiction what happens over there?"

"The editorial pages will jump all over her when they find out.," Sabrena said grimly. "They'll say she's favoring negotiations with terrorists. The *Post* will go nuts. So may the *Times*. They're all getting paranoid about any talk of moderation."

"No, she should simply say it was a fact-finding mission, on behalf of all the enclave residents. The Greeks, the Jews, the Italians, the Koreans, the Chinese, they're all upset at the deteriorating conditions in their own neighborhoods. That's what she should say. And besides, what's the alternative?" Cecil threw a hand up toward a window cracked by the blast. "More ghettoization and backlash, followed by more risk to us entitled souls in Manhattan?"

Sabrena drummed her nails on the white desktop. The intensity of her expression matched Cecil's: "Genesee will be crazy to just sit back and wait for Shrum to fall on his face anymore than he already has."

Cecil nodded. "She's got a huge opportunity here to exert some leadership, to take some control of this. To look presidential. She's got to understand that."

For a moment, Sabrena did not respond. Then she said: "Still, C, it's a huge risk. People want scapegoats. The enclaves are still everybody's victims of choice. She will have to be very persuasive about the crackdowns being self-defeating, and she'll have to come out of there with some sort of concrete action from the Imams. You know how damn problematical that's likely to be."

Cecil gave her a tight smile. "You're preaching to the choir, Sabrena. My public art has been warning of this for months."

Sabrena paused, then slowly nodded. Muffled sounds of heavy machinery could be heard rising from the street below. Finally, she said: "All right. If she'll let Fabreeze and a videographer go along, and we get this as an exclusive, you can assure her we won't break the story until the enclave visit is over. You can tell her she has my personal guarantee of that. First, you're going to have to convince her. That may take some doing, but she's got to know we're the most reliable media source to explain why something bold like this needs to be done. We're practically ground zero for this bombing, for God's sake; that's as good an excuse as any to bring us in on this. The Times and Post are both bound to call on Shrum to activate the State Guard and double the security around all Manhattan entries and departure points under the Emergency Decrees."

"If she agrees to see me, I can be on the fast train to Albany first thing in the morning."

"Good. The media will be bombarding her office with requests for statements now. If you call her on her private line...it will be a much faster. I've got it here someplace."

Sabrena wrote down the number and handed it to her.

Cecil stood up and embraced her warmly. "I love you, baby," she said. "We're going to do this."

Back outside, cleanup crews stood by as fire, police, and bomb squads worked amidst the wreckage. Cecil showed her identification card to a uniformed police officer, who scanned the card on his belt scanner and began to ask questions about what she had observed. Finally, he waved her through the cordon of police tapes.

As she waited for a cab, she noticed the biplane again, circling above the scene in what was now a clear blue sky. A cab pulled to the curb, and she stepped inside. As it pulled away, she dialed the toll-free number displayed on the banner. "We're sorry, your call cannot be completed as dialed," the automatic voice said, "please hang up and dial again."

Chapter Twelve

Cecil booked a seat on the crowded morning fast-train to Albany, the hour-and-a-half ride up the Hudson easier to endure than all the usual suffocating airport security. The train sped north at one hundred miles per hour, as placidly as a ship on a calm sea. There were electronic magazines and books, television monitors at every seat, light breakfast brought by white-jacketed stewards at the push of a button. At this hour, most passengers were lobbyists headed for the state capital or silver-haired seniors off to the Catskill casinos. The new gaming laws, enacted over Governor Genesee Wainwright's angry veto, had sunk Albany into an even deeper ethical pit than usual. Las Vegas gaming promoters had soon proposed using the new law to expand video gaming into the state's public schools--- a teaching aid, they said. This had presented Jack Flyte with a perfect opportunity to come to the aid of the public good by testifying strongly against the idea, an offer Governor Wainwright readily accepted. "This state should not be in the business of encouraging children to gamble under some veiled guise of teaching," he told a Senate committee at a critical televised moment. Cynics noted his testimony was hardly unselfish; the scheme hatched by Las Vegas gaming interests posed a direct threat to the Enterprise's near-monopoly hold over New York State's casino business. But the blatant breech of ethical lines had awakened the somnolent public to the larger outrage, and thanks to Jack's timely opposition, media coverage had ignited and the bill had promptly died. Governor Wainwright had applauded the Enterprise's effort. Jack had insisted Ben hang the framed appreciation on his own office wall; the bold public relations stroke had been his idea all along.

As the train sped north, the lines of television screens were now filled with replays of the Conde Nast bombing; the media, as usual, couldn't get enough of it. She watched raptly, but seeing nothing new reported (still no suspects in custody), she turned off her console and closed her eyes.

Fifteen minutes from Albany, she got up and walked back between cars to get some air. The automatic doors she had just passed through flew back open again and there, to her surprise and displeasure, stood Robert Thompson.

"Well," she said, puzzled, "this is a coincidence."

He smiled thinly. "I left you a text message this morning. I guess you didn't get it. We're giving all top people connected with the Enterprise an escort for the foreseeable future. Just a precaution. I heard you were in midtown yesterday. You were fortunate not to have been killed."

"Yes, I was very fortunate. It was awful. Have they any idea about who did it?"

For a moment, Thompson said nothing, pointedly appearing to be ignoring her question. He seemed to be watching the passing scenery without any special agenda; Cecil knew, however, Thompson always had an agenda. He turned and faced her again. "I must ask you what your business is upstate. I will need to include it in my report."

The two cars swayed. She grabbed at the safety handle to catch herself, but Thompson seized her wrist.

"Is this really necessary?" she said, pulling away. " You following me?"

"Just answer my question."

"Lunch with a friend. I will be in perfectly safe hands, I assure you."

Thompson nodded. "I see. Any particular friend?"

"I believe that's my business."

"As I said, it's merely a precaution. A prudent one, wouldn't you agree?"

"Escorts even for wives and husbands?"

"If warranted."

"Does Ben know about this?"

"He was sent the same message. He will be having an escort of his own from now on." Cecil stared at him with a particularly cold intensity. "Is there something else you want to tell me?"

"I've also had a call about that political mural that showed up last month on the wall of City Hall. There's a rumor around you might know something about it."

Cecil stared at him, then laughed derisively. "You're joking."

"You know what mural I am speaking about?"

"Of course. 'The Lost Mind.' It was all over the news last week. How could I have missed it? You think it's my work?"

"The mayor's office is concerned it resembles murals you did for the interior of the new Village Gate last Fall. Shrum specifically mentioned it. They are concerned about any politically motivated attacks that might undermine public support for the emergency decrees. You have artist friends well-connected in the immigrant community. If you have any information, you should report it."

"I know nothing about it. Still, he must understand not everyone agrees with him that these crackdowns are necessary."

Thompson frowned. "Must I remind you? You're the wife of an important Enterprise executive. We must maintain a cordial relationship with City Hall, the Enterprise's gaming licenses depend on it. I am only looking out for the company's best interests, as I would hope you would be. This mural was clearly an incendiary attempt to incite opposition to the decrees. The Enterprise must not be associated with such propaganda."

"If the purpose of this interrogation is to frighten me, Robert, you're failing. I'm merely becoming annoyed with you."

The train rocked, then began to slow. Air hissed from the hydraulics. The cars began to ease slowly down from their air cushions to the hard-steel rails.

The uniformed conductor stepped into the narrow passageway for an identity check. They handed over their cards. The conductor swiped them through his belt scanner, handed them back after examining the results, then moved past them into the next car.

"If you're assuring me you had nothing at all to do with this political rubbish," Thompson said, "I can put that in my report to the mayor's office and be done with it."

She held his gaze until it became uncomfortable for them both. "I don't believe," she said acidly, "encamping already angry people behind barbed wire barricades is a recipe for anything but more violence. And how I decide to use my artistic talents can hardly be of any of your business---or the mayor's. I suggest you tell him that."

Cecil abruptly turned and with an angry blush to both cheeks walked back through the automatic sliding doors to her seat.

From the consoles came the announcement that the Albany station was their next stop.

When she next looked, Thompson was nowhere to be seen.

***

Cecil was ushered into Governor Genesee Wainwright's ornate wood-paneled Executive Chamber and received a warm embrace from her former college classmate and longtime friend. It had been a year since they had last spoken. Genesee looked radiant amidst the polished woods and ornate furnishings of a room in which two

Roosevelts had held forth, dressed smartly in a sea-green suit that set off her short-clipped flame-red hair. Genesee motioned for her to sit. "I'm sorry to keep you waiting. As you can imagine, it's a madhouse around here today, even more than most days."

"I understand, of course. Yesterday, I happened to be on my way into the New Media Building to see Sabrena when that dreadful bomb went off. I have to say, it was a terrifying experience. We were both very shaken by it."

Genesee looked at her closely. "I had no idea. Are you all right?"

"Some bruises, but not like others; a poor woman near me was killed by debris, and Sabrena's offices felt the shock wave of the detonation. When I went up to see her, she was refusing to follow the mayor's orders to evacuate the building, giving his people holy hell, calling all her people back in to get their stories and other coverage out."

"Genesee shook her head. "I'm at the end of my patience with that man myself. An hour ago, he demanded I activate National Guard troops. We've been debating all morning the most appropriate response to that idea. Can you tell me what you saw, what you and Sabrena have been hearing? Every detail, please, no matter how unimportant you may think it is. I need some trustworthy ears on the ground down there. My advisers are as worked up about increasing security as the mayor is."

Cecil explained the circumstances surrounding the 42nd Street explosion; described what she knew about Ben and Jack's own personal encounters with the Brigades over just the past week---the Central Park execution euphemistically labeled an "intervention," the foiled attempted bombing at the Roosevelt Island racquet Club; Rabinsky's suicide. "All of it being used by the mayor to justify expanding the Emergency Decrees." Cecil voice had become shrill.

Genesee straightened in her chair and expelled a deep breath. "I told them all down there weeks ago if they went ahead with Shrum's plan for these damn encampments, it was just a matter of time before the violence moved out of the enclaves . There's just no reasoning with him. I almost hung up on one of his senior aides this morning when he tried to persuade me to activate the Guard. He wasn't specific about his plans for new crackdowns, but I am sure he's going to try selective roundups inside the boroughs, probably starting in Manhattan. The Midtown bombing is just the pretext they need."

Cecil took a deep breath. "That's what I wanted to speak to you about. Sabrena and I have discussed an idea addressing that very point."

Genesee's eyes widened.

"I know this isn't my place or Sabrena's place to be offering you advice like this, but I hope we're all still friends enough that we can give you some unsolicited counsel."

"Of course. I welcome it, more than you can know."

Cecil began to explain the idea she and Sabrena had discussed: a site visit to the enclaves by the governor, a way to see for herself what was really happening. As Cecil talked, the governor was interrupted several times by legislative pages rushing in with notes, but each time Genesee merely glanced at the note before sending the messengers away without a reply.

"I know this would be a tremendous political risk for you," Cecil continued, "and there would be every reason in the world for it to be branded a publicity stunt."

Genesee nodded. "To say nothing of infuriating bloody Shrum, stirring up the media, and giving extremists behind the violence me as their next target. My critics and political opponents will love that."

"Not if your true intent was made absolutely clear."

"And what is my true intent, dear? To negotiate with terrorists, as the media will certainly portray it---every one of my advisers' greatest fear?"

"Not if the moderate leaders of all three eastern boroughs have been the ones to invite you in?"

Genesee smiled. "Go on."

"My many artist and literary friends inside the eastern boroughs---the Bronx and Queens to the north, as well as Brooklyn to the south---tell me conditions in the immigrant encampments have become truly appalling over the last month---more overcrowding, criminals being thrown in with detainees simply awaiting citizenship applications to be processed. Even the more moderate Imams and Rabbis are talking about taking more extremist stands; they've lost all confidence in the city to manage anything in a humanitarian way. When a friend of mine tried to bring food to a family in Queens, she was refused enter and the food was seized. She said barricades have gone up all along Astoria Boulevard in recent days, limiting access even to side streets. Barricades are going up everywhere." She paused. "Now, we have this dreadful Midtown bombing, not just in spite of these crackdowns, very likely because of them."

Cecil suddenly stopped talking, too shaken to continue.

Genesee's frown had deepened. "I've not heard of any of these events, and I can see exactly your concern. Counter-pressures for more decisive crackdowns are enormous now; everybody is almost entirely focused on security after this latest incident. But I can see more here than just a security problem."

"Much more. I'm very glad you agree."

The governor dropped her gaze, then looked at Cecil. "I want you to agree not to divulge what I am about to tell you, Cecil, not even to Ben or to Sabrena, not yet, not to anyone. I have only told my two closest advisers what I have in mind. Will you promise me?"

"Of course."

"This morning, I told Shrum I was going to refuse any troop deployment, at least for the moment. I want him to appoint the police commissioner to take this over; and I want him to have the

Directorate stand down. The media will be full of that news very soon. He may still try to get the President to overrule me, since he has ultimate say over the Guard, but I doubt he'll succeed or even attempt it. The last thing the White House will want is to get entangled in any of this. They'll try to regard it as a local matter as long as they can. As for the Brigades, I told Shrum the attorney general is preparing a constitutional challenge to the decrees, one I plan to support." She paused. "Now, Cecil, I have a favor to ask you. It's why I was so glad you asked to see me. I need someone I can trust to bring a letter to my friend, Albert Longueille, the Algerian ambassador to the U.N. I am going to request his help in pursuing precisely the idea you have mentioned---a personal fact-finding mission by me to all three eastern boroughs, including Shrum's new barbed-wire encampments. I want the ambassador to be my back channel to borough leaders he thinks we can trust, and I want you to deliver that message to him personally through a trusted intermediary. Are you comfortable doing that?"

"Absolutely. But you've had something like this in mind all along,. We should have known."

"I've been on the fence about it, now, I'm not. I have you and Sabrena to thank for that. First, though, I must know if any local law enforcement can assist me with my security in the enclaves. They must also understand, as all enclave leaders must, that this is to be strictly fact-finding, with no guarantees of negotiations to follow. I will be asking them to suggest names of any insiders in the boroughs who are likely to be of help to us in making this visit possible. I want only people M. Longueille can vouch for to maintain confidentiality around this. Will you do this for me?"

"Of course. Absolutely."

"Shrum will be furious once he understands he's being bypassed. But he won't be able to stop me as long as he doesn't know beforehand. As I said, many of my own supporters and aides are demanding that I give Shrum troops right now. They want an overwhelming show of force. I will never agree to such a drastic step unless there is a clear emergency the local police cannot handle. Now, is there a chance you can stay the night in Albany? I'd like you to come to an important gathering I'm having tonight at the River Club."

"I booked a room at the Desmond this morning, just in case I needed to stay over."

"Good. I want to introduce you to the intermediary I will be using to contact Ambassador Longueille. She will be in attendance, the gathering is for her benefit."

Cecil was about to agree, then paused. "There's something I must warn you about. The Enterprise's chief of security has been watching me----for reasons of security and my personal safety, he told me on the train. I wouldn't be surprised if he knows I've come to see you. I hedged about who I was seeing, and I tried very hard not to be followed, but he can be very resourceful."

Governor Wainwright nodded. "I'm very glad you told me. I will make sure whatever car comes for you enters by way of the lower garage at the Desmond." The governor pressed a button at her desk. "Jenny, call the River Club and ask them to seat Cecil Collander at my table. And send a car for her to the Hotel Desmond. Tell them to make sure it's there for her at 7 o'clock sharp. Tell them to meet her at the usual basement elevator."

Cecil smiled at her old school confident. "I'm so very glad we've been able to help you with this."

The governor returned the look of affection. "You've already been a bigger help than you know, C."

Chapter Thirteen

Genesee stood with Cecil amidst the hum of guests assembled on the crowded back terrace of the River Club. Chloe Rothschild, ninety-year-old doyenne of countless controversial causes, walked slowly toward them with the aide of a pearl-handled cane, every wrinkle of character in her striking face a reminder that not everyone required youth enhancers to age beautifully. Diminutive in stature, stubborn by nature, Chloe had flown up from the city for Governor Wainwright's long-planned fundraiser for an Independent Palestine and Israel. The cause's most publicly visible and prominent Jewish proponent, Chloe had refused even to consider her nervous aides' attempts to send a stand-in in the wake of the security alarms that had greeted the midtown bombing. All this Genesee explained to Cecil as they waited for her to cross the terrace on her own power, Chloe's preferred mode of travel.

"You were brave to come," Genesee said when she had arrived, exchanging a warm embrace.

Chloe, her full head of silver hair pinned up carelessly, brushed back a stray wisp and smiled coolly, her penetrating gray eyes luminous under the lights of the gas lanterns surrounding the terrace. "How could I not? What better time to remind people there are many more sides to this story than one power-drunk mayor and a few fanatics causing trouble. Chloe paused, examining Cecil closely. "And who is this with you?"

"I'm sorry," Genesee said. "This is my friend Cecil Collander."

"Of course, the portraitist and muralist. I should have remembered you from the last exhibition of yours I saw last summer---your wonderful charcoal renderings of the famous poets. I especially liked your Dylan Thomas. It caught his tragedy perfectly. I knew him when I was a child in Paris, the poor, dear man."

"I'm flattered you remember."

"I've been looking for someone to paint my portrait. So far, I've had no luck at all. I want something along the lines of Sargent, your specialty, but no one seems to have the slightest interest in anything but impressionism. I think they're afraid to attempt anything that might actually require talent, which you most certainly possess, dear. Would you be interested in discussing it?"

"I would, very much," Cecil said.

"I'll be at my Gramercy Park apartment for the next month, before I return to California. Perhaps we could schedule a consultation."

"I would consider myself very fortunate," Cecil said. She reached inside her purse and handed Chloe her card.

Chloe took it and turned back to the governor. "Now, tell me, dear. Are you going to run for the White House or not? If that hand-picked successor of the President's is elected, every one of us will end up in jail for merely exchanging recipes."

Genesee, with a smile, shook her head. "First things first, dear. I'm not going to announce anything tonight. This is a gathering intended for your cause, not mine, whatever that may turn out to be. However, there is something else I must discuss with both of you before we begin the night's proceedings." She guided them to a bench in the adjacent garden.

The crowd was beginning to grow. Within its ranks, Cecil had quickly recognized countless liberal lights of New York philanthropy, the Hollywood film industry, and the New York arts scene, all mingling with surprising ease with an unlikely mix of conservatives---international business people and corporate CEOs, committed, for their own reasons, to thawing the Middle East permafrost. The unending hostilities had continued to put an intolerable hold on so many special interests, the Midtown bombing only the latest warning of how closely the unresolved Palestinian problem was to America's liberal and conservative interests alike.

Under the lanterns, they were able to share a bench, and after a waiter had brought them hors d'oeuvres, Genesee leaned close to Chloe, the bright moonlight sharpening the intensity of her expression. "As I recall, you were good friends with Monsieur Longueille, the new Algerian ambassador, during your years in Paris."

"You have an excellent memory, my dear. I haven't seen Albert in years, but, yes, when I read last month he'd been appointed the new ambassador to the United Nations, I sent him a message of congratulations; he responded at once, warmly if briefly."

"Do you think he might be willing to help me open an informal dialogue with a select group of enclave moderates about the deteriorating conditions for the residents there?"

Chloe's face lit up. "Whatever are you thinking, dear?"

"For the past month, some of the moderate Imams and Rabbi leaders in all three eastern boroughs have been reaching out to me, asking for help dealing with the mayor. It's still all strictly back-channel so far, a very delicate question of jurisdiction, as you can imagine.. However, it's clear now I have no choice. I must attempt some kind of dialogue with the most sensible Imams and Rabbis before this violence runs entirely out of control."

Chloe nodded. "What can I do to help, dear?"

"Would you be willing to inform Ambassador Longueille I have an important proposition for him, and that my close friend Cecil Collander will be contacting him personally on my behalf?"

She squeezed Cecil's arm affectionately. "Do you think the ambassador can be trusted to keep this in confidence? If Mayor Shrum or his people learn of this before I am prepared to act, it could be disastrous."

"If it is an effort to address this dreadful problem, I am sure he will be receptive," Chloe after a pause. "However, I will make some inquiries beforehand. There are always changes in loyalties when it comes to this impossible situation. I will warn you, of course, if I learn anything suggesting he's not the right intermediary for you."

Genesee nodded, then smiled. "I knew I could count on you."

Waiters appeared on the terrace with champagne.

"Enough of business then." Genesee got to her feet. "Let's attend to the more immediate matters--- support for your important cause."

Assisting Chloe back to the center of the terrace, she announced: "Ladies and gentlemen, please join me in a toast with our friend Chloe Rothschild to the goal that brings us all together here today---independent, secure, self-governing homelands for Israelis and Palestinians alike."

***

Cecil sat at a table at the edge of the terrace, a half-empty glass of champagne at her place. She had lost count of how many she'd had. Faceless waiters repeatedly stopped by with freshly poured glasses. Dinner and speechmaking were over. For some time, she had been sketching the crowd, the makings, perhaps, of another mural once the time and place presented itself.

Across the river, the lights of the Albany capitol dome lit up the hillside where the granite fortress of New York's state house overlooked the river. She glanced at her watch. It was nearly 11.

Genesee was bidding farewell to some of the guests. Chloe had left long before, deeply moved by the outpouring of support she had received in defiance of the partisan political polarization happening elsewhere beyond the River Club's walls. She folded the manila envelope Genesee's aide had just brought to her--- the governor's message to Ambassador Longueille--- and slipped it into her purse. Inside the cloakroom, she pressed in Ben's secure number on her communicator and left a message: She said only that her meeting had gone well and that she would be on the first morning train back to the city. Outside the club, she waited for the cab the doorman had called for her; she'd told Genesee the car wouldn't be necessary. Headlights flashed as a limousine pulled up. The valet handed over the keys to a young diplomat whose name Cecil could not remember, and they drove off. More cars arrived, more departed. She tried to remember if she had stopped to say goodbye to Genesee. Well, she would call her in the morning.

"Must the cabs come all the way out from the city?" she asked the valet, as time wore on and still her cab did not arrive. "Or is there a local company?"

The valet shrugged. "Depends. Your cab should have been here by now. I will call again for you."

Cecil thanked him, then suddenly felt a wave of dizziness come over her.

"Are you all right, ma'am?" the valet asked.

"A bit too much champagne, I guess."

"Sit here and wait, if you'd like."

He helped her to a bench. For some reason she could not feel her lips.

The doorman stepped back from the commotion of departing guests, opened a communicator and spoke into it. His voice seemed far away.

More time passed. She heard cars and laughter, countless car doors slamming. Those sounds seemed far away, too. Her head rolled back and she felt herself falling. A strong arm caught her, and helped her into the open door of a black town car. The deeply cushioned seat smelled of expensive leather, the cologne of the man helping her pungent and distinctive, a scent she did not know.

"Driver," she murmured. "I want to go to the Hotel Desmond."

She tried to make out the face of the driver in the car's mirror but could not, blinded by headlights of arriving cars. The engine sprang to life; the car moved away.

"Isn't that the road to Albany?" she cried. "Didn't we just miss it?"

"No, ma'am. This is the shortest way."

The interior of the car began to spin. She lay back and took a deep breath. Probably too much champagne. How much had she had? She couldn't recall. She would be fine if she could rest her eyes for just a moment.

***

She awoke in a large, crowded, high-ceilinged room---not her suite at the Hotel Desmond or anywhere even remotely like it. She struggled to get her bearings. Around her stood a raucous crowd, packed shoulder-to-shoulder around a roulette wheel, a chorus of voices shouting above the whirl and slide of the steel ball. High above the wheel, a crystal globe spun, casting a kaleidoscope of colored lights across the ceiling and below to the array of intense, anticipatory faces riveted on the wheel.

A tall, dark-haired man in a black open-throated shirt stood at Cecil's shoulder. "Now," he whispered in her ear, as if addressing a child. "All of it, my dear...on the 7 Red."

"All?"

He nodded.

Slowly, obediently, she pushed a stack of gold chips across the green felt betting surface to the square he had designated.

"Two thousand dollars on the 7 Red," the croupier called out. "No more bets." He spun the ball, then the wheel, and the crowd watched and cheered as the ball whirled. Finally, it clattered and dropped into its new home. "Seven on the Red. Seven on the Red is the winner," the croupier called out. Loud whoops and cheers went up again.

Cecil's expression did not change. Her eyelids had grown heavy again. She felt herself drifting ever so briefly back into sleep. Her escort took her hand, and she tried desperately to open her eyes. Tenderly, he kissed her hair and began leading her from the roulette station through the crush of people toward the cashier. Strangers stared, jostled, and congratulated her, their own appetites stoked by her success. One face in particular caught her attention---the face of a tall, slim man dressed as croupier, who seemed to be watching her with intense concern. Before she could speak, he had turned away and disappeared. Jack? She tried to speak out but could not, her lips numb again, her tongue too numb to form the actual words. Her escort tightened his grip, and she was forced to follow him. When she turned and looked again, the apparition had vanished. What was happening to her?

At the cage, the cashier counted out the chips, replacing each one on his counting table with a five-hundred-dollar bill. "One hundred thousand dollars in all, madam," he said at last, tapping the thick stack of cash into a tight pile, wrapping the money in a red elastic band and handing it to her.

"Now, put that in your purse," her escort commanded, as if speaking to a child.

She shook her head. "I feel sick. I want to go home."

"First, you must put your money in your purse."

"Please, I want to go back to my hotel room. I don't want to be here."

He seized her arm, snapped her purse open and stuffed the cash inside. He looked up at the puzzled faces of the watching crowd. "Just a little too much champagne," he said, then smiling, guided her surely and swiftly toward the exit.

Outside in the cool night air, a three-quarter moon lit the drive. A packed parking lot stretched out to a cliff. Just beyond the precipice, city lights blanketed the distant valley, Albany, she guessed. Now they could go home. The man helped her into the passenger seat and climbed in on the driver's side. No longer frightened, she moved closer to him and lay her head against his shoulder.

Suddenly, she heard a rumble of what sounded like thunder. Her eyes flew open. Just ahead, over the crest of a hill, came a squad of horsemen in visored helmets, their young grim faces caught in the town car's headlights.

The riders divided as they approached and streamed past at a fast trot on each side of the car. Cecil turned back and saw the squad dismount in unison at the front entrance to the casino. In seconds, they were bursting through the heavy double doors, sidearms drawn.

Before she could demand to know what was happening, her escort had stepped on the gas.

***

She awoke in her hotel suite at the Desmond, both temples pounding from a terrible hangover. The time on her travel clock stood at 5:50 a.m. She dialed the video message center that indicated she had five messages. Ben's worried face appeared on the screen and she heard his voice asking where she was, followed by four similar messages, each sounding progressively more alarmed.

She punched in his number, and he picked up on the first ring. "C, where the hell are you? You sound terrible. I've been calling and calling. Are you all right?"

"I've had a terrible night. I don't actually remember. I'm at the Desmond now. I guess I'm all right. Oh, Ben. I don't understand what happened to me."

"I've been calling since midnight. I was just about to phone the Albany police. "

"I have been feeling very strange ever since Genesee's soiree. I don't understand it." She paused. A wave of dizziness struck her again, and she sat back down on the bed.

"Cecil, are you there?" Quayle's voice sounded worried again.

"I'm sorry," she said finally. "After I left Genesee to come back here to the hotel, I began having dreams, but I don't think I was actually asleep. It's as if I've been sleepwalking." She stopped, pressing her fingers to her temples. She realized how bizarre this must sound. "The last thing I remember, I was waiting for a cab at the club. Then I got very sleepy. The next thing I remember is waking up in the Five Tribes Casino. At least, I think that's where it was. After that, I remember only certain moments, fragments. Then I woke up in my bed at the hotel, fully dressed. I don't even know how I got back here."

The digital connection was breaking up.

"Do you think you're well enough to make the 8 a.m. out of Albany?" Quayle asked. "Or shall I have Genesee send someone over for you?"

"I'm all right. I just can't remember things... I'm sure I can make the train. I have plenty of time...."

"Call me at the office as soon as you're aboard. But make sure you call me on the secure number."

"Ben?" She asked, then paused. "Have you heard anything from Jack?"

"No. Why?"

"I think I saw him at the casino. I was in such a state I couldn't be sure. Why on earth would he be there?"

She heard more interference.

"I didn't catch that, C. This is a terrible signal. We shouldn't be talking on an open line. Call me when you're on the train. On the secure line. Do you understand?"

Before she could answer, the signal went dead.

Chapter Fourteen

Thompson's communicator sounded. He took the call, then turned to the eight members of the executive committee for casino operations; only Jack's chair at the head of the long conference table stood empty. All were now poring over documents. "I have a visitor," Thompson said. "I'll need some time before we begin." He turned to Quayle. "You'd better be in on this."

The security chief's manner was abrupt; in Jack's absence he had the air of the man in charge.

In the hallway by Thompson's office, Police Detective Navarro was waiting. The security chief ushered him inside with Quayle and closed the door. "You have news?"

"An hour ago I had a call from a *Wall Street Journal* reporter. She said she's had a report from a reliable source that bookkeeping irregularities had been found at a number of Enterprise casinos. She asked if I could confirm that."

Thompson's jaw tightened "What did you tell her?"

"I told her I had no such information." The detective examined Thompson's reaction. "The rumor's not true then?"

Thompson's expression did not change. "We are conducting an internal investigation of all of Rabinsky's audits, routine in a case like this. I requested the Directorate's help in detaining Rabinsky so we could question him further. The Brigades were merely carrying out my request."

"You requested the Directorate's help?" Quayle demanded. "On whose authority? The protocols call for you to consult me before making any major decision in Jack's absence. We've been over that, damn it."

Thompson shot Quayle an equally withering look. "Again, as in the case of calling in the police, there wasn't time. I wasn't sure after Rabinsky quit how far he might get. It was a mistake for my people not to detain him until I could question him myself about exactly why he was resigning."

Quayle stared at the ex-CIA man speechlessly. Here was the second time Thompson had purposely gone around him on a key matter.

Navarro seemed to choose his next words carefully, speaking in his clipped, accented English: "Let me remind you, my friends, this is also a city police matter. I expect your cooperation. I should also warn you, the Directorate's been hearing from civil liberties groups wanting to know why the Brigades acted with such an intimidating show of force when Mr. Rabinsky had no police record and hadn't been officially declared a fugitive by our office." Navarro paused, looking from Quayle to Thompson. "Have either of you any reason to believe Mr. Rabinsky's suicide might be connected to Mr. Flyte's absence, or to this rumor concerning the Enterprise accounts? Could they somehow be connected?"

Thompson turned his gaze to the office window. Finally, he turned back. "We have considered that, yes."

Navarro continued to examine Thompson's reactions. "If you want my help locating Mr. Flyte, I would suggest you be more forthcoming. Have you had any further information about Mr. Flyte's location since we last spoke?"

"We still assume he's acting on a business matter. However, the more time that passes...."

Navarro turned to Quayle. "Wouldn't you suppose if he saw

media coverage of the Rabinsky episode, he would have called in?"

Thompson and Quayle exchanged glances. "It's fair to say it has been reason for added concern on our parts, yes," Quayle said.

"And because he has not, could it be he is already fully aware of the circumstances that may have led to Mr. Rabinsky's desperate act and had no reason to inquire about details he already knew?"

"That's absurd," Quayle protested. "There's no reason to believe any such thing."

"I agree," Thompson said. "None of the facts I have seen support it."

"Have you any reason to believe we may have a hostage situation here?" Navarro asked.

Thompson shook his head. "We have had no contact from anyone about Jack's absence. There have been no ransom demands, as has been the case in recent situations abroad. The media have been asking for interviews, of course. Mr. Quayle has been informing them he won't be reachable until the meeting in Dubrovnik. That's two days from now."

Quayle broke in: "If he was working on a particularly sensitive deal, he might be at some location where access to media might not be immediately available. In the past, he's been gone for as long as ten days without letting us know his whereabouts. It has always produced some sort of deal. It's how Mr. Flyte works when he's negotiating. He always remains focused on the business at hand. He hates distractions---especially the media, who have been responsible for complicating more than one deal."

"And are you aware of a major deal now in the works?" Navarro asked.

They both shook their heads.

"I see," Navarro said. His face went blank, then sprang to life again. "I presume you would have the name of the hotel where he is planning to stay."

"Actually we don't," Thompson interjected quickly. "We make reservations at several hotels under various pseudonyms, then never make the final decision until the night before arrival. Security precaution. All I can tell you is what I have just told you." Thompson paused, then added. "I assure you, detective, I will personally notify you the minute Mr. Flyte is located."

Navarro nodded. "One more thing. Do you plan to make a public statement regarding Mr. Rabinsky's death?"

Navarro had addressed the question to Quayle, but it was Thompson who answered it. "That is something I am about to ask the board to consider. We have not yet had a chance to address this matter."

"Of course, we will be making a public statement," Quayle interjected, but Thompson raised a hand to silence him. "As I said, detective, our public response is still to be decided."

Navarro looked from one to the other, then stepped into the waiting elevator. "Very good, I will be looking forward to our next conversation."

Thompson watched the elevator doors close, then facing Quayle directly, sensing the chief publicist about to protest, he said preemptively: "This is an emergency, Ben. Jack has given us new instructions. We're going to need to work out some new public information protocols."

Thompson wheeled and left Quayle to stare after him as he strode back to the conference room.

***

Inside, the faces had grown more alarmed as the seven other board members poured over the raft of documents strewn over the long table. Quayle and Thompson returned to their seats, the one vacant seat at the head of the long table normally occupied by Jack.

Quayle began to observe the board members' demeanors more closely than usual, wondering just how many he could count on if, as he suspected, he was about to clash with Thompson.

There was Cheevers, chief of the Mideastern casino division and a fair-minded chairman; Philip Damphousse, northeastern operations chief, with jurisdiction over both the Five Tribes Casino in Albany and the Starfire in New York Harbor, often in cordial contact with Quayle; Jimmy Hayes, California casino operations chief, remote and indifferent, who apparently regarded Quayle as part of the eastern establishment and therefore not to be trusted; Brent Jacobi, chief of northwest casino operations, new enough to the company to still be giving all the New York officers a respectful deference. Quayle's truest allies, he suspected, were the board's longest-serving casino committee members--- Doreen Silkhammer, southeastern casino chief, and Nancy Spiegel, chief of European casino operations. Like himself they were closest to Jack personally as charter members of the original organizing committee of the Enterprise's casino unit, now managed by this executive committee.

Thompson began to read from the top sheet: "I've asked for this emergency meeting to discuss what we believe to be strong evidence of fraud. Gerhard Ives, chief auditor for Banque Suisse, and James Grogan, chief auditor of the Coleridge Bank, principal holding company for all Enterprise casino operations have been examining the Enterprise's casino accounts since Mr. Rabinsky's departure. They will explain themselves what they have just told me following a preliminary audit of the Enterprise and Coleridge Bank casino accounts."

"As you can see in this first chart in your packets...." Grogan began, "...over the past nine months, cash receipts from several of the Enterprise's 35 casino divisions have been regularly diverted in relatively small amounts from the Coleridge Bank's money-market depository to unknown overseas accounts. As you know, the bank holds all casino receipts in the depository for 24 hours as a precaution against fraud. Only when they have been totaled again and reverified are they released to the Enterprise's own secure accounts. However, our new electronic scans have unfortunately revealed the Coleridge Depository has also been subject to numerous incursions during this 24-hour holding period, occurring over at least the last three fiscal quarters, possibly longer."

Grogan flashed new charts on the wall. "We have marked with red arrows all accounts where diversions have been detected. As you can see, the amounts are always relatively small---never exceeding $25,000 in any single casino account during any single day and never occurring more than once in any single account in any one quarter, making detection more difficult. While our scans have not yet determined the full amount, or the ultimate destination of the diverted funds, we know the diversions could not have been accomplished without help from someone inside the Coleridge Bank. With just a few computer strokes, the firewalls could be disarmed and diversions executed, then the firewalls could be restored in a fraction of a second."

"Even with our other accounting safeguards in place?" Nancy Spiegel asked, her face flushed with concern. "At the very least, wouldn't the tracking software have...."

Grogan interrupted, "The timing would have to be precise. The Depository firewalls were built to block outside incursions; they were never intended to block someone from inside disarming the fail-safe systems within the 24-hour holding period before the transfers were made to the permanent Enterprise accounts."

Brent Jacobi's basso voice boomed. "An insider? I don't understand. Do you mean this character Rabinsky?"

"We can't be certain what exactly Rabinsky may have done. His office would certainly have the opportunity. However, the

Depository's firewalls couldn't have been breached without the Enterprise's own alarms being simultaneously disarmed and simultaneous coordination between an insider at the Enterprise and someone else with an actual finger on the Coleridge computer systems."

"Rabinsky's remaining computer files are still being examined," Thompson interjected.

"In this way," Grogan went on, "no electronic footprints would be left. Our new system scanners have also provided us with some promising clues about how the diversions may have occurred and where they were rerouted. As you can see from this next chart," Grogan continued, "the Enterprise's losses in this last quarter have been in excess of $875,000. In the previous two quarters, the diversions were less---$100,000 over six months. The thieves may have been experimenting with the scheme before ratcheting up. We are now running scans further back to see if we can detect exactly when the diversions began to determine the full amount. However, I think it's safe to say we could be talking about a million dollars per quarter, per casino."

Thompson again broke in. "Mr. Ives from Banque Suisse will now explain how we plan to add a new security element to the cash-flow equation."

"Meanwhile," interjected Thompson into the silence, "Banque Suisse has already taken steps to change all computer access codes and protocols involving the Coleridge Bank's Depository accounts. I've also impounded all relevant Enterprise electronic files and documents. And I'm sure you will understand, Ben, from now on I must be the only Enterprise source to respond to all media inquiries, at least until this crisis has been resolved."

"Why?" Quayle demanded. "Why is that necessary?"

"This is now an internal security matter. I am chief of security. We can't have two voices speaking for the company. I'm sure you can understand the importance of that." Thompson's gaze swung back to the rest of the executive committee. "I'm also recommending that the executive committee invoke Section C of Jack Flyte's amended succession protocol, granting me full authority to act for him on all issues directly related to this grave security breech. Chairman Cheevers and I have already discussed this; he is in complete agreement."

The committee members stared. Those Quayle might have expected to protest on his behalf---Silkhammer and Spiegel, as well as Jacobi and Hayes, both of whom in the past Quayle had rescued from jams of their own making --- remained silent.

"On what grounds?" Quayle demanded finally. "This is not what Jack's succession plan calls for, at least not that I am aware of. We've been through all this. What's this Section C? I have never heard of it."

Thompson opened his folder and distributed down the table a stack of typed sheets, one for each committee member. "As you can see, Jack's memorandum, signed and witnessed four weeks ago, calls for me as chief of security to assume full command of the Enterprise in the event the executive committee determines an imminent threat to the company's financial security."

Quayle took a copy of the memorandum. "I tell you, I've never seen this before. I can't believe Jack would agree to such a thing without informing me."

"I urged Jack to write it into the regular succession plan as a precaution. All the major corporations are doing it in response to the rash of CEO kidnappings abroad. The emergency authority is subject, of course, to ratification by you acting as the executive committee. It can also be rescinded at any time by a majority vote of the committee. I will be fully accountable to you." Thompson nodded toward the Enterprise's chief attorney, R. Benson Stevens, there to answer questions.

Quayle ignored him. "I tell you, Jack wouldn't counsel this without informing me first." He looked again at the memorandum; Jack's signature was there, just above Stevens' signature as a legal witness. He had seen Jack's signature a thousand times; it was most certainly authentic. Sweat had broken out over Quayle's brow.

"I'm sure you must have questions," Thompson said calmly. "However, I assure you the document and Jack's intent are genuine and necessary given his continued absence."

"Are you saying," Silkhammer demanded, "we have no choice but to implement this?"

"The memorandum clearly specifies this shall be at the board's discretion," interjected Stevens, the officious attorney Quayle had never trusted "However, the committee's fiduciary responsibility to the stockholders of the Enterprise is paramount. As your legal counsel, I must advise that a failure to act could put the board at risk of serious investor lawsuits should it be found to have mismanaged a financial emergency."

"I would like to know what you intend to do with this authority," Parker-Smith broke in.

Thompson drew himself up in his chair. "Very simply, whatever is necessary to assure the markets that the Enterprise is on sound footing in the wake of our chief auditor's untimely death. That should be our top priority. Today, I am proposing that we publicly announce the Enterprise has launched an internal investigation to ensure all its accounts remain secure. Of course, the public statement will make no mention of Jack or of any other matters we have been discussing here today."

Nancy Spiegel cleared her throat. "There are already rumors about some type of investigation of bookkeeping irregularities after the Rabinsky suicide. I have heard them from my sources on the Street myself. If we confirm we are investigating, won't that just fuel those rumors? What about that, Ben?"

Quayle started to respond, but Thompson quickly rose from his chair and cut him off, his height, as always, an imposing barrier against dissent or rebuttal. "In the short run, I agree the stock will suffer and there will be talk. However, we can't allow these rumors to go unanswered; if Jack were here, I am sure he would agree. We must make clear that we are on top of this. It's decisions like this that call for fast action. I can also assure you that whatever losses the Enterprise has experienced will be recovered. We already have our forensic team assembled; we are developing preliminary leads. I think we must identify Rabinsky as our main person of interest in this matter as quickly as possible, before further rumors can spread."

"I have a hard time believing our auditor could do such a thing, Bob," Silkhammer said. "I have never known Julius to be anything but scrupulously honest."

Thompson frowned. "Then why did he act as precipitously he did? With the Piedmont Group scandals, no one ever suspected the chief accountant, either. Why was he so quick to take his own life?"

"Come off it, Bob," Parker-Smith interjected, "the Brigades scared Rabinsky out of his wits. That's why he panicked; they had him cornered. Simple as that."

"I absolutely agree," Silkhammer added. "Meantime, Jack's bound to turn up in Dubrovnik. That's only three days from now. I think we should wait to make any public statement until at least then. Ben already put out a statement early on that we're looking into Rabinsky's death. Why raise the subject of the accounts so prematurely? It will just fan the flames of the rumor mills before we have any facts."

"My point exactly," Quayle said.

"Maybe I haven't made myself clear," Thompson snapped. "You all must realize how this will look if we do not act quickly and decisively. There's no question funds have been diverted. Also, that our chief auditor has taken his own life and our CEO is still unreachable. At the very least, we must reassure the Street an investigation of all Enterprise casino accounts is underway. Only I am in a position to address such a matter, a circumstance I am certain Jack envisioned when he signed this memorandum." He looked at Quayle. "If Jack reappears at Dubrovnik, Clause C will be moot, of course But I ask you, where is he? Why hasn't he called in? Until he does, Ben, I think your loyalty to the Enterprise should trump whatever other personal feelings we may have about each other."

Quayle stared at the ex-CIA man. Now their rivalry was finally out in the open. "You have no grounds to question my loyalty. It's your loyalty to Jack and the Enterprise that I think is open to question here. I would say you are being far too quick to make Rabinksy a scapegoat here. This embezzlement---if that's what it is---has occurred on your damn watch."

Thompson's eyes flashed. "I tell you, we must start putting our house in order now. This investigation must be beyond reproach from the very start. That's what Jack would want. Don't you agree, Mr. Chairman?"

Cheevers nodded vigorously.

Whatever former allegiances Quayle thought he had now seemed to be evaporating. As this awareness flashed through his mind, something else occurred to him: Jack's memorandum was enabling this. Had Jack handed Thompson this new authority to see just what he would do with it? Was Thompson using Jack's absence to cook up a takeover attempt? He took a deep breath. There was only way to find out. "If the executive committee does not trust me to continue as the Enterprise's chief spokesman," he said forcefully, "I have no choice but to resign."

An awkward silence enveloped the room, punctuated only by the whir of Grogan's laptop computer.

"That's your prerogative," Thompson said after a long pause. "A regrettable outcome, of course. You should understand, if you leave the Enterprise, you will be expected to honor the confidentiality agreement. I certainly can't stand in your way if you think you cannot work with me during this emergency."

Quayle examined the faces of the executive committee. How many of the seven had known this was coming? Not all, he guessed, but enough to explain Thompson's confident, arrogant air. He took a drink of water, then looked down again at the signature on the memorandum. He had seen it a thousand times before; it was almost certainly authentic.

"Do I hear further discussion?" Cheevers asked. The pointed silence held. "There being none, all in favor of Security Chief Robert Thompson's recommendation to invoke Clause C of President and Chief Executive Officer Jack Flyte's memorandum of May 1, 2038, say aye."

Six hands went up. At Cheevers' call for the nays, only Parker-Smith joined Quayle in voting no.

Thompson nodded in satisfaction and turned his gaze back on Quayle. "Jack will be sorely disappointed you have chosen not to go along. Would you care to reconsider?"

Quayle's jaw muscles tensed. Jack would not have agreed to such a premature public disclosure of accounting problems. It was as simple as that. The moment Thompson made his public statement, Jack, like Rabinsky, could become a target of suspicion, just as Quayle would if he gave in to this impulse to resign in response to the board's no-confidence vote.

"I've said my piece," Quayle said quietly, more calmly.

He examined Thompson's stony countenance for any sign of disappointment that might belie the suspicion his resignation would be welcomed. He knew Thompson was certain he had won this confrontation and, most important, that he was now fully in charge.

Closing the door and settling behind his desk, he gathered up the code books and security gadgets that gave him access to all security systems in the Enterprise. If he were to resign, he knew the drill, having presided himself over employee departures. All personal access codes to the various computer systems, safes, doors, and files would be extracted, examined, and destroyed. Before he could find what he was looking for, there was a knock on the door.

"Say, old boy," a voice boomed as the door opened. Parker-Smith stood grimly smiling under his finely-trimmed, snow-white mustache. "Couldn't let this moment go by without shaking your hand, even if those cowards won't." Parker-Smith's bright blue eyes flashed as he seized Quayle's outstretched hand. "I know damn well Rabinsky had nothing to do with this mess."

"How?" Quayle asked. "I agree with you, of course, but how do you know?"

"I heard both of those fellows, Rabinksy and Thompson, arguing about some Hong Kong expense accounts Thompson had run up. Rabinksy had the goods on him. Rabinsky didn't quit; Thompson fired him. I'm sure of that. I'll also wager he then figured out Rabinsky could be even more dangerous running loose and had his contacts inside the Brigades bring him in for questioning, except Rabinsky must have known what was waiting for him and decided to end things his own way. You know what a church mouse Rabinsky was, except a damn brave one in the end."

"Why didn't you speak up?"

"Proof, old boy. My word against his." He turned, then abruptly stopped. "I'd watch yourself now."

Quayle met Parker-Smith's intense gaze. "I intend to. And thanks for telling me this."

After Parker-Smith left, Quayle sat down at his desk and wrote and signed a letter of resignation to Jack without an effective date. Under his signature, he scribbled a brief explanation of what had just happened and a request to Jack that he accept his resignation if he thought it was warranted He addressed the envelope to Jack's secret drop box at the Brooklyn P.O. and slipped it into his jacket pocket to mail outside the building. He then put as many documents from the committee meeting in a second envelope, along with an explanation of what had just happened, and addressed it to Detective Navarro at Metro Police. As soon as he could, he would also make sure Cecil knew what he had done; it was time to start covering his own ass for a change.

***

Outside the Enterprise, the neighborhood was a cacophony of noise, thick dust shooting skyward from workmen breaking up the street pavement with jackhammers directly in front. Quayle hurried through the barriers, stopped at the letter drop inside the foyer of an ATM, and dropped in his two envelopes. He returned to the sidewalk in search of a cab to take him home, the full implications of what had just happened sinking in. All he could think now was how urgent it was that he follow up his note to Detective Navarro with a personal interview as soon as possible. Despite any confidentiality agreement, Navarro would need to be told in detail and in person of this shift in the Enterprise's internal command structure. If for no other reason, he would need to inoculate himself from whatever spin Thompson might later try to put on the expense account matter. He just hoped his best instincts were guiding him in this, not his long-simmering resentment of Thompson.

The din of the jackhammers abruptly ceased. He glanced back. The three workmen had just set down their tools. Something ahead of Quayle seemed to be attracting their attention. At the far end of the street, an empty taxi sat idling at the curb, its yellow vacancy light brightly illumined. Suddenly, the three workmen were running toward it, forcing him aside as they pushed past. All three piled into the cab, dust masks still in place, gray powder puffing up from their overhauls. Before Quayle could react, the cab roared off, tires screeching. He turned back to the Enterprise. At the main entrance, the flow of pedestrians had abruptly stopped, as if seeing a warning in their sudden departure. At that instant, the entire block exploded. An impossibly powerful force lifted Quayle off his feet and catapulted him a dozen yards down the block, sending him crashing head-first back to the concrete. In the last few seconds before he passed out, all breath sucked out of him by the shock of the explosion, it was as if he'd been struck in the chest by a thousand-pound safe.

Chapter Fifteen

Cecil hurried through Penn Station on the midday tide of rail passengers, her communicator pressed to one ear. She left a message for Ben, then for Sabrena. Cellular, text, and cam service had all been unavailable down from Albany. Now, neither Ben nor Sabrena was answering, everything she said getting dumped into voicemail.

Outside, on the 37th Street Jumbotron, the main financial channel's news ticker was running, the Dow, Nasdaq, and S&P all trading fractionally up, Enterprise shares unchanged; each day without market-moving news for ENT had to be a good day as long as Jack remained unaccounted for. Had she really glimpsed him at the casino? With each hour that passed without news of him, her doubts deepened. Now, for the first time, she found herself letting her imagination loose. He might be dead from a fall off the balcony...he might have been pushed... or become someone's prisoner...was it just a matter of time before a ransom demand arrived?

At the Jumbotron's huge screen, she stopped, taking in a report of the international maritime summit Jack was scheduled to attend in Dubrovnik in two days. "Security is to be especially tight due to recent corporate kidnappings," the anchor reported. "With forty of the world's top corporate leaders gathering to resolve the sea lanes crisis, Croatian President Mihovil Babić has promised maximum attention to security."

Back in the apartment, the message center was blinking, a parade of faces flashing up on the video screen, a dozen new calls having arrived since she last checked.

..."This is Susan from Sabrena Tah's office calling. Sabrena says she's sorry but can't see you today. She will call you tomorrow with a more convenient time."

... "Cecil, it's Nonnie. Schuyler's been trying to reach Jack ever since the party. I do hope you've heard from him by now. I have a funny feeling about this, dear. Call me."

... "Olivia here, darling. I really am sorry about the other day. Honestly, it's this damn new job. No time for anything but details. I hope you'll forgive me for being such a bad sport. Please call me when you can. The Genesee project sounds amazing."

She listened to the remaining calls, all of them from media, all wanting to know if the Enterprise was reviewing its books after the Rabinsky suicide. No wonder Ben had sounded so stressed. However, there was still nothing from him. She saved all the messages and glanced at her watch: just barely 1:30. She tried him again but once again landed in voicemail. She still had not told him the details of her bizarre night at the casino, and her memory had not improved with the trip down; the whole episode remained a jumble of strange images, scattered flashes of lucidity, then pure blanks.

She called Sabrena's private number. "We're sorry, this number is not currently available," the recorded voice said. "Please hang up and dial again." She tried Olivia again, same result.

In the foyer, she could hear the ticking of her father's old grandfather clock, one of his prized possessions. On the mantle in front of her was a photograph. She stared at it, as she often did, the two of them pictured at the lake that summer, posed beside the clock, she a child of six holding his big hand, he looking unusually happy. He'd been the one to insist they go to the lake house without her mother; Cecil had been much too young to guess how unhappy her father had been behind that forced smile. All that would come later.

The phone on the secure line buzzed. A familiar face flashed up on the screen: Joyce Boles, Ben's secretary. Cecil picked up at once.

Joyce's voice was trembling. "Thank God you're there. Have you heard?"

"Heard what, Joyce?"

"There's been a bombing outside the Enterprise building. Fifteen minutes ago. We think Ben may have been hurt. It's all over the news channels now."

"Oh, God!" She turned on the wall screen. There it was: another all-too-familiar scene of pure carnage. Just what she was afraid she would see, except personal now, then even worse as her eyes darted from one terrible image to another, searching for but not wanting to see her own Ben lying somewhere amidst the bodies entangled in the rubble of the street,. What she saw instead was more impersonal but no less alarming, gaping holes torn in the sides of buildings, concrete slabs collapsed onto the sidewalks like waterfalls. Somehow the Enterprise itself seemed undamaged, its main entrances still intact. At that instant, a line of ambulances shot into view, then police cars, all of them pulling one by one into the street in front of the Enterprise building, paramedics scrambling out.

"Joyce," she said, scarcely recognizing her own whispered voice. "Are you sure he was out there when it happened?"

"He'd just left the building. He told me he needed to leave early, because of something that had happened in his meeting; he said he would explain later. Oh, Mrs. Quayle. I'm so sorry."

"But you can't be sure. No one can be sure, can they? That's what you're saying, isn't it?"

"Yes, of course. There's still no reason to think.... He could very well have left in a cab before it happened. Or he might have been on the next block. That's where he usually goes to hail a cab.

It's always impossible to get a cab in the front of the building. And there's been construction out there all week."

'Yes, yes," Cecil said into the communicator. Her voice stayed a whisper, but just below it panic was building. "He probably caught one on the next block," she said. "He always complains about having to do that."

She didn't believe it; how could he have escaped this kind of devastation?

Her gaze stayed on the disturbing images on the screen. She had no idea what to do. She looked down at her communicator, as if any second a message would come in from Ben, the one that would say he was all right. Each time she looked there was no message.

"The hospitals, Joyce...," she said suddenly. "We must call the hospitals --- as soon as those ambulances start leaving the scene. They always call in ID's to emergency rooms first, along with the injury reports for triage. Someone told me that once. You'll help me, won't you?"

***

Thirty minutes later, an eternity, Joyce called back. She said two hospitals were taking victims of the bombing but releasing no information. She would pick her up in her car so they could go and check both hospitals themselves.

"Oh, yes, Joyce. Thank you so much."

Hanging up, she grabbed her purse, trying to think what else she should bring. A few minutes later, the front door bell rang. Joyce already? It couldn't be. She rushed to open it.

"Mrs. Benjamin Quayle?"

Her heart sank. A short man in a steel-gray suit stood on the threshold. Beside him stood a heavyset woman in a khaki shirt and matching shirt.

The man showed Cecil a badge. "We're from the Directorate, Mrs. Quayle. We have

some questions to ask you. We need you to come with us."

"My husband may just have been hurt in the Enterprise bombing. I was just going to the hospital. I'm in a very big hurry. I really have no time..."

"I'm afraid that must wait. We have a court order to bring you in for questioning involving an important matter," the man said. "You'll need to come with us."

The woman stepped forward. Her almost muscular hand grasped Cecil's purse and removed it roughly from her shoulder. "We'll need to look inside this, Mrs. Quayle. We have a warrant."

Cecil stared at them in astonishment, two imposing figures at her door. The woman held an official-looking document in her other hand.

"This is outrageous," Cecil said loudly. She hoped someone was witnessing this. "I don't need to submit to this."

"I'm afraid you do," the man said calmly. "Things will go better if you cooperate. If you would like to see the warrant, of course, that is permitted.

"Yes, show me, damn it."

The woman handed her the document: a bench warrant signed by a judge of the Second Circuit Court of Manhattan, authorizing the Office of Special Investigations of the Directorate to interview one Cecilia Collander Quayle in the matter of the suicide of Julius Rabinsky, chief auditor of the Enterprise, LLC.

"But I know nothing about this." She stared at the Directorate's man with new alarm.

"This gives us the right to question you, voluntarily or involuntarily, Mrs. Quayle." He spoke as if he had not heard her. "It also specifies that we may inspect your purse as containing possible material evidence of a crime."

"What? Are you joking?"

"I assure you, Mrs. Quayle, this is no joke."

The woman removed the purse from her arm before she could react.

"I have never carried a gun," Cecil said sharply, "if that's what you're looking for."

The woman surveyed the contents of the purse, then unzipped an inside compartment. She parted the silk and withdrew from the sleeve a wad of cash bound in a Five Tribe Casino band.

"Do you ordinarily carry around such large sums of money, Mrs. Quayle?" the man said. He took the cash from the woman's hand and thumbed through it. "I'm guessing exactly one hundred thousand dollars---all in hundreds. Were you, by any chance, a lucky winner at a casino last night, Mrs. Quayle?"

Cecil stared. So it had really happened? "I can explain this," she said, her throat constricted with a new, more serious panic. She had no idea how she could possibly explain this.

"You will come with us now," the man commanded. "Assuming your answers are satisfactory, I assure you you will be on your way in no time."

The woman took Cecil roughly by the arm and led her toward a nondescript green Ford idling by the curb. The uniformed driver at the wheel was staring indifferently ahead, the usually busy sidewalk in front of the townhouse still strangely deserted.

Her escort opened the rear door for her and worked her thick bulk in beside her. The Directorate's man climbed in on the other side, Cecil now squeezed between them.

Outside on the street, a line of tour buses was starting to pass, their own way into the narrow side street momentarily blocked. She lunged suddenly across the lap of the woman and banged on the copper-tinted window of the car, crying out for help. More loudly, she banged and cried out again. No one seemed to hear.

"I'll take that, if you don't mind," the man said calmly, palming the communicator she had just attempted to snatch from her own purse which the woman now clutched in her lap. With Ben missing, she couldn't even think whom she would have called.

Chapter Sixteen

Quayle awoke in shadows. Unseen hands explored his body. All down his left side---shoulder, ribs, and hips, the back of his neck---came an aching, searing pain. It was as if he'd been savagely beaten. A hand moved to his chest and pressed. He thrashed and cried out. He just wanted it all to stop. A needle pricked his arm. Rivulets of heat shot through his veins. Slowly he began to breathe. Sweat poured. Someone began to sponge his brow. Goddamn it, what was this?

He opened his eyes wider. Above him appeared the black, featureless face of a white-jacketed man. An electromagnetic stethoscope hovered, a hand soon sliding the flat head of the instrument gently across his chest. From the man's lips came words that only gradually began to make sense.

"You're coming back, Quayle," the voice said. "I am Dr. McGreavy. You are going to be all right. Continue trying to breathe normally. Soon, the worst of the pain will go. Can you squeeze my hand now?"

Quayle squeezed weakly.

"Now, with your eyes follow my fingers, if you can."

Quayle managed to track the fingers moving from left to right along his sight line, then back. The pain that had been so severe in his neck dissipated. Whatever medication they had given him must be working. To Quayle's surprise, standing beside the doctor was a familiar presence: the Directorate's Noel Gatwick, chief of inquiries.

"Do you remember what happened to you?" Gatwick asked in his almost too-proper British accent.

"Not now," the doctor admonished sharply. To Quayle: "That's right. Breathe as normally as you can. Don't think about anything except that. Try not to notice anything else except your breath."

He gulped in fresh air, then shakily exhaled. The pressure weighing on his chest subsided a bit more.

He could now see he was lying on his back on some sort of padded gurney. IV bottles suspended from stanchions hung over him. Opening his eyes wider, he tried to focus on more distant objects, desperately attempting to assess where he was, to understand what had happened, why Gatwick was here. He saw an operating theater with a balcony high above him. The balcony encircled a cavernous room. In the front row, a bald man who appeared to be in his sixties sat hunched over the low rail observing him, details of the face obscured by the harsh lights beaming down from the high ceiling. Quayle realized now his arms and legs were strapped down.

"Don't be alarmed," the black man dressed in white said. "I am Dr. McGreavey. I understand you already know Mr. Gatwick. I'm glad to say, you're going to live."

Others in medical garb gathered around his bed, their faces now distinguishable---five in all---blank-faced young men and women who peered down at him as if he were some sort of specimen.

"We had to secure you," the doctor said. "You've been having seizures."

At that instant, Quayle's body shuddered. A searing pain seized his chest, and he could not suppress a groan. His feet began to thrash and kick. A white-gowned attendant reached out and touched his breastbone with an instrument. His body jerked against its straps, then fell back. Electroshock. He began to pant as the seizures began to subside. He wanted to demand that they not do that again, but no sounds emerged from his lips. Two attendants sponged his mouth and tongue. The attendant withdrew the wand from where it had remained poised and he fell back to the sweat-soaked sheets.

He could see Gatwick nearby more clearly, the chief of inquiries observing him carefully through the thick lenses of his spectacles, his thin bloodless lips pressed together tightly like pale rubber bands. His thick white brows seemed to rise and fall with each new circumstance. Slowly, Quayle relaxed a bit more.

"Nod for me again if you can understand me, Mr. Quayle," the doctor instructed.

Quayle obeyed.

"The concussion has affected your internal organs, as well as your optic nerves. Also, you've had a mild heart attack. You've been fortunate. In another era you might have died of internal organ shock, most certainly been blinded. Earlier, we removed the breathing tube the paramedics inserted at the scene so you would not choke on your own blood. That's why your throat is so sore. It also will pass."

Quayle waited for a full minute before he could find a way to speak.

"Where am I?" he finally managed, his rasp barely audible. Indeed, the soreness of his throat was almost intolerable. He noticed his ears were still ringing.

"You are in the Directorate's trauma center," Gatwick said. "By the time they dug you out, all the regular emergency rooms were full. You were damn fortunate to be found as quickly as you were. We have the best trauma specialists here."

"Three workmen...," Quayle rasped. "I saw them..."

Gatwick opened an electronic notebook. "Three workmen---

Go on."

Quayle blinked. "foreign men." He swallowed hard, catching his breath. "Young men with dark eyes, faces covered in dust masks. I remember their eyes. Cruel eyes."

"The surveillance cameras show them. They also show you exiting the Enterprise minutes before the bomb detonated. Can you tell us why you were leaving the building at that particular hour?"

Quayle looked up and saw the stocky, brooding man in the balcony hunched over the rail with a special intensity, his eyes large behind thick-lensed glasses.

Quayle shook his head and turned back. "I don't remember. I can't recall anything immediately before or after the explosion. My mind's a blank there."

"Temporary amnesia, " said the doctor. "Understandable, given the concussive shock. We should let him rest now. There will be time for this later."

Gatwick snapped his electronic notebook closed. "Yes. We will continue this in the morning."

Quayle was grateful. A wariness had overcome him, along with an exhaustion that weighed on him.

He saw the silent observer in the balcony rise and begin to move around the balcony toward the exit.

"I must speak to my wife," Quayle blurted, his body tensing against the restrains, but at that moment a nurse pricked his arm with a needle. Before he could protest, he felt himself slip inexorably back into the same blue haze that had enveloped him before.

***

He woke this time to the loud clanging of a bell. An orderly was pushing his gurney, rolling him fast down a narrow maze of corridors along a wide blue stripe painted on the floor. More bells sounding before and behind him. There seemed to be some sort of emergency, though exactly what was not clear. He wondered if all this was some form of hallucination. His tongue felt thick from sedatives and painkillers, and again he had no idea how long he'd been out.

The orderly brought him to a stop at a bank of elevators, rolled him inside, and stood beside him as they rose several flights. He lost count of the floors. They emerged finally into another corridor. At the far end, the orderly stopped the gurney again. On either side stood two sparsely furnished hospital rooms facing each other, their heavy doors propped open to reveal what they contained: a single bed, a writing table, to one side a toilet and shower only partially concealed behind a half-draw curtain. In one of these musty-smelling, decaying unoccupied rooms, Gatwick stood waiting. He lowered his spectacles and waited patiently as two orderlies wheeled Quayle in and unstrapped his arms, then lifted him carefully and slowly into the bed. Behind him, a cart of medical equipment was rolled in. They slid up bed stanchions on either side of him. From windows at the far wall a shaft of bright sunlight streamed in, striking Quayle full in the face. Gatwick reached over and cranked the blinds closed.

"Where am I?" Quayle managed to ask.

"The recovery wing of the old Downtown City Hospital. We had to reopen it to accommodate the overflow of wounded from a second bombing. More are being brought into ICU now; those bells are warning of the arrivals. We had to make room for them by moving you."

"Another bombing?"

"A smaller one, in the Brooklyn enclave. A Synagogue. It all appears coordinated, of course. Hardly coincidental. We're going to catch them, don't worry. It's just a matter of time."

Quayle stared at the director of inquiries with a look of astonishment, then around again at his surroundings. It had not occurred to him on his first visit to the Directorate anything like this might lie behind the copper-tinted windows he had seen looking up from Foley Square. Here was a maze of corridors and empty rooms, the air stale and pungent from old disinfectants and wasted bodies of former indigent patients. He wondered where the bureaucrats had ended up when they'd ridden up the gleaming elevators of the two towers that morning from the Directorate's Foley Square garage. Below, perhaps, or in some other wing of offices, or perhaps above where he now was, it was impossible to tell, his disorientation now seemed so utterly complete.

A silver-haired nurse in a starched cap waited as he settled back into his newly-upraised bed. She fussed over him as she adjusted the aluminum stanchions with their variety of bottles and tubes and monitors hanging down over and around where he lay.

Gatwick sat near him on a chair, hunched over his electronic notebook typing while they hooked Quayle up. He seemed in no hurry to resume the interview.

Quayle looked up at the wall screen the nurse had just clicked on. Before him was a placid, unremarkable scene of Midtown traffic flowing smoothly through Central Park. The time and date stamp on the screen showed 0900 hours, May 24, 2038. It appeared to be a live broadcast. The hour matched the time registered by a digital clock on the far wall. According to this, a full day had passed since the Enterprise explosion and his admission to the Directorate ICU, he could not guess how long since they'd given him his most recent pain injection; time was a scramble of indistinct reference points.

"When may I speak to my wife?" he said in a voice so hoarse

he did not recognize it. "Please, I must contact my wife."

Gatwick looked up from his electronic note tablet. "Oh, we've taken care of that. She has been notified. " He frowned. "However, your little seizure last night has created some complications. She's been told you need quiet for several more days." Gatwick's communicator buzzed. He listened, then snapped it shut. "I must go. More admissions I must attend to. I will be back soon. More time to rest, old boy. Take advantage of it." He got to his feet. "Nothing you need to do. We've taken care of everything. When the time comes, I hope you will feel free to answer some questions. We want you to help us get to the bottom of this."

Quayle stared at him, feeling miserable. No, there was nothing to be done.

The loud clicking of Gatwick's footsteps echoed down the corridor.

***

Quiet descended over his part of the hospital wing, the video screen on the wall of his room again blank. He tried clicking to other channels but the scene remained the same. His straps now no longer restraining him, he grasped the stanchion of his IV tube in one hand and tried to swing his legs over the bed. A piercing pain once again shot through his upper left shoulder and back. He sat for a few moments, breathing deeply. He tried again and managed to get to his feet. He reached his hand to the blinds Gatwick had closed and managed to open them, settling back hard onto the bed. Through the window, he was expecting to see Foley Square and the buildings of Government Center---some street scene outside---but instead what appeared was an inner courtyard of grass and dirt many stories below, while above at the roof a pyramid-shaped skylight shone refracted sunlight down on a slant against the far wall of the multi-storied space. He seemed to be on the topmost floor of the Directorate, the lowest point of sunlight striking the far wall just above a group of twelve Roman numerals that descended with identical spacing down the surface of this far wall. It was, he realized now, an elaborate, cleverly designed sundial, which by his calculation now read just a few moments short of ten o'clock in the morning. Far below, at the bottom of this four-sided expanse of walls, was a courtyard. There a single iron-barred door provided the one apparent entrance to the space, and in the center of the square stood a bandstand with a cupola roof accessible on two sides by two sets of wooden stairs.

The blank video screen blinked back on at the foot of his bed, startling him. He pressed the button on the master control to turn up the sound. He heard an unfamiliar news announcer declare: "In breaking news, it has just been learned that two top officers of the Enterprise are being sought for questioning following yesterday's bombing at the international conglomerate's West Side headquarters...."

At that instant the screen went blank. In the next, it was replaced by the same street scene he had witnessed before.

Quayle pressed the call button.

"Good morning, Mr. Quayle," a woman's voice answered. "Do you require more pain medication?"

"I want to speak with Gatwick. I demand to know what's happening."

In what seemed seconds, a nurse arrived at his bedside. "Up and around, are we," she asked sternly. "I wouldn't advise that. Let's just lie back now." As he described what he'd just seen, she frowned. "I assure you, Mr. Quayle, that screen is not activated for receipt of outside reception. It shows only recorded scenes. Now, you should not be walking around. It could induce more internal hemorrhaging. Perhaps you just had a reaction to your sedative. The doctor has ordered me to change prescriptions for you to make sure you rest."

She moved closer, her hand raised. Before he could protest, the needle she held over him again pricked his arm.

***

He awoke to an even more painful headache.

"Are you comfortable?" the nurse asked kindly. He felt a straw slipped between his lips. "Take some of this."

A foul-tasting liquid filled his mouth.

A white-coated technician took his pulse with a wrist-gauge; a circle of new faces now peered down at him. The technician fastened sensors to his temples, then connected the wires to a monitor. Green lines began to bound like gazelles across the screen.

"I thought you should see this, doctor," the nurse said.

Dr. McGreavey stepped forward, his eyes on the monitor. "You were right to call me." He leaned over, pried open Quayle's eyes with two fingers and aimed an orthoscope into first one, then the other. He pressed the lids back closed. "We will need to watch this. It could help explain the readings of the internal sensors. as well as the hallucinations. It appears to be an old wound, something he received as a child. I called up his history. Some sort of fall he took at a young age could explain it, re-injured from the force of the explosion We won't know for certain if the scar tissue's been traumatized by the force of the blast. We'd need a few more hours of readings."

Quayle attempted to speak, but no sound came from his lips. The people gathered around him did not appear to realize he had regained consciousness. He tried to breath evenly; his lips had gone numb.

"You're to be commended for getting him emergency attention so quickly," a new voice said. Quayle managed to open his eyes. Standing back from the doctor stood Gatwick, and beside him the squat balding man from the balcony of the ICU.

Dr. McGreavey lowered his instrument. "Well, our friend seems to have rejoined us," he said. "How are you feeling? You've given us a bit of a scare."

Quayle stared blankly. "What's happened? What's wrong?"

"The blast appears to have aggravated a childhood injury. Your brain scans spiked to dangerous levels a few minutes ago. You're being administered drugs to reduce the new onset of brain swelling."

"I want to see my wife."

"I'm afraid that's not possible. Your condition remains grave. As I mentioned, there's been further brain swelling."

Quayle stared blankly at the faces surrounding him.

"I don't want you questioning him for long," said the doctor, addressing Gatwick. " He still needs rest after this setback. A half-hour. No more."

"Of course."

The doctor pocketed his orthoscope and retreated with his team, closing the door quietly behind them.

"This is First-Secretary Simon Ross of the Directorate," Gatwick said, pulling up a chair. "We have a few more questions for you."

Quayle peered up as the man stepped forward. The name was one he recognized, the Directorate's first secretary --- Thompson had mentioned him once as his main liaison inside the agency's governing body.

"How did I get I here?" demanded Quayle hoarsely. "Why wasn't I taken to a regular hospital?"

"You might well ask," the bald man said coldly, eyes narrowing.

A faint wheeze came from his throat. "I want you to think back again, about your movements immediately before and after the bombing. It's important that we know every detail. You have said there were three men."

Quayle squeezed his eyes shut, then reopened them. The sedatives and painkillers were losing their hold on him.

"I remember workmen had been jackhammering for the past three days. They always wore dust masks. All of a sudden, as I walked past, they dropped their tools and made a run for it and got into the very cab I was hoping to take. A few seconds later, there was an explosion. I felt it lift me off the ground feet and send me flying. I must have come down on my back. I don't remember anything after that."

"Is it possible this was one of them?" Gatwick held up a black-and-white photograph of a dark-skinned male with a wiry tangle of black hair; his young-looking eyes scowled through a heavy black beard.

"I can't say it was or it wasn't. As I said, all their faces were partially concealed."

"But you cannot rule out this could have been one of them?"

"No, I cannot rule it out."

"Excellent," said Ross and leaned forward with a new intensity. "You understand, we need your help---that this is a matter of grave importance. Ten people died in this explosion,

Mr. Quayle, fifty others like yourself were injured." The first secretary paused, biting his lip. His eyes bore in. "We count on citizens to provide information. These men cannot be allowed to escape. It is important that you cooperate by telling us absolutely everything you know about this."

Quayle shifted his weight in the bed, growing more uncomfortable with each question. Something in the man's belligerent tone made this feel like an interrogation. "Are you in contact with Detective Navarro?" he asked, instead of answering the first secretary's question. " I would like to speak to him."

"We are cooperating with all interested agencies, Mr. Quayle. The police are being kept apprised of the situation, yes. However, there is another matter. We are also concerned about the whereabouts of your chief executive officer."

"He is due to attend a meeting in Dubrovnik shortly. I don't know more than that. I believe I issued a press release about it."

"Very good, you remember that. This meeting is just two days away now, but you do not know where your chief executive officer is?" Ross paused, blinking slowly as he examined Quayle's expression with an intimidating stare.

"He has not informed us. It's not unusual for him to be out of touch while engaged in sensitive negotiations involving Enterprise business. As you know, the Enterprise's reach is worldwide."

Ross nodded. "My sources inform me that on the afternoon of the bombing, shortly before it occurred, you nearly resigned your position as publicist for the Enterprise. Would you care to tell us why?"

Quayle shook his head. "I don't recall it. I told you, my memory is mostly blank both before and after the explosion."

"I am asking this, Mr. Quayle, because there is media speculation about cash-flow problems at the Enterprise. Our sources say Mr. Flyte may have special knowledge of this problem. What can you tell us about that?"

Quayle stared blankly at Ross, then slowly at Gatwick. "I have no idea what you're talking about. Even if I did, our financial circumstances are confidential. I would not be free to discuss it with you."

"You do not recall considerable discussion at the meeting about accounting discrepancies requiring an internal investigation?"

"I have no memory of anything like that. I don't know where

you're getting such information."

Quayle felt himself sweating, armpits soaked with perspiration.

"Could your memory have been affected by the explosion to a degree you would not actually recall the details of such a discussion, one so obviously important? Or is this memory difficulty a matter of convenience for you, selective perhaps?"

Quayle blinked angrily. "I'm telling you, I don't remember."

"Perhaps you can at least remember the last time you and Mr. Flyte spoke?" Ross demanded. He was no longer bothering to hide his impatience "You must tell us all you know about Mr. Flyte---his habits, his associates, his friends---or I can assure you this could end unpleasantly for you. As you must know, insolvency on the part of a company as influential as the Enterprise, an integral part of the corporate consortium over which we have security interests, can have worldwide repercussions. I must warn you. These rumors have become of growing concern to all the consortium's partners. When one member risks insolvency, the entire consortium has a right to be concerned."

Quayle's temples were throbbing now, an acrid metallic taste flooding his mouth. He fought to swallow the foul taste. Finally, he managed to compose himself. "I don't know why you are asking such questions. Are you saying we are suspects in some sort of crime?"

Gatwick shook his head. "We're not saying that, Quayle. The first secretary is merely saying it would be most helpful if you would tell us where we might locate Mr. Flyte. In this way, we can assure your board of directors we within the Directorate are exercising our responsibility to ensure the security of your firm, as is our charge under our contractual obligation to the consortium. Have you any reason to believe Mr. Flyte was considering pulling the Enterprise out of the consortium?"

Quayle closed his eyes, then reopened them. In fact, while his memory was a jumble of conflicted images, this question triggered a clear memory: Jack had indeed confided this. Whether he intended to act on it, that was another matter.

Gatwick withdrew a recording device from his briefcase. "Take your time before you answer, Mr. Quayle. Think carefully and tell us anything that might be useful in helping us locate Mr. Flyte. Then we will see if Dr. McGreavey will allow you that visit from your wife."

Chapter Seventeen

The next morning Gatwick returned alone, took the chair Ross had used the day before, and resumed his questioning, his laptop's recording devices fully activated.

"Your long-term memory seems intact, just as Dr. McGreavy predicted, Quayle. However, I want you to try harder today to recall more recent events. Do you remember how I informed you yesterday our conversations were being recorded?"

"Yes, I do."

"Excellent. You've also told us you have no memory of events immediately preceding or following the explosion. Has a night's sleep refreshed that part of your memory?"

"I vaguely recall a meeting now--- members of the casino executive committee of the Enterprise, I believe. I remember faces. I'm not sure about the details."

"All right. That's something. We can come back to that later. In the meantime, maybe I can help jog your memory about other aspects of that day. Security cameras outside the Enterprise show you left the building at 2:15 p.m." Gatwick activated his laptop's projector and flashed up images on the wall. "As I understand it, that was approximately ten minutes after your meeting adjourned. You are seen here depositing two envelopes in the public courier drop outside the entrance. The explosion occurred three minutes later, at 2:18 p.m. Unfortunately, the blast destroyed the cameras; however, the data banks have given us a number of views of the scene before the blast. Do you recall posting the envelopes?"

"No."

"But you do recognize yourself entering and exiting the courier drop?"

"Yes, or course. I still don't recall actually being there."

"Can you think why you chose that method of delivery, rather than leaving the envelopes at the regular collection point on your floor? That is the normal method of sending out documents, isn't it?"

"If I didn't trust it to be picked up in a timely way, I might have decided to use the outside courier drop. Or I might just have forgotten to use the inside mail drop and gone to the one on the street rather than go back up to my floor. I've done that on occasions in the past."

"Do you remember the envelopes' contents, and to whom you might have sent them?"

"No. I have no memory of even preparing them."

"Thompson told us there was a discussion at the executive committee meeting about missing funds in some of the Enterprise's casino accounts---funds that appear to have been diverted to overseas accounts from the Enterprise's depository at the Coleridge Bank. Does that ring a bell?"

Quayle looked at Gatwick. "No, I don't recall that. Except, I am sure now it was the executive board that was meeting. I remember Thompson notifying me about the meeting personally. He said it was especially important that I be there."

"Perhaps you will now remember the disagreement you had with Mr. Thompson over who should be addressing future media inquiries about this particular issue?"

"No."

"And who should be in charge of the investigation of the missing funds? Do you recall that?"

"No, I don't. Wait. We did have a discussion about chain-of-command protocols some time ago. Jack said Thompson and I should consult each other whenever a major decision had to be made in his absence, but I don't know anything about any change in that general protocol."

Gatwick paused. "Very well. Let me explain it based on our preliminary inquiries into the meeting. At Mr. Flyte's order, Mr. Thompson was to be the primary decision-maker and media liaison in the event a dire financial situation confronted the Enterprise during one of Mr. Flyte's absences. He took the trouble of putting the order in writing and signing it. The discovery of missing funds was just such a circumstance. The executive committee ruled it as such in respect to the matter of missing casino receipts."

"It doesn't sound like something Jack would do, at least not without notifying me first. I am certain I was not notified."

"That was what you told the executive committee, according to those who were present. I should also tell you, Mr. Flyte's signature on the change in protocol has been authenticated."

"I would have to see the document myself before I could be certain of that," Quayle said sharply.

Gatwick withdrew a sheet of paper from a folder and handed it to him.

Quayle studied it before handing it back. "It does seem to be Jack's signature."

"Thompson told us you were upset enough about the change that you threatened to resign."

Quayle shook his head painfully. "I have no memory of that. Did I actually resign? I have no memory of doing any such thing."

"At the last minute, Mr. Thompson says you thought better of it."

"He must have been disappointed."

"You think he wanted you to resign?"

"Isn't it obvious?"

"I'm sorry. I don't follow."

"Isn't it obvious Thompson has been using this document as a pretext to take control of the Enterprise in Jack's absence?"

"Or," Gatwick interjected, "the document merely prescribes what Mr. Flyte wanted to happen in a financial emergency in a case like this: for the Enterprise's chief of security to lead an investigation of a highly sensitive internal security matter, including managing the flow of information. Isn't that so?"

"Yes, I can see how you might construe it that way. However...."

"Frankly, Quayle, I doubt Thompson would have reason to misrepresent the details of this important meeting when those details can be --- and in all important aspects have been --- verified with other members of the committee. I think you may be taking your past rivalry with Mr. Thompson too far here. That was his opinion of the matter, at any rate."

Quayle shook his head in confusion, wincing again in pain. "I don't know what you mean. There is no rivalry between us --- not of any real substance that I can recall. I do admit I'm still not thinking very clearly."

Gatwick made a note, then looked up. "Mr. Quayle, is it possible Jack Flyte could have been responsible for a misappropriation of funds, notwithstanding your long association and friendship with him? Is that at all possible in your mind?"

"No. The company is his---created and built by him from the ground up. He would never..."

"Created and built with significant help from you."

"Yes, but I'd never be a party to...."

Gatwick shrugged dismissively. "It would not be the first time desperate circumstances caused a colleague to commit a desperate act without informing his partner. Was he despondent for some reason? Had he incurred unusual debts?"

"No. I remember nothing like that at all."

"Why do you think he wanted to pull the Enterprise from the consortium then?"

Quayle opened his mouth to answer, then stopped. The memory of the bomb scare at the Racquet Club came to him. He nodded. "I do remember he was upset about the Brigades' strong-arm tactics, I know that. And how they had handled a bomb scare in our presence. Very heavy-handedly. Earlier, I had witnessed an incident myself ---an encounter in Central Park where the Brigades ended up executing a man simply because he would not offer a defense against their charges of having helped drive a man to take his own life. As far as anyone could tell, all the man had done was refuse to answer charges, which, of course, was his right."

"You're referring to the Kidman encounter," Gatwick shot back. "That man was a spy for a Brooklyn terrorist cell, providing information about our security planning. We had been observing him for months. If you knew all the facts, I'm sure you'd agree that action was just and necessary under provisions of the Emergency Decrees. There is also the question of example. Insurrections first smolder, then ignite if you let them. We needed the Kidman case to be fair warning to all subversives that we mean business." He glanced down at his computer screen. "On this matter of the Enterprise's diverted funds, it's also come to our attention Mr. Flyte controlled one of the overseas credit lines issued by the Coleridge Bank. We have determined it has been activated and used over at least the past year, possibly longer. We believe that is how the casino receipts were diverted to as yet unknown overseas accounts. I should tell you, only two people were authorized to activate that account: Mr. Rabinsky and Mr. Flyte." He studied Quayle's expression. "Were you aware of that?"

"No, I wasn't aware of it. However, I suppose that information also comes from our security chief, Thompson."

Gatwick tilted his head, his eyes narrowing: "As a matter of fact, yes. He briefed me thoroughly about all this, as you can tell."

"Did he tell you Rabinsky was investigating his expense account vouchers?"

It was now Gatwick's turn to appear somewhat surprised.

Quayle continued quickly. "Rabinksy told me this himself several days before that he and Thompson had had a falling out. He suspected Thompson was holding meetings outside his scheduled itinerary, discussions with several Enterprise competitors Rabinsky wasn't certain Jack was being made aware of. Before he could investigate, Thompson fired him. You know the rest. Did Thompson also happen to mention this?"

Gatwick's thick brows rose. "Your loyalty to Mr. Flyte is admirable, of course. Even so, this does not explain why, if he had nothing hide, Rabinsky chose to take his own life rather than submit to our questioning."

A flash of pain shot through Quayle's temples . He pressed his hands to his forehead. "I don't understand where you're going with this."

Gatwick leaned forward. "Would you rather this became a public matter---a police matter? Wouldn't it be best to allow us to manage all this more discreetly, for the sake of the Enterprise brand? Let me ask you again, Mr. Quayle. Is it possible Mr. Flyte himself might have transferred these casino receipts to an overseas account for some reason known only to Mr. Rabinsky?"

"That they've been conspiring to steal from the Enterprise---Jack's own company? Embezzlement? Is that what you are insinuating"

"You do agree if a transfer of funds in the Coleridge Bank accounts was made, Mr. Rabinsky as the Enterprise's chief accountant would have most likely known about it?"

"Yes. That would have been likely. However, it means nothing without more facts than you've supplied me so far."

"So it's inconceivable to you that Mr. Rabinsky and Mr. Flyte could have been complicit in diverting the receipts for some reason you aren't aware of? Perhaps as payment for a deal you were unaware of?"

"No. I have usually been kept informed about any deal of importance that Jack might have had in the works."

"Except the one he seems to be working on now. Isn't that right? He hasn't kept you informed of this deal, has he? Your blind loyalty is a little premature, if not misplaced, in this case, wouldn't you say?"

Quayle pressed his forehead with shaky fingers. His skin felt on fire.

Gatwick leaned closer. "Perhaps this was why Mr. Rabinsky informed you he was investigating Mr. Thompson's expense accounts --- to discredit him in case he or his security team discovered a scheme to divert those funds to overseas accounts. Think about it. What could have provoked Mr. Rabinsky to take his own life, rather than to risk being questioned about all this, if he wasn't behind the diversion, or at least had knowledge of it?" Gatwick watched Quayle's reaction. "Let me ask this question again. Loyalty aside, isn't it possible Jack Flyte could be the one responsible for this misappropriation of funds, maybe for a reason you were not, and could not, be fully aware of because he had not confided his reasons to you?"

"No. That's impossible."

"Or ..." Gatwick paused. "....maybe you're not answering me forthrightly now because he did confide in you, and you were part of the whole scheme yourself."

"If Thompson's telling you that, then you can be certain it's a lie. Every bit of it." Quayle looked at his inquisitor directly, his gaze unwavering. “It’s as I told you before: it's my opinion that Thompson is laying the groundwork for assuming control of the Enterprise himself.”

Gatwick stared, his steel-gray eyes narrowing. “This possibility has occurred to us. I’m glad your memory has sharpened to the point it has occurred to you as well. Were you not capable of retrieving and piecing together certain facts, both from the past and recent present, I doubt very much you could have drawn this conclusion.”

Sweat broke out again over Quayle’s brow. Struggling to frame his words, he said finally: “I will say it again. Nothing you have been speculating about Jack Flyte is possible.”

Gatwick released his breath. “All right, let’s assume you’re correct. Let’s say in a few days he does appear at his scheduled meetings in Dubrovnik and reveals to the world a deal he has not explained to you, a deal having nothing to do with diverted funds from the Enterprise’s casino accounts. Could there be some political agenda behind it instead?”

“If you are asking if he has more than one agenda when conducting a business deal, yes, of course, it’s often the case.”

“That’s an interesting response.” He made a note. “He has political causes, then, is that what you are telling me, above and beyond the marketplace?”

Quayle nodded uneasily. “When he sees some injustice being done, he has been known to stop a deal, if that’s what you are asking me.”

“Precisely. Let me put it another way, as clearly and directly as I can. It is disturbing to us that Mr. Flyte was overheard mentioning possibly withdrawing the Enterprise from the consortium because he found fault with some of our methods. This has caused us concern about his loyalties to us. Can you understand this?”

“Surely, he can’t have been the only member of the consortium to find enclave encampments excessive?"

"In fact, he has been the only dissenter. There has been far more concern about the violence honest citizens of the city have been experiencing lately at the hands of these extremists. Aren't you concerned, as one of their victims now, and as someone whose own wife only narrowly escaped death from a similar bombing?"

"Of course the violence is of concern. But I believe it's possible to be concerned about violence however it may be employed. What cause has Jack Flyte given that he intended to in any way undermine what the Directorate is attempting to do to maintain the consortium's security and the city's? I have certainly never heard him express anything but legitimate concern about your recent tactics, which any citizen of a democracy could easily fault as extreme."

Gatwick smiled. "Calm yourself, Quayle. I assure you, we in the Directorate are interested only in facts. But to get to the truth, one must sometimes speculate. As the security arm of the city's most important enterprises of commerce, we recognize our legal and administrative boundaries. We do not act outside the law, or beyond the lawful powers granted us by the Emergency Decrees." Gatwick leaned forward, his gaze intense. "Make no mistake about it, however. We will do what needs to be done. We all have our vital work in these unsettled times---the police, corporate leaders like yourself, the Directorate and our Brigades, even our friends in government---all of us must heed the supreme goal: order, so those who obey the rule of law can remain free to engage in commerce, while those who will not follow the law can be firmly dealt with. As a patriot, Quayle, you do approve of this vital work of ours, don't you?"

Quayle, conscious suddenly of the recordings being made, nodded. "Whatever I can do to help, of course I will attempt to do. I am sure I speak for Jack Flyte as well. There can be no doubt about that."

"An excellent response, Mr. Quayle, at last! And your wife? Cecil Collander? Will she also be cooperative?"

Quayle stared, not expecting such a question. With each resumption of a more collegial tone, the interrogation seemed to have suddenly swung toward a new, more ominous turn.

"She has nothing to do with Enterprise business."

"Except for that interesting mural in the Enterprise lobby---undamaged by the explosion, fortunately. A heroic work of art, really. It inspired me to wonder what insights an observer of human character like your wife might have into a mind as complicated and opaque as Jack Flyte's."

"No more than you see depicted in the mural, I assure you. Jack wasn't much help to her. Most of the background came from me and her reading of his biographies, of which there are many. She's often referred to him as one of her most difficult subjects."

"Is that so? Also interesting."

"I've tried to be cooperative, Gatwick. Now, when may I see her?"

Gatwick rose from his chair. He patted Quayle's hand. "Not yet."

With that---before Quayle could protest---the Directorate's chief of inquiries was gone.

Chapter Eighteen

Cecil's Directorate inquisitors released her as unexpectedly as they'd taken her in, a two-hour ordeal she'd thought would never end. The casino winnings, the pretext for the questioning, had been discovered in her purse, but intimidation had seemed the true purpose. The part of the Directorate where they'd taken her had been a maze of cold and cheerless offices with scarcely a soul around. They'd shown her recorded scenes of her mystifying night on the casino floor from start to finish, the security cameras capturing everything that, until that moment, had seemed more like a dream: The tall stranger at her side goading her to bet; helping her cash out her winnings and placing them in her purse. She saw herself leaving the casino hanging on to his arm. He was a man they insisted she must have known, and she could understand why; they were behaving more like lovers than strangers. It was too unsettling, too disgusting. In fact, she had never seen the man before in her life.

More questions: How had she met him? (She couldn't remember.) Had it been at Governor Wainwright's soiree at the River Club? (How did you know I was there? Yes, possibly.) Had she ever seen this man before? (Not until, apparently, he practically kidnapped me).

In the end, they confiscated the $100,000---evidence of an as yet unnamed crime they refused to explain --- and sent her back into Foley Square feeling like a common criminal.

"There will be more questions as this investigation develops," the woman had warned. "I wouldn't leave the city."

They'd returned her communicator, and she immediately checked her messages. Joyce Boles explaining she'd been delayed, she was needed to help manage the office in the midst of the chaos. She'd been checking hospitals as often as she could, but still no word. Could she come after 5? By then, she might be free to help.

Exasperated, she headed for the first coffee shop near Foley Square she could find, took an empty booth, and pressed Ben's speed-dial number on her communicator. She heard: "Service temporarily unavailable." She tried Sabrena, needing to consult someone, anyone, to help her make sense of this. "In a meeting, unavailable."

"Goddamn it!

"M'am?" A waitress stood poised beside her ready to take her order.

"Sorry," she said with an embarrassed smile, "talking to myself." She ordered a coffee.

She looked up at the coffee shop's wall screen. The latest news break was replaying the aftermath of the Enterprise bombing. The eyes of every patron in the coffee shop were riveted to the wall screen. The images of the devastation were too much to bear. She jumped to her feet. Again she punched in Ben's number, her eyes not leaving the wall screen. She waited for an answer for as long as she could bear it, then snatched up her purse and bolted for the street. She had to go now. She had to be where news of Ben might be. At the curb, she charged ahead of a man about to enter a cab and leaped inside, slamming the door behind her. She shouted the Enterprise address at the driver.

"You in a hurry, lady?" the driver said in a heavy accent. "Too bad. Big mess here. Big mess everywhere. Gridlock, lady."

"I don't care. Here's $200. Get me up there as fast as you can."

She looked and saw what he meant: crosstown gridlock developing even downtown. She tried Ben's number again. Still no service---not even a normal ring. Frantically, she looked out the window again. Once on the West Side from Foley Square and the East Side, it would be another twenty blocks uptown to Columbus Circle, then over to Broadway and ten more blocks up to the Enterprise. At this rate it might be an hour or more before they arrived. Still, she had to do something.

She handed the driver two hundred-dollar bills and dropped the communicator into her lap. Almost immediately it chimed. She saw it was her mother calling, the familiar shrill voice crackling through the static. "It's mother, dear...the Enterprise bombing on the news...dreadful. Did you...(something indistinguishable)?"

The garble didn't matter. She knew her mother's M.O. Every violence-laced crisis triggered utter panic in her mother, at its root the memory of the suicide of Cecil's father. "I don't know what's happening, mother. I'll have to call you back." She was about to break off when the line cleared; in mid-sentence her mother's plea for information returned.

"Mother, shut up and listen to me!" Cecil finally managed to get out. "I can't understand what you're saying. I've been trying to get Ben on the line and can't get through, and now I'm caught in horrific traffic, and you're blocking my call. I'll phone you back as soon as I know something."

"Was he there? "Tell me he wasn't there."

"Yes, he was there. I don't know anything more, mother. Now, please....I'll call you back later." As long as the bombings had remained in the enclaves, they'd been distant thunder. Now, two bombings in Manhattan in a week. She could smell the panic even without her mother's added fuel. She prayed for the hundredth time Ben's line would answer, but again she only got the voice message.

Cecil began dialing hospitals she Googled off her communicator. She reached St. Luke's-Roosevelt, the circuits apparently working again. She waded through recordings before a live voice answered. "Yes, some of the bombing victims are being treated here," the voice said. "No, Benjamin Quayle is not listed here; it's possible he's still in emergency."

"For God's sake, then transfer me there, please. This is urgent."

More waiting. Finally, a nurse came on the line and told her Roosevelt ambulances had brought in just three injured and two dead from the Enterprise explosion. Benjamin Quayle was not among them.

"Where else might they have been taken?"

The nurse reeled off names and numbers of three hospitals.

She wrote down the information, thanked her, and rang off.

"Driver, can't you go faster?"

The way ahead looked as hopeless as before. Horns honked all around them. In another moment, the driver saw an opening and swerved the cab violently right over the curb and onto the sidewalk. Pedestrians leaped from its path. The cab hurtled over the curb back to the street, inching through an opening between two trucks, then accelerating until a new commotion quickly appeared and halted them. A blanket of rotating blue and yellow lights of ambulances and police vans warned of a new problem. Directly ahead, they could see the intersection at Columbus Circle and 59th Street blocked with barricades.

Cecil groaned. "Please, can't you get us around this somehow? I must get through."

A crowd, drawn to the commotion, was gathering: people heading home after work, laden-down shoppers, tourists with balloons from a street fair, children with school groups, all drawn to what appeared to be something going on at the Circle.

"For God's sake," she cried. "What's this now?"

Police were waving people back, throwing up more barricades. An unmarked van pulled up and stopped where the police halted them. Two helmeted Brigadesmen stepped out. They moved to the rear doors and stood at attention beside them.

"They got two guys under arrest who did the bombing in Midtown," the driver said. "Maybe it's them. The radio reports are saying they confessed. They're going to hang them right over there."

She struggled to let this sink in. He meant the bombers who had nearly killed her at Sabrena's offices. She could see by the driver's name on his hack license he was probably Middle Eastern as many cabbies were. He was staring pointedly at her in the mirror. Cecil's stomach turned over, first at what might be about to happen, next at what this driver might be thinking. And now, damn it, this new delay. This was too horrid.

A protester waved a sign that read, "Hang all terrorists!" More onlookers broke out signs. Someone began to chant the same demand. A cheer went up. Others took up the refrain. Like it or not, they were going to have a front row seat for this, whatever it was.

"Remain behind the lines," a police officer shouted over the barricades. "No one may cross. Stay behind the lines." He blew his whistle shrilly, waving his arms, loudly repeating the demand.

Cecil saw an adolescent boy in a school uniform walk in front of the cab. In blazer and pressed slacks, she could tell he was poised to bolt for the Circle. Cecil lowered her window. "Hey, young man, stay away from there! Where's your teacher?"

The boy stopped and stared at her. He looked back at the matronly woman he had just left. She was trying to keep half a dozen of her other young, unruly charges in tow. All seemed prepared to cross. "Are those your students?" Cecil shouted at her, catching her full attention despite the commotion. "You'd better get these children back. There's going to be trouble."

Alarmed, she called out: "Bobby, get back here! Right now!"

It was too late. Ignoring her, the boy laughed and darted in front of the cab to the barricades. He threw his arms over the top rail to see if he could see more. The rest of the pack raced to join him.

The Brigadesman stepped to the doors of the van and swung them open. Inside, two hooded figures could be seen seated side-by-side on a bench, wrists manacled, heads down and motionless.

The boy began to flap his arms: "Goony birds don't look so tough now. Hey, you gonna pay now, goony birds."

More of the crowd rushed over. The teacher tried wading into the crowd to herd her children back, grabbing at their arms, but they'd anchored themselves at the barricades closest to the open van. Word of the occupants seemed to be spreading now: the Madison Avenue bombers, somebody shouted. News crews clamored from nearby trucks. The crowd around the Circle grew larger, more excited. The teacher glanced back at Cecil helplessly, the same look she was sure her own expression was registering.

Beyond the barricades, wooden supports for some sort of contraption took on new importance, all but the lower parts of the boxed formation concealed by tarpaulins. Workmen now pulled off the tarps. There, a wooden scaffolding, accessible only by a single set of stairs, stood only feet from Columbus Circle's central monument and fountain. Two heavyset men in suits emerged from the crowd and took positions on either side of the steps.

"Damn it, driver," Cecil said. "Can't you get us away from here?"

The cabbie did not answer. It was obvious that for the moment there was nothing to be done.

Standing at the open doors of the van, a bearded old man in white robes of an Imam stepped before the doors and opened the pages of a book. He began to read what sounded like prayers from its pages.

The prisoner closest to the doors raised his head and shouted something at the crowd.

Cecil asked what the prisoner had said.

"He says, 'Allah be praised, curse all infidels, we have done nothing wrong.'"

"But you said the news media say they confessed? Was there no trial?"

The driver flashed a smile. "Two goats know they will always be found guilty of being goats. Big surprise to you?"

"But who do your people say did it if not these two?"

"My people?" the driver exclaimed with a laugh. "You crazy? I am American-born like you." He chuckled again. "Maybe we ask Allah; maybe this Allah will tell us."

At the open doors of the van, the Imam appeared to be reading to the occupants from a book. Finally, he closed the pages and stepped back from the van. Two Brigadesmen moved forward and reached inside. They pulled two bound prisoners onto the sidewalk, legs and hands manacled with chains, each set of shackles bound to the other. Slowly, they were brought in tandem to the stairs of the gallows.

"Why are we letting this happen?" Cecil whispered.

"Who will stop them?" The cabbie gestured at the crowd and laughed. The faces there registered none of the revulsion she was feeling. Instead, some began to clap as the prisoners were forced up the steps, the clapping matching the rhythm of the leg chains as the prisoners climbed. A guard on each side, ropes coiled over their shoulders, guided the prisoners to the high platform where they stopped and tossed two nooses over the sturdiest beams of what was now clearly a gallows. They positioned the nooses over the necks of both men and tightened the heavy knots.

The clapping stopped. A collective quiet settled over the park, the Circle, and the barricades. Without ceremony, a Brigadesmen yanked a lever beside the traps. The two hooded figures dropped together, reached the limits of their ropes, and with a sickening snap of knot against neck arched their backs, violently kicked, and finally, mercifully, grew still.

At first, the crowd did not cheer, then suddenly, as the outcome became clear, broke into a collective roar.

Close to the cab, the teacher and some of her charges looked stricken, shocked by consequences they should have anticipated but apparently, somehow, had not. A girl rushed sobbing into her teacher's arms; the boy who had taunted the condemned stared at the ground.

In a chorus of horns, a gridlock of drivers began to honk their impatience.

In a minute, Cecil's cab lurched forward. With painful slowness it passed by the motionless still-hooded corpses swaying from their ropes. The cab rounded Columbus Circle and crept onto Broadway, finally heading uptown again.

Outside her window, she could see a broad expanse of Central Park empty and tranquil, as if the scene just two blocks behind had never occurred.

***

At the Enterprise, street crews were removing debris; more barricades and police blocking their way. She decided to get out and walk the half-block more to the entrance. Save for shattered windows and doors, the building itself seemed miraculously unscathed. She threaded her way through the wreckage in the street: piles of shattered glass, twisted metal, crumbled concrete, bent lampposts, and remains of broken cars. It was as she had seen it on the coffee shop wall screen, a replica of the aftermath of the Madison Avenue bombing she had narrowly escaped. If only Ben had been as lucky.

At the security desk inside, she could see no evidence of the bomb blast at all, her mural intact, whatever bomb-proofing that had been done, impervious to the explosion outside. The Enterprise's security man looked at her pass, consulted a registry on his desk, and shook his head. "I'm sorry, Mrs. Quayle, I've been instructed to confiscate your pass."

"Excuse me? I have an appointment with Joyce Boles, my husband's secretary. You know who I am, for God's sake."

"Chief of Security Robert Thompson's orders, Mrs. Quayle, " he said, more officiously than apologetically. "All but employees must relinquish their passes for new background checks."

Cecil stared at him. Slowly, she handed over her family-member pass and received back the temporary yellow badge of a visitor. The guard spoke into his communicator and announced her.

At the elevator, a uniformed security man stepped in with her, standing so close she could hear him breathing as the elevator rose At the twenty-seventh floor, Joyce Boles awaited her. Glancing at the security man, who examined Cecil carefully before nodding his approval, Ben's trusted secretary motioned her into a vacant office. With another anxious glance back she closed the door.

"Mrs. Quayle, I'm so sorry about this."

"I want to know everything."

"I have called around to every hospital. None in the area

report admitting him."

"That could be good news then."

"Except why can't we reach him? Why hasn't he tried to reach us?" Joyce raised one eyebrow. "He must have seen the news about all this. The police say an ambulance took him somewhere, so he must have been injured. They just don't know where."

"I don't understand this. I don't understand it at all."

Joyce Boles opened the door to her office. Across the hall in a conference room, media were setting up for a press conference. She pressed something into Cecil's hand and leaned close to her ear. "Mr. Quayle gave me this business card before he left and asked me to call this woman and make an appointment for him."

Cecil examined the card as they stopped at the glassed-in entrance to the 27th floor's reception area. "What did the woman say?"

"I left a message on her voice mail asking for the appointment. I've heard nothing back. Mr. Quayle was very upset that the board had granted Mr. Thompson exclusive control of the company. He told me he had nearly resigned before he thought better of it. I'm so worried about him."

Cecil looked at her in dismay, then down at the card she'd just been handed: Raisa Amin, Doctor of Meditation. The name meant nothing to her; Ben was hardly the meditation type. What on earth was this about now?

At that moment, Thompson stepped from his office and waved to her through the glass windows of the reception area. Cecil quickly dropped the card into her purse. Joyce said hurriedly: "I'm sorry, I must prepare for the press conference now. Please be careful."

Cecil could see men in the uniform of the Enterprise Security Section filing out of the same office Thompson had emerged from. There were half a dozen of them. Several seemed to be sharing a joke, laughing. The sound of incongruous laughter sent chills up her spine.

Thompson greeted her and ushered her inside his office. Closing the door, he offered her a chair.

"I would prefer to stand."

"I know you're upset. However, the moment we learned he was among the injured, I asked Mrs. Boles to make inquiries." He glanced away before turning back to her, as if momentarily distracted by another thought. "I'd been hoping to have some good news for you before we spoke. That's why I haven't contacted you sooner. Unfortunately, we still don't know which hospital treated him. All the police can say is a witness saw him taken away in an unmarked ambulance." He looked at his watch. "I have very little time to talk now. I have a very important press conference in five minutes."

Cecil didn't move. "What happened at the meeting of the executive committee? I want to know at least that much. Ben only told me it was to be a very important meeting. There must have been some reason he decided to leave the building before the meeting adjourned."

"He walked out because he chose not to be a team player. It was his own fault he happened to be outside when the bomb went off. If he hadn't been so impulsive, this wouldn't have happened."

This remark, so much like her mother's evasions, infuriated her. "Why was he upset? Joyce said he almost resigned. Be clear, damn it! Tell me!"

"Jack signed an emergency authorization several weeks ago that authorized me to assume temporary control of the Enterprise if he was not able to manage any security matter that could endanger the financial health of the company. Ben refused to accept that fact. Ask anyone who attended the meeting. I presented the board with the authorizing document; it had been witnessed by our chief staff attorney. Ben still questioned its authenticity."

Cecil started to protest, then stopped herself. "You know where Jack is, don't you?"

"Of course not. What makes you say that?"

"I think you know exactly where he is, and I think you had something to do with his disappearance."

"You're being irrational."

"You know what else? I think you put something in my drink at Genesee's party, some sort of drug to make me lose control yet not knock me out. You did, didn't you? Then you had one of your men gamble money on a bet that was somehow rigged to let me win. The Directorate just questioned me about it. It was terrifying."

"I think you should leave now. I will have Mrs. Boles escort you out."

Cecil stood where she was, her gaze unwavering despite the force of his rising impatience forcing her departure. She repeated her accusation: "You did, didn't you?"

"I'm asking you politely."

She went to the door, then turned back to him. Tears stung her eyes. "Damn you," she said through clenched teeth. "Ben helped build this company long before you arrived." She stopped. "Do you think you can just steal it?"

Without waiting for his answer, she opened the door, marched into the glassed-in reception area through a sea of startled faces and out to the corridor, casting a glance into the twenty-seventh floor conference room now packed with media. She remembered something Ben had said to her once: "I know only one honest journalist left in this city." She wished she had asked him who that was.

As she waited for the elevator, the same big-shouldered

security man who had escorted her from the lobby followed her into the elevator again. She had a powerful urge to slap that implacable look of indifference off his chiseled, impassive face.

As she stepped into the lobby, she strode past her mural, this time scarcely noticing it. That seemed so long ago, a different time. Choking back tears, she turned in her visitor's pass and left the building with a sinking feeling of finality. Not since her father's death had she felt so alone---or more fiercely determined not to succumb to the helplessness threatening to engulf her.

Chapter Nineteen

The next morning at 9 o'clock sharp, the time she had been given for her appointment with Raisa Amin at 252 Park Avenue, Cecil pressed the button on the intercom marked "De-Stress." With still no word about Ben's whereabouts, she anxiously waited, hoping for some word, some news, that might at least explain his absence. Almost at once, a woman's voice responded in a heavy French accent: "State your name and references, *s'il vous plaît.*"

"Cecil Quayle My husband is Benjamin Quayle. I have an appointment with Dr. Amin on an urgent matter."

There was a long silence. She had the impression she was being examined by security cameras. At last the electronic locks buzzed. Two heavy oak doors swung open into a glittering low-ceilinged lobby bound by walls of flocked wallpaper and exquisite gold moldings. She walked down a narrow aisle of red velvet ropes and stopped at a security desk in front of a bank of elevators.

"Identification?" the uniformed guard asked in clipped English, his luminous sand-brown skin suggesting Middle Eastern origin. From his wide polished belt and holster hung a nickel-plated pearl-handled pistol. He examined her identity card, passed an electronic wand around her body, then nodded toward the elevators.

"Fifteenth floor, penthouse," he said to the operator inside.

At her floor, the elevator doors opened into an elaborate suite. Seated before her, blocking her way, was an enormous copper-colored Afghan hound. The dog examined her with otherworldly amber eyes.

"Yanille, it's all right," said a slender diminutive woman who stood directly behind the dog. She appeared to be in her early forties, a long black braid draped elegantly over one shoulder, her smooth skin almost tangerine in color, luminescent under the overhead lights. She bent over the dog, took its collar, and guided it to a corner. Over a sky-blue, ankle-length dress, she wore an elaborately embroidered tunic of emerald green; bracelets the color of the Afghan's eyes clicked on her wrists. The sum of her appearance gave off an energy and elegance that left Cecil momentarily speechless.

"Some believe a dog in the house is not healthy," the woman said, smiling. "Yanille, however, brings me luck, and she is a good judge of character. I believe she likes you." The woman nodded slightly but did not extend her hand. "I am Raisa Amin. I was just about to have tea. Will you join me?"

"Yes, please, thank you." Cecil answered. She could not help but be impressed by the luxuriousness of the surroundings. "I'm sorry I had to ask to see you on such short notice."

"It does not matter," the woman said and gestured to a chair facing her own. They sat facing each other on either side of a low ornate marble table.

"Bring madame her own service, Marie," she said to a housekeeper who had silently appeared. She turned to Cecil. "I can see you are distraught. Please, let us dispense with any further pleasantries. Tell me how I might help you, Mrs. Quayle?"

"My husband may have been injured or killed in yesterday's terrible bombing at the Enterprise. I spent all last night calling hospitals and friends trying to learn something, anything, about his whereabouts. So far there seems to be no trace at all of him, and now I'm desperate. Right before my husband left the building and walked down the street where the explosion occurred, he had asked his secretary to set up a meeting with you. He did not tell her why, but she's sure it was something urgent. I am wondering if you might know why he might have wanted to meet with you."

The cup and saucer arrived; Raisa Amin calmly raised the teapot and poured for Cecil. "It's Moroccan mint, already sweetened. I hope you like it."

Cecil raised her cup and tasted. "Thank you, it's excellent." She set the cup and saucer down. "All I've been told is an ambulance removed him from the scene. However, none of the borough hospitals or city morgues have any record of his being admitted. I'm frantic."

Raisa nodded. "Hospital records rarely keep pace with admissions in the chaos after a bombing. I can tell you, however, with certainty that your husband for the moment is out of danger and being well treated for his injuries."

Cecil let out a sharp sigh of relief, then just as quickly looked at the woman in alarm. "How do you know this? Where is he then?"

Raisa raised her hand. "I will get to that. However, you must give me your promise to say nothing about what we discuss here. After you leave, it must be as if you and I have never talked. Do you understand?"

Cecil blinked. "Yes, of course. As you wish."

"My associates and I wish to help you. We are people of mixed origins---Muslims Palestinians, and Jews, united with one goal: to stop the oppression in the enclaves and prevent the violence from spreading into other boroughs. It is urgent that we have your cooperation in this cause, Mrs. Quayle. Most in the city are not yet aware of it, but we are on the brink of a dangerous civil war in this city."

"You are the people the Directorate and Brigades call extremists?"

"Their way of demonizing anyone who opposes them. We prefer to see ourselves as patriots. And I assure you, our influence reaches well beyond just the enclaves." She paused. "Your husband is not in any ordinary hospital, Mrs. Quayle. He is being treated in the Directorate, and when he recovers, he will be interrogated. Perhaps harshly, if he does not agree to cooperate."

Cecil's spirits sank. Somehow, she had guessed this might be the case. "They questioned me as well yesterday, before the bombing. They wanted to know about my husband, and about his relationship with Jack Flyte, my husband's colleague and employer."

Raisa nodded. "We know they also had you shadowed at the Albany Five Tribes Casino, an evening that probably made no sense to you."

Cecil gave a start. "No, it still doesn't. I am almost certain I was drugged."

"It is common practice for them to invent pretexts for bringing in people for questioning. They wanted information. They didn't care about the money you won. It was all a charade to put you on the defensive and persuade you to cooperate."

Cecil shook her head, feeling sick to her stomach. "I didn't tell them very much. They wanted to know where Jack was. I had no idea. I still don't. That's what I told them."

"Good," Raisa said. She leaned closer, speaking with soft reassurance. "Please let me explain who I am. And why it's important that you help us. It is a complicated story, but I will try to be brief." She set her tea cup down and looked again at Cecil earnestly. "I am Algerian, of mixed race---my grandmother was Arab; her husband, my grandfather, was a Jew. Both had French citizenships and lived on a farm in Oran near Algiers---*pieds-noirs*, they were called, as were many thousands of other French citizens living in Algeria under the protection of the French colonial flag. Do you understand, this expression *pieds-noirs*?"

Cecil nodded vaguely. "I know it means black feet."

"Literally, yes. An insult at first, meant to describe the poverty of the settlers, many of them farmers with black soil of the land on their bare feet; later, it's said, it was an insult meant for the generations of French officials who colonized Algeria in their black boots. Later, it would become a badge of honor for those who saw Algeria and its lands as their true homeland and who demanded their French sovereignty be protected. In 1962, there was a civil war, a war of independence waged by socialists and generals against de Gaulle and his government. Much blood ---Muslim, Jew, and Christian---ran in the streets. The *pieds-noirs*, regardless of race or origin, found themselves abandoned as de Gaulle broke his solemn word. He declared Algeria independent---no longer under French protection. All *pieds-noirs* lands were confiscated, many families slaughtered or displaced, mainly by Muslim and other ethnic populations seeking retribution and reparation for years of oppression at the hands of the French colonialists; hundreds of thousands of Algerian French were forced to escape to France. The coffin or the suitcase, the new government and their police warned them, '*La valise ou le cercueil.*'

"Many of our people escaped unharmed, but it did not go well for them on French soil, either. The black feet were reviled by many French there, too, condemned as foreigners with no homeland --- outcasts---much like Palestinians remain now, you see; much like the poorest of the poor in our own New York City's eastern boroughs, ghettoized in the enclaves. Many escaped like animals into Paris' Muslim and Jewish neighborhoods, or into ethnic enclaves in Marseilles and other port cities, or, for the luckier, found their way to America to escape the persecutions. You understand what I am saying?"

Cecil nodded.

"But you still wonder what this may have to do with you and your husband. In the spring of that terrible year, my grandparents prepared their escape from Oran. The independence had just been proclaimed, the retributions had immediately begun. The first morning of the massacres, my *grandpere, grandmere* and many others were lined up in a square and shot. My mother then was just seven years of age. Fortunately, she had spent the night at the home of a friend --- a family of Jews, also *pieds-noirs*. Our different origins did not matter, only our bonds to the land, to our Algérie. At this house, my mother and her friend were hidden from the marauders. A day later, along with her family, they were taken by ship to Marseilles, then by train to Paris. There, they found safety in the Arab enclave of Belleville. If it had not been for those Muslim brothers and sisters taking them in, my mother and her Jewish friend might have perished."

"But again, what has this to do with my husband? I still don't understand."

"This family of Jews who helped my mother escape with her friend was named Lisset. Is this name familiar to you?"

Cecil leaned forward. "Julienne Lisset was the name of my husband's mother. She died in the World Trade Center attacks along with my husband's father when Ben was just a young boy."

"And your husband, how did he escape the disaster?"

"An hour before the planes struck the towers, he had been dropped off at a play group. He was only 4. He was raised by his grandparents. I distinctly remember they had told him his mother's maiden name was Lisset. They said she had come to New York in her twenties before her marriage to Ben's father."

Raisa Amin nodded. "Julienne Lisset---my mother's closest

Jewish friend."

Cecil stared. "But that's too incredible! I'm sure Ben knows nothing of this connection."

"I myself only recently learned these details. *Pieds-noirs* of those times kept details of their lives to themselves; they were often shunned if people knew of their pasts. Only in recent years have they begun to tell their stories."

Cecil stared at her. "How can you be so certain my husband's mother is the Jewish friend of whom your mother spoke?"

"Since my mother's death last year, I have spent many months researching these times. I wanted to know what had happened to these people, Muslim, Jew, Christian, *pieds-noirs* all, common people who had been so willing to cross ethnic and religious lines to do brave, uncommon things for one another. We wanted to find descendants of the refugees of those times now living in New York--- people we might recruit in our campaign against the Directorate's Emergency Decrees, laws that discriminate against immigrants regardless of origin or legal status, reminders to us all of those terrible days."

Cecil's brain was reeling, flooded with all sorts of images and emotions. She remembered the single photograph the New York authorities had managed to salvage from Ben's parents' half-destroyed apartment near the towers. He had that photograph in his study now, his parents' partially scorched wedding photo, the carefree faces of both young marrieds stopped in time.

"And this is why you wish to help us? Because of this connection to your mother and family?"

"In part, but that is not the entirety of it."

Cecil put down her cup. She shook her head. "I'm sorry, I'm having difficulty absorbing all this."

"Or also believing it, perhaps?"

Cecil nodded. "The coincidence, you have to admit, is rather incredible. How can I be sure your mother's information is correct?"

Raisa Amin reached into a handbag beside her and withdrew an envelope. She handed it to Cecil. "Julienne Lisset sent this photograph to my mother at the time of her marriage in New York many years ago. The date was June 4, 1985. Do you think this could be your husband's parents?"

Cecil took the photograph. With unsteady fingers, she turned it toward the light. She saw at once the youthful faces of Ben's happy mother and father. Cecil looked up, the skin on the back of her neck prickling. "He has a photograph identical to this one. Please, Dr. Amin. Please tell me what you want me to do."

The woman rang for the housekeeper to take away the tea. When the girl had gone, she leaned closer. Smoothing her long braid, she shifted it to a new shoulder and said: "We need you to help us find his colleague Jack Flyte. We must speak with him about these matters. We must enlist his help."

Cecil's eyes widened.

"To help us resolve these matters of extreme importance regarding the welfare of the city."

Cecil nodded vigorously, starting to understand better now. "Two terrorists were hanged before my eyes yesterday; a bomb nearly took my own life several days ago; another has just apparently injured my husband. If these are the urgent matters you mean, then I can assure you will do whatever I can."

Raisa Amin nodded. "When we have successfully freed your husband, we want you to persuade him to assist us in locating his colleague, M. Flyte."

The saucer clattered on Cecil's lap. She reached down and steadied it. "My husband does not know where Jack is right now. I explained that."

"We know this. We also know your husband's interrogators

want his help in locating him. They have very different reasons than ours. They are working to take control of the Enterprise."

Cecil rose from her chair with alarm, startling the Afghan. It raised its head.

"That's all right, Yanille. " Raisa motioned palm down to the dog, who lay her nose back on her paws.

Cecil shook her head. "How can you know so much?"

"We have many sources. I must warn you now, however. If you complain to the police about being detained, or report any information I share with you, it could go very badly for all of us. There are some elements of the city police who cannot be trusted any more than the Brigades. Both are now under control of the Directorate. Mrs. Quayle. I am placing my life in your hands telling you this."

"There is one detective my husband does seem to trust..." Cecil began, her voice quavering. Raisa raised a jeweled finger to stop her. "If you mean Detective Navarro, we have learned he has been reassigned. The Directorate is now fully in charge of the Jack Flyte matter, with the full cooperation of the Enterprise's chief of security, Robert Thompson." The activist looked at Cecil directly. "Will you persuade your husband to speak with us then, once we have helped to release him?"

"You have my promise, yes, yes, of course."

Raisa nodded with a look of satisfaction and handed her the folder. "Inside are also pages my mother copied from my grandmother's diary. They contain the names of others in your husband's past --- further proof I speak the truth."

Cecil took the folder and examined its contents. "Please, what exactly does the Directorate want?"

"Loyalty is important to the consortium, and the Directorate sees Jack Flyte, and now perhaps your husband, as increasingly disloyal. They are certain Flyte is prepared to support a public demand for repeal of the Directorate's Emergency Decrees."

"How can I help when I have no way to contact my husband?"

"There is a way." Raisa's voice rose sharply before dropping to almost a whisper. Again, she leaned forward. "When you leave here this morning, I want you to phone the Directorate at this unpublished number." She handed Cecil a scrap of paper. "I want you to demand that they allow you to see your husband. It's important they know you are aware he is there. They will know someone told you this before they had him reassigned; they will not be certain who. Secrecy always gives them more power, so we will remove some of that secrecy from them. If they realize you know they have your husband, they will have to be more cautious interrogating him."

The buzzer of the suite's intercom sounded. Raisa Amin lifted a finger. "I must go now. You can use the back elevator. My housekeeper will show you the way. Goodbye, Mrs. Quayle."

***

Cecil let herself back into the townhouse at East 21st. It was nearing noon now. She saw at once the message center blinking. She ran through the calls, listening only to each name before clicking ahead. Still hearing no message from Ben, the one voice she wanted to hear above all others, she reversed the disk and hit replay. While she listened to the stream of calls, mainly media looking for Ben to comment on the bombing, apparently also unaware of his situation, she sat down at her computer, punched in her password, and waited for access. She had no messages. She got up, entered his office, and sat down at his personal computer.

Behind her on the message machine, the babble of voices

continued: Olivia, Sabrena, and her mother, a long line of other friends were all wanting details, interspersed with more media people demanding information.

If she returned any media calls, she would be asking for trouble. Ben's advice in such circumstances was simple: When you don't know anything, don't say anything. His computer had two drives, one marked "Personal," the other "Business." She removed his locked metal box from his bottom drawer, opened it with her key, and found his list of passwords in case of emergency. She found the one for his personal file and typed it in.

Behind her, the message center chimed again. This time the voice she heard was a welcome one.

"Genesee," she cried punching in. "Thank God, someone besides the damn media."

"Are you all right, C?"

"No, of course I'm not. I'm wild."

"We probably shouldn't talk on an open line. I'll be in the city for a fund-raiser tonight. Have you at least heard if Ben is all right?"

"Honestly, Gen, I'm just not sure."

"All right. Can you meet me at the benefit? It's at Gramercy Park---a fundraiser for the World Hunger Institute. I know it's short notice but I need to talk with you. It's urgent."

"Yes, of course."

"Can you be there at 4?" Genesee asked. "I'll make a way for us to talk in private."

"Yes, and thank you. I'm so relieved you called."

She disconnected and quickly returned to Ben's secure computer. She typed in the personal drive's access numbers, and the screen sprang to life. She began to scroll. A long list of human resources memos came up, nothing more. In the "Personal" drive, the e-mail icon blinked on. She clicked and read down a list of half a dozen new messages. The subject line of the last one was an unintelligible garble. She was about to move on when she stopped. She clicked the file open. More lines of garble---numbers, letters, and symbols, how a screen looked when software could not read a language---SPAM more than likely. To make sure, she activated Ben's translator. It scanned seventeen computer languages before stopping at one it could read. The message it brought up seemed nearly as incomprehensible. In place of the garble, it read: "Play the orphans." She read the translated subject line, what appeared to be initials: "JF."

Puzzled, she examined the electronic mail's routing. She sent back a reply: a question mark. Her reply flew back, undeliverable. She looked more carefully. The date and time of the original message's arrival was there---today, just past 9 a.m., the same hour she had been meeting with Raisa Amin. The computer, maddeningly, refused to reveal the message's place of origin. She stared again at the subject line: "JF"--- surely a message from Jack Flyte, but, if so, what did it mean --- "Play the orphans"?

She opened her communicator and consulted the scrap of paper Raisa had given her, punching in the unlisted Directorate number.

"This is Mrs. Benjamin Quayle," she said as she got an actual person. "I'm seeking information about my husband. He was injured in the Enterprise bombing yesterday. I understand he's being treated for his injuries there."

"Please leave your name, address, and return number," the female responder intoned. "You will be notified."

"Please, I would like to know his condition."

"I'm sorry. I am not authorized to provide that. Leave your information where you may be reached."

"He is there then?"

"I am not authorized to provide that."

Cecil provided her callback number, then heard a click as the line abruptly went dead.

She put down the communicator, staring numbly at the computer screen blinking before her. The "JF" message suddenly flashed up with a warning. The damn computer was about to crash into sleep mode. She hit the save button, but it was too late. The message vanished, and the screen went black. As hard as she tried, she could not bring it back up. The message with its provenance, such as it was, had vanished.

Chapter Twenty

A strong scent of lilac hung in the air as Cecil passed through Gramercy Park East's security gate and entered the lush environs of the central garden of the exclusive compound, the lavish afternoon fundraiser for Governor Wainwright's World Hunger Foundation starting to get under way. The admiring glances would have pleased her if circumstances hadn't made the idea of how she looked seem so frivolous.

Sabrena emerged from a small cluster of people and embraced Cecil warmly, taking a step back to examine her. "You look far better than you should. Any news of Ben since you left me your voice message? I'm sorry I didn't get back to you. I've been incommunicado since last night."

"I believe he's alive," she said, unsure how much she ought to say, Raisa Amin's warning fixed in her mind. "The police told Ben's secretary an ambulance took him somewhere after the explosion, but no one can say where. I've called hospitals and morgues all over the city. I suppose it's good they have no news of him, but I've been half-crazed with worry by this."

Sabrena grimaced sympathetically. "And does Shrum really think public executions are going to stop this? It will only inflame whoever's behind the bombings. I've heard that fool Shrum's told Genesee flatly it's a city matter and that she'd better not interfere."

"I saw the hangings," said Cecil, red-faced. "I got caught in traffic at Columbus Circle. It was horrid." She leaned closer. "Also, some people from the Directorate took me in for questioning yesterday, dreadful people. They started asking me questions about Jack, trying to get me to say he was an insurgent sympathizer. The people he associated with. Where I thought he might be. I told them had no idea about his politics, and I only knew what Ben had released in his statement to the media about his whereabouts --- that Jack's due in Dubrovnik shortly. They finally let me go, thank God. Remind me to tell you why they took me in in the first place. That's another story."

Sabrena sighed. "I'm so glad Genesee's agreed to give us this interview. The timing couldn't be better, Ben's an absolute genius." Sabrena looked at Cecil closely. "He's just got to be all right, honey."

"I'm hopeful, too," Cecil said. "I can't say why, but I am."

Olivia arrived in the garden, Tommy Sung close behind her, and embraced Cecil effusively. "I was devastated when I heard Ben might have been injured. Any news?"

Cecil shook her head. "His secretary has been checking all the hospitals and health centers for me. Genesee's people have been doing the same. He's not been reported a casualty yet by any of the hospitals."

"I heard on the news this is really all about émigrés settling scores," Olivia said with undisguised disdain. "It's always so damn tribal with those people. Frankly, as long as they stay in the enclaves, I don't care what they do to each other. They're all savages, as far as I'm concerned."

"You don't mean that," Sabrena said.

Olivia looked her straight in the eye. "Of course, I do. At least I'm being honest about it, which nobody else is. Everybody's think it, and you know it. I totally agree with what the Brigades just did---hang them, make an example of them. It's completely justified. They should be closing the borders entirely. How much more of this are we supposed to take?"

Olivia's eyes darted past Sabrena and settled on Tommy. Wearing a coal black shirt with a string tie, the artist stood flirting with a young blond woman who looked enthralled at his attention. He spied Olivia, threw her an indifferent glance, and resumed his conversation.

Olivia made no effort to hide her anger. "That insolent bastard. After all I've done to help him, he won't even bother to be civil to me. I'm sorry I showed any interest in him at all."

"I thought you were in love," Cecil teased.

Olivia looked at her angrily. "I'd be crazy to take this any further, and you know it. That boy loves only himself. Would you believe it? All sorts of strange characters have been showing up at the gallery in the last few days. He takes them in the back of the gallery for these long, heated discussions --- in Mandarin, for God's sake. That would be just my luck, wouldn't it? To be sponsoring a terrorist?"

"Don't be dramatic, dear," Sabrena said. "He's just a sexy Chinese boy in an American candy store of round-eyed women, that's all. I have to admit I also find him rather cute."

"I wouldn't be too sure, " Cecil said softly. "See the man he's talking to now? That's got to be security."

Olivia looked and turned up her nose "I think you're right."

Cecil turned. Governor Wainwright was arriving, two uniformed state police bodyguards by her side. One leaned over and whispered in her ear as she stopped to greet her friends. Genesee glanced at a commotion starting around Tommy Sung. To Cecil, she said somberly: "It seems our intrepid Mayor Shrum has just announced random identification checks at all public gatherings. Obviously, he isn't wasting any time."

Tommy was protesting being told to hand over his wallet. Olivia's face had lost its color. "God, are they arresting him?"

"If the electronic background check shows he's legal," Genesee said, "he'll have nothing to worry about. Because of the bombings, however, I'm afraid it's something all city residents will have to endure for some time. There's not much I can do except to protest the randomness of his emergency order." She leaned over and whispered to Cecil: "Come find me inside the museum in ten minutes. I'm due to deliver some remarks, but we can talk afterwards. There are conference rooms in the back." She pressed Cecil's arm, turned, and walked with her security detail down the path toward the back gate of Gramercy Park Gallery. Beyond it, outside the iron fence and directly across 20th Street, stood the National Arts Club. It was there Genesee was scheduled to give a brief speech on behalf of the World Hunger Institute. Within the club was a gallery of some of the city's finest art, including several of Cecil's most recent celebrity portraits.

As Cecil, Sabrena, and Olivia joined the crowd following Genesee and her entourage, Cecil was startled to see Robert Thompson. He passed by them with scarcely a glance, heading in the opposite direction toward the front gates. He was walking fast, his broad shoulders rolled forward. Two plainclothes types trailed behind.

"What's going on?" Sabrena whispered. "Is that who I think it was?"

"Jack's chief of security."

"I met him once. He frightened me, I don't mind saying."

They watched as the Enterprise security chief and his men disappeared through the front gate. Beside them, Olivia was now staring in the opposite direction, at Tommy Sung being roughly escorted into the security tent by the men who had been questioning him. "They're going to arrest him," Olivia whispered. "I'm sure of it. Didn't I tell you?"

"All you did was vouch for him," Cecil said reassuringly. "They won't hold you responsible if he's in violation of his temporary visa. Didn't you say his father was someone high up on the Chinese Consulate staff? It's going to be his problem, not yours."

"Don't you see? I'll be questioned, damn it. I don't need this."

Sabrena's sharp eyes scanned the crowd. "I wish I knew what was going on. I wonder if there's going to be a roundup."

"Here, at the governor's fundraiser?" Cecil stared at the crowd. "Shrum wouldn't dare."

Sabrena did the same. "Didn't you tell me once Thompson once worked for one of the federal security agencies before he came to the Enterprise? What's he doing here if he isn't part of some general security sweep?"

"We'd better talk about this later. I've got to speak with Genesee right after her speech. She's promised to help me locate Ben."

"Tell us the minute you hear more," Sabrena said urgently.

Slowly, Cecil left her friends and worked her way quickly through the crowd and across the crowded expanse of lawn toward the gate that would take her out to East 20th Street and the elegantly appointed National Arts Club. Along the way, her progress was slowed by warm greetings from other artists, writers, and photographers, some she hadn't seen in years. Recently, many had been working abroad, fed up with the mayor's increasingly oppressive decrees. One was Catherine Parneau, her closest French friend even before her marriage to Ben; they'd been out of touch for months. Catherine pulled her aside, whispering in her ear: "The city's nothing but a police state now, Cecilia, how on earth do you stand it?" She grimaced more deeply as Cecil nodded. "Worse than Paris after the latest student antigovernment demonstrations. You look so worried, cherie."

"It's my husband. I have reason to believe he was injured in the Enterprise bombing yesterday. I've still not been able locate him. I'm sorry, I'm supposed to meet someone now who's promised to help me. Here's my card. Please call me as soon as you can."

"Yes, yes, *bien sûr*. Your husband is *très gentil*, I remember him well. I'm so sorry, *cherie*."

After their goodbyes, Cecil stared at the gate a dozen yards away. Instinctively, not sure why, she turned back. At the main gate, she saw Robert Thompson reappear. He was watching her from a position directly beside the visitors' main checkpoint, a communicator against one ear. In the street immediately behind him, sirens shrieked, scattering street traffic onto sidewalks. A line of half a dozen black vans appeared, then two police cars; the entire line of vehicles, lights flashing, drew up to the gate. Sabrena was right: a roundup.

Someone seized Cecil's elbow. In a low, commanding voice, one of Genesee's security men whispered in her ear: "The governor wants you to come with me right now."

He led her toward the 20th Street gate just as a clatter of horses could be heard, the unmistakable racket of a Brigades squad approaching. Cecil followed her escort, slipped through the gate, and walked quickly across the chaos of 20th Street to the entrance to the members-only Arts club. There, two more security men in dark suits were waiting for her; she was led quickly through the doors into the crowded, high-ceilinged foyer. The commotion outside was barely audible as the heavy doors closed behind her, a shoulder-to-shoulder throng apparently completely unaware of the ruckus outside, transfixed instead by walls filled with graphic, heartbreaking photographic images of the latest East African famine-and-relief effort. The security man guided her through the crowd into an expansive library, through more rooms, then down darkened steps. Then, unexpectedly, she found herself once again outdoors. In the small circular drive behind the club, a black unmarked town car stood idling. In the rear seat, Genesee waited and beckoned to Cecil. A uniformed state trooper helped her inside and closed the door behind her. The town car crept forward, tires crunching gravel. Entering Irving Place, the driver appeared to be preparing to turn onto 20th when he was forced to slam on his brakes. A half-dozen horsemen trotted by, so close to them Cecil could see the flash of their spurs and the shine of their boots. They passed, and the driver turned onto 20th, but a block further on the car instantly encountered a new commotion. Tommy Sung's gangly frame lay sprawled over the hood of one of the parked vans; a Brigadesman in khaki uniform was cuffing his hands behind him.

Cecil looked at Genesee anxiously. "For God's sake, Olivia must have been right?"

Genesee shook her head anxiously. "It could be anything. I honestly don't know. The Brigades have stopped sharing the city's arrest and detention records even with us. Unless charges are filed, no official public record has to be kept of civil arrests under the decrees; we're in the dark at the state level, the same as the public." The governor leaned forward in her seat. "Driver, move on. We must get to the bridge to Brooklyn before curfew. And notify the checkpoint so they don't stop us. I don't want to have to answer any questions from anybody connected to the city. Do you understand?"

"You've got it, ma'am," the driver answered at once.

At that moment, an unmarked car sped by, siren shrieking, a single blue light on its roof flashing. Tires squealing, it careened onto Third Avenue. Another roared past, following the first; at last they were moving faster, heading uptown with an escort.

Cecil dropped back into her seat. "Please tell me what the hell's happening." She looked at Genesee imploringly.

Genesee took her hand. "I'll try, C. This is a the first random roundup in Manhattan. The city's just had credible threats of more bombings, so the Brigades have been authorized to check all public venues. The minute the citywide bulletin was put out half an hour ago, my aids decided it would be wise if I was not here."

Cecil felt her heart racing. This wasn't happening. How could it be? The governor of New York's fund-raiser being raided by the Brigades, in tandem with law enforcement?

She leaned back in her seat, struggling to collect her thoughts. She let out her breath. "I think they may be looking for Jack." She began to explain what happened after the soiree for Chloe in Albany. "Afterwards, I found myself at the Three Tribes Casino. I'm not sure how I got there, but I was behaving and feeling very odd. I think I had been drugged, but almost sure I saw Jack in the crowd. Later, back in the city, the Directorate sent people to my townhouse and found money in my purse I had supposedly won at the casino. They took me to the Directorate for more questioning, then finally let me go. They confiscated the money, saying there was something suspicious about how I'd won it, but they never explained. I am almost sure it was all just a pretense to ask me what I knew about Jack."

Genesee did not answer. Instead, she settled back uneasily, her gaze directed out her own window into the snarl of traffic they had just encountered. A citywide security alert was obviously now under way, evacuation routes starting to jam.

"We'll be in a safer place soon," the governor said finally, squeezing her hand. "We'll get this sorted out, C, I promise."

At Roosevelt Drive and the Brooklyn Bridge, the car crept up the onramp and sped through the VIP lane as two guards waved them on.

Far below, Cecil could see the Starfire preparing to steam down river and into the Outer Bay for the evening's gambling. The casino ship's rails and decks were packed with people, its two passenger decks crowded to overflowing. She suddenly remembered the indecipherable e-mail on Ben's computer that appeared to have come from Jack --- "Play the orphans" --- and the equally puzzling command on Jack's red phone that Ben had told her about --- "Play the 7." Something trivial, or coded directives to someone? Given how swiftly the Directorate's investigator had gone to the winnings in her purse, and how obviously her bet had been orchestrated, she now strongly suspected the latter.

Chapter Twenty-One

The night nurse awakened Quayle with the arrival of her clattering cart. He watched groggily as she prepared medications. Day 3 was beginning for him on the ward, a little past midnight by the digital clock. The nurse handed him the now familiar two pills: two for pain, one a sedative. She watched him closely to see that he dutifully swallowed all three with water. Soon, she snapped off the lights, and he could hear her moving back down the corridor. Painfully, he got out of bed, turned his back to the blank wall screen and unobtrusively removed the sleeping pill from under his tongue. He watched it dissolve under a blast of hot water, then swallowed the two percocets.

Earlier, the doctor had explained why he still could not be moved to a hospital. "The brain scan shows a hairline fracture of your skull," Dr. McGreavey had said. " As you can see from the monitor, the damage is close to the head injury you suffered as a child. It's fortunate your digital history revealed that incident. There may still be some hemorrhaging. We'll need more tests, full brain scans, a regime of coagulants right away."

Gatwick had broken in to add: "And no visitors, no calls, total bed rest. We've been trying to locate your wife to inform her of the situation. Messages have been left on her voice mail but so far she hasn't replied."

At this, Quayle had looked skeptical. How hard could it be for them to locate her? If they had contacted her, her response would have been immediate; the Directorate's gatekeepers wouldn't have stood a chance keeping her away. Just as quickly, however, he had decided not to insist on it. There was no sense dragging Cecil into this when their intention was so clearly to interrogate him about Jack. As to that, he wasn't under arrest; how could they legally stop him from leaving if he could manage to find a way out?

He opened the door and looked out into the corridor. There was no nurse's station or security desk anywhere along the long, empty hallway. He took a tentative step forward from the room. At once, a buzzer went off above his head.

"Mr. Quayle?" a voice demanded through the intercom. He turned and stared at the wall screen; there, a night nurse's large, frowning face had sprung to life. "Do you require assistance?"

"I'm feeling nauseous. I need water. My call button doesn't work."

"Return to your bed at once. You are not permitted in the corridors."

Nurses swarmed, a bank of monitors was rolled in. Sensors were attached to his temples and chest, then along the veins of his arms and inner thighs. The monitors arrayed around him began to beep, green lines bounding like gazelles across half a dozen brightly-lit screens. The head nurse aimed a piercing light into his eyes; another took his pulse.

"If you need assistance in future, Mr. Quayle," she admonished sternly, "you will press the button and wait as instructed. Getting up is not good for you."

Before he could protest, a second nurse pricked his arm. Like a dust mite in a sunbeam, his body floated away.

***

When he woke again, the monitors were gone, the sensors detached from his body. A single IV drip remained, feeding him fluids through a tube in his arm.

"It's noon, Mr. Quayle," the duty-nurse said in a voice he barely heard. He had a strange ringing in his ears. "You've slept through the night. How are you feeling now?"

"Like somebody's hit me in the head with a crowbar."

"You've had a mild seizure. You gave us a scare. "

At that moment, the door opened and Gatwick appeared. Frowning, his shock of white hair disheveled, he sat down in a chair beside the bed and looked at him with annoyance. "You're a lucky fellow, Quayle. Dr. McGreavey says if they hadn't stabilized you, you could have had a grand mal seizure. Do you want that? Where did you think you were going?"

"When can I see my wife? She needs to know where I am, she needs to know what's happening. I don't understand why I even need to be here. You promised me I could see her if answered your questions."

Gatwick shook his head. "As I have said, seeing your wife isn't possible right now given your condition. And in any case, my people say she didn't return home last night, and her voice mail isn't recording messages. I was just about to inform you of that. Perhaps you can be of help to us by telling us where she might be."

Quayle stared at Gatwick. "I don't believe you. She must have spent the nights at our townhouse while I've been gone."

The directorate's chief of inquiries handed Quayle his communicator. "See for yourself."

With a trembling hand, Quayle took the instrument from Gatwick and punched in the landline number of the townhouse. He listened as the message center picked up, clicked, then failed to play the usual invitation to leave a recorded message. He tried again with the same result. He was about to punch in Cecil's communicator number when, warily, he stopped himself, realizing her number would be embedded in the memory of Gatwick's device even if she didn't pick up. Instead, he handed the communicator back. "She may have decided to stay with her mother. That could explain it. I don't have that number."

Gatwick looked at him, unconvinced. "Suit yourself, Quayle, but we're merely trying to assist you. At some point, I would hope you would return the favor; there are questions that must be answered, and being suspicious of me isn't going to help matters. We have left messages for your wife about where you can be found. At the moment that's all we can do." Gatwick clicked on the wall screen. An all-news channel sprang to life. "In the meantime, maybe this will convince you of how serious your situation is now."

Quayle had failed to get the news stations when he had tried before; the orderly had said the signal was down. Now the screen burst forth with the face of a black female anchor speaking urgently in a clipped British accent.

"BBC 4 News has just learned the U.S. Securities and Exchange Commission is pursuing leads regarding the disappearance of Enterprise founder and CEO Jack Flyte. Also reported missing are millions of dollars in receipts from accounts of the international conglomerate's casino empire. Authorities confirm an international search is under way. BBC 4 has been told by reliable sources the well-known corporate billionaire vanished from his Upper East Side penthouse apartment several days ago under suspicious circumstances. Stay with BBC 4 for further updates."

Gatwick clicked off the broadcast. "The fastest way for you to help is to tell us where he is."

"He should be on his way to the Dubrovnik meeting by now. It's what we've told the police, and what my press statement has said. As far as I know, there's still no reason to believe otherwise."

"The 19th Precinct says he has not appeared on any passenger logs of any commercial or private aircraft since his disappearance. How do you explain that?"

"Why don't you ask Detective Navarro of the 19th. He's the investigating officer. Handling Mr. Flyte's case."

"Detective Navarro has transferred to another precinct; Detective Salerno is handling it as a missing-person's case now."

Quayle stared at Gatwick, not concealing his surprise.

"Let's not play games here, Quayle. I will ask you directly: Do you think Jack Flyte has been skimming money from the Enterprise, and that explains his disappearance? And was Mr. Rabinsky an accomplice to that crime? Was that why he took his own life, to avoid interrogation?"

Quayle shook his head. "I told you before that's impossible. Who suggested this to you? Our chief of security? It sounds like it."

"That's not relevant. What matters is, the evidence points to both events as possibilities."

"Then am I also a suspect?" Quayle demanded. "Is that what you're saying?"

Gatwick examined his face closely, as if searching for hints Quayle was concealing something. "Not exactly. As a close associate of Mr. Flyte's, naturally you are a person of interest. I am certain if you have any legal exposure, we can make immunity arrangements. However, I would suggest you be as candid as possible with me now."

Quayle's throat felt constricted --- by the stress of the interrogation or by his head injury it was impossible to tell. He stopped to take a deep breath. "I will try to remember as best I can," he went on. "I can tell you that when Jack was reported missing, there was some reason to think he might have fallen from his penthouse balcony. Such a fall could have taken him into the East River."

"But you don't believe that's what happened?"

"No, frankly, I don't. I can't imagine he would have been at that particular part of the balcony; it's quite a distance away from the sliding doors. However, I can't honestly say what did happen."

"Perhaps he was pushed, or someone else decided to make it look like an accident to help him conveniently disappear."

"I don't believe it was something he planned, not for a minute. I suppose it's possible someone pushed him. However, there were no signs of a struggle anywhere inside or outside the penthouse. I've already told you what I and Security Chief Thompson told the media: we believe he decided to leave by way of the private elevator down to the parking garage. There is some evidence on a security camera that his car left the garage at the same time as his 50th birthday party, although it was unclear if he was actually in that car as it left. Still, it's not been unusual for him to act on the spur of the moment without informing anyone. I still believe he intends to keep his appointment in Dubrovnik."

"But you can't be certain of that?"

"No, I can't."

Gatwick nodded. "Indulge me a little more, Quayle. What did Rabinsky know about these casino accounts?"

Quayle paused. He pressed his fingers to his temples, trying to massage away the pain. "I was not aware he was investigating those casino accounts. The first I heard of it was during the Enterprise's casino committee meeting, when Thompson discussed the problem. I did know Rabinsky was investigating what he told me were discrepancies in Security Chief Thompson's overseas expense accounts. Thompson fired Rabinsky before I could discuss it with him. I have my own opinion about why Thompson did that."

"I hope you're about to enlighten me."

Quayle threw Gatwick a sharp look. He felt more clearheaded now, the disorienting fog in his mind lifting for the moment; it seemed to come and go. “Isn’t it obvious? He had come across something irregular that concerned him enough to investigate further. Thompson fired him because he was afraid he was about to reveal something about those accounts to Jack.”

“You have told me Mr. Flyte is politically active---politically aware at the very least. Would you say that would extend to an active interest in intervening in political matters such as the enclaves? Can you imagine him financing a counter-insurgency of some sort, for instance?”

“That sounds absurd to me. He was concerned when the tent cities and barricades were erected, as were many people sensitive to people's civil right. However, I never heard him mention what he might do about it. Certainly not countenance any sort of violence.”

Gatwick’s snow-white brows rose. “Other than planning to ask his board to pull out of the consortium, you mean? That provocative comment hasn’t escaped your memory, has it?”

“As far as I know, it was just that---provocative, spontaneously inspired by seeing the barbed wire fences had gone up, not any sort of call to action. If you heard the surveillance tapes of our conversation at the racquet club, you must know that.”

“Agreed. It did sound like he was merely thinking out loud, I’ll grant you. However, as you are aware, many throughout the city are praising us for that decisive action. In light of the bombings, they see containment of the insurgency in the enclaves as long overdue. You are aware of that?”

“Of course.”

Gatwick nodded with satisfaction. “Would you say he feels strongly enough about this to oppose us, to take this thinking another step forward, to some plan of action?”

“He has never agreed to finance any venture that might be in opposition to the city’s or nation’s stated public policies, and I have never heard him advocate such action. I would be very surprised if he ever would. He is a businessman first, not some political activist. As far as I know, the enclaves policy remains part of the city's official immigration containment policy. He just happens to disagree with it."

"Yes, you've made that clear. And I presume even if you were of a similar mind, you would not counsel such a subversion of public policy, either?"

"No, nor have I ever thought to do so. However, to disagree is not yet a crime, is it?"

Gatwick smiled coldly. "Save your sarcasm for another time, Quayle. This is serious. You were almost killed by a bomb whose makers may well be inhabitants of those very same enclaves. Let me ask you then: if a third party asked you to do something along those lines---something that might harm the general interests of the city, the country or your company---what might your response be?"

Quayle blinked. "I would refuse, of course."

"I see." Gatwick paused. He appeared to be considering something. "Let me be blunt. If you knew your employer and longtime friend was involved in just such a clandestine activity of financing terrorists, and you did not wish to be caught in the same net, what would you do?"

"I am sure I would resign."

"Which is just what I understand you nearly did at that meeting just before the bombing. Isn't that correct?"

"I was confronted with a decision by Mr. Thompson I disagreed with strongly, yes. He was encroaching on my own authority to deal with the public on public matters. He had decided to take over that responsibility, and Jack apparently had agreed. I was strongly opposed to that, and, frankly, I did not believe Jack had authorized it. But the evidence was there, and in the end I decided not to resign, which I am guessing you are perfectly aware of."

"I am, and I applaud you for your candor. I'm sure we will be able to make allowances for whatever complicity you may have in any other matters, provided you continue to cooperate. I hope our little chats from now on can become more informative and illuminating. I am counting on it, in fact."

At that moment, Gatwick's communicator again sounded. After listening for a moment, he closed it and informed Quayle the interrogation would resume later.

After Gatwick left, the nurses again began retaking his vital signs. One removed his IV. As they worked, Quayle realized he was sweating profusely. Gatwick, so seemingly affable at times, could also be unnerving when the questioning turned serious. He was under suspicion, of that he was certain. And it had been Thompson who had planted the seed. What did they know or think they knew? Just as disturbing, why wasn't Cecil reachable? Where was she?

Later that night, after his medications had been administered, they wheeled him down the hall. With electrodes all over his body and a protective screen over his face, they rolled him inside the full-body scanner and took another battery of pictures.

"Just a precaution," the nurse answered when he asked why they were doing this all over again.

***

When he next awoke, the digital clock on the darkened wall screen read 4 a.m. He did not know what had awakened him. He noticed at once his IV was gone, as were what had remained of the electrodes and monitoring devices the nurses had put in place during final night check. Suddenly on alert, he smelled disinfectant, then an even more pungent and incongruous stink of tobacco. The red light on the surveillance camera was no longer lit. Instead, the room glowed an eerie white. Moonlight was flooding in through the courtyard. Somewhere close by, he began to sense a presence.

A hoarse whisper came from the shadows: "Señor Quayle."

He gave a start, turning toward the dark corner from where it had come.

In the shadows, a diminutive form of what appeared to be a child squatted on his haunches directly behind the door. Eyes gleamed like black marbles in the sliver of moonlight pouring in from one window. The figure was positioned in such a way that even if the door were suddenly opened, he could not be seen. Quayle now saw a short but muscular man rise from the corner, locks of oily, intricately beaded hair drooping and clicking over a broad, low forehead. Gold earrings dangled from each earlobe, framing a dark, weathered face with skin the texture of leather---the face of a gypsy, Quayle quickly concluded, almost certainly.

"Who are you?" Quayle demanded.

The man did not answer. Instead, he smiled, exposing a set of magnificent gold teeth. He wore the green gown of non-medical staff, a name tag affixed to one pocket Quayle could not see clearly enough to read. With thick thumb and forefinger, the gypsy snuffed the remains of the glowing ember of a cigarette, went to the sink, and flushed down the remains.

"I am Nicu," he rasped. " A gypsy. You listen, ok? No questions." He glanced at the blank wall screen, then the door. He turned back. With a slight limp, he took a few halting steps closer to Quayle's bed. "Goddamn cameras come back on soon, then we got some big trouble." He pushed a finger to his lips and went to the door, pulling it open. He peered into the dimly-lit corridor, then rolled a canvas-covered housekeeping cart back into the room and let the door swing closed.

"Who sent you?" Quayle demanded. "Why are you here?"

The gypsy grunted. He withdrew another housekeeping gown, a pair of soft-soled hospital shoes, and a brimless green cap from the hamper inside the cart. "No questions, I said. You wear this. Soon the cameras come back on. You must get in cart quick now."

With his hand, he drew back the curtain, exposing the narrow platform inside --- just enough space for Quayle to crouch if he ducked and folded his legs under himself. The gypsy yanked the curtain back down. Soon, the cart began to roll down the corridor. Quayle could only see the gypsy's feet. Soon they stopped, and Quayle heard water being poured, the sound of mopping; he again caught the scent of disinfectant.

"Cameras back on," the gypsy hissed. 'You not move."

"Gypsy," a woman's voice called out from a loudspeaker. "You're an hour late."

"Pass code no work, mum," Nicu grumbled.

"What's the matter with it?"

"Code changed. They make me wait. They have to give me new one."

"Move along. There is only one patient in this ward. You've still got the whole ward to clean. Stop dawdling."

Nicu grumbled and started rolling the cart ahead, mopping, spilling, mopping, muttering, cursing. The cart rattled on over a connecting apron of tiles separating one corridor from another. The gypsy's rubber-soled shoes squeaked as he pushed on faster, the gypsy's limp more pronounced the faster he went. Abruptly, the cart rattled to a stop and he could hear elevator doors opening. The cart rolled in, the doors closed, and the elevator began a swift descent. His ears clicked from the rapid change in air pressure. He felt his heart race and his temples again start to pound. All this movement was probably bad for him, but that didn't matter now, someone appeared to be rescuing him.

The cart lurched off the elevator and rattled onto a new surface-- dank, cracked cement, some sort of underground passageway, bumpy and uneven under the cart's wheels, very unlike the tiles of the corridors above. The lights were much dimmer in this corridor, casting a yellow pall inside the cart. The skin on Quayle's forearm felt a sudden blast of cold air, as if a stiff wind were blowing straight at them from somewhere down the corridor.

A wall speaker crackled, a new voice shouting. "You! What are you doing in this tunnel? This is a secured area."

Quayle saw a Brigadesman's boots appear an alarming few inches from where he was crouched.

"This is a forbidden area," the voice boomed from the speaker box. "Where is your pass?"

"I am Nicu from housekeeping. I got the wrong elevator. Don't hurt me, boss."

Quayle was startled to see the gypsy's hand appear under the cart. He was being handed a pistol, muzzle-first. Quayle grabbed it, nearly fumbling the awkward handoff. The Brigadesman directly beside them spoke into his own crackling two-way radio: "This is Level 1. Gypsy from housekeeping in a forbidden area."

"Make him show his pass," the radio answered back.

"You there, where's your pass?"

"Here, boss."

"Ok. What else you got there?"

"Nothing, boss."

Quayle sensed the Brigadesman was about to duck down, maybe look under the curtains. At the same instant, he saw the gypsy's rubber-soled shoes turn, running back toward the elevators, away from the direction they had been traveling, abandoning the cart.

"You! Halt!" the Brigadesman shouted. "Halt right there, dammit!"

A shot rang out.

"Level 1, alert!" the Brigadesman shouted. "Fugitive in Tunnel 3.Seal security doors, power off all elevators."

In seconds, a Klaxon began to sound. Quayle crouched lower, his heart and head pounding.

The Brigadesman's boots drummed away. Soon, others in the same black boots thundered past. New shouts, a second shot, then a string of curses. Over the racquet of the Klaxon, the first Brigadesman yelled into his two-way: "I think he's knocked out the surveillance cameras. I can't see where the little asshole went? Can you read me?"

The wall speaker above Quayle's head crackled, the words indecipherable.

Quayle lifted the curtain. He peered out of the cart in the direction the gypsy and his pursuers had gone, the Brigadesmen's voices still audible but more distant now as they continued their pursuit. He guessed he had only a few minutes before they backtracked and returned. He swung his feet from the cart and stood in the freezing cold air of a narrow, low-ceilinged corridor. He raised his eyes. Along the upper walls, he could see the red lights of the surveillance cameras had gone dark. A few yards away, on the sweating, grimy tiles of one wall, a barely legible sign identified where he was: "Wall Street." This was most likely the old MTA stop, bypassed with the arrival of the new super-train. Quickly, he sized things up. Behind lay danger, while ahead, where the gypsy had at first been headed, might lie escape. All around him brackish water dripped from the tiled ceilings, the corridor ahead sloping down toward what appeared to be a subway platform. He slipped the pistol into the waistband of his hospital greens and moved carefully down the slippery slope of the corridor, finally emerging onto the dingy, gray-tiled platform under rows of mostly-blown-out banks of florescent lights. Just ahead, through turnstiles, he could see boarded-up elevators and cordoned-off escalators, while to his right, six feet below where he stood, lay the east and westbound track bed of the old subway system. The connecting tunnel between

Lower Manhattan and Brooklyn under the East River appeared to be nothing more than hard-packed dirt trail now, its steel rails long since torn out, and as he looked more closely, he could see along the center of the muddy path the unmistakable hoof prints of horses. This must be how the Brigades moved clandestinely with such ease; they had been using the city's old subway tunnels. Quayle slowly realized, too, he must now be standing directly under the city's financial district. Just a few blocks from there must be City Hall Plaza---and just beside it the Directorate itself.

The Klaxon abruptly ceased, and Quayle stood motionless where he was, listening to the steady dripping of water along the dimly-lit platform of the abandoned station. Where had the gypsy been trying to take him? Down into the subway tunnel itself? Or back up toward one of the stairways to the main station's exits, which might or might not be sealed? He could see the ascending ramp passed a fare booth with shattered windows and layered grit, the walkway passing through three sets of turnstiles, then up a second ramp to stairs rising to a platform marked Level 2.

He took several steps forward, warily paused, then drew back to listen. From the direction he had come came the unmistakable drumming of Brigadesmen's boots; they were returning along the tunnels of Level 1. Directly overhead in the ceiling, he heard a new sound: a soft scratching that quickly changed to rhythmic tapping. He saw now a square air ventilation plate slide back into the blackness of the ceiling. In the foot-square opening that had been exposed, the grimy face of the gypsy appeared. His dark, luminous eyes blinked in the light. The face vanished, quickly replaced by feet and dangling legs. Quayle reached up, grasped the Nicu's grimy ankles and held them. The little man tipped his shoulders and dropped through the opening directly onto Quayle's shoulders, then nimbly to the concrete floor. Crouching, a finger pressed to his lips, he urgently motioned for Quayle to crouch, too. Above their heads, video cameras suddenly flashed on. The gypsy motioned for him to remain on his knees. Finally, he waved him forward. They began to crawl one after the other, the gypsy first, along the wall out of camera range. A few yards more and Nicu stood and began to shuffle forward again along the corridor toward the main stairway that appeared to lead up to higher levels.

From the pocket of his hospital garb, the gypsy removed the magnetized key he had supposedly lost and slipped it into a slot in the wall. A door in the tiles snapped open and Quayle felt himself pushed through into a cubicle housing tools and cleaning apparatus. Nicu pulled the door shut just as Quayle heard the Brigadesmen mounting the stairs from Level 1, appearing to be heading their way. Through a crack in the door, the gypsy crouched and watched. The tread of boots on concrete drew closer, then passed by. In the blackness, the Nicu grabbed Quayle's arm in warning. A second pair of boots was approaching. As this Brigadesman began to pass, the gypsy opened the cubicle door and leapt to the startled man's back. Driving a knee in the man's spine, the gypsy drew a thick wire around his neck, bringing him down with a strangled grunt and clamping a hand over the quarry's gasping mouth. After a long moment, the thrashing stopped. The gypsy let go and scanned the corridor. Finally, he pocketed the garrote and jumped up. "You help me now quick, boss. They come back."

Dragging the body by the ankles toward the storage cubicle, he motioned for Quayle to help him jam the body inside.

"Where are you taking me?" he demanded.

"No questions," the gypsy snapped back. "We got to go quick. You come on now! More cameras coming back on any second."

He slammed the door of the cubicle, wheeled around, and began to limp his way down the corridor, breath coming in labored wheezes as he increased his speed. Back on the main platform, the little man dropped to his knees close to the wall, again below the reach of the camera above their heads. Quayle did the same, and the two crouched together, catching their breaths.

In the darkness of the cavernous Level 2 tunnel, whose entrance to the next platform appeared to lie just ahead, came bouncing flashes of light. Clearly now, too, they could hear the hollow clop of horses approaching from inside the abandoned subway tunnel. The gypsy pointed to a dark corner of the platform, and they crawled together behind a pillar of milk-white tiles, listening to the horses approach.

Their riders were moving at a slow, deliberate trot along the muddy path of the abandoned track bed, five riders and one riderless horse following close behind. Over the empty saddle of the last, a glistening body bag had been slung, the outline of a motionless form filling its length.

The gypsy spat, uttered a word Quayle could not understand and thrust him through an alcove leading toward a large steel door. Over the door, a battered, hand-painted sign read "Cellblocks 1 and 2."Behind them, in the corridor they had just left, the light of the closest surveillance camera remained out. The Brigades's central command had not regained their sight. Hurriedly, the gypsy began working his pass card into the security latch of the steel door.

"Level 2, Level 2, respond," the voice from the wall speaker demanded. 'What's going on down there? We need a new security team to report to Level 2. Someone report!"

The gypsy reversed the card, and the steel door snapped open. Stepping back to allow it to open, he rasped at Quayle in his pigeon English, "Give me pistol, boss."

Quayle reached under his hospital tunic and withdrew the gun. The gypsy took it and concealed it under his gown.

Inside this door was a wide corridor, well lit and airy, not like anything they had yet encountered. The gypsy grabbed Quayle's arm and pulled him inside, letting the door main close behind him.

He stepped up to the corridor's first secondary door and slid his passkey into its scanner. The lock released, and he pulled the door open. He yanked Quayle inside and clanged the heavy door shut.

A voice could still be faintly heard on the loudspeaker outside issuing commands, but the gypsy paid no attention. He was staring warily instead at the center of what was clearly a makeshift jail cell.

There sat a man at a small table under a single light bulb suspended on a cord above his head. The man's features were gaunt, his eyes open wide. He was staring at the farthest wall, seeming not to notice their entrance.

"Jack?" Quayle whispered. "Is that you, Jack?"

Jack Flyte, dressed in a yellow jump suit, turned his head and slowly blinked at Quayle in the harsh light of the bulb swinging above his head. His expression showed no sign of recognition.

Chapter Twenty-Two

The makeshift cell was small and spare, with a cot, two wooden chairs, and a metal table bolted to the floor. On one side were a portable toilet and sink.

"I brought him, boss," the gypsy said gruffly.

Jack did not respond. His gaze remained on the blank wall. The Enterprise chief looked gaunt, his unshaven cheeks darkened by stubble. It had been less than a week since his disappearance, but everything about him suggested he'd been through an ordeal.

"Ben?" He turned slowly, his blue-gray eyes, usually sharp and bright, now dull and empty, as if he were emerging from the sort of sedation they'd given Quayle to quiet him.

"It's me. I'm here," Quayle said finally.

Flyte's skin was as gray as the cinderblocks of the holding cell's walls. Tufts of his jet-black hair, usually combed straight back, curled like commas over his thick black brows in matted tangles. Despite bone-chilling dampness in the cubicle, Jack's forehead was beaded with sweat. He looked nothing like the charismatic figure Forbes magazine had once described as New York's "Superman of Business."

"We weren't sure you were all right, or where you were," Quayle said. "And there's been a bombing at the Enterprise. I was injured and they brought me here."

Jack looked dimly toward him, then the door, as if uncertain with whom he was really speaking. "How long have I been here?"

he asked hoarsely, pausing to catch a breath.

The gypsy answered. "Sunday now, boss, 4 a.m. You been here four days now." Without windows and overhead lights always burning, Quayle could see how it would be easy to lose all sense of time and place in here.

Nicu reached inside his housekeeping gown and withdrew the pistol from its waistband. "The 5 a.m. cellblock check coming soon, boss. We better wait for that before we go."

Jack nodded slowly, but from the listlessness of his expression the news appeared not to have registered.

"Have they drugged him?" asked Quayle worriedly.

"Cocktails, boss," the gypsy grumbled. "Make them all sleep. Then questions, questions, questions---ratatat-tat, food for Goddamn woodpeckers. He starting to come back now. I can tell."

From somewhere outside the cell door, a loud groan could be heard, followed by another.

"Others are here?" exclaimed Quayle in surprise. He wondered if would he have ended up here after he'd been discharged from the medical ward.

Nicu nodded, the motion rattling his hair beads. "Fifty rounded up now, maybe more. They putting in more cellblocks all the time now."

"It's all much worse than we ever imagined, Ben," Flyte whispered, a flash of lucidity returning with his steadier gaze. "Nobody gets charged here at first, just held and questioned. The damn Emergency Decrees allow it now." He cleared his throat. "I need more water. Please, get me some water."

Quayle rose, went to the sink, and filled a glass. Jack took it and drank it down. His hands trembled. With effort he handed the empty glass back. "Tell him, Nicu. Tell him what you've told me."

"News bad about the fascists. They on the move now. They look for us. Had to kill one, boss." Jack looked at him in alarm:

"Who, man? Who did you have to kill?"

"Brigades fascist was gonna find us. I kill him like a chicken." He twisted his fists in a garroting motion.

"I told you not to do that."

The gypsy shrugged. "We hide body, boss; they not find him for a while."

Jack shook his head, as if struggling again to clear his mind. He turned to Quayle "That morning at the Racquet Club, when we saw the encampments going up, do you remember? Nicu's been a spy inside the Directorate for the past year. He's seen, overheard and recorded a lot of what they've been saying and doing, reporting back to the insurgency leaders. Under the latest decrees, and with so much of the public and news media on its side, the Directorate has had little to fear. They've been getting much bolder. But also more reckless."

Muffled voices came from outside the door --- curses, shouts, a prisoner arguing or, maybe, dreaming. In a moment, silence finally descended again over the corridor. .

The gypsy checked the chambers of his pistol, limped to the door and put an ear to it. He pulled up his sleeve and examined the oversized watch on his wrist. "We wait now, boss."

He slid down the door to the cement floor, pressed his back hard against it, and closed his eyes. Almost immediately he began to snore, one oversized hand gripping the handle of the .38 in his lap.

Quayle moved his chair closer to Jack. In a low voice, he asked: "What have they done to you here?"

Flyte seemed to be regaining strength as the minutes wore on. Quayle guessed the drugs had to be wearing off. "The Brigades found me at Five Tribes. I'd gone after I left the penthouse, worried Thompson was going to have me arrested or worse. They were tipped off I was there, brought me here, and began their interrogations. They demanded that I cooperate. They wanted to know if I'd ever had dealings with that newspaper columnist you saw executed --- Israel Kidman --- or any of his enclave acquaintances. Subversives, they called them, sometimes terrorists. They said Kidman had been seen with me once at a party I attended, but I remembered nothing about him. They also seemed to know everything you and I had discussed at the Racquet Club that last morning."

Quayle nodded. "They had listening devices in there. They overheard you talking about pulling the Enterprise out of the consortium. They've questioned me about that as well."

Jack shifted in his chair uncomfortably. Quayle got up and brought him more water. He drank it down. Jack looked at the snoring figure blocking the doorway, then up at the light on the single surveillance camera pointed at them near the room's air vent; it was still unlit, the gypsy's sabotage of the system still holding. He nodded toward the sleeping gypsy. "The Nazis exterminated Nicu's ancestors. Thousands of Croatian gypsies were among the first to be rounded up and taken to the camps. His clan in Brooklyn fears the same may happen to them now --- a return of the pogroms. Now, in the enclaves whole neighborhoods are organizing, vowing to defy the decrees and force the barricades down. At first I thought he was exaggerating, but now I know it's true. There are people in this cellblock who have been here for weeks who tell the same stories. Their families have no idea they are being held, only that one day they went missing. Nicu's overheard them saying most of the Metro police precincts are now under the Directorate's full control, the media being bought off, too."

As Jack talked, Quayle felt a knot in the pit of his stomach, anxiety threatening to become panic, Still, at least some of the pieces of the puzzle were falling into place.

"The night of your birthday, the balcony rail was damaged," Quayle said. "What happened? How did you end up here?"

"That morning after we returned from the Racquet Club, someone with connections to the Algerian Embassy sent over a courier. She warned me Thompson had alerted the Brigades and they were going to question me." He gestured toward the gypsy. "I was told it was about my wanting to pull the Enterprise from the consortium; they were sure it meant I was helping enclave conspirators. I wasn't going to wait for them to come. Instead, I let everyone think I'd had an accident -- gone off the balcony. I managed to get past my security guard, down by the back elevator, and through the lower parking garage, but the security cameras must have spotted my car. The Brigades somehow found me at Five Tribes the same night Cecil was there. I'd gone up to make copies of forged Coleridge Bank disbursements Rabinsky had warned me about. The Brigades took me in, and brought me here for questioning. I had hoped Cecil would catch a glimpse of me, so she'd know I was all right."

"She thought she did see you but she wasn't certain; they'd given her some sort of drug. That must mean Thompson told them the surveillance cameras had spotted you. He must have known the Directorate had you all the time he was pretending not to."

Jack nodded grimly. "Rabinsky had warned me earlier about him; something about Thompson's expense accounts had raised red flags for him." Jack let out a breath. "Nicu told me what happened when the Brigades tried to bring in Rabinsky. He shouldn't have panicked like that. They were only fishing, the same as they're doing with me now. Nicu says they still have no hard evidence of a conspiracy, just theories they keep trying to get us to confirm."

Quayle nodded. "They tried it with me as well. Gatwick and Ross have been grilling me."

"Yes, those are the ones. A few days ago, I had Nicu send a message to your personal computer, again so you might guess I was still alive."

"I never saw it; maybe Cecil has. They say they haven't been able to find her to tell her I'm here. I'm sure they're lying." Jack leaned closer, gulped down more water, and set the glass back down on the table. "Do you remember in school, how we dreamed of creating the perfect corporate state -- Randian free markets, laissez-faire capitalism, as far as we could take it?"

Quayle nodded.

"Well, with the Directorate, we've just about succeeded, haven't we, damn fools that we are? We now control most commerce and mass media; our lobbyists protect us from laws and government regulations we don't like; the Brigades enforce the Directorate's Emergency Decrees."

"Yes."

"Now," Jack said. "Who the hell protects *us* from the Directorate?"

Quayle paused. "A devil's bargain."

"Exactly."

"Time to renegotiate," Quayle said.

Jack nodded. "If it's not too late."

Quayle remembered Kidman and Rabinsky's faces in their last moments, cornered desperation but stubborn defiance, too. He saw the very same expression in Jack's eyes now.

"I don't know," Quayle said. "This could be just Thompson's doing---his greed and ambition at work. You know I never trusted him. I should have been more insistent, not held back about that. I knew the minute he came to us from the Agency he had designs on taking over."

"You've been a loyal partner and friend, Ben," Jack said, his voice kind, deliberate. "I heard your concern about Thompson even when you thought I didn't, but I needed proof. Now I have it." He considered Quayle carefully, seeming to gauge something in his longtime friend's manner. Jack went on: "I know this may be difficult for you to accept, Ben. Here we are, so close to getting just what we wanted, and now I'm saying we must pull back. I know it may be too much to ask, and no man has already given me greater loyalty than you have. But loyalty to an idea as corrupt as this? I can't ask that of myself, and I would never ask it of you. It's not just the Enterprise they want to control; they want to create and rule a brand new corporate state. I need you to join me in opposing it before it's too late." Flyte paused, meeting Quayle's uncertain gaze with a nod. "I only wish it could be different. But seeing and hearing what's happening here, and the cruelty going on inside the enclaves outside the public's view, I know I must do all I can to extricate us from this. We must quash it now, before it goes any further. In the enclaves, they call those in control of the Directorate fascists. I don't know if they are right. I do know this is bigger than you or me, bigger than the Enterprise, bigger than our pathetic, gridlocked Washington. As New York goes, so may go the country. Do you see?'

Quayle dropped his gaze. Jack did indeed seem to him fully lucid; rarely had he heard him speak more clear-headedly or with more conviction. But this made it all the harder to hear. He noticed a battered book in his friend's lap; it appeared to be the one he'd seen in Jack's safe aboard the Starfire. He saw its title. The book was the same: *Bonhoeffer: Letters & Papers From Prison.*

He was about to ask the reason for it when Jack leaned forward and interrupted with an assertiveness he usually reserved for his final demand in a merger negotiation. "I want you to follow Nicu's instructions. He will guide you out of here. I am the one they most want, and I must continue to submit to their interrogations. This will give you time to escape. If eventually I fail to talk my way out, Nicu's friends have told him they have ways to free me when the time is right."

"What friends of Nicu's? More gypsies?" Quayle could not

conceal his skepticism. Remembering a gypsy could have planted the Racquet Club bomb, how reliable were gypsy elements really? Even Nicu seemed to operate on his own wavelength.

"If I tell you that now, and then you are caught," Jack said, "it could endanger you all. You will meet them soon enough, and gauge for yourself if they can be trusted. First, however, you must trust me."

Quayle nodded slowly. "Tell me what you want me to do."

Jack leaned forward. "Go now, before the surveillance cameras come back on. Nicu will give you my instructions once you are free."

Jack seemed about to continue when there was the sound of a door opening in the corridor outside. It was followed by boots tramping toward their door. Nicu sprang to his feet. Pistol in hand, he motioned for Quayle to join him to one side of the windowless door. If it opened, he would have a few seconds to decide if to fire.

Instead, a loud voice called out through the door: "No. 1, report."

Jack waited.

"No. 1, report!" the voice barked again.

"Present," answered Jack hoarsely.

The footsteps moved away.

"No. 2 report," the voice called out. A man's muffled voice answered. In all, five men and three woman repeated the ritual of what appeared to be a routine 5 a.m. bed check. The loud footsteps passed, followed by the clatter of the corridor door opening and slamming closed, before silence again returned to the cellblock.

Nicu removed a thin sliver of plastic Quayle had seen him slip into the door lock of the cell as they had entered, and opened the cell door a crack. "We go now, boss. I cut six camera cables, so we still got time. No worry."

Flyte nodded.

The gypsy leaned closer, his hair beads clicking, and looked at Flyte almost forlornly. "You come, too, boss."

Jack shook his head. "We've been through this. You and Ben must get out without me. No, I have my role here. When you're gone, I will tell them I have decided to cooperate; it's what they want from me. If I am convincing enough, they may release me, if for no other reason than to keep a check on Thompson. He's helping them, but I can tell they don't trust him. They know they need me to keep a check on him and to hold the rest of the consortium together. They're all consolidating power, Ben---a high-stakes poker game. I know that much now."

Jack stood up and moved toward the cell door as the gypsy leaned down and put his ear to it. Nicu pushed the door open and peered up at the camera lens monitoring their corridor. Quayle could see it was still unlit.

"We go now," the gypsy muttered.

Jack took the hand Quayle offered him and clapped in the back. "Good luck."

Quayle nodded, then moved into the corridor.

Jack stopped him and handed him the book he still clutched. "In case you begin to doubt, this may help explain. I promise you, Ben, I have not gone mad."

"Cameras back on soon, boss," the gypsy warned.

Jack nodded, and pulled the door closed.

As the echo of the door faded away, Nicu scanned the cellblock quickly. At the far end of the corridor, in shadows beside a door marked "Storage," his cleaning cart stood against the far wall. It apparently had gone unnoticed during the bed check. The gypsy limped toward it. He inserted his passkey to open the storage-room door, and waved at Quayle to come. The gypsy stepped aside to allow Quayle in, then pulled the cart inside too and closed the door behind them.

In the blackness, the gypsy clicked on a penlight he'd taken from his pocket and dropped to his knees, unfolded a jackknife and stabbed the blade between the seams of two concrete squares of floor. He pried up a square, then another, lifted and removed them both, and aimed the beam down a narrow flight of concrete steps that had appeared just below. At the foot of the steps, an empty chamber could be seen. The gypsy motioned for Quayle to start down. Following behind, Nicu muscled the slabs of concrete back into place above his head and descended to where Quayle now stood. At the far end of dank chamber stood a heavy oak door, its corroded brass hinges beaded with the same condensation that permeated every wall and ceiling of the abandoned subway station. Nicu next withdrew a plastic-coated map from his pocket. He began unfolding an old schematic for the entire subway system: its tunnels, electrical wiring, piping, intersecting air shafts, laid out over various pages like spider webs. The gypsy studied it.

"Where does that lead?" Quayle asked, pointing to the door ahead of them.

"Take us to tunnel under river."

"To Brooklyn?"

"Aye, boss."

The gypsy pocketed the map and pried open the old wooden door with his thick fingers. The rotted, partially collapsed frame gave way, and the door creaked open. Above their heads, a rotted beam was just high enough for them to squeeze under into the next tunnel.

Chapter Twenty-Three

At that moment, without warning, a thunderous explosion rocked the passageway, silt, mud, and brackish water cascading down around their heads. Once again, the "oogha" of the Klaxon could be heard from somewhere far above them.

The gypsy seized Quayle's arm and shoved him forward. At that instant, a whole section of tunnel collapsed behind them.

"Quicker," Nicu cried hoarsely, springing by him with surprising agility. More debris rained down. Overhead, rotted timbers creaked; it seemed as if at any moment they too might collapse and bring down the entire tunnel.

Soon, they heard a new sound: the squealing of rats fleeing inside the tunnel walls. Quayle looked down and saw more darting around his soaked pant legs. Shivering and shaking them off in disgust, he struggled to keep up with the beam of the gypsy's light bobbing up ahead. Ankle-deep muck ran along the floor, a small stream widening at their feet as they began to descend an incline. Lights flickered on above their heads.

"What's happening?" Quayle called out.

"Power back on. They search for us now, boss. Don't worry, they higher up."

"What was that explosion?"

"They think we still in upper tunnel, try to seal us off. They not know we down here."

He stopped and raised his hand. After listening a moment, he pulled out the map again and pointed to one of its thickest spiderwebs under the beam of his light. "Main tunnel under river here. They not blow that one up. They need that one, so we go there."

"All right. Let's go then. Why are you waiting?" "Not yet, Boss. Another squad due in that main tunnel soon. We let them pass first."

The gypsy squatted and braced his back against the wall a few inches above the mud. He continued to pour over the map.

Quayle stood where he was, finally removing from his waistband the plastic sleeve containing the book Jack had handed him. He paged through it, then asked: "What's this man Bonhoeffer got to do with all this? I recall seeing this in Jack's safe after he disappeared. He must have had someone bring it to him before his arrest. What's the significance of this book?"

The gypsy nodded. "Bonhoeffer, he *gadji* from Nazi times.'

"Gadji?"

"White man, *gadjikano*, not gypsy man. They say he part of plan to kill that fucker Hitler. Plan fail, so they shoot some generals, arrest him, then put him in prison. They have no proof, though, so for two years they hold him, maybe torture him, but he say nothing. One day American bombers come. Gadji pray for guards, tell them they not bad men, but one morning they make him give them his clothes then hang him. Two days later, asshole Hitler dead and Goddamn war over. This what Boss tell me about this book." Nicu stopped, cocked his head. "I go have a look up ahead." He moved off, feet squishing in the muck, his beam of light bobbing before him.

Quayle waited, opening the plastic cover and removing the book. In the dim lights above, he examined the first of many passages of *Letters & Papers From Prison* Jack had highlighted:

"The reasonable people's failure is obvious. With the best of intentions and a naive lack of realism, they think that with a little reason they can bend back into position the framework that has got out of joint. In their lack of vision they want to do justice to all sides, and so the conflicting forces wear them down with nothing achieved. ....Still more pathetic...The fanatic thinks that his single-minded principles qualify him to do battle with the powers of evil, but like a bull he rushes at the red cloak instead of at the person who is holding it; he exhausts himself and is beaten. He gets entangled in nonessentials and falls into the trap set by the cleverer people...."

Quayle quickly scanned the next highlighted passages:

'What lies behind ...the dearth of civil courage? In recent years, we have seen a great deal of bravery and self-sacrifice, but civil courage hardly anywhere, even among ourselves....The fact could not be escaped that the German still lacked something fundamental: he could not see the need for free and responsible action, even in opposition to his task and calling; in its place there appeared on the one hand an irresponsible lack of scruple, and on the other a self-tormenting punctiliousness that never led to action. Civil courage ... can grow only out of the free responsibility of free men. Only now are the Germans beginning to discover the meaning of free responsibility."

For Quayle, the passages could have been addressed to anyone trying to make sense of a government's monstrous betrayal of its own people, for clearly Jack saw his struggle as the same: how to shake the American public from the same paralyzing, murderous inertia that had cost Bonhoeffer his life and the lives millions of others.

Nicu had remained silent as Quayle had read the passages. Now, he said: "I find right tunnel up ahead, boss. Horses coming like I thought. First, we let squad pass, then we go."

Quayle listened. First, he could only hear the seepage from the walls and ceilings. Then, the sound of horses approaching, their hoofbeats growing louder.

Nicu sprang from his crouch and switched off his light. In the blackness, they waited. Loud splashing could be heard, the horses telegraphing conditions in the main tunnel ahead. The gypsy clicked the light back on. Its beam struck what appeared to be the end of this tunnel. There stood another heavy door. Its rusted hinges looked enormous, so encrusted by the elements it might be impossible to swing it open even if the iron bar that held it closed could be budged from its own rusted braces. The gypsy stood beside it for a few long minutes, one ear pressed against it, the grating sound of his wheezing more pronounced in the confined space. Finally, they could no longer hear the horses. The gypsy knelt, withdrew a slender aluminum cylinder taped inside his sleeve and motioned for Quayle to step back several paces. He inserted the canister in the door frame between the two rusted hinges, screwed the top back down, jumped back and turned his face to the wall. As Quayle did the same, there was a muffled pop. Quayle turned back in an acrid cloud of smoke and saw the door had been completely unhinged. Nicu pried it back until he had an opening just wide enough for them to squeeze through. The gypsy aimed the light downward then leaped from the doorway the four feet to the main track of the old subway tunnel just below the doorway. A line of dim overhead lights could be seen trailing along the high ceiling as far down as the next curve and back in the direction the Brigades had taken.

Quayle lowered himself from the ledge to the muddy floor of

the vast main tunnel. This surely was the Brigades' primary way into the eastern enclaves.

Until now, the Directorate's purpose had not seemed evident to him. Suddenly, it was clear: they were surreptitiously transforming the old subway system into an underground staging area, complete with detention and interrogation centers. Even after Quayle and Cecil's brushes with death --- in mid-town, the Racquet Club, and the Enterprise --- his predicament had not seemed all that personal. Now, however, after days of interrogation and imminent danger in these stifling, claustrophobic tunnels, his eyes had been opened. A flood of other recollections sprang to mind: the Brigades' expanded paramilitary presence, Mayor Shrum's Emergency Decrees passed in the wake of the bombings, the widening roundups of suspected illegal aliens and sudden appearance of barbed-wire encampments to hold them. Add to that Jack's abrupt disappearance and troubling imprisonment, and what Quayle now felt was a full-blown fear for his own safety and those closest to him.

As he walked to keep up with the gypsy, Nicu said over his shoulder, "We below river now, Boss." Abruptly, he raised a hand to stop. Ahead came sounds of more horses, perhaps a second squad deploying back to the Directorate, their riders calling to one other. Nicu dropped to his knees and motioned for Quayle to do the same. He covered his face with both arms and burrowed head-first into the muck piled up against the side of one wall, just feet from the center of the track bed where in any moment the horses would pass. Quayle did the same.

The hoofbeats grew closer, the ground under them shaking. Rider after rider began to pass, the shoes of their mounts striking so close Quayle was certain he would be trampled. He counted two-dozen horsemen, two full squads. He raised his head from his crossed arms and gulped for air, then slowly, painfully got to his knees. The gypsy was already on his feet scraping himself, every inch of the hospital gown he wore plastered with mud. Quayle tried to adjust his head bandage, worried about infection.

According to the glow of Nicu's wristwatch, it was now 6 a.m. By now, security must know he was missing.

The gypsy picked himself up, scraped more muddy layers from his clothes and motioned Quayle forward.

It was difficult to keep up. He stumbled and fell, his strength not entirely restored after his ordeal, his breathing labored. Fewer lights of the old tunnel were still working, and he tripped often and painfully in the rutted track bed that had begun a gradual and ever-steeper ascent. Streams of water and mire ran down the slope they were ascending. If they heard more horsemen, it would be more difficult to dive for cover again.

The travel grew steeper, even the gypsy now puffing. Finally they slowed. The sounds of more horses approaching could be heard again, this time from behind them.

"Fuckers!" spat the gypsy. "Maybe they see our tracks and come back." Nicu looked up. Quayle saw what had drawn his attention: a steel, moss-encrusted ladder rising from the tunnel floor to a small trap door in the ceiling. The gypsy pulled out his map, checked it, then began to scramble up the rungs. Reaching the ceiling, he grasped a rusted hatch wheel just above his head. He grunted and swore and forced his weight against it to unlock it. Finally it budged. Brackish water sprang from its rotted seals, sending a river of slime pouring down over him. One of his hands slipped, while the other held. The stream of black brine poured down, then finally dwindled to a trickle. The gypsy regained his balance and forced the hatch up and back with a loud clang. Wriggling his body up through the opening, his mud caked shoes disappeared. There was silence before the beam of the penlight once again flashed on Quayle from the hatchway. Nicu's grimy face appeared. "Ok, boss. You come. We go this way."

Quayle tried to climb but quickly found he did not have enough strength, his injured arm too painful. The gypsy scrambled back down and began to follow him up, forcing one broad shoulder against his thighs and buttocks as he forced him up one hand at a time and at last through the hatch. Wheezing and cursing, the gypsy hauled himself through directly behind him, reached back and pulled the hatch up. He tugged at the lock wheel to shut it. He clicked the light off then and waited. The sounds of horsemen could be again heard passing directly below them. The squad did not pause; they had not been discovered.

Fetid air now enveloped them in what appeared to be a large ventilation shaft. In the beam of the gypsy's light, they saw it stretching out before them, large enough for them to crawl through on hands and knees. They could see no hints of light ahead. They followed the light's beam. Nicu seemed on unfamiliar ground. From above, they began to hear the steady whir of what sounded like turbines. If, in fact, they were heading east under the river, they were perhaps now passing under one of the Con Edison power plants that sat at the edge of the East River on the Brooklyn side.

The whirring grew fainter as they crawled, soon replaced by what finally sounded like the heavy thrum of street traffic. The gypsy kept crawling. Directly ahead, in the beam of his light, they could see the air shaft had come to an end at a steel grate, an exit point that at one time must have served as a fresh air intake and was now clearly bricked over.

The gypsy cursed. Overhead, tantalizingly close, the rumble of cars and trucks moving along some nearby street had grown louder.

The gypsy reached through the grate and felt the bricks directly beyond it. The spot his fingers touched crumbled. Pushing a mud-caked finger between more bricks, he nodded to Quayle and handed him the light, working at the bricks with his jackknife. First one, then another, came loose, revealing plasterboard. Behind it must be a room. They stopped. Soon, they could hear voices. Nicu clicked off the light and pressed a finger to his lips.

They crouched low, waiting in the inky, stifling darkness for muffled, angry-sounding voices to stop. A man cursed, then a door slammed; soon, they could hear a woman weeping.

Sweat dripped from their faces; still they had no choice but to wait.

Quayle again withdrew Bonhoeffer's book. Turning the light back on, he began to quickly scan more of the passages Jack had highlighted:

"Folly is a more dangerous enemy to the good than evil. One can protest against evil; it can be unmasked and, if need be, prevented by force. Evil always carries the seeds of its own destruction, as it makes people, at the least, uncomfortable. Against folly we have no defense. Neither protests nor force can touch it; reasoning is no use; facts that contradict personal prejudices can simply be disbelieved---indeed, the fool can counter by criticizing them, and if they are undeniable, they can just be pushed aside as trivial exceptions. So the fool, as distinct from the scoundrel, is completely self-satisfied; in fact, he can easily become dangerous...."

Then:

"...But at this point it is quite clear, too, that folly can be overcome, not by instruction, but only by an act of liberation...a person's inward liberation to live a responsible life before God is the only real cure for folly."

Quayle shook his head, trying to understand. Had the social-justice bug bit Jack again, the one that in their last year at Yale had drawn him into the writings of philosophers and revolutionaries?

That brief fling with humanitarianism, while making a powerful impression, had abruptly ended when Jack had returned from his dinner with the Teamsters' Carmody and his father, to announce his plan to accept a $3 million union loan to help launch the Enterprise. Vouched for by Carmody, co-signed by his father, it would be the first of many strings-attached Teamsters' financing that would pour forth to help spawn the vast fleet of tankers and container ships, then, later, the casinos, all of which would become the backbone of the conglomerate known as the Enterprise. In return, the Teamsters had won rights to a broad array of Enterprise contracts. All Jack's talk of a life of good works had evaporated as quickly as the ink had dried on that loan. For Quayle, whatever he did not know about the Teamster's arrangements had been easily ignored. Ever since, he had prospered as Jack had prospered, a perfect synergy between them: Quayle burnishing the Enterprise's image, Jack making bold, profitable decisions. Yet now, almost overnight, Jack seemed to have circled back --- a pivot as impulsive as the reversal spawned at that New Haven dinner twenty years before. Was he suddenly ready to throw away everything based on the high-minded words of a long-ago martyred German pastor? He turned the page of *Letters & Papers From Prison.* There in the margin Jack had drawn an arrow to Churchill's foreshadowing of Europe's long-overdue awakening to the fascist threat: "Dictators ride to and fro upon tigers which they dare not dismount. And the tigers are getting hungry."

In microcosm, a Fourth Reich? Is that what Jack saw happening in America?

Quayle's attention was suddenly diverted by sounds of movement behind the brick wall --- the clatter of footsteps, a door opening, then closing, a key turning in a lock. In another moment, they could hear footsteps moving swiftly away behind the wall, then silence.

The gypsy rose from his crouch. He took hold of the air shaft's flimsy grate with his fingers and yanked it off its moorings. Using his knife blade, he dug at the mortar around the bricks that were now fully exposed, the disintegrated mortar powdering. Quayle moved forward in the narrow passageway to help. When they had removed enough bricks to see hints of light, they stopped and paused to listen. Finally, the gypsy sliced carefully through the thin plasterboard that lay behind the bricks, enough to allow them to pass through.

The gypsy shoved his way through first, then pulled Quayle after him. Once inside, they searched the small apartment and began to change into whatever clean clothes they could find in the closets. At the kitchen sink, they washed off their faces and arms of the remnants of the tunnels' brackish mud. In a closet, they found sweatshirts with hoods, and put those on. The gypsy rolled up the oversized sleeves and cuffs of his trousers, went to the bed, and picked up a phone. He listened, then dialed. Soon he was speaking rapidly again in a guttural language Quayle could not understand. He grunted once and hung up.

A single small window in the basement apartment faced the street. Nicu limped to it, knelt, and motioned for Quayle to join him. Just feet above their heads, they could see cars and trucks rumbling by.

"What now?" Quayle asked hoarsely, his lungs burning from having breathed in so much of the tunnel's acrid air.

The gypsy leaned closer. "We wait again now, boss. My friends....they come for us."

Chapter Twenty-Four

Entering the Brooklyn enclave, the Gramercy Park raid now well behind them, the governor and her unmarked car passed slowly through a neighborhood of pawn shops, abandoned row houses, and repo lots, then by the main checkpoint of the Brooklyn Immigrant Compound. The compound, Genesee explained to Cecil, was one of three hastily erected processing centers for undocumented aliens and others on the Brigades' watch lists now being trucked in by convoys of Army transports from the Staten Island intake station that had replaced the old Ellis Island arrival center. She had only just been briefed herself on the details, notified belatedly by Mayor Shrum's chief of staff almost as an afterthought. What the city did with its own immigrants and undocumented aliens was City Hall's business, he'd said, not a state matter; notification about the latest developments was therefore a mere courtesy. The media, preoccupied with its usual menu of political and celebrity gossip, had quickly tired of reporting it as news.

"Imagine," Genesee had snorted. "I had to send down my own chief of staff from Albany to pry this information out of Shrum's people."

She explained more: Inside the barbed-wire encampments, erected overnight along the East River, were Quonset huts and tents intended to hold and process new arrivals by the hundreds, manned and policed under the Emergency Decrees by the paramilitary units of the Brigades and U.S. Homeland Security's Immigration and Customs Enforcement division known as ICE.

Newly arrived foreigners hoping for green cards, along with anyone the Brigades had put on their watch lists, were now subject to roundups and random stops, along with background checks, a time-consuming process that was starting to result in a flood of deportations. Applications for permanent residency or political asylum, added the governor with gravity, were about to be stalled indefinitely by a mountain of mind-numbing new bureaucracy and paperwork. The idea, it was clear, was to close New York City's borders with whatever means allowed by the decrees.

The governor's words, along with the sight of the barbed wire and tent city, appalled Cecil. The scene reminded her of Al Jazeera images of refugee compounds in divided, bitterly-contested Middle Eastern territories like Damascus, Beirut, and Jerusalem.

The driver passed the encampment, and a dozen blocks more north turned the car abruptly through iron gates that led into an alleyway beside one of the more well-kept row houses that sat back from Brooklyn Heights' Pierrepont Street. The car slowed to a stop under a stand of shade trees leafed out in full spring bloom. Three men in expensive-looking suits, their leader speaking French into a communicator as they emerged from a side door, escorted Cecil and Gov. Wainwright inside.

The three-story home's curtains and blinds were tightly drawn. Inside, they found dozens of people taking refuge---Americans and foreigners alike, many of whom Cecil recognized from the Gramercy Park raid. They stood shoulder-to-shoulder in a smokey warren of high-ceilinged, plushly carpeted rooms and connecting hallways, conversing in hushed tones amidst repetitive refrains of what appeared to be an Arabic pop tune. A young Muslim woman in gray headscarf and black ankle-length skirt spoke in clipped English to a man in western dress, finishing a colloquy Cecil caught only in fragments. The hum grew louder as she and the governor were led through the first room and then quickly into the second: "the raid" ... "injustice"... "some detained" ... "what does it mean?" Here, clearly, was a safe house for insurgency organizers and sympathizers, becoming a refuge now even for some of the city's elite represented at the fundraiser, all put at risk by a common threat of Brigades roundups: what Cecil now began to hear described as "the Gramercy Park emergency."

Cecil recognized more dazed faces, some she knew unquestionably to be American citizens. Olivia, Nonnie, and Sabrena, whom she'd left behind before the raid, were nowhere to be seen. She could only hope they had not been taken in.

Most Muslims in the rooms seemed to be saying little, as if uncertain how much they dared speak. Or maybe, Cecil guessed, they were thinking: "Now you understand what we must endure in our countries; let's see what you will do about this." As far as she knew, a roundup of suspected illegals had never been conducted outside of the eastern boroughs before now.

Beside her, a young man in a white linen suit bragged to a young Indian woman in a *sari*: "They didn't have anything on me --- they had to release me when I warned them who I worked for. They will hear from my lawyers about this."

"An outrage," snapped an activist Cecil vaguely recognized from the "Duly Noted" page of the *Times*, her manicured nails tapping her digital camera. "I have all the proof I need right here."

"It's total bullshit," interjected a beefy American with a gray, close-cropped military-style haircut. "They wouldn't know a real terrorist if one fell on them. The Brigades think they can do anything to anybody. We'll show them the lie of that soon enough."

Cecil noticed a dark hallway leading to a series of back rooms. There, a line of people stood waiting. Genesee was nowhere in sight. She seemed to have been headed there when Cecil had been stopped by the crowd.

"I was born on this block!" complained a brooding pink-faced young man in a powder-blue tunic. "They made us move out anyway to eventually make way for these wretched encampments. I suppose they have something against us because daddy and mummy were foreign-born."

"You're gay, dear," his companion said, patting his arm. "That's all. You were lucky your family was displaced. Imagine living close to this sick oppression. It's disgusting."

"Cecilia, what do you know about this?" A familiar New York accent sounded close to her ear. Schuyler Schoenfeld --- Nonnie's husband and one of Washington's most influential lobbyists --- steered her into a corner.

"You here, too?" she whispered. "What on earth...?"

Casting a worried glance around the room, he said through clenched teeth: "My office warned me at the last minute to come here from the airport instead of going to the fundraiser. Have you seen Nonnie? She was going ahead to Gramercy. She hasn't answered any of my calls or texts since I landed. She wasn't detained, was she?"

Cecil blanched. "I was with her before the raid, but I had to leave when Genesee did, so I don't know. Sabrena and Olivia were with her at Gramercy, too, but I don't see any sign of them here either. What is this place? Genesee only told me it was some sort of safe house."

"The Algerian U.N. ambassador's residence, " Schoenfeld answered. "He has diplomatic immunity, so the city can't touch anyone here. Before I left Paris, I had a message from Nonnie Ben might have been injured in a bombing; also that Jack Flyte hasn't been heard from in days. Is that true?"

"Yes. We still don't know where Jack and Ben are. I've been worried sick."

"I'm damn sorry about this, Cecilia. I've been abroad for the past several weeks, purposely out of touch; there's legislation I don't want to discuss with the media right now. I came as soon as I could."

"Two people from the Directorate brought me in and questioned me for an hour about Jack. Of course, I had nothing to tell them, and it was as if they hadn't heard me at all when I mentioned Ben was also missing."

The lobbyist frowned, then warily scanned the faces of the increasingly agitated crowd. In a low voice, he said: "At first, I thought this was just another roundup of foreigners, but I can see this is different. They must be after anyone they suspect might be out to block enforcement of the decrees. Shrum said roundups would never move beyond the enclaves, but my sources say the latest bombings have caused him to rethink all that. He's starting to talk crazy, as if he's in a war. I think he may demand that the governor activate some National Guard units to help police the city."

Cecil shook her head. "She told me she has no intention of doing that. She's very suspicious of Shrum."

Schoenfeld pressed the speed dial on his communicator, stared at the blank screen, then closed the instrument. He tried again. Still no connection. He frowned. "My line is connected to a secure cloud server; it never goes down."

Cecil withdrew her own communicator from her purse and tried to turn it on, but her screen also stayed blank. She could see others in the room discovering the same problem.

Cecil noticed a diminutive woman dressed in a full *burqa*, all but her dark eyes concealed. She had just glanced at Cecil while speaking to a man with a salt-and-pepper goatee and fine-boned Arabic features. Had the woman recognized her? The woman suddenly glanced away. No, perhaps not.

Cecil turned uneasily back to Schoenfeld. If he, with so many connections, was worried, there must be greater cause for concern than even she knew. She scanned the room again. Before her own narrow escape from the Midtown bombing at Conde Nast, she had been all but unaware of her surroundings; now she was alert to every detail; everything seemed now to hold the possibility of danger.

She stared again at the woman. She met her gaze this time, before turning quickly away. Cecil was all but certain who the woman was: Raisa Amin.

"What's the matter?" Schoenfeld asked.

"I think I know that woman. Her voice. I am almost certain."

Schoenfeld leaned closer to her ear. "The man she is with is our host, the Algerian ambassador to the United Nations, Albert Rahid Longueille She must be someone very important."

Cecil gave a start. She remembered: This was the man Genesee had told her in Albany to meet with, using Chloe, the aged actress, as an intermediary. Now that wouldn't be necessary. Ambassador Longueille was standing just steps away.

She bent closer to Schuyler and whispered: "Her name is Raisa Amin. Have you heard of her?"

Schuyler shook his head. "I don't think so."

Cecil paused. "Ben encountered her at the Brigades' intervention of the theater critic Israel Kidman. After the Enterprise bombing, Ben's secretary told me he had left instructions for me to ask for her help if for some reason he wasn't available. I met with her for more than an hour. She was very sympathetic and knowledgeable."

"I don't believe in chance meetings, Cecilia, "Schoenfeld said softly but emphatically. "I would be careful, my dear. You must excuse me now. I must try to locate a working line to contact Nonnie. There are also congressmen who should know about this situation. Please inform Genesee when you see her that I'll be in touch with her; also that I'm prepared to help in any way I can."

Cecil watched Schuyler hurry through the growing swell of people. This must explain why Genesee had brought her here, not only to remove her from the risk of arrest at the fundraiser but also to meet with Ambassador Longueille. She shuddered to think what was happening to those who'd been detained, Tommy Sung among them.

She moved forward, stopped directly beside the woman who earlier had caught her eye, and said, "Please, forgive me, are you Raisa Amin?"

The woman's long black lashes flickered, then she slowly nodded. "Mrs. Quayle. May I introduce Ambassador Albert Longueille. He and I have been discussing your situation."

The rail-thin gentleman inclined his head in a low bow. "I have news about your husband," the ambassador said softly. "I was waiting for you to be free so we might speak. Please come with us."

The ambassador led the way through the crowd and into a narrow hallway. There, out of sight of the crowd, a glass sliding door led out to an expansive enclosed garden. A single electric lamp burned at the far end of the small walled space of trees and shrubs. Beside a back gate, two sentries in plain clothes could be seen standing watch, automatic weapons over their shoulders. The acrid scent of Gauloise rose in the air as the two broad-shouldered men stood puffing, carefully observing them.

In shadow beyond the lamplight, Cecil, Raisa, and the ambassador kept their voices low.

"My husband...," Cecil said. "... I've heard nothing more about him since Raisa informed me he was in the Directorate's clinic. Is he all right?"

Longueille's English was precise, cautious. "He is alive and out of danger from his wounds, that much we know." He paused.

"We've also learned Jack Flyte's in their custody."

Cecil stared dumbly at the ambassador. "My, God. Have they both been arrested then?"

"No. Not yet arrested. Under the latest decrees, they may detain anyone if they suspect they have information about a security matter --- indefinite questioning if they believe the situation calls for it. However, I must also warn you, other events are about to take place that will further involve your husband's well-being." He leaned closer. Cecil's face had gone completely pale. She bit her lower lip, determined not to cry. The ambassador continued: "Sometime tonight, one of our people will be coming to assist your husband; by early morning, if all goes well, this agent should bring him safely beyond the Directorate's reach. You must say nothing of this to anyone. I am only confiding this much because I must ask for your help in return."

"Who will be helping him? Who are you talking about?"

"I'm sorry, I can't disclose that. We've come to a critical moment. Your friend Governor Wainwright must be told of our plans to bring your husband to safety. She must be made aware of the true threat the Directorate poses, and that the steps we now take are in the best interests of the enclaves and the city. She must not intervene until we ask for her assistance. This is very important. Many lives are at stake."

Cecil examined the ambassador closely, searching for any hint of insincerity. For an instant Longueille's gaunt, deeply lined face moved into the lamplight. With a portrait artist's intuition, she saw from his clear-eyed gaze and the urgency of his tone this was a man she could trust. "What do you want me to do?"

Before the ambassador could answer, Raisa touched her arm. "We want you to vouch for me with Governor Wainwright. The ambassador must not be directly involved in any of this. One of the governor's aids is not loyal to her. If I can inform her of this, explain the sensitive and urgent nature of our business, I am certain she will assist us."

"Are you one of the people the Directorate calls insurgents, extremists? Is this why the Gramercy Park fundraiser was raided?"

Ambassador Longueille frowned, shaking his head. "You use this term as if in all cases it were a crime. Please do not be so quick to judge. Insurgencies arise when hope is denied, when oppressed people see no options. It is the Directorate and their Brigades that are the extremists. They have a watch list; perhaps you already know this fact. You are almost certainly on it. I am certain your husband is as well. I will join you all on it soon, I am also sure, once word gets out that I have offered refuge tonight to those who escaped the Gramercy raid. This is also why the governor's support will be so important. Without her, I will be unable to assure my own government in Algiers that this cause for our people in the enclaves is both just and achievable."

"Then, who are the people who have sought safety in your house? Tell me, please."

"Some are like yourself, unsuspecting artists, writers, philanthropists, average citizens, unwittingly caught up in recent events; others are on the Directorate's watch list, suspected of fomenting outright opposition to enforcement of the decrees, previously forced to endure questioning; others are foreign-born naturalized Americans, unable to remain silent as they see evils of their own pasts taking root in their adopted country. It is they who are at greatest risk of full arrest for the smallest infraction. It is for them I am risking my safety and position. For the rest, it is stopping these roundups that are the goal. In my country this is a common and tragic tactic of the regimes, fomenting fear and silence."

"The last group the ambassador mentions would also describe me," Raisa Amin interjected. "As I explained to you in our earlier meeting, there are many similarities between my family as *pieds-noirs* and what we see unfolding before us now. I want to tell the governor my story. I must see her in private. She must understand firsthand what steps we are planning. If she cannot see her way clear to actively help us, we need her assurance at least that she will not impede us."

Cecil dropped her gaze, then lifted it to look Raisa directly in the eye. "Why wouldn't the ambassador's introduction not be enough to open that door for you?"

"As I explained.," the ambassador answered, not waiting for Raisa Amin's response. "As U.N. ambassador, I may entertain anyone I choose in my home under the protection of diplomatic immunity. However, I must not appear to be engaged in any activity that might be viewed as contrary to my host country's local or federal laws. I am already taking a great risk that there may be spies in my house as we speak. My explanation for this gathering will be, if I am confronted, that I was offering refuge for people who were in fear of the Brigades ---a form of political asylum. The Brigades have few sympathizers beyond the Directorate and their own ranks. I have been amply briefed on this by our intelligence services. There will be none who will fault me for offering compassionate refuge. If they do, they will have my government to deal with."

"Hearing this, I am reassured enough to tell you that several days ago Governor Wainwright asked me to contact you, M. Longueille. I am sure because of the urgency, this was why the governor brought me along with her tonight---to speak with you about this matter directly. If you are telling me you have designated Ms. Amin as your intermediary, I am sure this meeting can occur tonight."

"I am greatly relieved to hear this," said Ambassador Longueille. He paused, eyes softening. "It's been many years since the governor and I last talked. People change over time, but I am happy to hear that it appears she has not altered her views on matters such as these."

"What more might I tell the governor about why Ms Amin

wants to meet privately with her?"

"At this time, all you need to know is that we believe the time has come for the office of the governor to reach out to those suffering the Directorate's most abusive oppression in the enclaves, the thousands who now find themselves with no option except to set things right by bringing the fight to the Directorate itself. The Directorate's recent actions are in danger of radicalizing all three eastern boroughs of the city. This, as you might imagine, could be seen as treason under the latest decrees. In that vein, Raisa will urge the governor to come here to meet with the most important leaders of all three boroughs. I am new to this role as U.N. ambassador, but I am not new to your country; I have great affection for it. The preliminary meeting I mentioned is now taking place a few rooms away from where we stand: a group of clergy, imams and rabbis from the three eastern boroughs, all deeply concerned about the dangerous path the Directorate and the mayor's office have been following, are meeting now with the governor. You understand, you must say nothing of this beyond our conversation here?"

"I won't, of course. Never."

Raisa stepped into the light and threw back the head piece of her *burqa.* "This," she said in a hoarse whisper, "was the present the Brigades' interrogators left me several months ago when they questioned me."

Cecil stared: A thin half-moon scar ran from left jawbone to right jawbone across Raisa Amin's throat. Cecil remembered now. When they had first met, a scarf had been stylishly wound around her neck. Obviously, it had been intended to conceal this terrible wound.

"They told me if I would not do as they wanted, give them names, provide information on my Muslim associates, they would finish the job. I refused. For some reason they let me go. Perhaps, because they did not want to murder a woman. Also, one of them spoke to me in Arabic, and said he was Muslim himself , and would try to spare me. So far, they have not made good on their threat. They know there are important people who support me, so they watch and wait. I dare not go out uncovered now."

At the far end of the garden, the two sentries had turned their heads toward the gate, distracted by some street sound. In the darkness some yards away from them, Raisa quickly replaced her headpiece. Slowly, the sentries returned to their smoking, their embers winking on and off against the stucco wall that marked the rear boundary of the compound.

"These are men I trust," Ambassador Longueille said, nodding reassuringly toward them. I cannot vouch for all of those who have made it here from the raid. I must assume some are spies."

"I still do not feel safe," Raisa whispered softly. "I am *Sufi*. This leader of the interrogators was *Sunni*. Do you understand?"

"No. I'm sorry, I don't."

"We do not believe in universal *jihad* espoused by the most extreme of the *Sunni*, evil men such as the 9/11 hijackers. We believe instead the true war against evil must take place within ourselves, not randomly, mercilessly, against all nonbelievers. The *Sunni* extremists revile us for that, as much as they revile you as a nonbeliever, for it does not fit their belief in universal *jihad*. That is why we must stand up to them. We must not be afraid. We must unite against their evil methods. We must begin to openly, publicly, denounce them before it is too late. Only moderate leaders in our midst have the power to do that, just as moderates like your own Governor Wainwright must be enlisted in this cause."

"But you said those people were questioning you on behalf of the Brigades."

"That is why we must speak with the governor. She must be made to understand this evil is not just within our walls. It is also within yours."

Cecil nodded nervously. "Yes, I see, of course."

"There is more, Mrs. Quayle, " the ambassador added softly, "we have good reason to believe the bombings of this past week have been the work of the Directorate itself, not of the *jihadists.* The purpose is quite obvious: to sow fear within the entire city as a pretext for ever more stringent powers under the decrees. This is what is most important for the governor to understand."

Cecil struggled to absorb this last alarming information. "Surely, you must be mistaken. The Directorate is concerned with national security. There are checks and balances. They could not have instigated the bombings, could they? Surely not."

"It is our belief they have. In the next twenty-four hours," Ambassador Longueille said, his face set grimly, "many more people of influence will be taken in for questioning---much like your husband ---if they're suspected of opposing the Emergency Decrees. Our sources inside the Directorate say more random roundups and interrogations are to follow the Gramercy Park incident. All brought in will be required to sign a Loyalty Oath of Cooperation before their release, or risk being placed on a watch list which will be circulated as a black list. Anyone on it will risk being sanctioned and shunned. Or worse."

Cecil shook her head, dumbfounded. "This is why have they detained my husband?"

"Most likely. Our sources also tell us your husband's employer, M. Flyte, has also been judged unreliable under Section 8 of the decrees. This is why he, too, is now in the Directorate's custody, also being subjected to their own brand of interrogation. We understand drugs are involved, sleep deprivation. There may be other methods."

Cecil paled. "Ghastly. It's the worst possible news! I'm stunned."

"This is why you must bring in person Raisa's courageous offer of assistance to Governor Wainwright before any more time is wasted."

Cecil looked at Longueille. For a moment, she was speechless. This was too unfathomable to comprehend. Yet circumstances and events of recent days --- her detention, now Ben's and Jack's --- had been sending warning signals. Taken together in their entirety, they pointed to the truth of what she was now being told.

Raisa reached out and touched her arm. "I understand what you may be thinking: 'Perhaps, this woman is an assassin?' I can only say if this were the case, the governor would not have made it here alive, and we would never be confiding all this to you. We, too, are taking a risk trusting you."

"She will not negotiate with terrorists," Cecil cautioned, guessing they might be asking this as well.

"No, no. That is not what we mean," the ambassador said urgently. "We wish Raisa Amin to act as a back channel for the governor --- between her good offices and my good offices and the many moderate voices in the enclaves now far too afraid of our own extremists to speak. Powerful factions within the Directorate welcome the escalation of violence; indeed, it is our belief they are fomenting it. If we can prove to her the Directorate is behind the latest bombings beyond the enclaves...." His voice trailed off. "...perhaps then she will understand the full picture. At last, we will be able to say to our most trusted leaders there is someone with great influence who not afraid to advocate for them and stand against the Directorate."

Raisa gripped Cecil's arm. Slowly, she reached inside the folds of her *burqa* and withdrew a paper folded into a small square. "When you show this document to the governor, I am sure she will understand the urgency of the situation."

Ambassador Longueille's lips tightened. "Mrs. Quayle, there are many of us now who believe there is no other way."

Chapter Twenty-Five

Cecil felt a rush of anxiety as she and Raisa walked from the garden to the back room of the ambassador's residence where Genesee waited. She felt disoriented, the world she had known replaced by a fearful, uncertain place she did not know, each new distressing scrap of information adding to her greater sense of panic. She could only imagine how it must feel to Ben, being so out of touch. For her, the lack of contact with him felt increasingly ominous. She took a deep breath, handed the security man at the door a note, then waited until she was ushered in. As agreed, Raisa stayed behind to learn if the governor would see her. Cecil found Genesee seated behind an ornate oaken desk in the ambassador's personal library. She was accompanied by a lone female aide Cecil remembered from Albany. Beside the rear door, where another visitor had just exited, stood the state trooper who had driven them here.

Genesee shook her head. "Cecil. I'm so sorry you've had to endure this. You look awful."

"No, I'm all right. I just don't understand what's happening. The more I hear about this, the more worried I am. " She took the chair the aide offered her. "Who are these people? Some I recognize from Gramercy, but who are these others? They look so desperate."

Genesee took her seat behind the desk. "I've been gathering as much information as I can about this roundup. I'm still not sure what to believe. There have been raids all over the city tonight.

Ambassador Longueille has been kind enough to offer his residence as a safe house."

"I've been hearing other disturbing things." At this, the aide handed Cecil a glass of water. She took it, swallowed some, then handed the glass back. "There's a woman waiting outside you must meet. She helped me after Ben's injury. Her name is Raisa Amin, a leader of a moderate Islamist group opposing the decrees on behalf of the residents of the enclaves. She says she has very important information for you. She has told me that Ben and Jack Flyte are both in the Directorate's custody. Yes, Jack, too; he's been there for I don't know how long."

"In custody? I thought you said in the car Ben was being treated at the Directorate's health clinic. Has something else happened?"

"They're both being questioned now. I have no idea why. I'm sick about it."

Genesee stared at Cecil. "This is terrible news. I will see this woman, of course. We are trying to develop some sort of public response to the roundups, but we need a lot more information.

Cecil nodded, choking back tears. "I'm terrified about what may be done to them."

The governor motioned to the trooper. "Bring in this woman right now. I must know what she has to say."

The trooper strode to the door leading to the front hallway and waited as Raisa Amin, still in full *burqa*, underwent a body scan. The governor greeted her and motioned her to a chair beside Cecil. Raisa began to unfasten her headpiece, then stopped as the govern resumed her seat behind the desk. "Madame Governor, would it be possible for this interview to be private?"

She nodded toward the aide and the policeman.

"Margaret," the governor said to the young woman, "I wonder if you and the officer will excuse us for a few minutes."

"Of course," the aide said. She got to her feet and gathered up her papers.

"That won't be necessary," said the governor. "You can leave those here until I've called you back."

The aide gave her a startled look, placed her notebook and paperwork on her chair and left with the officer through the rear door.

In the momentary silence, Raisa pulled back the hood of her *burqa* to reveal her face. "Please tell me about yourself," the governor said.

She began to speak in her careful, elegantly-phrased English, explaining the history she had related to Cecil in their first meeting. When she was finished, she bent forward. "I want to assure you, madame governor, we are not extremists. We only seek to ensure safety for all immigrants, the same justice America promises its own citizens, many of whom in generations past were immigrants themselves. We cannot continue to stand by and do nothing. We hope that you will help us."

The governor looked at this slight, fierce woman with undisguised admiration. "Will Ambassador Longueille vouch for you?"

Raisa's lips tightened. "Ambassador Langueille knows my mother from her days in

Paris, and also of my grandparents' martyrdom at Oran. My mother asked him to contact me once he had assumed his post here, which he did Algiers isn't the only Muslim capital alarmed by the decrees. We're hearing talk of Islamic leaders issuing a joint *fatwa* demanding an end to them and to these encampments that are becoming little better than prisons. You must understand this information must never be attributed to M. Longueille. He must not be seen as interfering in your country's internal affairs."

Genesee's surprise again was obvious. "I assure you nothing

will be said outside this room to compromise you or M. Longueille. But please understand, I must check your story and your credentials. Meanwhile, as I am sure you can imagine, for me to take a public stand against the decrees will put me at odds with powerful forces within my own government, and even my own constituency. These bombings have made it almost impossible to side with opponents of the decrees without appearing to side with terrorists."

Raisa nodded, but her expression hardened. "We are very aware of this, Madame Governor. This is principally the reason I have come to you---to explain the matter of these bombings." She moved her fingers to the yoke of her *burqa.* She pulled the fabric down to reveal the half-moon slash across her throat. Genesee saw it and winced.

"This is what the Brigades did to me when I refused to give them information about my group, a group I was able for the moment to disavow exists." Her dark eyes narrowed. "Tell me now, governor, who the true extremists are."

"I can't believe this. They did this to you?"

"Raisa covered the scar. "Yes. However, I am no stranger to such tactics, which is exactly the point I wish to make. As I said, my grandparents perished at Oran in the Algerian massacres. At war's end, when de Gaulle proclaimed independence for Algeria, armed men entered the city demanding all French, Islamic, and Algerian pieds-noirs landholders leave. French troops did nothing, local police did nothing, hundreds of men, women and children were massacred, thousands of others like my parents --- small children then---were forced to flee, living like animals in Marseilles or the Parisian slums of Belleville until the fortunate ones could emigrate to America. But in France, and within the de Gaulle government, there was no outrage. In just days, the war was over, the de Gaulle abandonment of the pieds-noirs ruled complete. There was no compelling reason within the official circles or the populace to pursue justice. My people had become non-people." She paused, clearing her throat, emotion overcoming her for a moment, but quickly she recovered and continued. "When I heard no outrage --- indeed praise--for the public executions of recent days, I remembered what my parents had always told me about Oran. No one protested Now, all these years later, we see what looks to us like a new Oran coming. Have such terrible things, and so many others like it, become lost to Americans' memories? The Directorate will never stop these roundups if we don't resist, and they won't be satisfied with that. We know what happens next, it's what always happens. We must stop this now before there is another Oran, another *Kristallnacht,* another Kosovo."

Genesee shifted in her chair uncomfortably. "What more do you know about this? You're not telling me something."

"The Directorate wants you to believe extremists are to blame for these bombings. We know that is a lie. We are compiling proof that it is the Directorate itself planting these bombs, using its special units within the Brigades. We too have spies inside the Directorate. Tonight, one of them is to escort Madame Quayle's husband out of the Directorate's custody; along with our man will come proof we need to expose the entire truth about these bombings."

The governor and Cecil stared at Raisa. Finally Genesee said: "You must know, this is very difficult for us to believe."

"Of course," said Raisa. "I would be just as skeptical if I were in your place. However, we have sources who are very well informed, and we have powerful friends. I will tell you, since you know one of them yourselves, one of those friends is Jack Flyte of the Enterprise. It was M. Flyte who came first secretly to us. It was almost a year ago. He had seen the extremes the Directorate was proposing under the decrees. When he had learned they had Mayor Shrum's cooperation, he contacted me. Without M. Flyte's encouragement and financial support, the resistance could never have gotten this far. We have been able to gather intelligence inside the Directorate for almost a year." She paused.

"Do you know what's happened to Jack?" Cecil asked with trepidation. Until this moment, she had sat with her friend speechless at what they'd just heard.

"M. Flyte is in the Directorate's custody, in solitary confinement, just as M. Quayle has been, and, I should add, many others. M. Flyte has chosen not to take part in the first escape effort. He believes as long as they have him and others held hostage, they will be able to discredit anything M. Quayle may say. We intend to make certain they cannot. I fear if the escape fails and Mrs. Quayle's husband and our people are caught, there will be retribution against all of us."

Genesee looked at her with new alarm. "Do you believe it could come to that?"

"I do." Raisa paused, slipped her fingers inside the sleeve of her *burqa* and removed an envelope. "There is one more thing." She handed the envelope to the governor.

Genesee removed the contents and began to read. When she was finished, she looked up with a new expression of alarm Cecil could not clearly read.

"Are you certain this document is authentic?"

"It came to me from Ambassador Longueille himself. He thought it urgent that you see it at once."

"Did he explain how he came to receive this information?"

"It came from someone close to the mayor's office who wanted a favor."

Gov. Wainwright's eyes had turned deeply green, a sign to Cecil her old school friend was greatly disturbed.

She turned to Cecil: "Have you seen this?"

"The ambassador explained only that it was urgent that you see it."

"It informs the ambassador one of my senior people is working secretly for the

Directorate's Office of Investigations."

"My God." Cecil looked at Raisa. "That's Noel Gatwick's office."

"I am aware of Gatwick," the governor said coldly. She turned to Raisa. "The mayor is also aware the Directorate has a spy in my office?"

Raisa leaned forward and nodded. She said: "There is something more you should know. The Brigades plan to execute two young students tomorrow for planting the bomb that injured Mrs. Quayle's husband at the Enterprise. It's certain to create an international incident."

Genesee stiffened. "I don't understand."

"The two---also falsely accused and convicted by the Brigades' secret tribunal---are the first sons of the Saudi prince Sheikh Mohammed Al-Harham."

"The Minister of Defense?"

Raisa Amin's gaze did not waver. "Yes, Madame Governor."

Chapter Twenty-Six

Cecil stood with Raisa outside the back gate of the safe house, waiting for Genesee's car to come around to take them back to the city. Beyond this neighborhood and the East River looking west, they could see the glow of the towering Manhattan skyline.

"Your friend, the governor, has courage, I could see that," Raisa said softly, her eyes shining intensely behind her burqa. "But will she help us? I could not be certain."

"You heard what she said. I am sure she will find some way. You've only asked her not to interfere with your plans. I think that was wise. It gives her some room to decide what will be best. My impression is, the ambassador vouching for you was also important for her to know."

Behind them, the two armed sentries had just emerged from the garden gate, leaning casually against the wall of the compound, their weapons slung loosely from their shoulders, muzzles pointed down.

To the north, somewhere in the Queens enclave, sirens began to wail --- police or ambulances, it was impossible to tell for certain. Cecil's hands trembled. Again, it came to her how different things felt now. How ominous it all seemed for Ben and Jack...damn, she couldn't stop trembling. Finally, the governor's unmarked town car backed slowly out of the alleyway beside the residence and turned back down the block heading toward them. Its headlights flashed on, piercing the darkness of the blacked-out street. Raisa took Cecil's arm, and they both stepped closer to the curb to wait for it, watching the car oddly speed up rather than slow down. Raisa said something in French, and the sentries unshouldered their weapons. The car picked up more speed. The first sentry raised his arm, but the car kept on.

"Where's the driver?" Cecil exclaimed. "There's no driver."

Raisa's grip tightened on Cecil's arm. "Bomb," she cried. She pushed Cecil back and yanked hard at the latch of the garden gate. It refused to open. The sleeve of her burqa caught on the iron spikes of the iron gate, and she tore it free, forcing Cecil back harder against the thicket of vines that covered the compound's wall. Bravely, she turned to face the onrushing car. The darkness suddenly exploded directly beside them, muzzle flashes tore through the night, the sentries' rifles sending tracer bullets ricocheting off the heavily armored vehicle. Raisa and Cecil pressed their backs to the wall and stared in helpless horror at the driverless car still coming.

"*Merde! A la droite la*!" Raisa shouted toward the kneeling sentries. "A guy there in the alley to the right. See him? He's got a detonator." The sentries' weapons came up. Another hail of bullets flew into the shadows of the alley she had been pointing to. From somewhere in the darkness came a grunt and a thump, then the sound of other running feet. Cecil saw the brief flash of two figures ducking down the alley, escaping the narrow beam of the sentry's flashlight, getting away.

The town car was nearly in front of the stoop. One of the sentries dropped his weapon, ran quickly to the driver's side, and yanked open the door. Hefting himself in, he grabbed the wheel and fought to steer the vehicle back to the center of the street. A few yards more and the car had passed the stoop it had been angled toward, then raced past the gate where Cecil and Raisa stood. It sped toward what looked like a vacant lot, still accelerating. At that same moment, the sentry dove from the open door into the street. An instant later the passenger compartment of the car exploded, sending a ball of flame into the sky. The ear-splitting blast rattled and shattered windows up and down the block.

The second sentry raced to his companion's side. When the man did not respond, he rose, aiming his flashlight into the alleyway. There, the motionless form of a man lay, blood pooling beneath his head.

Raisa and Cecil approached.

The sentry stooped and picked up a palm-sized device from beside the body.

"Just as I thought," declared Raisa. "A detonator."

The sentry nodded, then shone his light directly on the lanky body dressed in black sprawled before them. Cecil stared. "There, looking up at them with lifeless eyes, was the pale, hollow-cheeked face of Tommy Sung.

Chapter Twenty-Seven

Quayle crouched with the gypsy on the floor of the basement apartment and peered through the grimy street-level window into the early-morning dawn breaking over the congested heart of the Brooklyn enclave. It appeared they had emerged from the old subway tunnels just off the intersection of Flatbush, 4th, and Atlantic Avenues. The three streets, clearly marked where they converged, now formed one of the borough's most congested commercial districts. Iron security bars in their windows separated them from traffic, already flowing heavily despite the early hour, comprised of every manner of vehicle-- cars, pushcarts, bicycles, trucks. They rumbled and rattled and jounced all in the same direction toward blinking electronic signs that pictured the famous Prospect Park Grand Arch and ticked off the distance to the famous landmark. Across Flatbush Avenue, in plain view of where Quayle and the gypsy knelt, Muslim and Hindi women in *hijabs*, caftans, saris, and *burqas* fought for places in a long, snaking queue at an open-air market set up in a vacant lot up the block. They seemed the only people ignoring the southward press of what appeared to be a rapidly assembling mob.

A squad of Brigadesmen on foot came into view, marching shoulder to shoulder down the thoroughfare, clearing a path from curb to curb through the advancing crowd. Nicu glared as the Brigadesmen approached in their black high-topped boots, grumbling at them under his breath in his strange gypsy language.

Now suddenly uncommunicative, except for such mutterings, he seemed to be waiting for the people he'd telephoned half an hour before to arrive.

Quayle had questions he wanted to ask, but so far the moment had not presented itself. It was still astonishing to him he could have missed Jack's involvement in this unrest, yet in hindsight he knew the signs had been there: absences, fewer completed deals, negotiations inexplicably abandoned. Quayle had felt a need to ratchet up damage-control because of such lapses, but until the overt comments about wanting to pull out of the consortium that Jack had let drop at the racquet Club, he'd had no reason to suspect his involvement in what now clearly appeared to be some sort of insurgency. He had to learn from the gypsy how deep it went, and where it was now going.

Out on the street, a troop truck crept into view, its canvas top flapping as it rattled over the potholed street. Its driver rammed the truck into low gear in front of the apartment, and at that sound Nicu jumped up and threw open the front door. He looked both ways and motioned Quayle to follow. Limping up beside the driver, he waved at the uniformed man, then fell back and leapt onto the rear bumper. To Quayle's surprise, a uniformed policeman leaned through the flap and started to help Nicu inside when the truck jerked to a complete stop. The gypsy cursed and dropped off the bumper to the street. Ahead, Quayle could see a lone mounted officer of the Brigades, one hand raised, his mount blocking the way. The Brigadesman glared down at the driver of the truck and demanded: "Who are you? State your business."

"Metropolitan police. Get out of our way."

"State your business, I say. Why are you in this truck. This is no regular police vehicle. This is an Army vehicle. What's going on?"

"Security and crowd control," the police officer shouted. "Now make way."

The Brigadesman looked momentarily confused. Warily, he peered down the side of the truck, spotted Quayle and the gypsy ducking away, and shouted: "You there! Stop right there! Halt!"

Instead, they kept backing into the crowd.

"Halt, there!" The Brigadesman cried again and spurred his horse forward as they began to run.

From the passenger side of the truck, a captain of metro police sprang out directly in the horse's path and brought the rider to a stop "I am Police Captain Singleton. What's the problem here?"

"Brigades business," the uniformed rider snorted and yanked his horse's bridle away from the police captain's outstretched hand.

"Who are you after?" the officer asked calmly.

The Brigadesman looked down the side of the truck where the gypsy and Quayle had just vanished. The Brigadesman cursed. "Out of my way, you idiot, they're getting away. Hold those people," he shouted to the crowd. "I want to talk to them."

Two burly men grabbed Quayle and pushed him with Nicu roughly back into the street.

"You there, gypsy!" the Brigadesman shouted. "What's your name?"

Nicu stepped forward, blinking in the sun. "*Aljenicato*, fishmonger, boss."

"And you?" the Brigadesman demanded, his gaze fixed now on Quayle. "Who are you? What are you doing with this guy?"

Quayle saw a knife handle slip from the gypsy's sleeve into his palm.

"On our way to the market for work," Nicu answered. "We don't want no trouble, boss."

"Show me your identification."

Quayle saw Nicu deftly prick the horse's flank with the knife. The animal sprang violently to the right and reared, throwing his rider to the street. The Brigadesman's black helmet cracked back down hard on the pavement. The crowd shrank back from the whirling horse, its reins still gripped by the Brigadesman's hand.

Down the block, they could see the Brigademan's squad turning back, drawn to the commotion. Their leader raised his baton and clubbed a man on the shoulder, demanding the crowd move. Before them at the truck, a uniformed policeman leaned through the flap and said angrily to Nicu: "You're on your own. We'll have to send someone to find you." He yanked the transom flap down, but not before Quayle had glimpsed what was inside: more uniformed police, flanking what appeared to be two bound and hooded men.

The driver blew his horn and swerved away from the squad of approaching horsemen, plowing through pedestrians scrambling away, vanishing down a side street in a cloud of exhaust. The squad of Brigadesmen fought to regroup, but the heavy traffic and crush of the crowd prevented them from doing anything but reining in their mounts and falling back.

Quayle and the gypsy darted into the crowd. It was now impossible to go anywhere the Brigades or the mob did not dictate. Ahead, a huge billboard stood on the roof of what remained of a warehouse. Its message in Aramaic bordered a life-sized photograph of two young men in Muslim skullcaps. Just ahead, a roar went up. Someone shouted in English, "No more blood!" All around them, voices took up the chant. Overhead, an unmarked jetcopter appeared over buildings and swooped low over the crowd. A uniformed man in khaki could be seen leaning far out the side door filming.

Quayle heard the thud of more batons. He lost sight of Nicu, then saw him again, crouched against a brick wall near the entrance to an alleyway allowing the mob to stream by.

Quayle pushed his way over and knelt beside him, pointing up at the billboard. "What's that say?"

"Sign says terrorists die today,'" he said, then looked ahead at the commotion up the avenue. "Another one of those Brigades fuckers coming now," he muttered. "Don't move, boss."

A Brigadesman approached on foot, a communicator pressed to one ear. He was looking ahead, his gaze passing above where the two sat crouched. Soon he was swallowed up by the crowd.

"Who were those men in that truck?" Quayle demanded amidst the commotion.

"Our people."

"They looked like cops."

"They just dressed like cops. They going to stop the executions. Those Saudis not plant any bombs."

"What are you saying?"

"Brigades plant the bombs, boss. A trick, boss. So Brigades can blame bombs on foreigners."

"What are you saying?"

"Arabs, boss, blame the Arabs, so Directorate do what it wants. So it take over everything, run everything." Nicu rose and suddenly pointed to the alley. He pushed a scrap of paper into Quayle's hand. "You take this and go now, boss. You go to this place. They catch you with me, they arrest you for sure."

Quayle grabbed the gypsy's arm. "No. You can't leave me here. I want to know what's going on."

"Ok, ok, boss," he said peevishly. With his surprising strength, he pulled Quayle by the arm into the alley. Quayle took a stumbling step, stopped, and looked back at a new commotion starting outside the alley back on the sidewalk. The gypsy's black eyes were scanning the same scene, his beaded braids rattling with nervous jerks of his head.

"Move, move on!" a Brigadesman on foot was shouting, plowing his way through the crowd in the street toward them: "Get out of the way, damn you," he shouted. He lunged and stumbled and grabbed a young man in a jacket trying to run. Quayle heard the crack of a baton on bone. The boy dropped to the ground, hands clutching his head. The Brigadesman stood over him, his baton raised. "This one is mine. You people step back." He wasn't after them, he was after this student. The Brigadesman started handcuffing him.

Out on the jammed street, another of his compatriots on horseback had spurred his mount straight for the scene of the arrest.

"We go now," Nicu demanded.

"What about those guys who were supposed to pick us up?"

"We go!" Nicu ordered, and sprang from his crouch, limping swiftly down the length of the narrow alley. At the far end, they found themselves entering another broad street. There, a new crowd streamed by, more posters marking the way. At that moment, a lone policeman fell into step beside them. He mumbled a few words to the gypsy, then walked rapidly ahead, turning left onto Lafayette Avenue and advancing more swiftly.

Nicu gave Quayle a sign to follow him and with his limping gait struggled to keep up. Nicu seemed to have no fear of this policeman, in much the same way he had welcomed the troop-transport arriving, showing no sign of alarm until the mounted rider of the Brigades had appeared and confronted them. He sensed something peculiar happening within law enforcement --- a schism of some sort, perhaps, between the Metro city police and the paramilitary Brigades. Maybe this explained Detective Navarro's sudden and unexplained transfer out of the Manhattan precinct before his investigation into Jack's disappearance could begin.

As they walked, the crowd was continuing to swell along the adjacent Flatbush Avenue, multiple lanes of vehicles slowing to a crawl as crowds continued to form in a relentless push toward Prospect Park.

Up ahead, the police officer turned and suddenly crossed. Nicu followed. A few moments more and they found themselves passing the rear of a building marked Howard Gilman Opera House. At a clearly labeled stage door almost entirely hidden from the street, they glimpsed the police officer entering. Following close behind, they soon found themselves in a long, dimly-lit hallway that almost immediately brought them to the lower mezzanine of the cavernous performance hall. There a set of stairs could be seen, the policeman's shadowy figure rapidly descending them.

Another low-ceilinged hallway stretched before them, leading into a cluttered, musty-smelling prop room filled with theatrical costumes, mirrored makeup stations, and rows of curtained dressing rooms. Further ahead, behind a wooden door, came the sounds of muffled voices. Quayle's heart jumped in his chest. Many voices, exclusively men's voices, their precise words indecipherable but clearly foreign, came floating out and down the dimly-lit hallway. Quayle saw the police officer knock on the door. It flew open, and before them stood a broad-shouldered, thickly bearded man in a black wool skull cap. A Glock machine pistol hung from one shoulder. The man smiled broadly. Removing a toothpick from one side of his mouth, he clapped the gypsy's sturdy shoulders with a meaty hand and exclaimed in a heavy accent: "Little one, don't look so worried. You've made it. You are safe."

Chapter Twenty-Eight

The hard black eyes of the man with the gun examined Quayle carefully. Behind the tangle of beard, he looked intimidating, but something in his manner also struck Quayle as kind. He turned to Nicu: "This the one you called about?"

"Flyte's main man, boss," Nicu said.

"Good," the man said. He turned to Quayle. "You are welcome here."

The policeman who had brought them entered the room, removed his visored cap, and sat down at a long crowded table laden with food. Around him were two dozen or more men in all manner of dress, forking rice into wooden bowls. The attire of the group seemed common to the enclaves' multinational ethnic diversity: Muslims, Jews, Greeks, Africans, others in western attire --- baseball caps and team jerseys --- and some dressed overtly as religious men.

"I am Rabbi Isaac Schulman," a short balding man in a *yarmulke* said as he rose from the head of the table and moved to shake Quayle's hand warmly. His accented English was thick and guttural. His dark brows lifted as he pointed to the gathering. "As you can see, our group is of many faiths and persuasions."

Two beefy men rose from the table where the rabbi had been seated and also came over to shake Quayle's hand. One wore a sweatshirt over a black tunic with a Roman collar, the other the distinctive head-covering of an Imam. "This is Father Kaminsky from the Brooklyn Catholic Diocese," the rabbi said, "and Imam El Hamad of the Brooklyn Central Mosque."

"I am Benjamin Quayle."

"We have been expecting you," the priest said. We are well acquainted with your friend and colleague, Jack Flyte. We had all hoped he would be with you."

Quayle looked at them in surprise. How could they be this informed so quickly?

"It was by his own choice he decided to stay," the rabbi broke in, sparing Quayle the need to answer. "He was afraid they would unleash a citywide search for him. Nicu the gypsy is the one in greatest danger now. He's managed to make fools of them." A round of applause erupted for the gypsy. He smiled quickly and sat down before his rice. The rabbi waved his hand toward the group to begin eating while to Quayle he said quietly: "What you see here would not be possible without the assistance and support of your friend and colleague Jack Flyte. We have food for you now. Please join us."

He motioned for Quayle to sit beside him as the gypsy filled his plate and went to a nearby wall and squatted against it, beginning to fork rice quickly into his mouth.

Quayle realized he was also famished; he had not eaten since he had left the clinic. He was surprised, too, his injuries had not slowed him down. Whatever medications they had given him must have long since worn off, yet he had almost complete movement of his arm. To the rabbi, he said: "Is it possible for me to contact my wife? I have not able to speak to her for days. I know she must be very worried."

The Rabbi shook his head. "Not possible. We are about to begin an operation soon. If you will give me an address where she can be reached, I will have someone contact her once it is under way. The Directorate is monitoring all communications traffic, no standard devices are secure. We have had to resort to couriers now for everything."

Quayle took the pencil and scrap of paper the rabbi handed him, wrote down the townhouse address, and returned it.

As he looked up, he noticed four large video screens on the far wall of the room. Each flickered with live views from four different angles of what appeared to be a grassy expanse of well-manicured lawn and forest On the fourth screen was a view of the Grand Arch of the Army, the signature attraction of Prospect Park. As Quayle looked, he could see more and more people spilling into the park's venues.

"What is all this?" he asked as he began to eat, gesturing to the crowd in the room. "What are all these people doing here?"

"You saw the mobs outside. Two young men are to be hanged, two students accused of planting the bomb that killed nearly a dozen people outside your company, the Enterprise. We are going to help stop their executions."

Quayle looked at him with a start.

"Yes, that's right. They are accused of planting the same bomb that nearly killed you. However, these men are entirely innocent. Nicu has brought proof that these bombings have been carried out by none other than the Brigades themselves."

"That can't possibly be true." Quayle looked at him in astonishment.

"I'm afraid that it is. With each new bombing, the decrees have gained new popularity with the general citizenry, as has the Directorate. It is a ruse to sew fear and enhance the power of the Brigades." He looked over to where the gypsy was squatting. "Nicu, join us."

The gypsy rose from his haunches, his leathery face drawn, world-weary. It was impossible to tell his age, the creases around his forehead and eyes as weathered as hardpan. Like Quayle, he still wore the sweatshirt he'd taken from the apartment they'd broken into, emblazoned with NYU across its front. Dried brackish water and mud from their time in the tunnels still caked his hands, face, and tangled brows. Quayle guessed he must look, and smell, the same.

"What have you brought us, my friend?" the rabbi asked softly.

The gypsy reached inside his sweatshirt and untied a cord wound around his chest. A small leather pouch dangled from the cord. He handed it to the rabbi. "Flash drive with surveillance, boss. All there, six months' worth."

"You will be handsomely rewarded, my friend."

The gypsy pocketed the pouch, smiled, and limped back to his wall, once again squatting.

The rabbi turned back. "When you're finished eating, Ben , my friend, you can both go back to wardrobe and get cleaned up. There are showers and fresh clothes. We have two hours until the first units are to go. I am in charge of the operation, Father Kaminsky and Imam El Hamad have helped us draw up the plan and the strategy. The Brigades will not expect such unity of purpose from us. They do not understand how the decrees have brought us all together. It's as it should be when there is no other way."

"I want to help in whatever way I can."

"Good. We want you and the gypsy to be our eyes and ears at the park." The rabbi touched his shoulder. "Now, bring your food back to the surveillance screens. I am about to give the final instructions. You can hear the plan for yourself."

The rabbi rose and clapped his hands. Everybody moved their chairs to face the screens. Quayle counted twenty eight men in all, not counting himself and the gypsy. They had separated themselves into groups of six, each stationed at one of the screens. Before them, the priest and Imam stood with the rabbi as he began to speak, carefully and clearly, in his accented English.

"The time has come to act. When you have heard my final instructions, you will put on whatever civilian clothes you'll find in the bins by the front door. Precisely at 11 o'clock, unmarked trucks will pull into the back of the opera house to drive your groups to their two designated quadrants to the west and the east of the Grand Arch. This is where the gallows are to be erected. There you will wait for a courier to bring further instructions. Take no communicators or other electronic devices with you; bring no identification or weapons. We know the Brigades' horse squads will not appear in full force until the park has been fully occupied. At that time, they will form a perimeter around the crowds, blocking all entries and exits. Their purpose will be to seal off the gallows and the Grand Arch in case there is any attempt to interfere with the executions, any attempt at all. Under no circumstances are you to leave the vans until a courier has given you the word. There will be people monitoring the scene from our command post here. Is this understood?"

An Arab man in Palestinian headgear was frowning from his seat. "Rabbi, we have seen no weapons here for us. We must have weapons."

"No, Jamal, my friend. We have been over this before. You will have them if they are required."

The Arab frowned angrily. "I must know how we will have them. We must know the rules of engagement. You have not told us enough. We must know more."

More voices grumbled in agreement.

"I am getting to that," said the rabbi. "You all know me, and I know you. It is why you have been selected for this action. Do you really think I would not have your safety in mind? Have you ever known me to speak an untruth? You have been plucked from your mosques, churches, temples, and community organizations, all for the same purpose --- to stand up to the decrees with a unified voice. Disunity is fatal. I will repeat what I just said. There will be weapons only if they are needed as a last resort. They must not be our first line of defense. Your codes of conduct and mine abhor violence. We have talked of this many times before. Now is the time to put our resolve to work. This will be a civil disobedience, not a war."

"Jamal is only stating the obvious, rabbi," said a burly fellow in a Greek fisherman's cap. "What if the Brigades attack without provocation?"

"Weapons will be available if they are required. I have already said that," the rabbi repeated calmly. "We won't be the ones to attack or provoke, however. Is that clear?"

"When then?" demanded the tallest man in the room. Quayle guessed his attire and lilting accent suggested his origin as African. Standing, he said: "I am Moussa, a Kenyan. My family was arrested by 'dem last month. I not see my family again. Fuck 'dem, I say. We already wait too long."

"No," the rabbi said. "Listen to me, all of you. I will not kill a man just to kill a man. Do you understand? Not even for revenge. I promise you, they will not be willing to fire on us without some sort of cause. To that degree, they still fear a public backlash. Our spies inside the Directorate have told us that." The rabbi's eyes blazed. "So, it must be as I say," he said firmly, "or I will not be the one to lead you." In the silence, he waited. When he heard no one protest, he said: "Then here's how it will be: When the two prisoners are brought to the gallows, you will do nothing.

Whatever is to be done at the gallows will be done by others. Our job is to monitor the rear ranks of the Brigades and hold them in place so the crowd remains between them and the gallows. They will think they are containing us; in fact, we will be containing them. The crowd will be with us. They must be made to see we are standing against the Brigades. You must stand your ground. The mob must see that we are brave. Then they will have reason to be brave and join us."

"Only twenty-four of us against them, rabbi?" demanded a slender man, also in a *yarmulke*. "How will it be possible? What if the crowd does not stand by us? You ask too much of us."

The rabbi shook his head. "No. We know the cameras in the park will be broadcasting the executions. All the more reason to show them we are unarmed and then make our voices heard. We will demand release of these two innocents. The Brigades will always have more guns. We will never defeat them that way. It's never wrong to use non-violence to stand up to a bully. We must do this to prove to the public we are in the right."

Imam el Hamad broke in. "All wise men have urged this course. The great Mohammed, Jesus, Buddha. Rabbi Schulman is right. We must all have courage to do this without the force of arms, instead we will use our force of will."

The priest nodded toward the Imam. "We in the churches, temples, and mosques of the enclaves are united in this. We ask that you trust us. We must also ask that you have the courage to trust in the righteousness of your demands. These two young Saudi men are innocent. We demand their right to a free and open trial, so we may have a chance to provide the world with proof of who the true criminals are."

Despite these words, Quayle felt fear still clinging to the room. He tried to imagine himself in the shoes of these men. For an instant, he felt moved to join them in their vans, but he knew just as quickly this was not the way. He would be more useful doing what the rabbi asked. He was more certain than ever this is what Jack would want of him: to be a reliable witness.

Chapter Twenty-Nine

The car bomb had sent scores of frightened people scrambling from the ambassador's residence into the street. Firefighters were quick to arrive, followed by ambulances and a dozen squad cars from the 78th Precinct. In front of the ambassador's stoop, onlookers still strained to look beyond police barricades into the alley where the body had lain before being taken away. Those who had glimpsed the dead man thought he'd been Asian; for Cecil the sight of Tommy Sung sprawled in the alley had shaken her to the core. To her surprise, Cecil now saw Detective Navarro combing the spot where the body had been found, too occupied now, it seemed, to notice her. (So, she thought, the Brooklyn Borough was where he had been transferred!) Raisa, meanwhile, was nowhere to be seen amidst the crowd; she seemed to have vanished.

Cecil returned inside to find Genesee waiting for her in the hallway with a police officer. "This is Captain Singleton of the 78th Precinct," Genesee informed her quickly. "He needs statements from us."

"My people have your preliminary statements," the captain said, "but we need to consult with you both about some related matters. Would eight o'clock tomorrow morning be possible? I will have a dispatcher send a police car around. It will be strictly off the record."

Genesee looked at Cecil, then nodded. "Of course, captain.

Ambassador Longueille speaks highly of your precinct. Your men have been very thorough. We promise to provide you with as much help as we can."

As the officer left, Genesee began taking control. "Call Albany on a secure line," she ordered her aide. "I want Chief of Staff Cosgrove and his team down here right away. I will also need some space for a command center. Maybe the ambassador can find us something nearby."

Glasses and bottles of Perrier had been prepared for them in the library; it was just what Cecil needed, her throat raw from the bombing's aftermath; everyone's clothes reeked of fumes. When the door closed, the ambassador activated a satellite phone, tapped in a code, and handed the receiver to Genesee. She sat down and demanded Cosgrove. She cupped the receiver and motioned to the ambassador and Cecil. "Please give me a few minutes?"

The two of them stepped from the room and closed the door. Cecil knew what would be foremost on the governor's mind as she spoke with her chief of staff: the Directorate spy who had been reporting back to Shrum. Just what on earth was going on there?

The ambassador took Cecil's arm and led her down the hallway out of earshot of the state trooper guarding the door. "What do you know about that young man out there who was shot? My security team said you recognized him."

Cecil breathed an exasperated sigh. "Yes. He's the son of the Chinese ambassador to the United States. His name is Thomas Sung. An artist friend of mine has been mentoring him, acting as his American sponsor. I'm stunned, utterly stunned. When we were leaving Gramercy Park to come here, I saw him being taken in by the Brigades. This makes no sense."

"Did you see the others with him? My security team said two others in the alleyway escaped."

"I couldn't see faces, only others running away."

The ambassador fell silent, examining Cecil carefully. "This could be extremely important information. This man was not killed by my own security men; they are certain of it from the look of the wounds. The fatal shots entered from behind."

Cecil shook her head in confusion. "I don't understand."

"His accomplices executed him---to cover up Brigades' involvement. He may have been coerced into detonating this bomb."

"Yes. Good God," Cecil whispered.

The ambassador smiled grimly. "This may be the evidence we need to help clear the students they plan to execute tomorrow, if we can only find a way to prove the Directorate has been behind these bombings, not the insurgents as they are claiming." He gently touched Cecil's arm; she was trembling. "It's your very good fortune, my dear, that you and the governor weren't injured or killed out there. It was a narrow escape."

"My second one," Cecil said. "As I mentioned before, my husband's was an even closer call. It's all been so terrifying."

The ambassador nodded. "When Islamist insurgents were fighting to seize control of Algeria from the French, our capital of Algiers experienced bombings every day. Now, ironically, so many years later, my country's experiment with Islamist democracy is finally making progress, while your democracy is slipping away." The ambassador paused, then looked again at Cecil in earnest. "Worst of all, your tyrants are among you --- your powerful corporate and political elites. They already have keys to all the doors of power --- and to the safes ---yet still they want more. Meanwhile, your government allows them to act in their own interests and against those of the people --- a corporate takeover of government, as it were." He shook his head. "It's very sad for us foreigners to see, this silent tyranny eating away at the core of your democracy. Since my troubled nation's independence from France, we have seen more betrayals, terrorism, and deceits, too, but never with so little awareness or shame as you Americans are showing now. Your husband and his colleague, Jack Flyte, have been islands of inspiration for us --- and now your governor, too. We had almost lost hope that the oppression would be resisted."

Cecil looked at him. "Sometimes, I think Americans have become too spoiled, or complacent, to imagine deceit on a scale this size, much less finding courage to resist it."

Ambassador Longueille met her anguished gaze. "Others are no better, Mme. Quayle, believe me --- Americans may be blinded by their corporate oligarchies, but so are Islamists by their infernal tribalism, Zionists by their Masada complex, Indians by their cruel caste system. For my Islamist government to appoint me U.N. ambassador --- a non-Muslim with French colonialist blood --- is a remarkable development in itself. Each of us has something to learn from such moderation and modernization; the world would be a better place for it, don't you agree?"

Before Cecil could answer, the door to the library opened, and the governor's aide beckoned them back.

There, seated behind her desk scribbling notes, the governor seemed composed. She lifted her eyes. "It seems Mayor Shrum has left for Washington, so I'm going to do what I should have done when he first authorized these damn detention camps. Albert, cher ambassador, I have just checked with New York's attorney general. You mentioned to me a man detained in the Brooklyn compound is seeking political asylum and may have important information for us. The attorney general tells me because of your diplomatic status, under the new protocols governing stateless peoples you do have the right to personally interview any detainee requesting asylum. I want to accompany you into the Brooklyn compound to make certain you are allowed to conduct this interview."

"Tonight?" asked the ambassador.

The governor nodded. "Mayor Shrum isn't in town to interfere, and I don't think we can wait with executions scheduled for tomorrow."

"Then of course I will do as you suggest," the ambassador said with visible relief. "It is almost 11 o'clock now, however."

Genesee nodded. "If we arrive without notice, they won't be prepared for us. I suspect they won't dare turn us away if we arrive with a police escort. "Cecilia and Margaret," the governor interjected. "I want you to accompany us. We will need corroborating witnesses for this."

"Have you seen Raisa?" Cecil asked suddenly.

Ambassador Longueille nodded. "She disappeared just before police and media arrived."

* * *

The car's digital clock read 11:15 p.m. as they turned off the elevated expressway and entered the riverfront redevelopment district. Directly to their west, the lights of midtown were sparkling in the night, while to the north they could see the delicate filigrees of lights that defined the graceful spans of the Brooklyn Bridge.

"The 78th has just assigned two patrols to us as I asked for, governor," said the state trooper at the wheel. "As I mentioned, I think very highly of Captain Singleton.

"I have similar confidence from my brief encounter with him," Genesee said. "How far is the Columbia Street Waterfront District now?"

"Just another mile."

"How many gates?"

"Two. Main gate, and a service gate off Congress, just north of the redevelopment area along the river."

"All right. Let's go to the service gate. What sort of security will they have?"

The trooper consulted his satellite GPS. "Barricades, same as the main gate, only one man in the guard house. The whole encampment is under subcontract with a private security outfit, so it's technically outside the city's jurisdiction. The controlling entity is the Directorate."

"No city oversight at all?"

Genesee's aide handed her a folder marked Brooklyn Central Compound 2038 budget Document, Confidential. "The city provides it with some public monies, but it seems from these documents it's off the regular budget."

"The contract specifies only that this is for special services, effective in January of this year. Is this all there was in the council budget records, no supporting documents?"

Her aide nodded. "As I said, it deals with city security matters, so it's not part of the public record."

"That's convenient for Shrum."

The governor closed the folder. "Make a note that I want a full report on this."

"Yes, ma'am."

The trooper turned into the warehouse district, found the service entrance, and stopped at the barricades.

Genesee looked ahead at the rows of Quonset huts beyond the barricades. "This has the look of a Japanese internment camp after Pearl Harbor, for God's sake---it's a bloody prison in all but name."

A man in khaki wearing a sidearm came out of the gate house and walked to the trooper's window.

The ambassador leaned over to address the sentry. "I am Algerian Ambassador to the United Nations Albert Longueille. With me are Governor Genesee Wainwright and her party, here to see Superintendent Tashian."

The guard demanded their credentials and they waited.

Just when it seemed he might not return, the gates lifted. "Stop at Quonset 3, and wait there," the guard called out through the window of his booth.

At Quonset #3, they did not have long to wait. A rotund balding man with a black mustache tapped at the passenger window. Ambassador Longueille lowered it.

The man peered into the back seat. "What do you people want? Why wasn't I notified you were coming? It's late, my staff has left."

"We know it's after hours, but we have urgent business. I am Governor Wainwright." Genesee showed herself in the beam of the man's flashlight. "We have some questions to ask Superintendent Tashian about one of his detainees who has demanded political asylum with the Algerian Embassy. It's very urgent that he be interviewed."

"I am Superintendent Tashian. Who are these others?"

"Algeria's Ambassador to the United Nations Albert Longueille; also, my assistant Margaret Sensabaugh and Mrs. Benjamin Quayle. They are to be witnesses to the interview."

"You do understand, it's within my rights to insist you schedule a meeting another day through normal channels? You may also be unaware that we are not under any of your jurisdictions here."

The ambassador nodded. "We are grateful that you have agreed to speak with us. I would not ask for this meeting at this hour if I did not think it was urgent."

The superintendent opened the door for the ambassador. "The more people you take off our hands, the better, as far as I'm concerned. We're getting overrun, with no place to put new people as it is."

Inside, the superintendent stood at the head of a long table and looked down at them impatiently. "All right, I'm listening."

The ambassador withdrew a notebook from his suit jacket and opened it. "Under the United Nations High Commissioner for Refugees, you are obliged to permit me to interview anyone who has requested asylum through our Embassy's channels. One of your detainees has made such a request."

The superintendent looked at him blankly. "Which detainee?"

The ambassador opened the notebook. "His name is Ahmad Chadi, age 48, a resident of Brighton Beach, Brooklyn. He's been a naturalized American since the age of six, still with immediate family in the city of Algiers. He has been an upstanding American citizen with no police record, but claims he was about to be put under arrest for reasons that he says are politically motivated. It is clear that his fears have come to pass."

The superintendent broke in. "Yes, I know of this man. He is assistant to City Comptroller Urban Bartholomew, an important man in the city administration."

"Can you tell us then why he's being detained?"

Cecil watched the superintendent carefully. From his expression, the question was being weighed carefully, but obviously Tashian was not eager to cooperate. However, it was late, and here before him were the governor of the state and a high-level foreign diplomat.

"The Directorate does not provide us with anything but names, addresses and occupations," he said finally. "Our job is to hold people until their cases have been reviewed. Whatever happens to them is not our affair. We merely do as the Directorate tells us. All I know is the Brigades are to transfer him to the Directorate next week for indefinite questioning."

The ambassador's jaw tightened. "Then it is all the more urgent you allow us to interview him first. International law prohibits coercion or intimidation, direct or indirect, by the country of origin when sanctuary is sought. I will be relying on these people with me to be my neutral and official witnesses. Is this understood?"

The superintendent shrugged. "How you conduct your interview is your affair. In my own birth country of Chechnya, there are no trials, much less what you call political asylum. There is only death. I suppose it will cost me nothing to allow you to speak to this man, as long as you will vouch for me that as governor you demanded it."

***

Soon, Ahmad Chadi sat before them, a short, beetle-browed man with dark skin. He wore an orange jump suit stenciled "Detainee" front and back; it hung on his thin frame like an oversized semaphore. He peered warily at the group through horn-rimmed glasses, a bureaucrat through and through. The ambassador waited for Superintendent Tashian and the guard to leave, then withdrew a handwritten letter, unfolded it, and pushed it across the table in front of where the nervous man sat.

"M. Chadi, I am Ambassador Albert Longueille, chief representative to the United Nations from Algeria. With me are Governor Genesee Wainwright and several neutral observers. Would you kindly confirm you are Ahmad Chadi of Brighton Beach, Brooklyn, and that the document I have placed before you is your handwritten request for political asylum under the protection of the Algerian Embassy?"

The man lowered his gaze to the letter, then looked up. He pressed his spectacles back against his forehead with his thumb. "Yes, sir, this is the letter I wrote. I assumed they would not have permitted me to see anybody while I was here. I did not expect this. I am very grateful to you."

The ambassador consulted his notebook. "I have made

numerous inquiries after receiving your letter from my embassy in Washington. I see before your detention you held a key position in Comptroller Bartholomew's office."

"I've been his executive assistant since 2030 when he was first elected. I had previously served as his chief bookkeeper for the Metropolitan Transit Authority. Mr. Bartholomew liked my work and brought me over to City Hall with him."

"Why have you been detained?"

"I've been told nothing, except that I am to be questioned."

"By whom?"

"I don't know. A week ago, shortly after I mailed this letter to the embassy, the Brigades came and took me from my home. I had suspected I was being watched, so I decided to do this as a precaution. I am a careful man, ambassador. My family will tell you this. The Brigades brought me here." Chadi paused, his gaze fixed on the letter, then looked at the ambassador. "Are you recording this?"

"No, that's not allowed. I'm taking notes so I will have it all down correctly. You have nothing to fear from us."

He nodded.

"Why does the Directorate want to question you?" asked the ambassador.

Ahmad Chadi shook his head. "I have information about them, and about some of the city's highest officials, that could cost me my life if they knew I intended to report it to authorities."

The ambassador leaned closer. "Mr. Chadi, I will do all in my power to assure your safety. But you do understand, I must have details in order to take your case to my embassy. They will want to know why you believe your life will be in peril if you are not granted political asylum."

Chadi nodded, then his hands began to tremble. It was as if some inner voice was urging him on, even as fear outwardly gripped him. "Three weeks ago, I reported to Mr. Bartholomew I had discovered the city was using public monies to finance criminal acts---funds being transferred into a secret Directorate account intended for the purchase and deployment of explosives. He thanked me for coming to him with this information, and denied any knowledge of it. However, one day later, I was taken from my home and brought here by the Brigades. I have not been allowed to speak to anyone, even my own family. I now see I was a fool to think he could have been unaware of what was happening."

Governor Wainwright leaned forward. "Mr. Chadi, as you know, the Directorate is assisting the city with its anti-terrorism efforts. Could you have mistaken these funds disbursed to the Directorate for legitimate anti-terror efforts? Just this evening, for instance, I barely escaped a bombing myself. Tomorrow, there is to be a public execution of two men found guilty by a Directorate tribunal for bombing a West Side corporation known as the Enterprise. That happened scarcely a week ago. Don't you agree such bombers are murderers who deserve to be apprehended and punished?"

Ahmad Chadi bit his lip. His small eyes darted anxiously between the governor and the ambassador. "Everyone knows those Directorate tribunals are fixed. I tell you, I have been detained here for only one reason--- to silence me. Also, I am not the only Muslim in the Shrum administration being rounded up now for questioning. Inside city government, a citywide purge is beginning." He slammed a hand on the table. "I still have family in Algiers who will give me refuge. I demand to be joined with them. I fear for my life. You must believe me."

Longueille stared at him calmly, then nodded. "You must understand, Mr. Chadi, I must know everything in order to speak for you. I must have this proof you speak of."

The man dropped his gaze back to the letter. "How can I be

certain you will not go to the Directorate and report to them what I have just said?" He lifted his eyes and scanned each of their faces.

The ambassador shook his head. "That would be a violation of my diplomatic neutrality, a very serious offense for me and for my government, as well as for the governor. I am here because you have demanded asylum. I have an obligation to act for you with my government."

Chadi stiffened, then slowly, haltingly began to speak again: "I took the precaution of collecting records and notes of all the meetings that led to the Emergency Decrees, all of the weeks of discussions. There were secret city appropriations approved which those documents also show. It was always left to Comptroller Bartholomew to work out the details of those expenditures with the budget committees. I now realize he had to be aware of it all. I was a fool not to have realized that before I went to him."

The governor stared. "These expenditures would not be reviewed even by rank-and-file committee members?"

"No. Not even by the City Council. Only the committee chairman knew the purpose of these appropriations The items included any money spent on the detention camps; also the Directorate's secret criminal tribunals where the most dangerous terrorist suspects were to be tried." He paused. Chadi was now unburdening himself. "There is more. This off-budget money was also to be used to fund the Brigades' special operations units."

The governor looked at him. "I don't understand. Special operations units? To do what?"

With trembling fingers, Chadi pressed his glasses against his forehead. "I see I have already said too much. I don't know why I should trust any of you."

"Tell us," the governor insisted. "We're here to help you. The fact that you're telling us this could very well inoculate you against any retribution. As the ambassador has said, we are empowered under the asylum law to act on your behalf. I must say it's remarkable, disgraceful really, that a naturalized American has found it necessary to seek asylum in Algeria, a young Islamist democracy still trying to find its way. I am personally mortified to hear you say you fear political persecution by an entity of the American government."

Chadi let out a breath. "All right. The funds were to be secretly used to combat what they refer to as the insurgency --- anyone opposed to the Directorate's Emergency Decrees. The first requisitions were for plastique explosives; also for steel canisters and detonators. I have secured the requisitions in a safe place."

"For bombs requisitioned by the Directorate?" the ambassador declared, as if still not quite believing this.

"Yes, sir."

The ambassador and Genesee exchanged horrified glances.

From somewhere outside the compound, they heard the roar of motorcycles starting up, quickly followed by the whoop of sirens --- some new emergency possibly taking their police escort away.

"If you tell me where these documents can be found, you will have given me enough to take to my embassy, M. Chadi," Longueille said finally. "Meanwhile, I will do everything I can to have you released from here immediately."

"As will I," added the governor. She looked at him. "You have done a very brave thing, Mr. Chadi."

Chadi glanced down at the letter, finally shaking his head. "People become brave when they have no other choice. In my predicament, only a true coward would fail to act. I am no coward."

Chapter Thirty

At eight o'clock the next morning, Cecil and Governor Wainwright entered the 78th Precinct in Brooklyn and were escorted by Captain Singleton into a vacant interrogation room out of sight of the main squad room. Waiting for them was Detective Anton Navarro. He reintroduced himself to Cecil, then shook the governor's hand.

"I remember you, of course, detective," Cecil said, taking a seat. "It was a shock when I learned you were no longer assigned to the Manhattan Precinct and Jack Flyte's disappearance."

"No less a surprise to me, Mrs. Quayle."

"Detective Navarro and I were in the Police Academy together," Singleton interjected. "There's not a finer detective in the city. I am very pleased to now have him back in my own precinct."

Singleton tapped a finger anxiously. "I know you must be shaken by last night's events --- Mrs. Quayle, as well. I'm sorry I had to call you both down here. However, I feel personally responsible that this happened in my precinct on my watch. I can assure you, had I been notified of your presence here, we would have provided you with first-rate security at the scene."

"I'm afraid that was my doing, captain," Genesee said. "I would have had staff warn you at the checkpoint if I had not been worried about the mayor interfering. I learned too late from my friend Ambassador Longueille that the 78th Precinct was reliable. It's no secret Mayor Shrum and I are not on the best terms."

Singleton nodded. "The mayor, in fact, is precisely why I have asked to meet with you. He's become a huge problem for us. I wouldn't be surprised if he attempts to blame us for the security lapse, just as he's blamed other precincts for the recent Manhattan bombings."

"I will be happy to disabuse him of that idea," Genesee said sharply. "Please go on, captain."

"As we just discussed, Detective Navarro was abruptly pulled from the Flyte case and transferred here."

Navarro leaned forward. "Just before the Enterprise bombing, Mrs. Quayle, your husband was able to send me a memorandum by special courier. In it he implicated the Enterprise's security chief Robert Thompson in a plan to seize control of the company by skimming casino receipts. Your husband believed he and Mr. Flyte would be falsely blamed for the missing funds.

The very day I received the memorandum I was pulled off the case and transferred to the 78th. They confiscated all my case files, the memo along with it."

Singleton continued: "Since passage of the Emergency Decrees, the 78th has become a Siberia for officers the police commissioner doesn't think are toeing the line like Navarro. The Brigades' blatant encroachments on our community policing duties have been increasingly upsetting to borough commanders. Morale problems have been worsening all over the city. And if it gets back to the mayor or Commissioner Daggett that you and I have had this conversation, it will go very badly for us here."

"I admire your frankness, captain," Genesee said. "We were already aware of some of this trouble from our own sources; the eastern boroughs have become regular items on our cabinet agendas. However, we had not heard that relations had soured so completely with Daggett. We rather thought he would be defending his own people against the Brigades. Now more executions are scheduled for today. They are foremost on my mind now."

Singleton turned to Cecil: "We understand the man with the detonator who was killed at the ambassador's was known to you, Mrs. Quayle. Could you elaborate on that?"

Cecil sipped some water. "He's a young artist from Beijing, a son of the Chinese ambassador to the U.N. We have the same representation, Olivia Gardner Steele's Fifth Avenue Gallery, where he made his New York debut. He seemed a typical precocious young artist --- full of himself, perhaps political, but I couldn't say for sure. When the governor and I were leaving Gramercy Park yesterday as the roundup was starting, we saw him taken into custody by the Brigades. I am certain Olivia knew nothing about his role in the bombing and would be mortified to hear it."

Singleton made a note. "Our data base shows this Thomas Sung was facing deportation for overstaying his visa. It's a pattern we are discovering about all these recent bombings---the Brigades intimidating surrogates to plant explosives and cover their tracks. When the job was botched last night, Tommy Sung was executed so he could not point fingers."

Genesee shook her head grimly. "Unfortunately, this does not come as a complete surprise to us, captain. We have sources who have reported similar suspicions. But why are they committing such treachery? And who would give such an order?"

"An assassination of the governor would be just what the Directorate would need in order to call for imposition of some sort of citywide lockdown. Had it succeeded, the mayor, police commissioner, and city council would have had cause to put the Brigades in charge of counter-terrorism operations in all five boroughs."

At this, all four fell silent.

Finally, Genesee said: "You mean martial law?"

Singleton nodded gravely. "Using the Brigades instead of the

National Guard, whose mobilization would require your approval as governor."

"Do you have proof?"

"So far, the bombers themselves have had no connection to terrorist groups that we are aware of. Instead, they're people in trouble with the law forced to do the Brigades' dirty work, then eliminated afterwards --- either as Sung was, or by public executions such as the ones scheduled for later today. We believe the goal is to spread enough chaos throughout the city to justify extending the mayor's decrees indefinitely, which the public and the media so far have not resisted."

"This is treasonous!" Genesee exclaimed. "This is a war on every citizen of the city! And the mayor? Is he involved?"

"We suspect there's been regular communication between the Directorate and someone in the mayor's office immediately before and after every detonation, but so far we are still pursuing those leads. We have purposely kept the commissioner out of our own investigation. Our precinct budgets in the eastern boroughs have been cut to the bone by the City Council, and Mayor Shrum's been more than willing to go along with the Brigades taking more control."

"I can't believe the mayor could be unaware of the Directorate's complicity," Genesee said, staring at a stunned Cecil.

Captain Singleton nodded encouragingly. "You were about to say?"

Genesee shook her head. "No, go on with this, captain."

"We suspect he is not unaware," Singleton said. "And we feel the situation is dire. For all intents and purposes, the Brigades have become a private militia in the city, taking their orders from the Directorate."

He stopped for a moment and took a breath. His voice then rose with more urgency. "So far, we have been forced to conduct our investigation with no support or backup from any of our higher-ups. Meanwhile, the corporate consortium either does not know how much power the Brigades and the Directorate have been amassing under the decrees, or has made a bargain with the devil. Either way, the situation is intolerable."

"I am in total accord with you, captain," Governor Wainwright said. She removed her communicator from her bag. "In fact, I am certain Ambassador Longueille will be able to corroborate your accusations against the Directorate, but give me a moment."

She removed her communicator from her bag and began texting. Almost immediately came the reply.

She looked up. "Ambassador Longueille has just agreed to cooperate with your investigation." She replaced the communicator. "Late last night, as you may know, he and I drove with one of your motorcycle escorts to the Brooklyn Incarceration Center to interview a man in city custody awaiting interrogation by the Directorate and who had requested political asylum from the Algerian Embassy. He provided us with information about a black budget used secretly by the city controller to finance antiterrorism operations conducted by the Brigades, approved by the City Council and signed off on by the mayor. He can provide documentation. I am sure you understand this is a very delicate matter for the ambassador, captain, since he will be putting his diplomatic immunity in jeopardy if he is ever identified as the source of this information."

Singleton smacked his fist into his hand and exclaimed: "Best damn news we've had in months!"

"There's something more you should know, captain," Genesee said. "I have been warned there is ab informant in my office who's been reporting directly to Mayor Shrum. My people are looking into those reports as well."

Singleton said: "It's my turn to thank you for your frankness, governor. I also think it crucial for you, governor, to send word to the locals you are supportive of their efforts to resist the decrees."

Genesee looked at him puzzled. "The locals? Whom do you mean?"

"Citizen groups who have been secretly organizing for months to overturn the decrees. It would mean a great deal to them if they could count on you. As you know, New York's city police force isn't the only one facing privatization. It would mean a lot to New Orleans, Chicago, and Los Angeles to see a governor finally stop this insane abuse of power at local precinct levels."

Genesee paused. "As you must know, there will be jurisdiction problems if I attempt a state-level intervention. However, I have asked the attorney general to research my options. To stop enforcement of the decrees, I must have both cause and precedent. There was a state intervention by Governor Carey during the 1975 financial crisis, when the city nearly went bankrupt; he stepped in on an emergency basis and put the state in charge of city finances to avert a fiscal disaster. I've also asked Attorney General Romero for an executive order that would allow me to do the same to avert a civil liberties crisis of at least the same magnitude. If we can make the case the Directorate has been complicit in bombings, and that City Hall has been secretly financing those bombings, a state court should have no trouble granting an injunction against the city decrees. For the moment, at least, we have surprise on our side. The mayor isn't due back from Washington until tonight."

"Respectfully, I must ask, governor, if you are absolutely certain you want to take such drastic measures? There won't be any turning back once you decide. They will most certainly try to destroy you politically. For me, it won't matter. Even if I do nothing, I suspect at best my days in this precinct are numbered. For you...."

"Haven't they already just tried to assassinate me, captain?" the governor snapped. "Isn't that drastic enough?"

Chapter Thirty-One

Quayle exited the Brooklyn Academy of Music through a back door and watched as four unmarked black vans pulled out of the parking lot, taking the rabbi and his almost two-dozen hand-picked interveners to their assigned places at Prospect Park's Grand Army Plaza, site of the scheduled executions. He and the gypsy had slept only an hour before they'd been awakened by the rabbi and given instructions to act as reliable eyewitnesses first and foremost for what was about to transpire. They were both operating on pure adrenaline.

Nearby, Nicu fussed with a contraption he'd just dragged out of a shed, a dusty bicycle with a sidecar attached. He squirted oil on the chain, ran the chain back and forth over its rusted sprockets, then began wiping off layers of dust from the sidecar. Soon, his work had exposed a stenciled sign that read "Brooklyn Parks & Recreation." He hauled a shovel and rake out of the shed and dropped them inside, then looked up at Quayle with his gap-toothed grin. "You drive, boss," he said, and jumped into the sidecar.

Both wore green ball caps and matching uniforms embroidered with the words "Prospect Park Grounds Crew." Rabbi Schulman had given them the uniforms and the task of meeting a contact at Prospect Park's Revolutionary War memorial, Battle Pass. From there, they were to find their way back to the Grand Plaza Arch at the northern entrance to the park to await the scheduled hangings.

Nicu tugged the bill of his cap low over his eyes, tucked his beaded braids out of sight, and motioned for Quayle to turn onto Lafayette Street. Quayle pedaled, easing them into the flow of traffic that was crawling bumper to bumper along Lafayette heading south.

"You know where we're going?" Quayle asked.

"I know the area good, boss. I was groundskeeper at park. I know all about this place. I show you everything."

A motorcycle roared by, swerving between cars and weaving back and forth through congested traffic ahead. They reached Fulton Street, and the gypsy waved for Quayle to take it. It, too, was jammed with vehicles and walkers. Quayle started ringing his bell to warn people darting in front of him. It seemed the entire borough was out on the streets now, determined to occupy the park. On Vanderbilt, they passed a block of bars and restaurants jammed with people; some began yelling at a Muslim-throng of pedestrians walking just ahead of Quayle and the gypsy. "Go back where you came from, you rag heads," someone shouted. The marchers shouted back with cries of "no more blood, no more blood." It was a protest chant they'd been hearing erupting spontaneously everywhere they went. All along the route, it was easy to see groups taking sides, waving signs and carrying banners.

At the intersection of Vanderbilt and Flatbush Avenues, police barricades were blocking all side streets, preventing any vehicles from going anywhere but into the Grand Army Plaza and its roundabout. Here, the rabbi had told them, they should stay on Flatbush until they found the easternmost park entrance and their rendezvous point. Towering before them now was the

Soldiers and Sailors Memorial Arch, the city's answer to the Arc de Triomphe of Paris, where a dozen traffic cops stood. At the sight of their official park insignias, the cops waved them on, and as Quayle pedaled forward they could see another phalanx of local police surrounding a barricaded expanse of concrete encircling the arch itself. Inside the circle of uniforms stood the gallows, suspended within the arch a dozen feet above ground by a gleaming stainless-steel frame and portable stairs.

The midday heat was rising, the sky a smokey blue. The sun was almost overhead, a spectacular translucent ball of orange in the haze. Nearby, a ragged gang of boys clamored up the pedestal of a larger than life statue of Lincoln, fighting and shouting for the best possible view.

As Quayle pedaled back onto Flatbush, a loudspeaker boomed: "Observers must remain behind police lines. Violators will be subject to arrest. Repeat: No one is permitted beyond police lines."

Just ahead, on a broad expanse of emerald-green grass, two electronic screens had been erected, displaying black-and white still photographs of the same young bearded Saudis they had seen pictured on posters and banners lining Atlantic Avenue when they had first emerged from the tunnels.

The loudspeaker boomed again, repeating the warnings. This time, a hail of rocks shot up from a gang of workmen gathered at a construction site off the plaza, stones raining down on a cluster of Muslim protesters. Retaliatory chants began again, many more voices joining in now, the chorus taken up by others all around the Plaza: "No more innocent blood. No more innocent blood."

Nicu turned and shouted to Quayle: "Stay on Flatbush. We get into park by zoo, a little ways down now, boss. "

Quayle saw he could not have turned directly into the park here anyway, signs for the East Drive marked one way toward them. Instead, he merged with cars, trucks and pedestrians streaming down four-lane Flatbush, ringing his bell as pedestrians darted in front of him, some racing into grassy areas bordering the park. Now and then Nicu yelled "Hey, make way, we got official business."

The scene was as chaotic as any Quayle had yet seen. At the Willink Entrance down Flatbush, the narrow path was jammed with protesters as they jockeyed to get in, many dodging around to pass them. The path now passed by the Prospect Park Zoo, curved gradually back north, and soon reconnected with the clearly-marked and wider East Road. This was now teaming with walkers and runners moving as one back toward the Grand Plaza and, they would soon see, the vast open area called Long Meadow, central gathering place for the overflow crowds spilling in from Grand Army Plaza. Several hundred yards on, they arrived at a large stone resting against an embankment with a bronze plaque commemorating "Battle Pass, site of George Washington's ill-fated first Revolutionary War battle." Nicu raised a hand for them to stop.

All around, walkers and bikers streamed by in all manner of dress, jabbering in many languages, as diverse in ethnic makeup and appearance as the Brooklyn enclave itself. Nicu jumped from the sidecar and motioned for Quayle to park and join him with rake and shovel. "Do some work, man," he muttered under his breath, head down. "Look busy. We can't be sure where they got cameras on us, or when this guy's coming."

Quayle began raking brush and debris, uncertain what would happen next. In minutes, a very tall, rail-thin black man emerged from the throng and stopped at the plaque. At first glance, Quayle thought he was one of the Africans he had seen at the arts center, but on closer inspection he saw this was a different man. Wearing a beaded *kofia* on his head and a gray flowing robe, his large eyes scanned the bronze plaque; he must have been nearly seven feet tall. A communicator dangled from his waist.

As the rabbi had instructed, Quayle approached and said: "I have an urgent call to make.

May I use your phone?"

"Sorry, sar, no service here. You come with me, sar."

It was the response the rabbi had said to expect. Nicu exchanged a few whispered words with the man, who then quickly turned and rejoined the walkers, his *kofia* bobbing along above the crowd.

Nicu climbed back in the sidecar and Quayle pedaled off. Several hundred yards further on they passed an expanse of meadow marked Nellie's Lawn, and then arrived at Long Meadow. This huge expanse of green grass and shade trees was rapidly filling up with people pouring in from all sides of the park. Here, two more electronic screens displayed live shots of the nearby Grand Army Plaza and the nearly completed gallows, so the overflow crowds could see. Ahead, their gazelle-like contact strode swiftly across the grassy slope of the meadow, then along the macadam through a thick canopy of trees. Quayle was forced to pedal faster after him, finally finding him waiting under a thick stand of oaks. Ahead, further along the paved road, the Grand Army Plaza with its gallows was now looming before them again.

"What is your name?" Quayle asked.

"I am Kenyan man, named Moussa, sar. You have something for me?"

Nicu handed him a brown paper bag he'd pulled from the sidecar. Inside was a pistol the Kenyan quickly slipped inside his robe. His gaze went to the nearest electronic screen visible from where they stood. "They bring prisoners in soon. Big crowds all over now. Leave 'dis machine here or you not get through 'dem."

Nicu ran the pedicab in under the trees and concealed it behind a thicket of brush. The Kenyan hung back, then drifted away back into the trees as Nicu lead Quayle out of the meadow along the macadam of the north entrance to the Grand Plaza. As they reentered the plaza, they heard a loud cheer as a young bearded man jumped a barrier before the gallows. He was shouting and shaking a fist at the workmen standing high above him preparing the nooses. Two men in the uniforms of the Brigades suddenly appeared on foot from behind the barricades and lifted the man off his feet, carrying him away. From the crowd came jeers, then the chanting again began: "No more innocent blood; no more innocent blood."

Nicu scowled, shaking his head as the young man was taken away. "I know that guy. He a spy for Brigades. He make trouble so they can crack heads. All for show."

The Kenyan nodded. "Lies, always they lie."

Quayle stared blankly into the commotion. Before Jack's disappearance, he'd been indifferent to injustice; now, it seemed, injustice was everywhere he looked. He remembered the rabbi's instructions, that he and Nicu should serve as reliable witnesses to the executions, instructions identical to those Jack had given him before he'd left his cell. They were all doing their parts to build a case against the Directorate, that much was clear. He felt comfort in that, and the fact they all now seemed to be executing someone's carefully conceived plan.

Soon, they saw the Kenyan reappear at the eastern side of the Grand Arch. He had entered the heavy vehicular traffic now clogging the roads around the perimeter of the plaza, crossing the road with long, loping strides and ducking under the cover of an apartment building's awning.

Immediately, they heard familiar sounds of horsemen. They turned and looked along the path through the trees along which they had just come. From out of the Long Meadow, a long line of mounted Brigadesmen could be seen trotting through the break between the two lines of trees, helmets, body armor, and Plexiglas visors in place, reins and hard rubber batons in hand. They entered the plaza, scattering people out of their way, then began fanning out into a single line, squeezing the crowd closer to the barricades and police lines surrounding the arch.

"You there," one of the Brigadesman called out. A man staggered, then fell to his knees. The horseman spat on the ground as his horse barely missed trampling the fellow as he frantically crawled away.

Looking again across the Plaza, Quayle saw the flash of a flowing gray robe and a red *kofia.* The Kenyan was moving swiftly from one van to another, perhaps passing on the rabbi's final instructions.

Preparations at the gallows now looked complete, stairs in place so the condemned could be brought to the platform where two nooses now hung from ropes. In the pit of his stomach, Quayle felt the same dread he'd experienced when the Brigades had cornered Kidman in Central Park and, later, Rabinsky on Roosevelt Island. It felt to him like one execution too many. No more innocent blood, he found himself thinking.

Two ranks of uniformed police officers from the Brooklyn Borough's 78th Precinct stood at parade-rest before the barriers, while two others stood on either side of the stairs leading up to the scaffolding. Rounding the plaza now was a canvassed-roofed troop transport, unmarked but similar if not identical to the one Quayle and the gypsy had encountered when they had first emerged from the tunnels. Nicu had expressed no fear of the Metro police in that encounter. Yet why were they and the Brigades now acting as one? He started to ask, but Nicu was preoccupied, scrambling to pull a small hand-held video camera from between his feet and aiming it at the scene.

At the gallows, a captain of police stepped from the passenger's side of the truck and strode through the barriers surrounding the platform. Quayle recognized him as Captain Singleton, the same officer whose truck had been transporting the prisoners and who had intervened to prevent his and Nicu's arrest by the Brigades. Quayle stared at the scene in new confusion, for directly behind the captain came Detective Anton Navarro, his thin, angular face turning for an instant as the ranks of police snapped to attention. And why was he here? Was he still on Jack's case, or had he somehow been co-opted by the Directorate as well?

At a bank of microphones, both Captain Singleton and Detective Navarro stopped. At that moment, a mobile television truck entered the plaza from the rear and halted at the Bailey Fountain, its occupants scrambling out. At the film crew's appearance, the crowd began to jeer, raised a placard and again took up the chant: "No more innocent blood! No more innocent blood!"

Singleton raised his hand for silence. As the refrain died away, he withdrew a sheet of paper from his breast pocket. "I am Captain Singleton of Brooklyn's 78th Precinct. The prisoners being bought before you today have been convicted by a tribunal of the Directorate, the city's special homeland security agency, for conspiracy to commit terror in violation of Emergency Decree #7 and for unlawful association with terrorists in violation of Emergency Decrees #8 and #12."

Around the park, Quayle saw the electronic screens flash on; a camera operated by an unseen hand began to pan from gallows to crowd and back again. Across the side panel of the truck on whose roof a cameraman stood, CNN's call letters could be seen. The executions, it seemed, were to be broadcast live.

At that moment, the police line parted, allowing into the plaza two mounted horsemen led by a Brigadesman wearing silver epaulettes and clearly in command. The two halted before the gallows, watching as two prisoners were pulled from the truck and led to the gallows by two policemen. Their hands bound behind them, ankles in chains, orange hoods over their heads, the two were led slowly up the makeshift stairs to the scaffolding.

Quayle looked back into the sea of faces of the waiting crowd. Behind them, more and more horsemen were emerging from the Long Meadow. More also approached through both the park's eastern and western entrances, drawing up and halting directly behind the crowd's outermost perimeters.

The defiant stomping of feet resumed, the angry chants growing louder: "No more innocent blood! No more innocent blood!"

At the gallows, Captain Singleton ordered nooses placed around the necks of the condemned.

"No more innocent blood!" the crowd roared more loudly, urgently. One section of the throng attempted to surge forward but once again was blocked by the barricades and the upraised batons of the front ranks of police defending the gallows. Behind them, out of the Grand Meadow, came more horses and riders, the throng now completely hemmed in on one side by police, on the other by the Brigades, fifty Brigadesmen on horseback, more on foot, by Quayle's estimate, facing off against an equal number of police.

How many times had Quayle cursed enclave protesters, annoyed like so much of the city at the public-relations black eye their repeated chaos had caused? In the seconds before it was clear the trap doors were about to be sprung, the crowd fell silent. Quayle looked for some signs of action from the interveners' vans parked at the main exit points of the plaza, but there was none.

Captain Singleton stepped up to the lever beside the two nooses, but instead of springing the traps, he tore away the orange hoods from the heads of the condemned. The faces the crowd now saw were not those of the young Saudis students that had been plastered all over the borough. In their place, blinking out at the angry crowd, were two middle-aged men most in the crowd had probably never seen but Quayle knew all too well--- the Directorate's two most powerful and secretive inquisitors, Director of Inquiries Noel Gatwick and Chief Superintendent Simon Ross. Like the crowd, he stared in astonishment at the two terrified captives peering out into the angry mob as if waking from some terrible dream. House-sized images of their frightened faces flashed up on the electronic screens all around the park. Under their names, a single, damning word blinked: "TRAITORS."

Chapter Thirty-Two

Captain Singleton stepped to the microphone, his image on the electronic screens replacing those of Gatwick and Ross. In the next instant, live images of the throngs on Long Meadow and three other venues sprang up on the screens, tens of thousands of people still massing to witness the executions. Those multiple images were a far cry from the static single-camera work normal for the Directorate's surveillance operatives who so often managed to trick or bribe network and other news sources into running pure propaganda.

Quayle leaned down to the gypsy so he could hear him above the noise. "Who's controlling the cameras?"

"Our guys, boss," Nicu said, his gold tooth flashing. "They hacked into the Directorate command center. Next, they try to free Jack Flyte."

Quayle stared. "How do you know that?"

"Moussa, the Kenyan. He give me the news back there just now. He heard it from another runner out of the Directorate. Phones not safe now, boss. We got to use runners."

"You're sure about Jack?"

"Sure, sure, boss. They say he's off the drugs and ok enough to try."

"Good," said Quayle excitedly. "Very good."

Singleton began to speak to the crowd. "As commander of the Brooklyn Borough's 78th Precinct, I have an important announcement. Under a warrant signed by Attorney General Romero, I am placing these two men under arrest for acts of terrorism against the citizens of the state of New York. I order all units of the Brigades to stand down immediately. There will be no executions today."

Atop the gallows platform, two police officers from the 78th quickly disarmed the Brigadesmen attempting to take control of the prisoners. The crowd's confusion at seeing Gatwick and Ross, not the faces of the young Saudi students whose executions many had come to protest, was as evident as the Brigades'.

At that moment, a commotion arose along the western perimeter of the plaza. Two of the vans carrying the twenty-four interveners Quayle had met with at the Academy of Music rounded the Grand Arch and pulled up directly in front of the line of mounted Brigadesmen surrounding the crowd. The rear doors of the first two vans flew open and the first dozen men, led by Rabbi Schulman and Imam El Hamad of the Brooklyn Central Mosque, jumped into the street and abruptly turned. Linking arms, they faced the startled horsemen, blocking their way into the plaza. An identical scene was being repeated at the Grand Plaza's eastern perimeter, the second group of twelve leaping to the street from the two parked vans. They, too, quickly confronted a second cordon of horsemen positioned near the Grand Arch.

"Do not impede us," a mounted Brigadesman, in the silver epaulettes of a commander, shouted at Rabbi Schulman's group. He wheeled his mount into their faces, close enough to the bank of microphones for the loudspeakers to pick up his words. "Who are you people? Why are you blocking us? Identify yourselves."

"We are community leaders of this borough," the rabbi shouted back. "Do as the police say. Order your riders to disperse. We don't want you here."

"No, don't be fooled," Gatwick shouted from the gallows.

"These police have gone rogue, defying the Emergency Decrees. The men you really want are Saudi terrorists the Directorate's tribunal has just convicted of bombing the corporate headquarters of the Enterprise. We are innocent men, in the lawful employ of the Directorate, a private agency hired by the city of New York to help maintain security. By order of the mayor under Article 13 of the Emergency Decrees still in effect, and until further notice, the Brigades have authority to pre-empt all local police forces in the eastern boroughs."

"Order your riders to stand down, commander," Captain Singleton insisted again, his voice ringing out across all venues of the park through the loudspeakers. "Officers of the 78th, take these two men into custody."

The uniformed officers atop the gallows seized the two prisoners. At that moment, the Brigades commander wheeled his horse, raised his pistol, and fired a shot in the air. "No one move!" he cried. "We are taking these men into our own protective custody. Everyone stand aside and let us pass."

Rabbi Schulman, joined by his dozen companions, arms still linked, took a step directly into the path of the agitated horsemen. To the east of the Arch, the second group of interveners did the same, blocking the second cordon of Brigadesmen threatening to move in on the gallows to take control of the two prisoners.

Standing beside Rabbi Schulman, Imam El Hamad from the Central Mosque of Brooklyn, raised his own voice above the commotion: "We come here unarmed, exercising our lawful right to peaceably assemble in this public park. Our acts of civil disobedience pose no threat to anyone. We will not yield."

At Quayle's side, Nicu was squirming. "Brigades not gonna pull back, boss. Maybe they shoot somebody."

The Brigades commander's jaw stiffened. "You are impeding a lawful Brigades enforcement action." He pointed the barrel of his weapon directly at the rabbi.

Holding his gaze on the commander, the rabbi said calmly: "I am Rabbi Isaac Schulman of Brooklyn Heights Synagogue. At my side is Imam El Hamad of the Brooklyn Central Mosque. With us are other community leaders from the Brooklyn Borough. The men you now see assembled to the east of the Grand Arch are Father Kaminsky of the Brooklyn Catholic Diocese and Pastor Jeremiah Stevens, president of the borough's Council of Protestant Churches, joined by ten of their congregates. Is this what you want, commander, for the world to see your men shooting down unarmed religious and community leaders, when all we ask is that these prisoners be fairly tried by legitimate courts instead of some secret Directorate tribunal?"

"These men may be unarmed, commander," Captain Singleton called out, "but we are prepared to return fire if you are foolish enough to challenge us."

Nicu suddenly handed Quayle his hand-held video camera. "You record them now. I be back."

Quayle tried to stop him, but the gypsy had already ducked under his hand. Slipping into the crowd, soon he skirted the westernmost flank of the cordon of distracted Brigadesmen and headed for the stand of trees where they'd parked the pedi-cab. The gypsy dragged out the contraption, jumped on, and began pedaling furiously away back toward the Grand Meadow.

Activating the camera, Quayle aimed back toward the gallows.

To the north along Flatbush Avenue, sirens began to wail. In moments, a black limousine appeared, escorted by police motorcycle units. It rounded the plaza and rolled to a stop behind the barricades. To Quayle's astonishment, Genesee stepped out and moved quickly to the microphones, flanked by two uniformed State Police officers. Her sudden arrival and the ensuing commotion appeared to have been enough to allow the stalemate between the mounted Brigades and the rabbi's police-backed groups of interveners to hold.

Looking out over the mass of people, Genesee began to speak in a firm, authoritative voice: "People of Brooklyn. I am Governor Wainwright. I have just signed an executive order immediately suspending the city's Emergency Decrees. All executions ordered by the Directorate under those decrees are hereby declared null and void, including those of the two Saudi men originally scheduled to be executed here today. The two men you see before you, the Directorate's Noel Gatwick and Simon Ross, are not these men. They are masterminds of a citywide plot to spread terror and chaos through all the boroughs, a plan intended to justify imposition of citywide martial law. These top leaders of the Directorate are to be placed under arrest, their cases remanded to the city's Joint Terrorist Task Force for prosecution before the authorized federal court of the Southern District."

Cheers swept over the throng. The full meaning of the governor's words were now becoming clear: The hated decrees were being suspended, as were all executions!

The governor went on: "I will look to the Task Force to ensure justice is done in this case, and in the case of the two young men we believe the Directorate's secret tribunals falsely accused and convicted of the Enterprise bombings. There will be no more searches without warrants, random roundups, or secret trials by the Directorate. This I pledge to you"

The crowd burst into sustained cheers. On the ubiquitous electronic screens, jubilation was erupting all across the park.

Suddenly, out of the mob stepped a bearded Muslim dressed conspicuously in black robe and knitted skullcap. Addressing the governor, he said: "Madame Governor, I am Sheik Kaleem Jamil, a naturalized American citizen and a lifelong resident of Brooklyn. I was detained and tortured by the Brigades, then released when my family was permitted to prove my citizenship. We want to hear from these two men you are arresting. We demand that they be required to speak. We will not disperse until we have heard them admit their crimes. How are we to know this is not all a trick, that you are not in league with them?"

The crowd sent up a roar. "They should be made to confess and be hanged now," cried an old man standing close to Quayle, shaking a fist. "Why do we wait?"

The mounted Brigadesmen reined back, struggling to hold their ground as the crowd began closing ranks behind the interveners, linking arms to form a more formidable wall of resistance before the gallows.

Media helicopters now came chattering in overhead, three aircraft in all, fuselages displaying news-station call letters. Swifter, more agile, police jetcopters soon buzzed them and turned them away, forcing them out of what must have been a designated no-fly zone around the Grand Arch.

"I assure you, Imam, this is not a trick," the governor shouted as soon as the noise overhead began to abate. "From this time on, all of the eastern enclaves, including all citizens of the eastern boroughs, will be under the protection of the 78th Precinct, backed by special units of the state police. As of now, all laws of the state are again in force here, with all appropriate due-process guarantees that existed before the decrees."

"You have no right to suspend the decrees," cried Simon Ross, the Directorate's superintendent, the agency's highest authority. The noose still slung loosely about his neck, his hands remained tied behind him, his round pink face contorted with anger as he addressed the crowd. "The decrees are city ordinances, lawfully enacted by the City Council and signed by the mayor. I demand you inform Mayor Shrum before you take any actions against us."

Without glancing back at the gallows, the governor retorted: "Under the precedent established during the City of New York's financial crisis of 1977, it is within my power as governor to intervene for the greater good of both the city and the state. This threat to the civil liberties of free citizens of the city of New York is a threat to the rights of all citizens in this state, one at least as dire as that long-ago financial crisis. I will not stand by and allow this unconscionable subversion of the rule of law to go any further."

A single rank of Brigades pushed forward, rubber batons of its riders raised. Clearly preparing to charge the crowd, the lead commander raised a hand to order them forward.

The rabbi and his men, backed now by the crowd, stayed still, arms locked. "We will not yield," cried the rabbi.

"Brigades, disperse!" Captain Singleton shouted again into the microphones. "My officers will fire on any Brigadesman who harms any citizen. You have heard the governor. Under her executive order, the 78th Precinct and the State Police are now the lawful authority here."

Directly behind Quayle came a new commotion, the sound of horses squealing. Quayle had never heard such a sound of panic before. He whirled and saw riders furthest from the gallows fighting to keep control, their curses and whips having no effect. One after another the horses reared, wheeled, and galloped away from the Arch, back toward any open expanse of meadow or pavement that offered room for escape. Rider after rider was unhorsed as more and more of their mounts squealed and bucked in panic. Suddenly from the crowd came raucous cheers, then incongruous peals of laughter as every electronic screen in the park lit up with the cause of the equines' consternation. A flock of giant birds, five feet tall at the shoulder, taller still at neck and head, came rushing and squawking out of the trees --- emus, Quayle guessed, set loose somehow from the park zoo. Close behind came Nicu, snapping a buggy whip, the long ungainly strides of the birds eating up ground as they charged ahead in a single flock toward the closest lines of startled horsemen like predators closing in on a larger prey. Nicu whooped at the animals as he pumped the pedals of his pedi-cab as fast his short legs would go, forcing the birds on with clear purpose. Horsemen who had given no attention to defending their mounts' blind spots, found themselves helpless as the birds bore down at them from the rear, scattering riders and horses alike.

"The emus are coming, the emus are coming!" a fat man in a ball cap whooped gleefully.

Quayle lost sight of the gypsy as the havoc continued. All over the park, the crowd could be seen fleeing stampeding horses and charging birds. Others in the crowd took up the taunting chant: "The emus are coming! The emus are coming!" Shots suddenly rang out, Brigadesmen still aboard their erratic mounts firing point blank at the attacking birds. Their wild firing only spooked their horses further.

"This is a trick," the Directorate's Simon Ross cried from his place at the gallows, microphones easily sending his angry voice across the park through the loudspeakers. "There are jihadists in your midst. This is only a diversion. Do not yield to this ruse."

Captain Singleton glared at Ross. "Take them into custody," he shouted to his officers on the gallows.

"Wait!" a voice called up from the crowd, demanding a microphone. Quayle saw it was again Imam El Hamad of the Central Mosque. When he had his microphone, he raised a hand and addressed the governor. "My friend Sheik Kaleem is right to be worried. How can we trust any of your words when officials in City Hall and the halls of the state government have been deaf to so much of the suffering in the eastern enclaves for these many months? How shall we know you will keep your word when all our past calls for help have been met with indifference, when our suffering has been greeted even by so many of our fellow citizens elsewhere in the city with ridicule and scorn? Shame, I say! Shame on you, and on them!"

"I can only urge you to judge me by actions," Genesee said. "Beginning tomorrow, I will bring my personal assurances of solidarity to all the churches, synagogues, and mosques of the three eastern boroughs, also to all civic groups, fraternal organizations, and community centers. I will hear your grievances, I will do all I can to assist you; these will not be empty promises. We must stand together against this tyranny. Down any other road lies certain failure. I know you have suffered, and I am prepared to do all in my power to see appropriate reparations are made."

Appearing surprised, Imam Hamad paused, then answered: "You will be welcome in our places of worship, governor. Indeed, we are commanded to open our doors to anyone who offers to come in peace. It will be our honor. "

"And ours," called out Rabbi Schulman.

Singleton called to his men atop the gallows: "Officers, remove the prisoners at once."

A new wave of emotion swept the crowd as Gatwick and Ross were forced down the gallows' steps and back into the troop transport that had brought them.

Quayle turned. Behind him, the Brigades' leaders began calling for their men to regroup. Those who had been unhorsed caught their animals and remounted, galloping to rejoin their still-mounted squads. Two by two, side by side, they rode back up the macadam from the Grand Meadow, their commander again easily recognizable by his silver epaulettes shouting for them to follow him back toward the Arch.

Quayle could guess their goal: to break through the police lines and retake the prisoners.

But then something happened that at first only Quayle seemed to notice.

To one side of the gallows stood the statue of Civil War General Henry Warner Slocum. From its pedestal, a young boy dropped silently into the crowd. Frail, clothed in a ragged robe, he could not have been older than fourteen. At that same moment, the cordon of police around the Arch was pushing forward through the crowd to solidify their stand against any further advance to the gallows by the Brigades. Bomber! Quayle thought, as he saw the boy rise ominously from his crouch. At that instant, he saw Moussa, the tall Kenyan, lope out of the crowd, shoving people aside, heading straight for the boy. Quayle turned his camera on the scene just as Moussa caught one of the boy's frail arms. The boy shouted in Arabic, but Moussa bent over and tore open the boy's cloak. Taped to his small body appeared to be a suicide belt packed with explosives. The boy clawed at it, struggling to activate it, but the Kenyan caught at the boy's hand and pried open his fingers. The boy lunged and broke free, heading for the barricades and the governor. Without thinking, Quayle dove at the boy from behind, tackling him around the legs, bringing him down just feet from where the governor and Captain Singleton stood before the microphones. The boy's hand groped inside his ragged cloak again, his frightened face growing taught. His fingers twisted, then twisted again, but there was no explosion.

From the nearby crowd came gasps. Imam El Hamad rushed over and grabbed the struggling child. He said in Arabic as he pointed to Quayle sprawled on the ground, loud enough for the loudspeakers to pick up: "*As-salamu alaykum*" In English, he seemed to be repeating the same sentiment of praise for Quayle's benefit: "Peace be upon you." He turned then and shook the boy by the shoulders. "Speak, boy! Who has told you to do this?"

The boy shuddered, his sharp black eyes darting left and right.

"Speak, I tell you," the cleric cried again.

The would-be bomber finally turned. He stared for a long moment at the line of horsemen now looming above the heads of the crowd, their mounts now at a dead halt. Trembling, he lifted a finger, pointing directly at the Brigades commander still sitting tall atop his chestnut horse. Epaulettes flashing, the commander raised his pistol and fired over the heads of the crowd. A spot the size of a bindi appeared between the boy's startled eyes as the bullet struck, then widened into the shape of a crimson star. The boy tumbled back into Quayle's arms. Officers of the 78th Precinct, their own pistols raised, rushed forward through the rabbi's men. Two dragged the commander of Brigades from his saddle and disarmed him. Other police officers commanded the Brigadesmen to drop their weapons. Those who resisted were quickly subdued. Across the electronic screens, identical scenes could be seen playing out elsewhere in the park.

The emus, like the apparitions they had first appeared to be, had vanished, perhaps escaping to some distant corner of the park where they could be corralled. In the chaos, the gypsy and the Kenyan, too, had disappeared.

Quayle could imagine the *Post's* sly headline now: "Governor Gives Prospect Park Executions the Bird."

That might be as deep as the co-opted fourth estate might go --- trivializing another bloody incident as just one more sensational but easily replaced spectacle.

Except this time the governor was involved, as were hundreds of citizens, some of them prominent and powerful community leaders; the mayor, too, could soon be implicated in a burgeoning scandal.

"No," Quayle thought. "This time they can't ignore us."

As this collective noun passed through his mind, he felt an almost imperceptible, yet profound, shift. His allegiance no longer belonged to the power brokers. It belonged to "them," people he had so rarely --- if ever --- considered his equal, the distressed, angry crowd that now stood in noisy solidarity around him, once again shouting "no more innocent blood."

Chapter Thirty-Three

Quayle stepped off the cable car of the Roosevelt Island funicular onto the Manhattan platform and watched as his escort, one of Captain Singleton's plainclothes detectives, vanished down the escalator into the mid-afternoon sunlight. The escort had helped him thread his way from the chaos of Prospect Park through a series of back-street borough neighborhoods to Queens. Finally, they had passed safely through the Roosevelt Island checkpoint and boarded the overhead tram, which took them over the East River to the 60th Street Station. Now, a black limousine pulled up, its driver opening the rear door for Quayle, briskly motioning him inside.

Cecil waited anxiously. Beside her sat a woman in a *hijab* partially covering her face. Cecil threw her arms around Quayle's neck and wept softly. "You look awful, you smell awful, but here you are, thank God." Her voice was trembling. She stared at him and hugged him again. "We weren't sure you would be able to escape the Prospect Park mob. News reports made the situation seem so grim, like the Brigades were trying to regroup...." She gave him a worried look. "Are you all right, Ben?"

"Exhausted is all...very exhausted. My injuries weren't as bad as they claimed, though; I think they made some of them up. I'm so glad to see you, C, so glad to be free." He paused, struggling to clear his thoughts. "The borough police are doing their best to maintain control in the enclaves, but there's still a hell of a lot of chaos over there."

The woman in the *hijab* lowered her face covering. "I'm Raisa Amin. Do you remember me, Mr. Quayle?"

"Yes, of course, the Kidman intervention. I gave your business card to my wife before the Enterprise bombing."

Cecil's eyes brimmed again with tears. "Thank heavens you did. I don't know what I would have done without her. She's been my guardian angel."

"The gypsy was ours, Mr. Quayle. One of our most resourceful agents. He didn't tell you?"

"Not much of a talker, that Nicu. I didn't realize how organized you and your people were until he took me to the Academy of Music. The insurgency's appeal is growing fast. I see that now. It's no wonder the Directorate fears you."

The car sped off. Quayle and Cecil hadn't spoken since she'd left Albany, and to Quayle it seemed an eternity. She began explaining what happened since then: her own interrogation by Directorate agents; the chaotic Gramercy Park roundup; the barely averted assassination attempt on the governor at Ambassador Longueille's Brooklyn residence; finally what they had learned at the Immigrant Processing Center about Mayor Shrum's black budget. She paused before blurting out the most damning information: "We've learned the Directorate is secretly behind the bombings."

Quayle nodded grimly. "When the gypsy told me that, I couldn't believe it at first. Then I remembered. At the Racquet Club, the Brigades disarmed an undetonated bomb in Jack's locker and tried to arrest one of the housekeeping staff for it. The poor woman was so frightened she swallowed cleaning fluid just to avoid being interrogated. The bastards claimed she was connected to the insurgency. Now it all makes more sense."

Raisa nodded, her dark eyes flashing in the bright sunlight. "They wanted to create a personal threat to show you why you needed to support the decrees."

Quayle glanced out the window. "Where are we being taken?" His face had turned ashen, distrust lingering from his traumatic week of interrogation.

"To Chloe Rothschild's at Gramercy Park," Cecil said. "She's loaned us her driver and car for as long as we need them. I didn't have time to tell you she was at Genesee's Albany fundraiser."

"The retired actress? She must be over 90 now." He pressed a palm against his forehead. His temples were throbbing again, another persistently recurring aftermath of his ordeal "Yes, I remember now. You asked to do her portrait, and she agreed."

"Active and as feisty as ever, a huge fan of Genesee's. She's also offered us one of her guest rooms as long as we need it."

"Why can't we just go home?" Quayle asked.

"The townhouse is being watched by the same Directorate agents who detained and questioned me while you were in custody. They wanted to know what I knew about Jack." She took his hand again. "Look at me, Ben? You're so pale. Are you sure you're all right?"

Quayle nodded, just half listening. His thoughts had turned back to the Directorate's rows of cinderblock cubicles, holding people nobody seemed to have missed. Even the social media had gone silent amidst the rising tide of roundups and disappearances, relatives of the detainees apparently too afraid to speak out and risk their own detentions. Paranoia in certain circles was becoming contagious.

"I'm worried for Jack," Quayle said abruptly. "I haven't heard anything since I escaped the Directorate. He refused to leave with us, afraid it would bring out a full-blown Brigades search party. Raisa's man, Nicu, was a lifesaver." He looked at Cecil grimly, his temples pounding. "This ride is splitting my head. Will we be there soon?"

Cecil matched his anguished look with one of her own. "What have we gotten ourselves into, Ben? The entire order of things has been turned upside down. So much has changed in such a short time. I want our old life back." She stopped. "That's an absurd hope, isn't it? Who can we possibly trust now?"

Raisa looked at Cecil. "You can trust the insurgency, I promise you that much --- and Governor Wainwright and Ambassador Longueille. I cannot tell you how much we appreciate what you both have done for us, Mme and M. Quayle. By now, you must realize we have all become allies. Those of us present in this car are most certainly bonded by this understanding. We are in something like wartime now."

Quayle and Cecil looked at each other. Raisa was clearly speaking the truth.

The driver exited FDR Drive and headed for Lexington Avenue. In the streets ahead and around them, there were no signs of the chaos occurring scarcely a mile away across the river. Quayle glanced down at a dried spot of blood on his sweatshirt --- the young boy's. He had never felt so clearly the disparity between these two worlds that were now so rapidly breaking apart.

Just ahead, through the car's front window, they could see a police helicopter move in low from across the East River, then hover over the rooftops of nearby Bellevue Hospital, probably, Quayle conjectured, bringing in the body of the boy. He tried to clear his mind of the dimming light in the dying boy's eyes. He knew he must stay focused. There was still much to be resolved.

***

In the outer foyer of Chloe Rothschild's Gramercy Park mansion, a uniformed guard announced their arrival. Inside, they passed down a hallway of red velvet drapes and exquisite art and entered a high-ceilinged morning room. There, Chloe greeted them dressed in a two-piece silk tunic with black pants and elaborately embroidered slippers. Her snow-white hair was done up in an imperfect bun, wisps of silver hair out of place. One pale hand rested on the silver handle of an ebony walking stick. Despite her advanced age, she was still the elegant actress Quayle remembered from her countless film roles, from a young Eleanor Roosevelt to the heedless and cruel Madame Defarge. Her clear blue eyes still sparkled with the same fiery, often defiant luminescence of strong women. Cecil went quickly to her, leaned down and kissed her cheek. "I've brought Ben back safe and sound. We're both so grateful you've given us refuge."

"Forgive me for not getting up," she wheezed in her trademark throaty rasp. "I must save my energy." She looked at Quayle carefully. "That boy armed with a bomb, how dreadful. They've had the two of you all over the television screens all afternoon. You're quite famous."

Quayle tightened his lips. "They intentionally sent him on a suicide mission. The bomb didn't detonate. Did they report that?"

"Of course not," Chloe said. "They called him a terrorist, as if he could be. Imagine. Just a little boy."

"It was identical to the bomb at Ambassador Longueille's," Cecil interjected. "Olivia's protégée, Tommy Sung, was executed, so he couldn't testify to what the police are now sure he was forced to do."

"It sounds like you are learning the truth now," Chloe said. "Soon the world will know it." She reached out and patted Cecil's arm. "You are not alone, my dear. I am completely supportive, as are many of my well-connected friends. After today there are a lot of us who will not rest until there's a just end to this awful business."

Throughout this exchange, Raisa Amin had been silent; she and Chloe appeared to be acquainted, though neither had made an effort to acknowledge the other. Chloe turned to Raisa and said: "My dear. Is everyone aware of the fact Ambassador Longueille is your own kin?"

Raisa blushed. "There's been no need for that."

"But there is," Chloe said huskily. "If they attempt to arrest you, you must ask your uncle for diplomatic immunity."

"I could never endanger him like that," Raisa interjected. "They would assume at once he was working with the insurgency."

"My dear, the ambassador insists on it. Besides, they can't take retribution against him as long as his own government stands behind him; he's told me himself he's been assured by his superiors the government of Algeria will stand behind whatever he chooses to do to protect their own people in New York from this treachery."

Chloe turned to Quayle: "The ambassador also tells me Governor Wainwright now has clear proof Mayor Shrum is using sheltered tax funds to finance secret Directorate operations, including these bombings."

Quayle nodded grimly. "We were just discussing this on the way over. They are truly diabolical."

Chloe stiffened. "Listen to me. All of you remain in grave danger, I am sure of it. It's why you must allow me to offer you refuge. They won't dare arrest me, even if they learn I am helping you. They know I am a hornet's nest they dare not kick over."

"I wouldn't be too sure of that, Chloe dear," exclaimed a voice from the next room.

The double doors leading into the library now stood open. In the passageway, the tall and gaunt figure of Jack Flyte stood motionless. Two men in suits, briefcases in hand, moved past him, strode to the front foyer and let themselves out.

Quayle and Cecil looked at Jack, speechless. Now clean-shaven, the Enterprise chief executive was dressed in plain gray slacks, white dress shirt. His expression was alert, not dulled by the effects of drugs as Quayle remembered him slumped over in his chair inside the Directorate's makeshift cell. He seemed to have just showered. His black hair was damp, combed straight back, amplifying the paleness of his hollowed cheeks.

Cecil jumped up and embraced him. "You're here. I can't believe it. The police were able to say only that they had information you were still alive."

Jack kissed her cheek, then reached over and grabbed Quayle by the shoulder. "I'm so glad to see you, old friend. You can't imagine how glad."

"We can all imagine, for God's sake," Quayle said softly. "But how did you manage it?"

Jack nodded toward Raisa, then went to the side board, uncapped a Perrier, and drank it down. "Two of Raisa's men came to my cell late last night. At first I thought they were officers of the Brigades, taking me out to be executed. There were rumors prisoners were being hanged. By then I'd started refusing food, and I had been told there would be nothing they could do to spare me if I persisted in defying them. Instead, I was taken into the old subway tunnels. There, they had a horse waiting for me and a Brigademan's uniform to wear. The tunnels were dark, all lights extinguished. We had to go by flashlight. I don't know how long we rode before we finally reached the Brooklyn side. Still riding, we went half a dozen blocks to a building just off Flatbush Avenue, the Brooklyn Academy of Music. There were crowds everywhere. It wasn't until I was led inside that I knew I was safe. An hour later Raisa and her people came for me in a car. She explained the details of the insurgents' plans to rescue the students the Brigades planned to hang, and how the Directorate's top men had already been taken hostage in their place." His hand shook as he put down the empty water bottle. "When the faces of Ross and Gatwick appeared on the CNN screens, arrested, I couldn't believe my eyes. The scope of the thing." He looked at Raisa. "A truly astounding feat."

For the first time, Raisa smiled. "There was a multitude of others. I am merely one among many."

Chloe leaned forward and examined Jack, concerned. "I've called a doctor to come have a look at you. Who knows what things they might have done to you!"

Cecil reached over and rolled up Jack's sleeve; needle marks tracked up his arm.

"Injections, pills," he said dismissively. "They had worse methods for others, undocumented immigrants they'd rounded up and weren't afraid to bloody up to get information about the insurgency. We could hear their screams. I just told the FBI all this. You needn't worry about me. In a short time, I'm sure I'm going to be all right."

"Can any of these federal agents be trusted?" Raisa asked worriedly.

Jack slowly nodded. "Before the FBI came just now, I was on the phone with the governor. She warned me the mayor's office was compromised now --- top to bottom, all the way from the city council and treasurer's office to the police commissioner. Only the 78th Precinct in Brooklyn and the Manhattan FBI office are reliable. She's working with them, also with Attorney General Romero and the federal prosecutor for the Manhattan District. She's determined to get to the bottom of all this."

Cecil nodded. "Raisa and I have been with her and Ambassador Longueille since yesterday. Still, no one knows the Directorate's exact long-term purpose." In exasperation, she said, "What could these horrid people really want?"

Without hesitation, Jack answered her: "Under the city's Emergency Decrees, the FBI's special terrorism task force now believes their intention is to transform the consortium into a corporate oligarchy, protected by the Directorate and the Brigades, an Ayn Rand sort of free enterprise city-state in which New York's most powerful corporations, the Enterprise included, can conduct business unshackled from all city regulation, taxation, and public oversight. Casinos of a merged Enterprise and Sun-Yung Resorts would all be exclusively licensed by the city comptroller's office, for all intents and purposes becoming cash cows for the city, the consortium, and the Directorate, a triumvirate of secretly unified interests. The Directorate would then control disbursements of all monies drawn from the consortium's Swiss bank accounts. Even before the Wall Street financial bailouts way back in 2008, there had been many signs of this coming --- a secret corporate city-state, clandestinely run, operated independently of normal governmental constraints --- much like Vatican City, accountable to no one." He looked at Quayle with chagrin. Slowly he shook his head. "I was so consumed by our own empire building, Ben, I didn't see any of it coming, to be honest --- yet there it was, right under my nose in the guise of Thompson, an ex-CIA man." He groaned softly. "I'm doubly ashamed, since you warned me he couldn't be trusted. It's so much like the financial trap Carmody set for me twenty years ago with that loan to help start the Enterprise. All along, he knew he would eventually use it as leverage to force me to cut the Teamster's locals out of all future contracts on the West and East Sides docks, effectively undercutting my father and everything he'd built for the union movement, a lifetime of hard organizing work. I know in the end that's what really killed him." At this, Jack winced. His parched lips trembled. He picked up another water bottle and gulped from it. "So when Rabinsky discovered the casino receipts were being secretly diverted to Swiss accounts, it was clear Thompson planned to blame me, as well as you, Ben. I knew then I needed to buy time to work out a plan for us." He passed a hand over his perspiring forehead. "As I told ben, the night of my birthday party, I let everyone think I'd gone over the railing. I escaped, leaving the parking through my private entrance."

Chloe stirred, looking at Jack intently. She put her cup down in its saucer. "Shrum," she said, expelling the name as if it were caught in her throat. "He's the most dangerous one here. I'm sure there's no way you could see the whole picture, his whole plan. He despises anyone who dares oppose him, rich or poor--- and he won't be happy until he's privatized every public service in the city for his own personal gain and finds a way to control everything."

Quayle added sharply: "It must have been particularly annoying to him when he learned you opposed the decrees and planned to take your concerns to the consortium. I can just imagine Shrum's reaction to that."

Chloe cleared her throat. Indignantly, she said: "I had a run-in with him myself a year ago when I was on the City Film Board. He was secretly working to kill a grant application we had before us for a public-service documentary exposing rent-control manipulation in the city. A group of Shrum's pals owned most of the rent-control properties in New York. I knew exactly what he was worried about. Someone close to him in City Hall was tipping off anyone in a position to do favors for him about upcoming vacancies. His Wall Street cronies stood ready to buy up thousands of properties as soon as Shrum persuaded the City Council to lift all rent-controls, which a few weeks after the board's vote they did. Their kickbacks were going to Shrum. The week before the vote, I told the Film Board what my reliable sources had told me about this. A few nights later, two of Shrum's thugs showed up at my front door. They threatened foreclosure for code violations if I didn't help kill the grant. I told them to go to hell." Her pale lips quivered. "It didn't matter that I reported the intimidation attempt to the board. The other board members caved in. They all sided with the mayor.

Still, I never imagined he'd stoop this low, countenancing bombings to kill and terrorize his own citizens. That just goes to show how naive an old lady can be. He's worse than any terrorist; he's a traitor to his own city."

Jack looked at her, his simmering rage barely concealed. "Do you feel well enough to come aboard the Starfire with us tonight? We're going to need all the reliable witnesses we can find for what we have in mind. We're about to give our longtime mayor a surprise."

Her blue eyes flashed. "I have never felt better, my dear."

Chapter Thirty-Four

Jack boarded the launch to the Starfire just after sunset. Across the placid East River, the lights of the casino ship blazed a few hundred yards ahead, rails jammed on all three decks with gamblers admiring the lights of the Manhattan skyline. At precisely 7 p.m., the ship's bell would clang to signal the crew to weigh anchor for the 3-mile limit, the point where gaming could lawfully begin.

Flyte and the helmsman sat side by side in the launch, a low-slung skiff with a powerful engine, no running lights. The vessel forged through gathering darkness in a light chop; it was a perfect late spring evening. The two men were wearing hooded Starfire crew slickers, so the Enterprise chief could board without being recognized. Jack felt the exhilaration every freed prisoner must--- an exquisite sensation of euphoria at his first real breath of fresh air. Just to starboard, the dark aspects of the Lower Bay stood in sharp contrast to the lights of the Staten Island and Brooklyn coastlines to port. He felt like a different person now than when he had ripped out the railing to fake his death. Then, he had been thinking only of Thompson's threat to the Enterprise and his empire. Now, he now knew false claims of terrorism were camouflaging a far graver threat to the entire city --- flames of government scare-mongering threatening to spread like Hitler's *Kristallnacht* through an indifferent city, its citizens still dozing despite the upheavals of the last days. How soon, Jack wondered, before the country itself might start to feel this same oppression at its foundations?

He made his way up the crew's private gangway and ducked into his cabin on third deck, avoiding the throngs assembled along the decks below. He went to the television, turned up the sound on the all-news channel, and reached over to the main control console to click on the three security cameras keeping 24-hour watch on the ship's casino. The CNN coverage had just shifted from talking heads to a shot of Governor Wainwright stepping before a bank of microphones. She'd chosen to make her first official statement about that morning's Prospect Park confrontations in front of the nondescript walls of the Directorate---a backdrop as forbidding under the harsh klieg lights as her face was resolute and unreadable. The consensus of the pundits debating the matter while he awaited her arrival appeared to be one of shock. Based on the early reports of the governor's astonishing intervention, she appeared to be siding with the insurgents, or, as one pundit asserted derisively on air as she mounted the podium, "certain terrorist elements."

"My fellow New Yorkers," she said into the banks of microphones and a throng of reporters, cameras, and citizens. "I come before you tonight to explain why earlier today I stayed the executions of two accused terrorists and arrested in their place the two most powerful men in the city's private security agency known as the Directorate. Also, why, as of today, the State of New York will no longer honor the city council's Emergency Decrees that earlier this year empowered the Directorate to make warrant-less arrests. I have taken these actions to restore the rule of law as we have always known it. I also pledge to you that should the mayor or the City Council attempt to countermand my decision, I will stand against them as forcefully as our state courts and Constitution will allow. I submit to you that the city's decrees were not only unconstitutionally imposed, but also that even their intent has been breached for the sole purpose of instilling fear among our citizens.

At the same time, the very patriotism of those who have unlawfully enacted them has been called into question, as well as it should be."

Jack watched the screen, transfixed. Genesee Wainwright was as formidable a politician as he had ever encountered, but he had never seen her to be as transformative and courageous a presence until now.

The governor pressed on: "As you know, two bombings have occurred in the Manhattan borough in the past two weeks, the most recent one on the West Side blamed---without proper hearing or defense---on the two young men I have just ordered to be retried under the laws and rules of criminal procedure in force before imposition of the unconstitutional Emergency Decrees. In fact, I now have in my possession recordings and documents that will plainly show these bombings were secretly ordered by Directorate officials --- specifically Directorate Chief Commissioner Simon Ross and Director of Inquiries Noel Gatwick --- and carried out by undercover paramilitary operatives of the Brigades acting clandestinely on the Directorate's behalf. Further, Attorney General Romero will bring forth incontrovertible evidence that certain men and women in both public and private life have been unlawfully detained, questioned, and imprisoned by secret tribunals conducted by the Directorate. Witnesses to these crimes are now being freed as I speak. They will testify not only to their own innocence of the crimes for which they have been detained, but of the civil right violations they and others have suffered or witnessed over these months in custody. As governor, I will not allow such flagrant violations of New Yorkers' civil rights to go unchallenged."

Murmurs of disbelief arose from the crush of reporters and bystanders.

"The sole purpose of these deadly bombings of the past few days, including an assassination attempt on my person, has been to enable certain political and corporate factions in the city to strengthen their own nefarious influence." She squinted into the bright lights. "I therefore implore you, the media and my fellow citizens, not to allow the rule of law to be further subverted by the Directorate's campaign of fear. It is not enough that we as public citizens attempt to do no harm. It is important for each of us to demand that justice be done. I submit to you the time has come for us all to demand of our leaders, both public and private, the truth."

Genesee turned and faced the cameras directly. "To all foreign-born people in the enclaves waiting for naturalization, I now make the same appeal to you. You have suffered enough, often at official hands, and I pledge to you the rule of law will be restored." She stopped. "However, just as we in the public and private arenas must take responsibility for our crimes of both commission and omission, so, too, the leaders and people of the enclaves who are not yet citizens must accept responsibility for bringing your own extremists under control. As Sheik Kaleem Jamil eloquently said at Prospect Park earlier today, when bearing away the body of a boy taught by his elders to choose the path of a suicide bomber, we must not permit more innocent blood to be spilled."

A reporter pressed her: "Mayor Shrum's spokesman has said you have no authority to make such pronouncements, much less take any unilateral action regarding city security. How do you respond, governor?"

"My response is simply this: When order breaks down, as it has in the enclaves, I have a responsibility as governor to act in whatever lawful way I can to protect the lives of New

Yorkers wherever they may be."

Although she had made no direct reference to Shrum or his administration, it was clear to Jack the governor's actions would fuel media speculation. More proof was needed, hard proof of criminality on Shrum's part, and the FBI's intervention might help provide it. But it was Shrum whom Jack was counting on to soon sow the seeds of his, the Directorate's, and Thompson's undoing.

As the media's questioning of the governor continued, Jack's gaze now shifted to the ship's security cameras trained on the main casino. One of four monitors showed a television screen beaming the press conference into a crowd gathered around the casino bar. Toward the back of the crowd stood Bob Thompson, a head taller than most, his expression a mixture of anger and agitation.

Jack picked up his phone and punched in a number. "Have master control kill the television monitor at the bar---and the outside feed to every television screen on the ship except mine. Block all wi-fi's, too. Don't turn any of it back on until I say so. From now on, I want the attention of the crowd on the casino action."

In a moment, the security camera showed the television screen at the bar go black.

Thompson cursed, downed his drink and went for his communicator, no doubt trying to re-access the press conference. He swore at the device and quickly pocketed it, all ship's communications to the outside world now blacked out.

On his own monitor, Jack watched a local television anchor in the front of the media scrum raise his hand. "Governor, what do you say to those who see your lifting of the decrees as an opportunity for *jihadists* to escalate their bombings? How can you assure citizens they will be safe without the Brigades? "

Genesee's eyes narrowed. "I have placed the National Guard on standby to ensure local police have adequate backup should there be further terrorist incidents. However, as I have said, I am not convinced any of these bombings have been the result of local insurgents."

Another shouted: "It's being said by Mayor Shrum and other political opponents of yours, even by some supporters that you have made these claims to further your presidential ambitions. How do you respond, governor?"

Genesee's eyes flashed. "I would have to be politically foolhardy to imagine any act so controversial to be a winning strategy for the White House. Until more facts are known, at worst I fully expect I will be condemned as siding with terrorists, at best I will be deemed misguided. Of one thing I am certain: to act otherwise would be to so undermine the integrity of our system, so as to make any political office not worth having."

***

As the Starfire steamed up to its anchorage at the 3-mile limit, Jack went to his house phone and speed-dialed the pit boss, Jarvis Smalley. Smalley was the longest-serving man on the casino deck and the one he could best entrust to carry out the instructions that would now set his plan in motion. On the overhead camera he could see Smalley making the rounds of the stations before the gaming could begin. His well-trained eyes were methodically scanning the room for the ubiquitous card counters and other scammers. Smalley had a genius for spotting them. Tonight, though, he would be asked to perform an entirely different task.

"Who is this?" Smalley asked when Jack got him on his communicator.

"It's Jack. Come to my office at once. We need to talk."

In moments, Smalley stood stiffly before him in black tie, his sharp eyes assessing his boss's demeanor. The Starfire's crew must have been speculating the entire time Jack had gone missing, but Smalley knew not to ask questions. Jack had nurtured his loyalty from the moment he'd personally hired him and was counting on his unquestioning cooperation now.

He handed him a sheet of paper the FBI had given him at

Chloe's. "Here is a history of calls someone made to Robert Thompson's red security phone in my Penthouse office during the past two months. I need to know which croupiers were on duty at the Starfire on each of these six occasions."

Smalley took a communicator from his pocket and consulted the Starfire's duty roster.

After a moment, he said: "In each case, Sonja Plaque was in the chair until midnight. She's very reliable. Smart. She came to us three years ago from the Casino Barrière at Biarritz."

Jack leaned forward. "Who's her replacement when the betting limits are lifted at midnight?"

"Danny Fontaine. The high rollers respect him. He's all business."

"He handles all bets until the 1 a.m. closing hour?"

"Right. Bob Thompson told me he wanted it that way because of Fontaine's knack for spotting scams and keeping high-rollers' bets straight."

"Who's in the chair tonight?"

He looked at his screen. "Same schedule --- Sonya starts first shift at 8, Fontaine relieves her at midnight for the last hour."

"Tell Sonja to come to my cabin before she clocks in, but I don't want anyone knowing I'm back yet. When does security say the mayor and his people are to arrive tonight?"

"Sometime after 11, by helicopter."

"If they reschedule or cancel, I want to be informed at once. Use my secure number." He paused. "And I want you armed tonight. Understand?"

'Yes, sir."

Half an hour later, Sonja Plaque stood before him, a look of surprise on her face. She was dressed in dark blue skirt and a croupier's orange jacket with the ship's coat of arms on its breast pocket. An ID badge hung around her neck. Her blond hair was pinned straight back, part of the dress code that allowed in-house cameras to observe all casino employees at all times. Any sign an employee might be doing any signaling was grounds for immediate dismissal.

"Mr. Flyte," she said, composing herself. "I hope you're not displeased with my performance."

"Any reason I should be?" he said with his usual brusqueness. When it came to dealing with staff, he was always all-business; still it was rare for anyone to complain of being treated unfairly or to have reason to question Jack's judgment. He had always tried to be scrupulously fair.

"No, sir. I hope not."

Her personnel folder lay open in front of him. "It says here you came to us from the casino at Biarritz where you worked in security. Yet, you're still a croupier, not a shift manager here or in the security office. Why is that?"

"Not sure, sir. I've put in for those jobs when they've opened up, but so far I've been passed over." She shifted uneasily in her chair.

"Let me make this easier for you," he said, pressing more forcefully. "Mr. Smalley tells me you are very reliable, but for some reason Security Chief Thompson doesn't have a high regard for you. Have you had problems with Mr. Thompson? You may be frank, Ms. Plaque. Whatever you tell me won't get back to him, I promise. Despite my recent absence, I am, after all, still in charge here."

The young woman nodded slightly. "I've asked to be allowed to remain in the chair during no-limits nights but have been refused. There are nights when I've been replaced even in mid-shift without warning or explanation."

"Also by Mr. Fontaine?"

"Yes, sir. I hear Mr. Thompson's keen on seniority, chains of command, that sort of thing. Danny's senior to me, so I know I'm not supposed to complain. I just assume it's for some legitimate security reason, but I keep wondering if I've done something wrong." Her lower lip began to quiver.

Jack raised his eyes to the overhead monitor. He saw Thompson finish his drink at the casino bar, stand, and move out of camera range. At the exit to the main casino, another camera picked him up talking to a man Jack recognized as one of Shrum's advance men. They moved onto starboard deck where the outside cameras showed them joined by a third man coming up the gangway from launch side of the ship. For an instant, Jack glimpsed the face under the deck lights and gave a start. Another vulture had arrived to see the Starfire's bones get picked. It was Michael Carmody, his father's old nemesis, and, now, his own.

"It's all right," he said, turning to Sonja, "But listen. I want you to use my secure phone to call this number." He made a note on a scrap of paper and handed it to her, then reached inside his desk drawer and removed a black enamel rotary phone. He used it whenever he needed to make a call untraceable by modern methods. "Listen to the response and tell me what you hear."

She dialed and waited. In a moment, she looked up. "It's a recorded message. It says 'Play the orphans.'"

"Do you recognize the voice?"

"It sounds like Danny Fontaine's, though somewhat garbled."

"What are the orphans he refers to? Do you know?"

Her expression tightened. "They are the 11 black and 29 black, the only numbers on the American betting table that break the normal alternating red-black color sequence. On the wheel itself, this anomaly does not occur, so one must know that distinction between the wheel and the betting table to understand a "play-the-orphans" command at any of the Enterprise casinos."

Jack nodded. "Smalley has instructed you well. The recorded

message, therefore, is telling any person calling Thompson's emergency telephone in my office suite to bet the 11 Black and the 29 Black."

Sylvia looked at him. " Telling a caller what to play on the Starfire tonight?"

Jack nodded. "It should be easy enough for authorities to verify with proper equipment who recorded the message, as well as the identity of the caller."

Worriedly, she looked at him. "I don't want to make any trouble, Mr. Flyte. Please, I had no idea the police would be involved."

"Merely follow my instructions, Ms. Plaque, and you'll be in no trouble. When Fontaine comes to relieve you tonight, I want you to refuse to leave your chair. I will take full responsibility for whatever happens next. Under no circumstances leave your post until I have instructed Smalley to have Fontaine replace you. Then I want you to return up the back gangway to my cabin. Someone else will be filling in for you at blackjack. I'm going to need you here. Any questions?"

"No, sir."

As she left, he remembered what Bonhoeffer had said about every person's responsibility to play a part in the thwarting of evil, no matter how small or seemingly insignificant. At Flossenberg Concentration Camp, Bonhoeffer could not have known the good his part in the German resistance had done as he had walked his final paces to the gallows. Yet, he had been at peace, a witness would later write, in his vigilance against evil. To Jack, Bonhoeffer's faith in the power of good acts had made all the difference in how he viewed his own role in combatting this current evil. Whatever the risks to himself seemed small in comparison.

Chapter Thirty Five

Moments before midnight, all eyes turned toward the mayor of New York as he made his way out of the Starfire's heliport elevator into the packed casino. He and his entourage headed directly for the roulette table, his wide bulk laboring through the crowd like a tanker entering port under full cargo. One deck above the casino in Jack's main cabin sat Raisa Amin, smuggled aboard just as Jack had been, now scanning the ship's monitors for signs of Directorate spies. With the arrest of Gatwick and Ross, the agency had no doubt been rocked back on its heels, but as Jack knew, thanks to the FBI surveillance tapes, the Directorate's reach now extended well beyond City Hall and state government, its tentacles worming into federal and even international spheres of influence.

Shrum drew close to the roulette table for an unobstructed view of the wheel. As Sonja looked up from her chair, she smiled politely at the mayor, who threw her a salacious wink. At that moment, the ship's bell clanged, announcing the start of the no-limits round when half of all winnings in the next hour would be dedicated to the charity of the evening. On this night the designated charity was the Waterfront Redevelopment Project, a public-private collaboration to revive the West Side docks, whose principal architect was none other than Michael Carmody.

The short, stocky frame of Danny Fontaine emerged from the crowd. He tapped Sylvia's shoulder, but she shook her head. The monitors registered Fontaine's annoyance as Sonja set her jaw and refused to budge.

Smalley moved in to deal with the impasse. After listening to Fontaine's complaint, the floor manager reached for the house phone.

Jack's end buzzed. "What's wrong? " he prompted. "What's going on?

"Shrum says Fontaine's always been good luck for him. He says he won't bet with anyone else in the croupier's chair."

"Good. That's what I want everybody to hear. Put Sonja on now."

"Sonja," Flyte said when she came on. "This is Mr. Flyte. Tell the mayor now that Security Chief Thompson has ordered you to give up your chair. Then I want you to leave and come up to my cabin."

As Sonya Plaque nodded and repeated what Jack had said to the mayor, Jack could see a relieved smile break over Shrum's fleshy face.

As she departed, around the table organizing their chips were six CEO's, all members of the Consortium, men familiar to him and with whom he'd been at odds back at their contentious meeting over the matter of the decrees.

A security monitor now showed Cecil wheeling Chloe slowly through the crowd, her scowl fixed on the mayor. Behind her wheelchair stood Cecil, and several rows back Quayle, his earpiece tuned to Jack's radio frequency to communicate with him from the floor. All three could eventually become witnesses for any court action against the mayor and his accomplices.

Jack had made clear to them before leaving Chloe's that the FBI wiretaps had revealed a the evening was to be about anything but charity. For Shrum it would be about snatching for himself a huge share of the Starfire's cash reserves, while helping the

Directorate and Sun-Yung Resorts seize control of the Starfire and its easy money. If Thompson's scheme went as planned, two huge rigged best on the “orphans” would first bankrupt the Enterprise's flagship casino, while within the next 24 hours similarly rigged bets would do the same at seventeen other Enterprise casinos. Such a devastating cash-flow hemorrhage could never be covered without endangering the solvency of the entire conglomerate. To raise the cash, Jack would be forced to put every Enterprise casino on the auction block, Sun-Yung Resorts of Shanghai poised to pick up the pieces at fire sale prices.

In short, with Thompson and Carmody's help, Shrum was about to stage a staggering financial coup and power play, attempting to steal the Enterprise in the process. But Jack, once the naïve young man with a hunger for power and fame, would not be outmaneuvered by Carmody. He had thus once destroyed his father. He would not be duped again.

Out on the third deck's covered breezeway, Thompson and Carmody could be seen returning. Just outside the doors, they stopped to watch, seeming to play disinterested observers, Jack surmised, in case something went wrong.

Inside the casino, Quayle moved closer to the wheel and circled Cecil’s waist with his arm. She turned and lightly kissed him. Seeing that small intimacy, Jack felt a surprising stab of loneliness. There never seemed time for anything like that for him, nothing beyond careless, meaningless encounters. Wealth had always clouded his ability to trust anyone to love him, the Enterprise a far too jealous and all-consuming lover. Yet he had envied the depth of Quayle and Cecil’s natural affection, respect, and easy collaboration, both professional and personal. They were a formidable team.

At the wheel, Shrum pushed what appeared to be a stack of 10 thousand-dollar chips onto the betting surface. At 37:1 odds, a bet of $10,000 on any one winning number would deliver $370,000, half for the Waterfront Development Project, half for Shrum and whoever had staked him, most likely Carmody. But how were they going to make the wheel deliver the orphans, not just once but twice? This particular stroke of magic the FBI wiretaps had not revealed.

So far, neither Fontaine nor Shrum seemed to be behaving in any way out of the ordinary. Fontaine sat back calmly and watched as bets were placed. After a few moments more, the dapper croupier pressed the bridge of his loosely positioned glasses back against the bridge of his nose, and sent the ball whirling counterclockwise against the clockwise turn of the wheel. The action was smooth, expert --- unremarkable. He called out, "No more bets." In a few moments more, the ball slowed, clattered and bounced over a dozen more numbers before coming to rest.

"Eleven Black is the winner," Fontaine called out.

Jack leaned closer to the monitor as he watched the action unfolding. Shrum smacked his fist into his palm. "My lucky night," he cried, the microphones of the monitoring system easily broadcasting his exclamation. As the mayor stacked his winnings, the two women beside him giggled. On the monitor, Jack saw him suddenly remove his trademark unlit cigar from his cheek and stab it into the breast pocket of his suit jacket. From his vastly increased stack of orange chips, he took a single one and bet it on the Red. At even 1:1 odds, the loss or the payoff this time would be only a thousand dollars. Around him the other six players at the table placed their bets and again waited for the spin and the call of "No more bets."

"Six Black , the winner," Fontaine called out as the ball came to rest.

Shrum had lost his thousand. He shook his head good-naturedly.

Up in the cabin, Jack acknowledged Sonja Plaque's arrival and motioned for her to take a chair beside Raisa.

"You did well.," he said to her. "Now, watch carefully. We're not certain how they're doing it, but Shrum and Fontaine must have some kind of system."

At once, Sonja nodded. "It looks to me like he's playing to lose some and win some. When the final big bet comes, it won't look so suspicious."

"Yes, that's our thinking, too," Jack said.

The final hour wore on. The mayor won, then lost, then won again, always conservatively, his losses slightly exceeded by his wins. His hefty reserve from the initial big win on the first orphan, however, remained very much intact. While he appeared calm, he had begun sweating more profusely.

So far, nothing in Fontaine's manner or Shrum's suggested anything out of the ordinary. One of the hostesses passed by the betting table with champagne. The mayor snatched a glass and drank it down. Several others joined him as they waited for the board to be prepared for the next round of bets. The mood was festive, easy, the size of the stakes disguised by the normality of it all. The ship's clock read 0140 hours; twenty minutes to go before the wheel would be shut down and the ship prepared for return to harbor.

It was that moment Jack had chosen to emerge from the casino's side entrance and take up a post along the ship's ocean-side bulkhead a few paces back from the wheel. All Shrum had to do now was lift his eyes and he would see Jack standing there, but Shrum was too preoccupied for that now. In contrast to Jack's tall and gaunt figure, his hefty girth inelegantly slumped over the betting table as he pushed his entire stack of remaining thousand-dollar chips onto the single square marked Twenty-Five Red. This no-limit $50,000 bet of 50 chips at 37-1 odds would deliver a total payoff of $1.8 million if Twenty-Five Red turned out a winner. It stood to become the largest winning bet ever cashed out aboard the Starfire.

As Jack and Smalley watched, Shrum pulled his cigar from his breast pocket and jammed it back into his cheek. Fontaine waited for the other six players to organize their bets. Once again conspicuously pressing the frames of his glasses back more firmly against his nose, he leaned over slightly and launched the ball into its spin. At that instant Shrum shifted his entire 50-chip stack. He moved it quickly --- $50,000 in chips off of the Twenty-Five Red and squarely on the Twenty-Nine Black, the second orphan.

"All bets are down.," Fontaine called.

Sonya's excited voice came through Jack's earmike: "It's got something to do with the cigar."

The ball sang in its groove, whirling fast, starting to slow, then dropped and bounced with a clatter before finally coming to rest in the slot marked Twenty-Nine Black."

Fontaine announced, "Twenty-Nine Black, the winner!"

The crowd burst into whoops. The $1.8 million unofficial calculation of the winning bet now flashed across the electronic tote board.

"This is one fucking beautiful night...," Shrum howled in triumph, "... especially for the people of this great city!"

Jack motioned to Smalley. The floor manager moved around the wall and stopped beside him. He leaned over and whispered : "They've got to be using some sort of radio transmitter to control the final drop."

"The cigar?" Sonja said into Jack's earpiece from up in the cabin.

Jack leaned in to pass on to Smalley what she'd said.

"And the glasses," Smalley said. "They must be using them to connect a coded pulse through a digital chip right to the wheel."

Smalley abruptly raised a hand before Fontaine could begin his ritual of paying off the winners, shouting "Hold on!" At those words, plainclothes security began to appear.

Shrum scowled. "What's the meaning of this?"

"Just a formality, Mr. Mayor," Smalley said calmly. "You know the rules. A big bet and a big win like this means an automatic review."

The electronic tote board still flashed Shrum's big score, along with the totals for secondary winners. Then, just as Smalley had said, came the streaming message "Under Review."

At that moment, Shrum finally noticed Jack, the mayor's entire face boiling over into a mix of anger and disgust. Turning on Smalley, he snarled: "It's for charity, for Chrissake. What's the matter with you?"

"The rules are the rules," Smalley insisted calmly, extending his hand. "And now I'm going to need to see what you just put in your pocket."

"The hell with you."

Smalley gripped the mayor's arm before his hand could reach his breast pocket. Deftly, he withdrew the cigar, and before the outraged Shrum could snatch it back, he lightly tapped it on the betting table, looked at the mayor, then rapped its tip more sharply. The cigar broke apart, revealing not the carefully rolled tobacco of one of the mayor's fine Cuban cigars but the casement and wiring of an electronic device, most likely the miniature transmitter Smalley had suspected.

Smalley turned and motioned to Fontaine. " I want to see those glasses of yours."

Fontaine shook his head.

"Hand them over," Smalley snapped. "I'm not fooling around." He opened his tuxedo jacket to show his holstered gun.

As the croupier hesitated, one of Smalley's plainclothes security men gripped his shoulder and pushed him down in his chair hard. A second yanked the horned-rims from his face. Turning the glasses over, the officer examined the underside of the nose band carefully. The band bore all the earmarks of a quartz computer chip.

Jack looked up suddenly as his gaze caught movement at the rear of the crowd. Just outside the casino doors, Thompson was ducking away. Jack motioned to one of Smalley's nearby plainclothes security men to go after him. Through the portholes, Jack could see Thompson break into a run down the outer passageway, probably headed for the aft gangway that would bring him directly down to first deck and the boat-launch. He nodded to Smalley, who quickly gave the order into his intercom to have Thompson intercepted and stopped.

As the mayor was led out of the betting area by uniformed police, he turned to Jack. "You? Here?" he snarled through clenched teeth. "You'd better have all your ducks in a row, boy. You're damn well going to need them."

Chapter Thirty-Six

Cecil sat sketching in a canvas-backed chair on third deck just below the Starfire's bridge, a story board of sketches across her lap. The ship hissed smoothly through the calm waters of the Outer Bay, headed back to Pier 57 for its 2 a.m. disembarkation. Charcoal in hand, she drew with broad, sweeping strokes a multi-paneled panorama that would dramatize the astonishing events she had witnessed over the last several days: the scores of frightened faces of newly rounded-up immigrants lining the freshly-erected barbed wire enclosures of the Brooklyn Detention Center; debris-strewn streets of Midtown, Uptown and Brooklyn in the aftermath of three separate bombings; bloodthirsty crowds cheering the Columbus Circle hangings. Next came the startled, wide-eyed expressions of Gatwick and Ross, unhooded and arrested before an angry Prospect Park crowd; Governor Wainwright before the banks of microphones at the Directorate, declaring an end to the city's Emergency Decrees; finally, a Boss-Tweed-like rendering of Mayor Shrum being led away in handcuffs. All of it was rendered in Cecil's signature style, an amalgam of "Banksy" and a lush John Singer Sargent, about to be digitally recast on computers by her crew for projection onto the giant multiplex screens of the four-story Times Square Jumbotron. There, at sunrise, in just a few hours, tens of thousands of commuters crossing one of the world's busiest intersections would be compelled to witness the past week's atrocities blinking and flashing across the boulevards in 50-foot relief, disturbing images impossible for the morning shows to ignore just outside their doors. Their lazy producers would soon be compelled to repeat the scenes in loop after loop, guaranteeing, in turn, a second life over social media. By day's end, in just one news cycle, the message would have become so watered down and overexposed, so trivialized by repetition, that Cecil would be compelled to create something more shaming and alarming, until finally, maybe, public outrage would swell to the tsunami proportions needed to wake a dull-witted citizenry out of its somnolent indifference. They needed to be jolted out of their complacency, just as she'd been by the bombing and other events she'd witnessed. She must drive her message into the public conscience --- the Directorate and its paramilitary Brigades were the true terrorists, the insurgency the last best hope to save the city's democracy. Of one thing she was certain: her assault could not stop until the Directorate's conspiracy against the public good had been fully, completely exposed.

Satisfied with what she'd done, she took out her communicator and began photographing the drawings. Soon she was sending the images to her waiting Soho crew. Quayle and Jack walked down the gangway from Jack's cabin where they'd been meeting with two FBI agents. Jack whistled softly as he saw the raw drawings. "You've captured the essence, Cecilia. By God, you have. Good for you! It's damn remarkable."

Cecil blushed at such uncharacteristic effusiveness from the Enterprise's normally dispassionate CEO. "Outrage," she finally said, "has a way of wonderfully focusing one's mind."

Quayle smiled. "A photographic memory doesn't hurt, either.".

From her perch just below the Starfire's bridge, Cecil could see the moon steadily rising above the lights of Staten Island. At this angle, the deck from aft to stern was alight with a pale eerie glow, lifeboats in their stanchions casting shadows of almost human shapes onto the bulkheads. The ship's passengers had turned boisterous following the arrests, the approach of the Manhattan skyline and the closing of the gaming tables drawing the crowd back outside to the rails. Just above the two passenger decks, close to the narrow gangway leading up to the bridge, Jack, Cecil and Quayle huddled, struggling to sort through a new problem: Thompson's apparent disappearance.

"What did the federal agents say?" Cecil asked, her frown of concern matching theirs.

"They've discovered the auxiliary launch missing," Quayle said. "He may want to get back to the Enterprise to destroy files and buy time before they take him in for questioning. I'm sure he wasn't expecting any of this."

Jack looked into the horizon, his pale lips tightening. "We're still a good two miles out. I reminded the agents he's also ex-CIA and bound to have some tricks up his sleeve. He could have cast off the launch just so we'd think he left in it, then stowed away. I urged them to keep searching the ship. Harbor patrol's been alerted to watch out for him."

Cecil said: "If he'd come up anywhere near the bridge while I was here, I'm sure I would have noticed. This far from the crowd, it's pretty quiet up here."

Indeed, the only audible sounds, except for occasional outbursts from passengers on the two decks immediately below, were the thrum of the ship's engines and the hiss of the bow waves as the Starfire sliced through the rolling swells of the Outer Bay. Cecil breathed in the night air as she listened to Jack and Ben discussing their next moves. She realized how close all three of them had come to death at various points during this ordeal, a bond as powerful as their family histories: Ben orphaned by 9/11, her father's and Jack's father's suicides under different but equally devastating circumstances. Now, their lives were being drawn together even more tightly by the need to confront a power structure run amok. To Cecil, predestination would once have been a foreign idea, but now it somehow seemed the only logical explanation.

A cold breeze sprang up, a change of weather coming in. Quayle pulled off his jacket and draped it over Cecil's bare shoulders. She folded her sketches and collapsible storyboard and put them inside her shoulder bag, watching as Jack took up a position at the rail, the Manhattan skyline drawing steadily closer. At the East Side pier, throngs of media would be waiting, held at bay by the 3 miles of ocean the Starfire had put between them, no doubt clamoring for firsthand news about the mayor's arrest now that he'd been choppered off the Starfire.

She saw movement to Jack's right. A new, different sort of shadow drifted silently along the bulkhead. She tugged on Quayle's sleeve.

"Who's there?" Jack demanded.

The shadow stopped. Someone was clearly waiting at the bulkhead. Thompson stepped into the moonlight, allowing himself to be seen. It was impossible to know how long he'd been waiting there, perhaps long enough to hear everything they'd been saying. His face was sallow in the moonlight, his tight smile suggesting a darker agenda. Both big hands were jammed into the pockets of his light overcoat; again Cecil sensed in his posture something ominous. She jumped to her feet and trembling grabbed Quayle's arm.

"The FBI's been looking for you, Thompson," Jack said finally. "They have some questions for you. They thought you might have taken the launch back."

"It's what I wanted them to think," he answered with a guttural growl, then stepped threateningly closer.

"Why are you here?" Quayle demanded.

"I'm glad I've found the three of you alone," he said incongruously, for a moment looking almost animated, as if they'd been merely fellow travelers on a cruise. "This is not what you think.

There's been a misunderstanding."

"There's no misunderstanding," Jack said coldly. "You've been setting up the casinos for months with these rigged bets. We know all about it --- secretly siphoning casino receipts into Swiss accounts, misleading the Enterprise board about your secret merger talks with Sun-Yung Resorts. Ben and I are prepared to testify to all that."

"It will be my word against yours. And you'd be surprised to know I have the votes from the board to have you removed as CEO as soon as you return. As for the mayor and this little episode tonight, this was a test of the Starfire's security systems. Smalley and his crew failed it, and I just told them to pack up and get out, that they're all fired."

"They're reporting to me now, so that's a moot point," Jack said savagely. "And your little story won't fly. The FBI has you on tape setting up this so-called test. It was an elaborate fraud, pure and simple. You thought you could hit the Starfire the way you've been hitting the other casinos."

Quayle broke in. " I know you were behind the rigging scheme, because you took Cecil to the Five Tribes Casino in Albany after the governor's fundraiser. You had somebody drug her and go through the motions of placing a rigged bet so she would incriminate herself. As for the other casino raids, Rabinsky knew about those before you ever had the Brigades round him up. By that time, he was too frightened by what he knew about the Directorate and the Brigades to let them take him in." Quayle paused. "Also, right after the Enterprise board meeting, and just before the bombing outside nearly took me out, I sent Metro police a memo by private courier detailing why I resigned. The Feds knew all about that meeting, along with the Swiss bank accounts holding the diverted casino receipts."

Cecil looked up "I also remember just enough of the Albany encounter to know the whole charade was your doing, starting with drugging my champagne."

Thompson stood perfectly still. For the first time, he appeared to have been knocked off balance. "You've all been watching too many cheap thrillers," he finally said. "It's still your word against mine. Next you'll be blaming me for the Enterprise bombing."

Cecil interrupted angrily. "Stop lying, Bob. The governor also has proof Shrum's secret slush fund has been financing these bombings. I was present at the Brooklyn Detention Center when a source from the Comptroller General's Office provided documentation. There's no doubt the bombings have been a secret Directorate and Brigades operation."

"And why were you and Shrum going into the Directorate together the day before the Midtown bombing?" Quayle demanded. "I saw you myself."

Thompson blinked in the moonlight, first at Quayle, then Jack. "I'd hoped you and I could reach an accommodation about all this, but I can see now that's not going to be possible. Let me repeat, tonight's little exercise at the roulette table was a test of Enterprise and Starfire security, nothing more; the Enterprise won't be out a dime. As for the rest, I have no idea what the three of you are talking about."

Jack rose to his full height. His gaze locked on the ex-CIA man's impenetrable mask and quickly reached for the rail to steady himself against the growing swells. On the horizon a few hundred yards off, a squall was kicking up. "You don't think this is just about money, do you, Bob?"

Another gust of wind sent one corner of a nearby lifeboat's tarp flapping, its brass fasteners knocking loudly against the thwarts, the thrum of the engines growing louder as the helmsman increased speed to hold course. Cecil had the ominous feeling Thompson had them cornered, isolated from the rest of the ship.

"I'm sure you'd like to make a conspiracy out of this, my friend, but it isn't going to work," Thompson finally retorted. "Everybody knows what Wainwright's up to, laying groundwork for a 2040 presidential run. Do you think the Emergency Decrees are going to be overturned just on the governor's say-so, without eyewitnesses. This case isn't going anywhere. Even the wiretaps will be inadmissible before we get through."

"No witnesses?" Jack scoffed. "You think Ben and I haven't seen enough to bring evidence of criminality to a grand jury? Make no mistake, old boy, you, the mayor, Gatwick and Ross, the Comptroller General, and many of their associates, are in deep trouble. Others also know what we know and more, thanks to the spy insurgent groups have had inside the Directorate for the past year."

Thompson stared darkly down the deck. He seemed to be dropping his mask, preparing to put his cards on the table. "The gypsy, you mean?" he erupted suddenly. "We're aware of that treasonous little rat and the rest of his scheming cohorts. We'll be dealing with all of them soon enough. Where's your loyalty to this country, Jack, that's what the hell I'd like to know. What sort of unpatriotic turncoat are you?"

Jack arched a brow. "You could only know about the gypsy if Gatwick had told you --- more proof of your complicity with those thugs. And now you're telling me that defending the rights of citizens against a tyrannical government is treasonous and unpatriotic? Does the American Revolution ring any bells?"

"Damn right I'm accusing you," Thompson roared. "The real tyranny here is the insurgency, underhanded Muslims --- the last people we should ever trust --- along with the dregs of all those other Third-World countries trying to overthrow the duly elected government of this city and undermine our country."

As he erupted in this diatribe, Thompson's hand emerged from his coat pocket. It clutched an automatic pistol --- snub-nosed, especially cruel-looking because of its deadly compactness. Cecil sucked in her breath. Standing motionless ten paces away from the ex-CIA man, Jack looked directly into the barrel and said, as calmly as Cecil had ever heard him: "You're going to kill us all, Bob? Is that the idea?"

"Two or three short bursts," Thompson said indifferently. "That should be enough."

"Then what?" Jack asked in his own measured way. "How will you explain it?"

"That I was confronting you, the real conspirators, trying to bring you in. You refused. You were about to overpower me, dispose of me over the side."

"Desperate explanation, Bob," Jack said with a shake of his head. "No one will believe it for a minute." He stepped forward as Quayle moved a few steps to one side, perhaps to make it more difficult for a single burst to take them both out.

"I'm warning you," Thompson said. "You're not going to be telling these lies to anyone." It will be my word against yours. You will be the ones brought to justice for violating the Emergency Decrees. Or we could make some agreement. I assure you, if you'll work with me, we can make this right."

"That's not our world you're talking about, Bob. That's the world you and your twisted friends have created --- as if that were ever your role. Who elected you, Bob? Who elected any of you except Shrum, that miserable specimen of a public servant? Who are the real terrorists here? It's not so obvious now, is it, my friend?"

Jack took another step forward.

"Stay where you are," Thompson warned. "I mean it. Don't make this any harder."

Suddenly, Cecil really understood: Thompson was going to execute them. Maybe he'd intended to do it all along, or maybe now realizing how much they knew about the flimsiness of his defense, it was his only option. No eyewitnesses. She would have to be killed, too. Conversely, she could see Jack daring Thompson to act, the

Enterprise chief 's fatalism never far from the surface from the moment she'd met him that first afternoon when he'd sat for his portrait, a risk-taker to his core. Her hand went to her shoulder bag. She had never actually used the flashlight-sized device she was about to take from it. Her index finger found the firing button that the nice woman at the personal weapons booth at Macy's had showed her. "Point the two prongs of the device at the perpetrator and press here," she'd said. "You will observe a laser dot appear on the target. Press the button again. The device will fire two barbed electrodes into the perpetrator's body at the laser's point of light, sending enough voltage into your attacker to incapacitate him." She remembered what else she had said: "It won't kill a healthy man, only shock him, so he'll be marginalized until you can summon help."

Jack began to advance on Thompson. The ship rolled in a swell and Quayle struggled to hold his balance. Cecil didn't dare wait. If Thompson began firing, none of this would matter. She softly whispered "Robert," as if to a lover. He looked at her, startled by her tone. She pressed the button to mark her target, then quickly pushed again. With a loud, nasty snap, the device went off, the first barbed electrode penetrating a pectoral muscle, a second piercing the trousers, then the skin of his left thigh. With an anguished groan, Thompson dropped to his knees. His entire 6-foot, 3-inch frame convulsed, crashing down to the deck. Curling into a ball, he uttered a string of anguished curses and cries.

Quayle bent down and picked up the pistol. He and Jack looked in astonishment at Cecil as she stood over Thompson, Taser still in hand. She was trembling, sobbing softly. Finally, she said: "Can we please just go home now?"

ACKNOWLEDGEMENTS

I am indebted to *Letters & Papers from Prison*, the personal reflections of German philosopher and pastor Dietrich Bonhoeffer, executed in 1945 for his role in an unsuccessful plot to assassinate Adolph Hitler. Bonhoeffer's struggle to define a citizen's personal responsibility to resist malevolent leaders inspired this fictional account.

Also, many thanks to numerous patient readers who gave of their precious time to offer constructive comments or encouragement during the long slog of this manuscript's preparation, especially: Bobby and Irene Fischer; John P. Kennedy, Jane McCullough, Catherine Menninger, Grant and Peggy Monsarrat, Bonnie Stratton and Roger Hamstreet, Robin Wilkins and Joan Anderson, Frank Grundstrom and Cynthia Dickstein, and my three children. Most crucially, to my wife and editor, Barbara Ann Curcio.

Also, many thanks to my former agent, Frank Weimann, of Literary Group International, who worked hard to give *united states* at least a fighting chance in an otherwise unwelcoming world of mainstream publishing.

ABOUT THE AUTHOR

Author photo by Kerri Courtney

Nick Monsarrat edited and wrote for Vermont newspapers for 27 years, taught journalism at St. Michael's College and co-chaired an exchange of Soviet/U.S. editors both here and in Russia in the 1980s. Most recently he helped start up a new Vermont online investigative newspaper, VTDigger.org.

www.nickmonsarrat.com

www.ingramcontent.com/pod-product-compliance
Lightning Source LLC
Chambersburg PA
CBHW030821310726
48980CB00006B/576/J

* 9 7 8 0 9 9 6 0 1 7 6 1 9 *